Praise for Phil and Kaja Foglio's Girl Genius Series

"Filled with Foglian touches—Borscht-belt comedy accents, things that go *sproing*, adorkable sentient machines, and laugh-a-minute slapstick—*Agatha H.* is a tremendously fun addition to the Girl Genius canon."
—Cory Doctorow, award-winning author of *Little Brother* and *Down and Out in the Magic Kingdom*

"The Hugo Award–winning Foglios present their popular gaslight fantasy comic in novelized form, maintaining the zany energy, witty repartee, creative characterization, and innovative world-building of the original."
—*Publishers Weekly*

"This volume by the creators of the Eisner Award–nominated webcomic Girl Genius (Volumes 1–9) is a fantastic reintroduction to the Girl Genius world and will definitely capture new fans. It will appeal to fans of the steampunk genre who like their books riddled with mad science and adventure, along with a liberal dash of humor."
—*Library Journal*

"Simply said, Girl Genius has everything I look for in a story."
—Patrick Rothfuss, bestselling author of *The Name of the Wind*

". . . the Foglios appear to have been liberated by the [webcomics] format—and that sense of buoyant imagination and unbridled fun runs through every page."
—*The Onion A.V. Club*

". . . ridiculous, and funny, and a little bit sexy."
—*Portland Book Review*

"Phil and Kaja Foglio's awesome new fantasy . . . pushes the boundaries of steampunk past the polite boundaries of pseudo-Victorian and into full-on techo-madness!"

—Matt Staggs, *Suvudu.com*

"Fans of the series will enjoy another trip into Agatha's world, and it is not too late for new readers to jump aboard."

—*City Book Reviews*

"I will confess to being a big fan of Phil and Kaja Foglio's Girl Genius"

—Charles Stross, author of *Halting State* and *Rule 34*

". . . a madcap comic adventure combined with steampunk and some well-used fantasy tropes."

—*EscapePod*

". . . bursting at the seams with creativity, humor, and outright weirdness . . . an infectious and incredibly fun read."

—Sarah Kuhn, *ign.com*

"If Jules Verne had written comics, he wouldn't have written Girl Genius. He would have been jealous of it, though."

—*Comics Buyer's Guide*

"Girl Genius is brilliant. It really is. It's fun and funky and unlike almost anything else, and it's Phil and Kaja Foglio doing what they do best."

—Eric Burns, *Websnark.com*

AGATHA H AND THE SIEGE OF MECHANICSBURG

A GIRL GENIUS NOVEL

PHIL & KAJA FOGLIO

NIGHT SHADE BOOKS

NEW YORK

Night Shade books may be purchased in bulk at special discounts for sales
promotion, corporate gifts, fund-raising, or educational purposes. Special
editions can also be created to specifications. For details, contact the Special Sales
Department, Night Shade Books, 307 West 36th Street, 11th Floor, New York, NY
10018 or info@skyhorsepublishing.com.

Night Shade Books® is a registered trademark of Skyhorse Publishing, Inc.®,
a Delaware corporation.

Visit our website at www.nightshadebooks.com.

10 9 8 7 6 5 4 3 2 1

Library of Congress Cataloging-in-Publication Data is available on file.

ISBN: 978-1-949102-27-7
EISBN: 978-1-949102-28-4

Cover illustrations by Ondřej Hrdina
Cover design by Daniel Brount

Printed in the United States of America

To Science!

AGATHA H AND THE
SIEGE OF MECHANICSBURG

A GIRL GENIUS NOVEL

PROLOGUE

⟪◦⟫

Lucrezia Mongfish slotted the last components securely into their places inside the great engine, slapped the hatch closed, and cackled. Her assistant, the defrocked priestess Mozek, shuddered at the sound. "You shouldn't be getting so worked up, Mistress," the old woman said, as she tightened the final bolts. "Not in your condition."

Mozek felt the presence of Glimtockka, the taciturn Geisterdame who never left Lucrezia's side, looming beside her. She didn't bother to look up at the frowning warrior. "And don't you even pretend you don't agree with me, White-eyes."

The Geister snarled at the overly familiar address, and Mozek fully expected to feel the usual stinging rap to the back of her head. Instead, to her astonishment, she heard the warrior clearing her little-used throat. Mozek had diligently studied the language of the Pale Ladies, partly because it helped serve her mistress's purposes, and partly because she learned many potentially lifesaving secrets when people didn't think she could understand them.

"Your slave speaks truly, Lady. Her impertinence rises in a legitimate cause. If she who you carry within you is indeed the Holy Child—"

Lucrezia ended this by slapping Glimtockka sharply across the face. "Silence!" She stamped her foot. "I've told you that stupid prophecy is wrong! It is predicated on failure! *My* failure!" She spun about and regarded the two figures that were strapped to the large steel tables.

1

One of them, a furious construct of flesh, metal, and black leather, writhed impotently against her bonds. She roared, cursing Lucrezia in Old French. "*That which you have done here is blasphemy!*"

"Oh, I know!" Lucrezia hugged herself and twirled about. "It's so *exciting*! I'm positively giddy!"

Lucrezia's pirouette took her to the other table. Strapped to this one was a clank, made all of metal, in the shape of an angel almost three meters tall. Even restrained, it was imposing, although it was evident it had been neglected for quite a while. Its clothing was frayed and tattered; its wig, once elegantly coiffed, was now a dusty rat's nest sliding from its place. The great wings were now little more than almost-bare struts still adorned with a few tarnished silver-foil feathers. Its face, as well as the rest of its body, was still and lifeless. *But not for long*, Lucrezia promised herself. She turned back to the other slab while patting the inert clank.

"I'd think you'd be glad to be out of this old thing. I mean, it must have been *terribly* boring being chained up in that forgotten hallway for over a hundred years . . . "

To Lucrezia's discomfort, her words merely caused her prisoner to smile. Lucrezia felt ghostly icicles of dread slide down her spine. "You have no idea what it was like," the creature on the slab said with obvious relish. "But I take comfort in knowing that if you continue in this madness, *you will.*"

Lucrezia considered giving this impudent wretch a slap as well, but . . . even shackled, there were those terrible teeth. They had seemed like such a funny idea at the time . . .

She was saved from further indecision by the sound of Mozek clearing her throat. "It is done, Mistress."

Lucrezia looked over her minion's work and could find no fault. Thick cables were now attached to the metal figure. The engines themselves were awash with green lights as they quietly thrummed.

"It won't work, Lady Heterodyne." The creature on the slab's voice was different now. There was no trace of anger or malice. It was a voice that begged to be heeded. "You are attempting to pour the ocean into a teacup." She glanced at the prone figure beside her. "And you have actually found a teacup strong enough to hold it."

Lucrezia tipped her head to one side as she considered the construct. "That's very impressive, that voice thing. Some sort of harmonic pitch. Is that how you got old Andronicus to actually listen to you?" She patted the inert clank. "It might actually have worked if you'd been able to use your original vocal mechanisms, but even so, it was *very* persuasive. I'll have to remember that."

She strode over to the switches. "But I am tired of listening to you. Tired of being under the thumb of my husband's House and tired of being a good little wife!" She gestured towards Mozek, who threw the first switch. There was a hum and then a roar. The lights flickered and the air became heavy as, unseen and malevolent, the vast presence of Castle Heterodyne filled the room.

"What is this place?" The Castle sounded confused. "It is a part of me, yet it is not." It paused. "Lady Heterodyne," it said in a voice filled with suspicion. "This is *your* doing. You are meddling where you should not!"

Lucrezia laughed scornfully. "And that is the last time *you* will tell me what I should or should not do!" She grasped the final switch. "Things are going to be *different* around here!" With a shout of triumph, she threw the switch—

And things were very different indeed.

CHAPTER 1

⤳◕🙰◕⤶

L ucrezia blinked as she awoke. She had been outdoors, with dear Klaus[1]—she had him, and his empire, very nearly under her thumb—but now he was gone and she was indoors. She realized with surprise that she was in the secret laboratory she had established beneath Castle Heterodyne . . . oh, how long had it been since she had worked here? Since she had been the young rebellious spark with such a malicious delight in her schemes? Her head swam. It seemed an eternity. So much had happened to her since then. The room was dusty now, damaged and neglected since the fall of Castle Heterodyne, but she still remembered it well. Someone was standing over her. A girl. "Oh! My goodness. Who—?" she began weakly. It couldn't hurt to play vulnerable, put whoever it was off their guard. Looking vulnerable was easy in the body she currently wore—that of the youthful Agatha Heterodyne.

The girl looked down at her and smiled. "Hello, Auntie Lucrezia. I'm here to help you."

Lucrezia rocked back in astonishment as she beheld the face of her long-estranged sister hanging ominously above her. She looked as if she had never aged beyond the carefree days when all three Mongfish sisters still lived in their father's fortress and gloried in their fame

---

[1]   A scene detailed at the end of one of our previous textbooks: *Agatha H and the Clockwork Princess*. This was the first time the Lady Lucrezia had possessed the Lady Heterodyne.

as the three beautiful daughters of the supremely evil spark Lucifer Mongfish. "Demonica?"[2]

Zola laughed in delight. "Yes, everyone says that I look just like dear Mama!" She drew herself up. "But no. I am Zola Anya Talinka Venia Zeblinkya Malfeazium."

Lucrezia looked haunted and glanced around. Her fingers twitched towards a nearby wrench. "First Serpentina's boy, then you. I swear, if Daddy is waiting to pop out from around a chair . . . "

Zola waved a hand dismissively. "Oh, Grandfather died years ago, in a freak airship explosion." Lucrezia raised her eyebrows. Zola shrugged, "I know! Such a cliché.[3] We still laugh about it at Christmas. But no, no, it's just me."

"Excellent," said Lucrezia, as she swung the wrench upward, knocking Zola cold with one smooth blow.

Zola awoke with an aching head and the realization she was restrained. A few subtle tests revealed that whoever had secured her knew her business.

"Now don't bother trying to escape, dear," Lucrezia sang out from a workbench. "I gather from the wide variety of items you were carrying—some in rather uncomfortable places, I'd imagine—that you are *very* well trained." She used a forceps to exhibit a cleverly made sheath housing several small, wicked-looking knives.

She put the knives down and fastidiously wiped the forceps with

---

[2] Lucifer Mongfish, the reluctant bête noir of the Heterodyne Boys, had not one beautiful daughter, but three. The most famous of these was, of course, Lucrezia, who eventually wed Bill Heterodyne. Serpentina Mongfish eschewed the family business and ran off with the science-adventurer Prince DuMedd, while the third, Demonica, remained in the family lair, which occupied an extinct volcano somewhere to the west of Minsk. There she continued her father's work. You don't hear much about Demonica Mongfish, which is just the way she wanted it.

[3] Airships—at least in the lurid pages of the pfennig dreadfuls—are expected to, on a regular basis, burst into flames, be attacked by sky-pirates, struck by lightning, grapple with air kraken, and be caught up in freakish air currents that swiftly and unerringly transport them thousands of kilometers to hidden civilizations and lost continents. Surprisingly, according to the empire's records and statistics, this is in fact the case, but it is still the safest form of travel.

a moldering rag. "But you won't get out of that, dear. I've been tying people up since before you were born."

"You don't have to do this! We're on the same side, Auntie," Zola protested. "I've been spying on your daughter and her minions even before they shut down the Castle!"

Lucrezia stared at her. "She . . ." Lucrezia looked down at the body that her mind currently occupied. "My daughter has shut down Castle Heterodyne?"

Zola blinked. "You couldn't tell?"

Lucrezia waved a hand at the cavern walls. "Not from down here, darling. This little retreat was so perfect because that interfering Castle wasn't even aware it was here." She gnawed gently at her lower lip. "Dead. Well *that* changes a few things . . ."

Zola tried again. "Auntie, I was going to help you."

Lucrezia raised an eyebrow and smiled wistfully. "My, you *are* just like dear Demonica, aren't you?" She twirled around and whisked a dust sheet off of a mid-sized machine that sat lifeless to one side. "Well, don't you worry, my dear, you *are* going to help me."

Zola looked at the device and flinched. "AH! That's some kind of Beacon Engine!"

Lucrezia was a bit thrown by this. How did the girl know about the Summoning Engines? That would need to be answered, but later. For now, she tried to hide her confusion. "Not exactly, darling, *this* is some of my *earlier* work. It produced some amusing results and was very helpful in developing my later, most useful, devices. With a few simple adjustments, I think it will do very well for what I have in mind today."

So saying, she lifted a panel off the machine and began tinkering. Zola stared and then, with a small shudder, looked aside. Trying to watch a spark at work was just asking for violent headaches and disturbing flashbacks.

Lucrezia blithely chatted on as she worked. "You are obviously familiar with the plans of the Order's Inner Circle. That will save us all so much tedious exposition." Lucrezia looked at Zola expectantly, but the girl kept silent, eyes narrowed and averted. Lucrezia sniffed and continued to tinker with the machine. Finally, she could stand the silence no more. "Well, if you *must* know," she continued, "my poor, stupid admirers in the Grand Sycophantic Order of the Knights of Jupiter, or whatever nonsense they called their ridiculous secret society, were supposed to do little else but search for this girl Agatha—my daughter. She was supposed to be the perfect receptacle for me. For my mind." Lucrezia slumped back against the bench and frowned. "But now that I'm in the girl's body, no thanks to them, it appears that I might have made a . . . a mistake depending on her."

Zola spoke slowly. "I don't understand. A mistake? How? She was—"

"Yes! Yes, yes, yes! My child! Prepared and conditioned—and maybe if those fools had found her ten years ago. Or if that *Barry*—" she spat the name "—hadn't interfered by giving her that wretched locket . . . "[4]

Lucrezia turned with a glare, and Zola spied the locket shining amidst the clutter atop the workbench. Lucrezia seemed to deflate slightly.

"But . . . maybe not." She picked up a small mirror and stared into it. "Maybe she simply has too much of her father in her after all." Zola was astonished to see a tear well up in one of her aunt's eyes. "This is all his fault," she whispered. Lucrezia became aware of Zola's interest and slammed the mirror down hard enough to crack it. "The *point* is that, for whatever reason, Agatha is too strong. It has become too

---

[4]   The locket under discussion was given to Agatha by her uncle, Barry Heterodyne, when she began to display signs she was about to "break through," i.e. transition into a full-blown spark. Whereas this was something to be expected, considering her lineage, Agatha began to do this at the unprecedented age of five. The locket, in brief, acted as a governor on young Agatha's brain, effectively retarding its development. Every indication we have was that this was supposed to be a short-term fix. Unfortunately, Barry disappeared and Agatha wore the locket nonstop until it was removed when she was eighteen years old. At that point, a lot of the preliminary neurological processes of a spark's breakthrough had already begun, but had been allowed to develop incredibly slowly. As a result, Agatha did not so much *break* through, as *ease* through. This goes a long way towards explaining her relative sanity, despite her otherwise worrying pedigree.

easy for her to seize control of this body and keep me from taking it back. I am not *winning*. And worse, she's learning things from me! Reaching into my mind and pulling out my secrets! She knew to look for this place! She intuitively grasps the principles of my work!"

She took a breath and Zola dared to interject, "But that's not uncommon. Your own work, while magnificent in its own right, of course, is a recognizable extension of some of your father's theories. Many sparks within a family have a natural insight—"

She flinched as Lucrezia's fists slammed down on the bench before her, punctuating her words. "SILENCE!" she shrieked. "This! Girl! Must! *Die!*" She glared, panting, at Zola, who wisely said nothing. After a moment, Lucrezia regained control of herself and straightened up. Zola was immediately reminded of a cat that had fallen off a table and was nonchalantly pretending this was exactly what it had wanted to do.

"Ideally," Lucrezia muttered, "I would just destroy this body now while I still have control."

Zola blinked. "*That's* ideally?"

Lucrezia was obviously thinking about something else, but a part of her blithely chatted on. "Of course. Now that my priestesses have my Summoning Engine working, all they need to do is call me into some other suitable vessels. I've managed to expand the operating parameters so I should have ever so many more choices now. Destroying the part of me that's occupying this wretched girl won't destroy me at all. Not even close. Redundancy allows one to be much more relaxed about sacrificing individual iterations."[5] She frowned, "But . . . but in this calling, I have gained valuable information. Killing this girl before I have had a chance to pass it on . . . " She shook her head and, once again, focused her full attention on Zola. "Luckily, I won't have to go through the whole 'summoning' rigmarole with you, dear." She smiled

---

[5]   Statements like this have helped convince behavioral psychologists that, wherever the original Lucrezia was, she was either incredibly mad or no longer human. A large majority of those questioned opined for "both."

reassuringly and patted the machine's carapace. "That wouldn't help me at all in this situation. The new calling would have none of the knowledge I have gained in this body. No, instead I can simply use this lovely old toy of mine to copy myself from this troublesome girl into you. *Then* I will kill her." She smiled at Zola. "After that, I shall rendezvous with the Sturmhalten hive, round up a few more suitable girls, and then give myself all the important information over tea. Yes, that sounds perfect. I think I'll have those little jam sandwiches. I've really missed them . . . "

"No."

Zola's quiet but emphatic statement caused Lucrezia to laugh with delight. She regarded Zola with genuine amusement. "Oh, I do so love a truly defiant subject! They're so much fun! If only I had the time to do it right!"

Zola kept talking. "It won't work, auntie. If you try to force yourself into my brain, you'll suffer *rezzok tig-zaffa.*"

Lucrezia's hilarity cut off as if a switch had been thrown. Zola nodded, "That is what your Geisterdamen call mutual brain death, yes?"

Lucrezia scowled. "I see you are *very* well informed, aren't you?"

Zola nodded. "Yes, I am. All those years ago? When you sent the Geisterdamen here to build your machines and hunt for your daughter Agatha? Some of those priestesses began to question the divinity of the great goddess they served so blindly. They began to *think*, to *ask questions*, and to *see you for the fraud you are.*"

Lucrezia's slap threatened to dislocate Zola's jaw. "FRAUD?" Lucrezia's fury was palpable. "How dare you! You know nothing! NOTHING!" She reached overhead and brought down a headset encrusted with components, then slammed it down on Zola's head. "I shall simply blast your mind from your body and rebuild your neural pathways!"

"You can't," Zola screamed from under the helmet. "Just like you can't use the Geisterdamen! For pity's sake, *listen* to me!"

Lucrezia—a live, sparking cable in her hand—paused. Zola continued. "Mother found your Loremistress Milvistle. She jumped at the chance to study such a high-ranking Geister. She learned everything Milvistle knew. One of the things she learned was how to block you, if you ever came back and tried to pull just this sort of nonsense. Even if you brainwashed me to the point where I *wanted* to sacrifice myself, I couldn't let you take me over." She peered out at Lucrezia. "And it would get very messy. Go on, test me. Run a blue phase engram alignment. I'll wait."

Zola could see Lucrezia's fury rising. Now was her chance. "But! I *can* let you ride along inside my head! I can tell you how to do the modifications that will let you get out of here, if you'll stop menacing me long enough to actually *listen*."

Lucrezia stared at her and then carefully put down the cable. "Good heavens, dear. You seriously did intend to help me? But why didn't you say so?"

Zola simply glared at her. Lucrezia shrugged. "Oh, I know. Working with family really can be infuriating. Fine. I'm listening."

Zola nearly sagged with relief. "About time. So . . . You want the Heterodyne girl dead? I am all for that. But unless you work with me, you'll lose everything you've learned here. Including everything you've just learned from me about the family."

Lucrezia slowly tapped her finger. "Do get to the point, dear."

Zola licked her lips. "Just what I said. I can let you in—you can share my mind—"

Lucrezia slapped the bench. "Share my power, you mean. I do see where this is going, you presumptuous little—"

"Precisely. I want to play too. Now, the Order has been very busy while you've been away. They have gone to a lot of trouble to set me in place as the lost Heterodyne heir. Their plan has gone wrong in every possible way, but it has its good points. Together, we can still make it work."

Lucrezia growled. "Those fools in the Order with their stupid, shortsighted 'plans.' I knew I should have killed half of them years ago. The difficulty was in deciding which half."

Zola felt a flash of sympathy. "Fools, yes, but most of them are still loyal to you."

"Oh lucky, lucky me."

"But the family—"

Lucrezia smiled. "Oh hush, dear, I already know everyone is plotting against me. But, purely by accident, you might have a valid argument." As she said this, Lucrezia removed the helmet, then wheeled over an alarming-looking device that consisted primarily of a number of loaded syringes—which were all aiming at Zola's head. Lucrezia picked up a switchbox and the device lit up and flexed slightly. A drop of solution fell next to Zola's hand and a wisp of acrid smoke puffed upwards.

Lucrezia studied a small screen. "Now, lie to me. Just for calibration purposes, darling. Are you male?"

"Yes."

Lucrezia nodded. "Good enough."

Zola jerked in her seat. "What? No, it isn't. To properly calibrate—"

"Boring," Lucrezia sang out. "Just stick to the truth, darling. It's usually easier to remember, anyway." Zola stared back at her. "Is Klaus Wulfenbach really the ruler of Europa?"

"The Baron? Yes! Yes he is!"

"And everyone accepts this?"

Zola stared fixedly at the needles above her. "The Fifty Families don't *like* it, but no one can resist him."

Lucrezia sighed nostalgically. "I can believe *that*. And his empire— it's stable?"

Zola paused. "He's done nothing but expand it for the last sixteen years. He's never had to deal with the problems of stability, per se."

Lucrezia sighed. "That impossible man. He's too good a piece to lose." She nudged the syringe rack away with a foot. "All right, my dear, lucky for you, I simply *must* stay. We have a bargain."

Zola allowed herself to relax back against the chair. She heard Lucrezia humming to herself as she began fiddling with a device on one of the work benches. She frowned. "Um . . . Auntie? Aren't you going to release me?"

"All in due time, darling."

Several minutes later, Lucrezia swept over lugging a complicated device that trailed several wiry cables behind her. She hooked it to the helmet and once again placed it on Zola's head. "There we go," she said cheerfully. "Now obviously I've had to make a few modifications, but this old equipment should prove quite adequate." When she was satisfied, she placed another helmet on her own head and hooked up several more wires. Several lights came on and she nodded in satisfaction.

Zola spoke up, sarcasm thick in her voice. "Is there anything you need me to do?"

Lucrezia considered this and flipped a knife switch. Instantly a surge of power ripped through both women, causing Zola to gasp and driving Lucrezia to her knees. As abruptly as it began, the power cut off. Lucrezia took a deep breath and lifted the helmet from her head. "Try not to pass out?"

The girl in the chair stirred and her eyes flicked open. "Ooh," said Lucrezia from Zola's own mouth, with Zola's own voice. "This *does* feel different."

The first Lucrezia leaned over and gently tapped her forehead with Agatha's finger. "And is our dear little niece still in there?"

"Yes, she's here." Lucrezia/Zola frowned. "It's a bit odd . . . this head feels wrong."

Lucrezia/Agatha giggled as she began releasing the chair's restraints. "Hardly surprising, dear, it *is* wrong. Whatever else I will say about my daughter Agatha, she is a very comfortable fit."

Lucrezia/Zola levered herself out of the chair and stretched. She frowned. "Oh. I'm getting some of her surface thoughts." She looked pensive. "She's . . . gloating?"

Suddenly Zola froze; her eyes widened with astonished admiration. "Good heavens, Auntie! You got the Baron with a slaver wasp?"

The Lucrezia-within-Agatha rocked back. "What! How—?"

Zola's eyes opened even wider. "Oooh, and that's why no one's ever been able to find the Citadel of Silver Light! Amazing! It explains so much!"

"Get out of those memories," Lucrezia screamed. "Lucrezia, darling, are you even still in there? Fight her off!"

Zola shrugged. "Oh, she's trying, but she can't."

Lucrezia rushed forward, a heavy wrench held high, but Zola pivoted smoothly and drove a foot into Lucrezia's midriff. "The family has had *years* to prepare for your inevitable reappearance and Loremistress Milvistle was *ever* so much help!" She smirked down at the gasping Lucrezia and tapped her forehead. "My copy of you is now safely ensnared in a neural trap where I can sift through your precious secrets at my leisure."

Lucrezia snarled in outrage, "You said you wanted to help me!"

Zola looked contrite. "That's true." Her expression changed to one of hurt surprise, "And yet— Oh dear. I see that you planned to vivisect me the minute you got your information back to your other selves. Oh, Auntie, really."

Lucrezia screamed with rage and tried to climb to her feet. Zola casually swept them out from under her. "Don't worry, *darling*, I'll keep my end of the bargain. A version of you *will* make it out of here. Your plans will go ahead beautifully. And no one, not even your other selves, will ever suspect that *I'm* the one in control." She smiled sweetly and drew her pistol. "Now, as we agreed, it's time for Agatha Heterodyne to die. Then I can take my time with those three fools you so conveniently locked up for me . . . " A peculiar look crossed Zola's face. "Wait . . . I'm getting . . . " She looked at Lucrezia blankly. "You only found two? No, there were three. Violetta and Gil . . . " Her eyes widened. "That means you missed—" She jerked back in surprise, which is why when Tarvek dropped from where he'd been hiding in the rafters, the cudgel he swung viciously at her head only cracked firmly across her wrist. Zola's pistol spun away as she shrieked in pain and surprise. Tarvek was about to finish her off when he saw, from the corner of his eye, Lucrezia diving for the pistol.

Without hesitation, he swung his foot against her jaw, sending her crashing into a bank of machinery.

"Tarvek," Lucrezia cried, "Don't be a fool! Aid me! I am the Agatha girl!"

Tarvek rolled his eyes even as he dived for the gun. A jar of desiccated leeches shattered against his side and his hand missed the pistol by scant centimeters.

Zola followed. "Don't listen to her, Prince Sturmvoraus! She's the Other! We have to stop her!"

A small machine smashed into Zola's forehead, stopping her dead in place.

Lucrezia followed, doing a full body dive for the gun. "If *I* die, your precious Agatha dies too! You dare not work against me!"

A wheeled tea cart caught her full in the face and dropped her to the floor. The three rose to their feet simultaneously and realized they were all equidistant from the pistol. There was a tense moment while they all appraised each other . . . and then all moved at once.

Tarvek leapt towards the gun and was astonished when he reached it unimpeded. He rolled to his knees, pistol in one hand and cudgel in the other, to find himself alone.

A clacking sound caused him to spin in time to see Zola snapping shut a large machine rifle of some sort, a triumphant grin on her bruised face.

An amused "ahem" drew both of their gazes to the other side of the room where Lucrezia stood smiling. When she saw they were both focused on her, she flipped a delicate switch. Instantly, the doors slammed shut and a series or red lights began blinking. A scratchy recorded voice drifted down from the ceiling: "Hello, intruders! The blast doors are now sealed, and my laboratory's self-destruct mechanism has been engaged. Shouldn't have snooped, darlings, but it's too late now. You're going to die horribly in sixty, fifty-nine . . . "

"What are you doing?" Tarvek demanded. "Stop it! You'll die too!"

Lucrezia threw her head back and laughed. "No power on Earth can stop my perfect death-trap! This iteration's death is unfortunate, but the two of you are *so* annoying that I consider it worth it!"

Zola's lip curled. "No, I don't think so." In a single smooth movement she drew, pointed, and shot a high-pressure grappling gun upwards into the ragged shaft in the ceiling. From high above came the solid *thunk* of the hook. Lucrezia and Tarvek, after a momentary surprise, dashed towards her, but Zola engaged the winch and, with a laugh, was pulled up and out of their reach. "Later, Tarvek," she sang out. "Or . . . maybe not. Bye Auntie, I'll be sure to say 'hello' to your other selves! Hee hee hee . . . "

And, still giggling, she vanished from sight. The two stared upwards. Tarvek looked at Lucrezia. "If she's got that big gun, why didn't she just shoot us?"

Lucrezia considered this. "Well, it only shoots marshmallows, so the real question is why did she bother taking it at all?"

Tarvek sneered. "Oh, by the way, nice 'death trap.' "

Lucrezia looked embarrassed. "That hole in the ceiling was not part of the original design! You're not supposed to get in by tunneling straight down."

Tarvek conceded this and peered up again. "Well, Agatha, myself, and the others came *in* that way, perhaps we can—"

A flash of light was followed by a hollow *BOOM*. "Blue fire," Tarvek yelled, "She's blown the shaft!" Instinctively, he tackled Lucrezia, pulling her with him as he dived for cover. "RUN!"

The room shook as a small avalanche of rock crashed to the ground. A torrent of dust and smoke poured from the shaft and filled the air, spreading like a wave. Tarvek landed with Lucrezia in his arms, sheltered by a row of huge glass tubes. The avalanche of material flowed around them, demolishing and covering machines and furniture before grinding to a halt.

Then, there was silence. For a moment they huddled, breathing deeply. Tarvek buried his face in "Agatha's" hair and closed his eyes. Her hair was still soft, but smelled of oil and electricity mixed with stale sweat and dust. None of them had been able to wash for quite some time, and he knew he was in a similar state. Agatha was safe, and somehow that knowledge made her smell wonderful. He pulled back slightly to gaze into her eyes and met Lucrezia's smirk as she batted her eyelashes up at him. In his panic, he had only thought of keeping Agatha safe, momentarily forgetting Lucrezia was within her. He jolted back in revulsion. "You—!" he snarled. His startled movement made it easy for Lucrezia to slam him back even farther, so that he toppled and fell through the open hatch of one of the tubes. He swung up in time to see Lucrezia shut and bolt the tube's door, sealing him in. "Me!" she crowed.

It was then they both remembered the self-destruct mechanism. Its patient, automated voice had continued to count down the seconds. Lucrezia looked tired. She glanced over at Tarvek.

"Really, it would be so much easier to just kill everyone here and start over with a new calling. I could see sacrificing all the other knowledge I've gained, but I mustn't allow myself to forget that one of me has been captured by that traitorous niece of mine. She is simply too dangerous." She sighed and gingerly picked her way through the rubble to the control panel. "No, I'm afraid this body must continue to live for now." So saying, she flipped a switch and the voice stopped in mid-sentence.

"You said no power on Earth could stop that," Tarvek protested, his voice muffled through the thick glass of his prison.

Lucrezia nodded. "I did, didn't I?" She turned to face him and a look of pleased surprise was on her face. "It looks like we've learned something else useful, hm? Little Zola should have *known* how to turn off my self-destruct system."

Tarvek nodded. Lucrezia was poisonous and he hated her, but he was always reluctantly fascinated when she talked about her work. "Perhaps if Zola had time to concentrate . . . perhaps your copy is able to hold some things back in the heat of the moment."

"Or can confuse her with *false* memories." Lucrezia clapped her hands. "That *is* what I would do! Little Zola may not find my memories as useful as she thinks they will be."

This cheered her up considerably and she began humming as she cleared debris away from the tubes. Tarvek hammered at the door, which didn't even rattle. Earlier, he had seen Lucrezia place his comrades Gilgamesh and Violetta in the adjacent tubes and they were still there, slumped and unconscious.

"This may work out nicely after all," Lucrezia mused as she worked. She patted the glass on Tarvek's tube as she passed. "Oh, don't worry, I'm not going to kill you, that wouldn't be fun at all."

She sashayed over to a control box and flipped a switch. Lights slowly glimmered into existence. "Now these old mind-control devices of mine were an early effort. My beautiful wasps are ever so much easier to administer, but since you're already there, they'll do quite nicely." She gazed at the row of tubes and unconsciously licked her lips. "To have Baron Wulfenbach's son Gilgamesh *and* you, the nascent Storm King under my control—" she gazed down at herself and smiled "—the possibilities make me quite giddy." Lucrezia began to chuckle, which turned into an angry squeal of surprise as she was yanked to the ground.

Lucrezia struggled, but found her ankle trapped in a grip of iron. The battered face of the vicious construct Von Pinn glared at her with furious eyes. "What the deuce are you doing?" Lucrezia screamed. "You're supposed to be dead!"

Von Pinn grinned, a wide nasty grin full of sharp teeth. She slowly began to drag her broken body forward across Lucrezia's legs. "Not quite," she whispered.

"Release me this instant," Lucrezia said imperiously. "That's an order!"

Von Pinn hissed in amusement. The leather encasing her body creaked as she advanced. "That will no longer work, you filthy thief of souls. It was not easy, but I have found ways to break your hold on me."

Lucrezia's efforts to escape took on a new urgency. "Ridiculous! You cannot resist me! I made sure of that when I built you! Stop, I say!"

Von Pinn's metal claws hooked into Lucrezia's belt and the construct pulled herself higher. "Ah, you built this cage, but you did not build me. Have you forgotten your 'greatest triumph'? Even trapped in this miserable flesh, I am Otilia—the Muse of Protection." Lucrezia opened her mouth and a hand of steel and leather closed on her throat. Her eyes bulged in terror.

"No . . . " Lucrezia choked out. "Can't die. Too . . . important . . . "

Von Pinn's face drew close. She glared into Lucrezia's eyes. Her terrible jaws snapped together in a fearsome grimace. "Then *run*," she snarled.

Lucrezia shuddered once, her eyes began to lose focus and close. "Curse you," she whispered. "I'll be back . . . "

She retreated.

Agatha opened her eyes and gave a strangled choke of surprise. "What? Von Pinn! Stop!"

With a smirk, Von Pinn released her grip and collapsed fully atop Agatha.

"What was *that* all about?" Agatha asked, as she struggled to extricate herself.

"Your mother was always a coward," Von Pinn said dreamily. "She could never tolerate pain. You should remember that." Her voice trailed off as she slipped into unconsciousness.

Moloch von Zinzer sat brooding. Ordinarily, he would be assisting the sparks in refurbishing the great cat-like security clank that lay stretched out on the floor. Today, however, with four different sparks crowding around the clank—arguing, jostling, and attempting to work on it all at the same time—he merely watched from a safe distance, perched on a crate that had been pushed to one side of the room.

Beside him sat Fräulein Hexalina Snaug, Doctor Mittelmind's minion. They were sharing a small sack of raisins. Snaug was observing Moloch closely. The little mechanic had undergone a radical transformation in the last day or so.

Ever since he had been sentenced to work in Castle Heterodyne, Moloch had earned a reputation as a clueless screw-up. The general consensus was that the only reason he was still alive was because no newer prisoners had arrived to take his place in the Castle kitchens.

But that had changed ever since the Heterodyne had appeared. Something about her presence had shaken him so badly that he had undergone a startling transformation. He started handling other minions, sparks, and the Castle itself with an artless efficiently that was the envy of the other minions, and had even been noted by some of the other sparks.

Thus it was with some surprise, and no little embarrassment, that Hexalina found herself entertaining certain fantasies that had her blushing. Moloch heard a faint sigh and glanced over at her. A touch of concern appeared on his face as the girl beside him appeared slightly flushed. "You okay?"

Snaug nodded. "Just worried about . . . " she waved her hand to encompass everything in sight. Moloch nodded. "What are *you* thinking so deeply about?"

"The Castle. Didn't I once hear Professor Tiktoffen say that it was alive?"

Snaug nodded. "It's a point of some contention amongst those sparks who dabble in artificial intelligence, but Tiktoffen said the Castle—that is, not the walls, exactly, but the part that's, well, *dead* now, I guess—" she threw out her chest and waved her arms about "—exhibits many of the prerequisites that would allow us to classify it as an intelligent entity."

Moloch snorted at the accuracy of the imitation.[6] "No, I don't mean smart. That's obvious. I mean . . . alive. Like you or a . . . a construct."

Hexalina paused. "Oh. I see. Well, that's what Tiktoffen believes. He claimed it was an entirely new form of life. Why?"

Moloch slapped a stone. It shifted slightly. "Because when you kill something, it usually starts to rot."

The two of them absorbed the implications of this, then hurried to the sparks to offer assistance.

Unfortunately, not a lot of constructive work was getting done around the mechanical cat. One of the sparks, Theopholous DuMedd, happened to glance down in time to see a small clank dragging off the micrometer he'd been using. His yell caused a modest swarm of similar small clanks to flee, all clutching tools and equipment. Theo chased them until they disappeared into a large crack in the wall, dragging their spoils behind them. With an oath, he flung his work gloves to the ground. His fury doubled when another tiny clank popped out, grabbed the gloves, and dragged them out of sight as well.

"This is not going well at all," he snarled. "Those confounded little clanks of Agatha's have gone out of control! They steal parts! Tools! When we repair something on this beast, they nip in and rip out

---

6   Many minions have developed the knack of imitating various sparks. It only becomes a problem when somebody gets interested in the whole mind-swapping thing. It's one of the reasons why, by common consent, this is a field of science that is never pursued, or if it is, it stays between consenting adults.

something else!" He gave the clank a kick. "We'll never get this thing moving at this rate!"

Moloch nodded and began checking the hoist controls on the makeshift lift. He stared down into the hole Agatha had blasted in the floor of the Castle and gave a resigned sigh. "Guess I'd better go get spooky girl and Wulfenbach and let them—"

"NO!" Professor Caractacus Mezzasalma drew himself up on his mechanical legs and glared. "We do not need to run to a Wulfenbach every time we have a problem! We are sparks! We can solve this!" The others nodded in agreement. "It may take years! Endless toil! The blood of thousands of minions! But our science will triumph!"

The other sparks cheered. Moloch rolled his eyes.

Princess Zeetha and Airman Axel Higgs regarded the cavorting sparks from a safe distance on the other side of the room. They shared a significant glance. Zeetha nodded and pulled a small mechanism from her pocket. "Oooo—kay. I think it's time for this."

Higgs leaned in to examine it. It was a small, decorated metal sphere. "What is it?"

"Don't know," Zeetha admitted as she hit the only switch, "but Agatha said it would help, and really at this point—how much more trouble could it be?"

The sphere shivered. Small panels slid aside releasing a set of arms and legs that unfolded with a snap. A mismatched pair of eyes swiveled open and examined the room. It turned back to Zeetha, nodded once, and leapt to the ground and scuttled away.

Higgs cocked an eyebrow. "I guess we'll find out."

The walls of Castle Heterodyne contain unusual spaces. Places where corners come together in odd ways, secret places sealed away for forgotten reasons, and, of course, places where the mechanisms that allow the Castle to perform its many wonders are housed.

In the Castle walls, two separate teams of dingbots, each led by a small commander, were busy assembling devices intended to crush their opposite number. Each of these primaries[7] was fiercely territorial and regarded the presence of the other primary as a direct challenge to their control. They marched among their troops clicking and whistling with smug self-importance.

An unearthly music unexpectedly began in the room outside. Both teams of little clanks froze. Dreamily, they dropped tools and began to move towards the sound. They thronged into the room and gathered around the hulk of the security clank, waiting. The sparks who had been rebuilding it danced backward, trying their best not to trip over the single-minded tide of clanks. Standing atop the security clank was the music's source: the little round clank that Zeetha had activated. The rest stared up at it, mesmerized. The two primaries pushed their way through the group until they stood at the front, gazing upwards in evident astonishment.

The music ended and the singer gazed down on the assembled crowd. The two primaries blinked, then each understood—with fury—that it was standing next to its hated rival. They moved to fight, but the round clank rang out a single clear tone and both primaries dropped to their knees. Atop the new clank, a small hatch folded open with a crisp snap and revealed a minuscule crown. The assembled clanks stood frozen before their new ruler. It clapped its jewellike hands once and, without a word, the clank armies became one. Surging forward, they overran the giant security clank like ants on a hill.

Everyone stared at this flurry of activity in amazement. Theo

---

[7]   The diminutive clanks, now colloquially known as dingbots, were constructed by the Lady Heterodyne as lab assistants and were fascinating entities. The ones the Lady constructed herself served as primaries. Once activated, they operated independently, scavenging parts and constructing additional, secondary dingbots. These would then go forth to construct tertiaries. Persons of a nervous disposition have allowed themselves to become overly concerned about a future where all of Europa is buried hip deep in duodenary dingbots busy disassembling the Earth itself for parts. Fortunately, secondaries were not as good at building dingbots as the primaries are, and the tertiaries were barely capable of performing simple tasks, let alone constructing more dingbots.

leaned back and nodded in approval. "They're repairing it." he said. "This looks promising."

Doctor Mittelmind gripped his arm. "A promising *disaster*," he growled. "Can you not see it?"

Theo blinked. "Um . . . no?"

Mittelmind indicated the organized chaos swirling before them. "Observe! Those little clanks are building! Designing!"

Diaz' eyes widened. "Spitting in the face of the creator!"

Mezzasalma gasped. "Warping science!"

They all looked expectantly at Theo, who felt like he was letting down the home team. He shrugged. "So?"

Mittelmind smacked the back of his head. "They are taking our jobs!"

"We are doomed," Diaz declared.

Mezzasalma concurred. "DOOOOOMED!"

Theo rolled his eyes. "Nonsense! These things are but tools!" He scooped up a clank that had been attempting to straighten a steel strut with only a tiny hammer. He tried not to notice it seemed to be succeeding. "New, complex tools, certainly. But surely there are unique strengths that we, as men of science, can provide that these little mechanisms cannot."

The three sparks looked abashed. Mezzasalma rubbed his jaw. "Oh. Well, certainly . . . "

The others nodded and looked like they might relax, when Moloch, who had been deep in conversation with Snaug, wandered up and took notice of what was happening. "Oh not these things again." he groaned. "They start by being helpful, but soon they'll build something terrible that could kill us all!"

The three older sparks went white. "DOOOOOMED," they moaned.

Suddenly there was a shudder and a prolonged rumble. A huge billow of smoke and dust erupted from the shaft now opening in the floor. When the room stopped shaking, they all crowded around the edge and peered downwards. Higgs lit a torch, dropped it—they were able to follow it even through the dust—and saw it bounce and land on a heap of rubble almost a hundred meters down.

"That happened faster than I *thought* it would." Moloch muttered to himself.

Diaz shook his head. "I do not know what you were expecting, but *that* was an explosion from a bomb. Someone did this deliberately!"

Zeetha looked stricken. "Agatha," she whispered.

Airman Higgs carefully put his pipe in his pocket. "Master Gilgamesh is down there too. Guess we'd better go see if they're all right."

Moloch raised an eyebrow. "You ain't going *this* way."

Higgs nodded. "Lady Heterodyne carved this hole. There are other paths."

"Well . . . sure. But where are they?"

Higgs paused, and realized that everyone was looking at him. "I . . . think I can get there." Moloch looked skeptical. Higgs hesitated, then continued. "I . . . found a map."

"A map!" Professor Diaz perked up. "That could be useful indeed! Where is it?"

The airman shrugged. "It's down in the lab."

Diaz frowned. "That does not do us much good, then."

Higgs tapped the side of his head. "I remember maps." The professor opened his mouth, but Higgs continued. "Who's coming with me?"

Zeetha stepped up. "I am."

A tiny smile scurried across Higgs face. "Good." Zeetha felt inordinately pleased at this reaction. She tried to hide it by looking to Krosp. "How about you?"

"Of course," the cat responded. "Agatha'll be lost without me."

Higgs turned towards Moloch. "How about you?"

Moloch looked alarmed. "Why me?"

"You're useful." Higgs slid a glance towards the huge security clank and the little clank army that swarmed it, working furiously. "Don't think you're needed here. Of course, the madboys could probably think of something to do to you . . . "

Moloch clapped his hands. "Let's go."

Theo DuMudd and Sleipnir O'Hara, friends of Gil who had helped him gain entrance to the Castle, were standing to the side, watching. Sleipnir leaned in towards Theo. "A map?" Her voice was the barest whisper, practiced during countless pranks and adventures back on Castle Wulfenbach. "Of *this* place? That doesn't even—"

Theo answered with a matching whisper. "I know. But he says he can get us back to Gil and Agatha." He narrowed his eyes as he studied the airman. "If he's got to claim there's a map in order to do it? Fine. He found a map." He raised his voice to call: "We'll come too."

Zeetha nodded. "Yeah, you can handle the spark stuff." She turned to Professor Mezzasalma. "Can the rest of you get this thing running?"

The professor gave an offended snort. "Of course!" He then paused. "If those wind-up mice will *let* us."

Zeetha nodded, then strode up and confronted the queen clank. "Hey! Agatha needs this cat monster thing up and running as soon as possible! Help these guys make that happen, got it?" The diminutive ruler reared up, clearly offended. It then considered the warrior princess who stood before it and gave a clear nod of acquiescence.

Zeetha turned, caught sight of Mezzasalma's smirk of triumph and buttonholed him before he could move. "And I'll be checking to make sure that's *all* you had them do, so no bright ideas. No extras, no deviation from what's already here. I know how sparks think."

The professor looked into her pitiless eyes and swallowed. "That's . . . quite a reasonable demand, considering the circumstances." He swiveled his eyes back. "Don't you agree, my dear fellows?" Both Diaz and Mittelmind looked like they were sucking on persimmons, but they gave stiff nods nonetheless.

Fortunately, Doctor Mittelmind's natural ebullience could not be contained for long, and with a sigh, he shrugged and declared, "To work everyone!" He leaned towards Fräulein Snaug. "Prepare a list!"

Hexalina shuffled her feet. "Um, actually, Herr Doktor, I'd like to go help find the Lady Heterodyne." Her master turned towards her, astonishment writ large upon his face. She continued, "Please, sir?"

Mittelmind glanced over at the security clank and its busy repair team. It was a fascinating sight. "But why?"

Moloch stepped up to her and touched her shoulder. "Hey, are you coming? I'd feel better having someone at my back who wasn't completely nuts."

Snaug glanced at Mittelmind. "Maybe. In a minute."

The mechanic nodded, grabbed a toolbox, and legged it back to the group assembling around Airman Higgs. Snaug watched him go, a look of longing on her face. The doctor observed this and a knowing smile softened his features. Fräulein Snaug looked back up at him hopefully. "Ah. Yes, of course." Mittelmind awkwardly patted her head. "Off you go, girl." He then snapped out a hand and prevented her from darting off. Once he had her attention, he raised an admonishing finger. "But no *permanent* damage. He belongs to the Lady, now." A quick pout crossed Hexalina's face and her hands clenched in frustration—but Mittelmind was adamant. She gave a small huff and nodded. "Yes, Doctor." Mittelmind smiled and released her. Snaug caught sight of Moloch and repressed a small thrill of anticipation. *Permanent* was such a delightfully high bar.

Violetta closed the fastening with a satisfying snap. "There!"

Everyone gave a sigh of relief. Once Lucrezia had retreated, Agatha had scooped up her locket, holding it close to her with one hand as, with her other hand, she rushed to release the others from their glass prisons. Zola had damaged the necklace when she yanked it away, so Violetta repaired the clasp while Agatha held it in place.

Now, the locket was, once again, firmly held at Agatha's throat.

"Thank you, Violetta." Agatha gave it an experimental tug and frowned. "Maybe I'd better just weld the thing onto an iron ring."

Violetta rolled her eyes. "Don't be overly dramatic. A good solid lock will work fine." She cast a scornful eye towards Gil and Tarvek, who were busy seeing to Von Pinn. "Whose adolescent slave-girl fantasies are we indulging here?"

Agatha quickly changed the subject as they joined Gil and Tarvek beside one of the lab's operating tables. "How is Madame Von Pinn doing?"

"I'm amazed she's still alive, actually," Tarvek confessed.

Gil shrugged. "Constructs of this type are notoriously tough, and we've managed to stabilize her for now."

Tarvek shook his head, "But her body is definitely on its way out." He began ticking items off on his fingers. "We need to extract the Castle entity from the body of the Muse, Otilia. Then we need to transfer Otilia's mind out of the body we know as Von Pinn and into a suitable clank body until the Muse can be repaired. *Then* we have to transfer the Castle entity back into the Castle system."

Gil nodded. "It's like a sliding puzzle in that we can't do anything until we do the first step, and we can't do that until the others get back with that watchdog clank."

"No." They turned at the firmness in Agatha's voice. "We can't wait. We have to leave as soon as we can." Agatha strode over to a bench and grabbed a brass tube and began stringing wires through it. "Zola now has access to all of my mother's—Lucrezia's—memories, right?"

Tarvek waggled his hand. "Yes, for the *most* part . . . "

Agatha turned to Gil. "And your father is probably still planning on destroying the Castle."

Gil nodded. "I'm sort of counting on him not doing so while I'm inside . . . but, yes."

Agatha selected a coil of copper tubing, snipped off a length, and began bending it into a fanciful hook. "That's two very powerful enemies, one inside the Castle and the other outside." She laced wiring about the base of the coil and began attaching it to the tube.

"Nobody here—" the wave of her hand indicated the room, the Castle, and probably Mechanicsburg as a whole "—is safe until I get the Castle running again." She glanced down at the construct on the slab. "That includes Madame Von Pinn here."

She stared intently at a small electronic device that was sitting on the bench before her. She selected a large monkey wrench and, with a fluid movement, smashed the device sharply and precisely, causing the case to disintegrate without damaging the components inside. With a satisfied nod, she picked them up and began inserting them into the end of the brass tube. "We'll have to leave notes for the others. They're smart, and Theo and Sleipnir care about Von Pinn too, I imagine. Once they find their way back here, they should be able to get started on her without us."

Agatha turned to face them. Idly, she swung the copper and brass wand through the air, testing its weight. "Our first priority is repairing the Castle." She pointed to a small collection of equipment piled up on a bench. "I've gathered what I think I'll need to transfer the part of its consciousness that's in Otilia's body back into its main system." She looked over to the shattered hulk of the Muse. "That's assuming we can find a place to hook you up . . . "

The clank jerked its head up. "I-I can show/guide you. But even with the four of you, you have t-t-too many/much equipment. I am too large and heavy. To transport this/me/me/me alone will require—"

As the Muse was talking, Agatha snapped a switch on the wand. It sparked to life and a crackling bolt of energy burned between the points of the hook. With a deft swing, Agatha sliced the Muse's head cleanly off and caught it before it hit the ground. She turned to the others. "I have that covered. Any other problems?"

In the shocked silence there was a burst of static and then the head tucked underneath her arm spoke. "N-n-no. We are good."

The great flying armada that accompanied Castle Wulfenbach was slowly regrouping. Mechanicsburg's newly reactivated Torchmen clanks had driven it away like a swarm of bees fighting off an invasion of wasps. It now hovered two-and-a-half leagues[8] to the north of the town as it saw to its reorganization and repair.

A squadron of damaged ships flashed a departure signal, then peeled off towards the already overtaxed repair yards at Sturmhalten. Other ships were covered with swarms of rigger-rats, busy replacing canvas or repairing hulls even as they hung at dizzying heights above the ground.

Aboard one small, unobtrusive vessel, an inner door burst open. The occupants of the room, who had been examining a large map of the town and its surroundings, leaped in surprise. One produced a knife, seemingly from thin air.

In the doorway stood Boris Dolokhov, second in command to Baron Wulfenbach and the man currently running the Empire of the Pax Transylvania while its master recuperated in hospital. Boris had a reputation as being perennially annoyed, but the man who stood framed in the doorway now radiated a controlled fury that had those who saw him, seasoned fighters all, slowly rising to their feet and flexing their claws. Boris's normally fastidious appearance was marred by several bruises on his face and one of his four arms hung limp. His suit was tattered and looked as though he had been in a fight. Several fights.

General Khrizhan, who was easily the most level-headed of the three Jägermonster generals, gave him a wary nod. "Gospodin Dolokhov. How did hyu find us?"

Boris removed a handkerchief from an inner pocket and delicately dabbed it at his lip. "Your messenger told me."

The three generals glanced at each other. Khrizhan raised his chin defensively. "He vould not."

The Baron had been declared hors de combat, and Boris was in the process of coordinating the current situation vis-a-vis Mechanicsburg.

---

[8] After some experimentation, it was determined that the defense system of Mechanicsburg defines a league as 5.556 kilometers.

There had been a sudden disruption at the door, and a Jägermonster officer had sauntered in. "Hey dere, Meester Boris bug man!"

Boris swore under his breath. Then a sudden realization made him frown. "Wait a minute . . . " The Jägers had been created by the Heterodynes. Because of this, the news of Agatha's existence had been carefully kept from them. In advance of the empire's sally into this neighborhood, every Jägermonster that served the empire had been plausibly dispatched to far-flung locations. He flipped through a stack of troop movement reports. "What are you even doing here? All of you Jägers are supposed to be up north."

The Jäger carefully collected a stack of paperwork, then sat on it. "Heh. Yez, vell, sveethot, ve gots a message for hyu." He smiled at Boris. "Ve quit."

Boris carefully adjusted his pince-nez. "I don't have time for jokes."

The Jäger shrugged insouciantly. "No joke, sport. Iz a message direct from de generals."

"Obviously I need to talk to them. Where are they?"

The Jäger laughed uproariously. "Vell dey ain't got time to vaste talkin' to hyu." He unwound himself from his chair and leaned over to gently pat Boris's cheek. "Iz hyu disappointed ve ain't gunna be around anymore?" He smiled toothily. "Tell hyu vat. Hy let hyu get vun punch in to treasure in hyu old age." He then cracked his knuckles. "Or ven hyu vakes op."

Without breaking eye contact, Boris dragged his fourth arm into view. Grasped firmly in his hand was a severely beaten and battered Jäger, whom he allowed to drop with a *thud* to the deck. "Oh," he allowed, "not right away . . . "

The generals stared down in shock until Zog, the oldest, threw his head back with a roar of delighted laughter. He tossed the knife in his hand upwards with a flourish, and it performed a delicate pirouette before sliding cleanly into the scabbard at his hip. "Hyu haz earned the right to a tok." He turned to the astonished Khrizhan

and smacked him on the arm. "Alexi! Get some tea for our guest."
He reached back and spun a chair into place at their table. "Zo tok."

As the injured Jäger was taken away, Boris nodded, took a seat, and
fastidiously adjusted his cuffs. A tall glass of tea was quietly set down
before him. Zog sat opposite and studied him openly. In his opinion,
Boris was under a great deal of stress. More so than usual. The man did
periodically take over the reins of the Baron's empire without trouble,
but these were, unquestionably, extraordinary times.

Boris took a deep breath in through his nose. "You say you are
leaving the Baron's service."

Zog nodded. "Dere iz a Heterodyne. Dot vos the contingency."

"She is not official. She has not taken the Castle. The Doom Bell
has not rung."

Zog ground his teeth together in annoyance. "Feh! Technicalities!
Ennyvay, ve half not entered de town, yah?"

Boris rolled his eyes. "You mean your troops haven't climbed up
a set of stairs!"

Zog was unpleasantly surprised. "Oho!" He blustered, "Vot hyu—"

He was interrupted by Boris slamming two of his hands on the
table. "No! Nonono! We cannot fight! Not now!" He looked at the
other generals. "We need you. The empire needs you."

Zog waved a hand dismissively. "De Baron haz gots lots of troops.
Thousands." He smiled. "Sum ov dem might even gif us a goot fight."

To his disappointment, Boris did not rise to the bait, but nodded
seriously instead. "Granted. But everyone knows that the Jägers serve
the House of Heterodyne. If you acknowledge this girl prematurely,
it could fuel trouble all over Europa."

Zog shrugged and scratched at his chin. "Yah, dot's true. Could
be ve's in for goot times. Lotsa fightin'. Lotsa fun."

Boris folded his arms. "Oh really? And how will your new
Heterodyne like that sort of chaos—if she takes after her father and
uncle?"

Zog looked like he had bitten into a particularly bitter bug. He glanced at his compatriots. General Goomblast considered this. "Her papa?" He wiggled a hand to indicate that it was an open question. Then he sighed, "But she does seem more like her oncle den her papa, yah?"

The others nodded. General Khrizhan cleared his throat and tried to look reasonable. "Hyu said 'prematurely'?"

Boris took a sip of tea. "I did." He looked at the three old generals. "Wait. Wait until she takes the Castle. Wait until the Doom Bell rings. Wait until the Baron formally releases you back into her service." He spread his hands. "Let the people of Europa see that the Law of the Wulfenbach Empire still holds."

Zog frowned. "Und let de pipple see dot de Heterodyne *submits* to dose laws, hey?"

Goomblast clicked his claws together. "Brodders, Meester Boris makes a goot point."

Zog's fur bristled. "Empire law . . . "

Khrizhan leaned in. "Dun alvays tink ov youself, Zog. Dis vay, *Meez Agatha* ken choose her first var."

Zog's eyebrows shot up and he looked at his fellow general with new respect. "Ooh, dot is very true, Alexi." He leaned in to Boris and explained, "A gurl haz gots to be *picky* about her first var." He glanced back at the other generals. "Remember de Lady Roxalana?"

To Boris's astonishment, he saw the other two generals blushing. He opened his mouth to ask, then realized he really did not want to know[9].

As Zog chuckled, Goomblast stepped up and made a formal bow. "Hokay, Meester Boris, maybe ve do dis hyu vay."

---

[9]   Intriguingly, there is no written record of a Roxalana Heterodyne. However, in a hundred kilometer radius around the town of Mechanicsburg, one will find assorted geographic features, clearly caused by the unleashing of cataclysmic forces; these include "Roxalana's Chasm," "Roxalana's Blight," "The Melted Mountain of Roxalana," and a vast wasteland where nothing grows known as "Roxalana's Comeuppance."

Boris let out a sigh of relief. "Excellent."

Goomblast held up a delicate finger. "Eef hyu agrees to certain trade concessions ve is gun discuss now."

Sweat broke out on Boris's forehead. Still, it could have been a lot worse—

A voice rang out from behind the group. "Sirs, if you agree to this, the Lady Heterodyne will die."

Everyone spun about to see a tall, jaunty man sitting in the window. Boris started to his feet, unwelcome recognition obviously showing on his face.

The man in the window continued. "Do forgive me for letting myself in, generals. I am Ardsley Wooster. You might recognize me as Gilgamesh Wulfenbach's manservant, but in actuality, I am an agent of British Intelligence!"

General Goomblast impatiently waved a hand. "Yez, yez, *efferbody* knew dot. Now vat vos dot about de Lady Heterodyne?"

Wooster sighed. Apparently, his secret had been safe . . . with everyone. Oh well. "I regret to say that Herr Dolokhov is not playing straight with you."

Boris gave a desperate shout and tried to leap forward, but was easily kept in check by one of Khrizhan's large hands. "Keep talking, Herr Wooster."

Wooster nodded. "What he isn't telling you is that, if you stand by and do nothing, there won't be a Mechanicsburg to return to. The Baron plans to destroy the Castle and your Lady Heterodyne."

Khrizhan stepped forward. "Dis is a serious charge."

From inside his leather coat, Wooster produced a thick oilskin courier packet. He tossed it to the general. "Here are orders. Troop movements and instructions for the attack and its aftermath."

Khrizhan snapped open the packet and began flipping through the papers within. Suddenly he paused, then began to scowl as he flipped faster. Within seconds, papers were blizzarding throughout the room as he screamed in rage.

Boris broke free and advanced, fists balled in rage. "Do you know what you've done?"

Wooster leaned back out the window and grabbed a rope that was hanging beside him. "Destabilized Britain's greatest rival *and* aided an innocent girl," he replied smugly. "A mighty good day's work, I'd say."

Boris screamed in frustration. "She's not innocent, you dupe! She's the Other!"

Wooster looked serious. "I believe you're wrong, but if she is, then rest assured that Her Majesty will take an interest."

"You damned spy," Boris screamed. "I'll kill you!" But as he leapt forward, Wooster simply fell backwards into the open sky. Everyone rushed to the window and peered downward in time to see Wooster pull a small personal flight unit from inside his coat. It was too small to actually fly anywhere, but the British agent was now in a controlled fall that was taking him back towards the town below. A last faint "*dosvedanya*" wafted upwards.

As Boris stared at the receding figure, a large hand fell on his shoulder. A great feeling of peace washed over Boris. He really had done his best. He closed his eyes and wished his coat was not ripped. "All right," He said evenly, "Fine. If you're going to kill me, just do it quickly."

There was a pause. Then, to his surprise, a second hand grasped, lifted, and turned him around until he faced the trio of menacing monsters who regarded him from troubled faces. Zog nodded. "Perhaps. But first . . . " He gently set Boris down onto his feet. "First hyu weel tell uz about Meez Agatha and de Other. Ve iz *listening*."

CHAPTER 2

One would think that sparks—being on the whole, psychotic megalomaniacs with little regard for human life and poor impulse control—would have no friends or indeed any use for people. Quite often they believe this themselves, and can often be heard making dramatic statements to this effect. The reason these diatribes are heard by more than just the occasional potted plant or captured hero is this: sparks quite frequently find themselves surrounded by people whether they want to be or not. We are not just talking about the stereotypical traveler whose cart breaks down during a storm and thus must seek shelter at the lone castle glimpsed through the trees and so finds himself at a timely ringside seat for the revelation of the latest abomination of science (although there is no denying this happens far more than is statistically probable). No, your seriously steeped-in-madness dabbler in the esoteric sciences usually finds themself taxed with a rag-tag collection of hangers-on, typically consisting of minions, constructs, adventurers, and those unique, unclassifiable, individuals whose raison d'être appears to be to remind us of what a strange world it is. Even more interestingly, it appears that the greater the spark, the more of these individuals they spontaneously accumulate.

Philosophers and other underemployed persons have theorized this is a natural phenomenon, and is simply "Nature's Way" of trying to insulate the world from the direct effects of sparks by constantly distracting them. The argument goes that if they were left alone to their own devices (so to speak), they would soon reduce all of human existence to naught but mathematical formulae, and I do not believe that I am speaking figuratively. This theory goes a long way towards explaining the enormous collection of odd persons that have, over time, accreted around Baron Klaus Wulfenbach.

Those who believe this phenomenon does represent some sort of cosmic defense mechanism, and that the greater the spark, the greater the number of distracting persons required to prevent them from bringing about Armageddon, noted with trepidation the number, quality, and sheer strangeness of the people that had already begun to fall into the orbit of the young Lady Heterodyne less than a week after she had publicly revealed herself in Sturmhalten and became known to Europa as a whole. From this, they had drawn rather alarming conclusions. All of which, it turned out, seriously underestimated the events to come.

—An excerpt from the Introduction to Professor Thaddeus Brinstine's *What the Hell Was That? Trying to Understand The Legacy of the Long Wars* (Transylvania Polygnostic University Press)

ॐ

Airman Higgs reached out and grasped a mildewing set of draperies. These disintegrated into tatters with a firm tug, allowing a wan, dust-filled shaft of light to illuminate the hallway. The doors that punctuated the walls were more elaborately carved than any others they had seen in the Castle, and some effort had been made to soften the usual style of decor they had found throughout the rest of the building. Oh, there was still a plethora of fanged monstrosities threatening hapless humans, but here, at least, everybody involved seemed unnaturally cheerful. Higgs nodded in satisfaction. "I'm betting this is where we need to be."

The others looked at each other in confusion. Zeetha glanced out the window. "But we haven't gone down anywhere near far enough. We're still above ground."

Sleipnir had opened the nearest door and peeked inside. "These look like they're all bedrooms. Pretty fancy ones too." She raised an eyebrow sardonically. "Read your 'map' wrong?"

Higgs regarded them blankly. Then he gave a slight sigh. "Thought you folks were smart." He started walking. "The Castle told Herr von Zinzer here that the Great Movement Chamber was so secret that even the Heterodyne Boys never knew about it. But Miss Agatha found the Lady Lucrezia's secret lab in a set of small rooms hidden *underneath* it." He pulled his pipe from his pocket and gave it a ruminative suck. "Sparks are like balloon bees.[10] They like to spread out to fill as much space as they can. If the Lady Lucrezia was set up in those small rooms, it's because she didn't know about, or couldn't *get* to the larger room right overhead."

He gave the wall a gentle rap as he kept walking. "A place like Castle Heterodyne—even if you was the boss—I'm betting you'd want to get away from it occasionally and to do that, you'd have to put your secret room somewhere the Castle couldn't see. The Great Movement Chamber was as deep as the Castle's perception went, so they stowed it below that."

He stopped outside a bedroom door that, even compared to the others, was ostentatious in the extreme. Gargoyles and assorted monstrosities frolicked in all directions and the door itself sported inlaid panels of gold and jade. "And the only person who'd know about it would be the Heterodyne."

"Oh!" Sleipnir snapped her fingers. "The Heterodyne Boys' father

---

[10]   Balloon bees (*urinaria apis caeli Europa*) are a species of cave-dwelling honeybee that has adapted to living within airship cells. Their signature characteristic is that they spread out in an enclosed space until they are as far as possible from each other. They then construct small, solitary dens.

was killed by their mother. He might not have *had* the opportunity to pass that knowledge down to his son."

"This does make sense," Theo chimed in. "From stuff I've heard from my family, Lucrezia could get anything she wanted from her husband, Bill Heterodyne." He pushed open the great door and revealed an extremely ornate room, complete with a bed that could easily have comfortably slept a half-a-dozen people. "And knowing her, I'll bet she even convinced him to give her the master bedroom."

The room was large, but one could see that, even in ruins, it conveyed a feeling of comfort and power. The outer wall was dominated by a large set of cracked windows and a set of French doors that at one time must have led out to a balcony. This had been ripped away, but there was still a breathtaking view of the town spread out below. In addition to the bed, there was a parlor, a row of elegantly carved armoires, and a spacious, sunken marble tub. The walls were paneled from top to bottom in a reddish wood that even under the dust and grime of almost two decades conveyed richness and extravagance. The walls were hung with numerous paintings.

It was Zeetha, while studying them closely, who realized: "Hey. These all feature the same woman."

Theo examined them and nodded. "That is the Lady Lucrezia," he confirmed. "I saw portraits of her in the family gallery back home." He shook his head. "My mother said she always loved looking at herself."

Everyone examined the pictures with a renewed interest. Lucrezia had been a curvaceous blonde, with large, heavy-lidded eyes, a small nose, and sensuous lips. In every picture, the artists had managed to convey a sense of mischief and the underlying cruelty that one found in the most pernicious of practical jokers.

"So that's Agatha's mom?" Moloch asked. "She doesn't look that dangerous."

"Nevertheless, that's the woman who became the Other, destroyed a whole bunch of the Great Houses, and rules the Geisterdamen," Krosp reminded him.

While everyone else examined the paintings, Higgs was slowly walking the perimeter of the room, tapping lightly on the walls. Finally, he stopped, reached out, and gave a nondescript section of paneling a firm shove. With a faint groan, a narrow door fell inward, raising a cloud of dust. He nodded in satisfaction. The head of a darkened stairway could be seen.

"I'll bet *that* goes straight down to her hidden lab."

Theo nodded. "A nice little chain of logic there, Mister Higgs. Well done."

As they filed through the door, Zeetha laid a hand on Higg's sleeve. "Wait a minute—how did you know where the master bedroom was?" she asked quietly.

Higgs looked at her with raised eyebrows. "It was on the map."

The passage wound down and down and down. They descended in single file, with Higgs leading the way. Krosp was fascinated. "This thing must connect to secret doors throughout half the Castle."

Moloch hunched his shoulders. "I'm just amazed there wasn't a trap every two meters."

Snaug considered this. "This is a place the Castle intelligence didn't go. Maybe there weren't any."

Moloch snorted. "If I was one of the wackjobs who built this place, it's where *I'd* make sure there *were* traps."

Higgs listened as he stealthily disarmed yet another trap. He nodded. *Young von Zinzer would fit in just fine.*

Eventually they came to a door that, when opened, revealed the ruins of Lucrezia's secret lab. They all exclaimed at the sight of the collapsed ceiling and immediately spread out to look for Agatha and the others.

Krosp and Moloch gazed back at the stairway, which continued on deeper into the earth.

Moloch scratched his beard. "So—there are secret rooms under the secret room?"

Krosp grinned. "Exploring this place is going to be very interesting." He clapped Moloch on the back. "You'll have to tell me all about it."

Zeetha was searching near the pile of debris when she stumbled against an unstable rock—striking it with her shoulder. A small cascade of rubble began and Higgs yanked her out of the way just as a large stone block dislodged and fell. She looked at the cracked floor beneath it and turned to Higgs. "Thanks. I was careless."

This was clearly not the response Higgs had been expecting. To cover, he gestured at the pile with the stem of his pipe. "We have to risk it to find the others, but this whole thing is unstable. Could come down at any time. You keep searching. I'll keep my eye on you."

Zeetha nodded, but at that moment there was a shout from Theo. "It's okay! They all survived!" He was holding a wad of notes that had been placed on the same bench as the comatose Von Pinn.

"Then where are they?" Krosp asked.

"They've gone to fix the Castle." He read further and frowned. "Ah. They say that the fake Heterodyne girl is still loose. Huh. Gil says she's someone he met in Paris—and she's a lot more dangerous than she looks," He looked up. "They want us to take care of Madame Von Pinn." He shook his head. "I can't say they left us with the easier job."

Moloch leaned into Fräulein Snaug. "Oh, I dunno. You mean I get to stay in a fortified secret room while a bunch of sparks race around trying to fix this death machine of a castle? Twist my arm."

Snaug looked at his defenseless little arm and shivered. *Soon enough*, she promised herself. Aloud she said, "But first we'd better shore up this ceiling."

By Von Pinn's bedside, Theo was finishing up a quick examination and frequently referencing the sheaf of notes he'd found.

Sleipnir stood by passing instruments as requested. She bit her lip. "Poor Von Pinn. She looks so . . . vulnerable."

Theo nodded. "At least she's stable." He laid down his stethoscope and shook his head in admiration. "This setup they put together is amazing. I think she could lie here for the next few months if she had to."

"So what should we do?"

Theo again shuffled through the notes. "They didn't leave me any specific instructions, which is flattering, but not particularly useful." He flipped a page and then frowned for a second. "Ah. Look here," he said, not showing Sleipnir anything. "Gil, Agatha, and Prince Sturmvoraus all worked on this. They've annotated each other back and forth." A light seemed to go on inside his head. "Oh! Yes! I see! Amazing! And I think I can even improve this." He looked up and his voice began to drop into the registers associated with the activation of the spark. "Yes! I've got everything I need already here! By the time you—" he pointed at Mister Higgs "—get that watchdog clank down here, I can have all of the preliminary work done and then some!" He wheeled about and gave Sleipnir a crazed grin. "I can do this!"

Sleipnir gave a tiny growl and slipped her arms around Theo's neck. "Now that's the brilliantly sparky beast I ran off with!"

Theo swept her up in his arms and cackled softly, "Care to *assist* me?"

Sleipnir gazed up at him through half lidded eyes. "Oooh. Yes, master."

Moloch's overly loud throat-clearing barely registered. "We're just gonna leave. And . . . and go tell the others how to get down here." He began backing away. "And we're gonna do it *really slowly.*"

Zeetha nodded. "Yeah, and, um, we're going to go with them."

Higgs glanced down and noted the heat coming off the couple before him had spontaneously ignited his pipe. "And then we'd better go look for the Lady Heterodyne."

Krosp waved a paw. "Eh. Too much running around. I'll just wait here." Two seconds later, he had been forcibly hauled out of the room by the collar of his coat. "What is your problem," he groused as the party trudged back up the stairs. "Haven't you ever watched that sort of thing? It's hilarious!"

Privately, Zeetha had to agree with him. "Everybody deserves a bit of privacy."

Krosp shrugged. "Whatever."

Moloch stomped upwards, shaking his head. "Sparks," he muttered. "They're crazy, the lot of them."

Beside him, Fräulein Snaug glanced at him coyly. "I think it's romantic."

He glanced at her with a touch of concern. "You've been hanging around sparks too much."

"Oh, come now, Herr von Zinzer. Have you no romance in your soul?"

A look of mild regret passed briefly through the man's eyes, then he shrugged. "Dunno. Never had a chance to find out."

Hexalina looked skeptical. "No! A dashing fellow like yourself?"

Moloch snorted. "The word you want isn't 'dashing,' it's 'fleeing.'"

"Oh, but surely there's some girl somewhere who's caught your eye?"

"Well . . . "

Hexalina was astonished at the feelings that swept over her at this. "Yes?" she prodded.

Moloch concentrated on putting one foot in front of the other, but his face slowly went red. "Well, I do kinda like Sanaa."

Snaug stopped dead. "Sanaa? Sanaa Wilhelm?"

Moloch nodded. "I knew you'd know her, she's been in here longer than me." He glanced at the look on Snaug's face and gave a self-deprecating shrug. "I know. Crazy ain't it?"

"*She will die,*" Snaug whispered.

Moloch blinked. "What was that?"

Snaug grinned maniacally and gave him a jaunty "thumbs up." "I *said*, 'never say die!' You know? Good luck?" Her canines glinted in the light.

Moloch smiled. "Thanks." Some vague feeling urged him to change the subject. "So how is it—working with Mittelmind?"

Snaug blinked. "Oh, he's very supportive of my needs."

"Yeah? That's good."

Snaug glanced down at her hands. The hands that would never be *truly* clean . . . "I wouldn't call it *good—*"

At that moment there was a scream and a brilliant actinic flare from the room directly before them—the room where they had left the three scientists.

With a blur and a gust of displaced air, Zeetha and Higgs shot ahead. They paused in the doorway just long enough to see the scientists sprawled about and Zola furiously clutching at a smoking hand. She gave an animal snarl and, without hesitation, dove into the great shaft melted into the floor.

As she dropped, she produced her grappling gun and fired it upwards, catching a protruding beam. With a jerk, she swung herself to the side, released, and gracefully rolled into a pile of crumbling old furniture on a lower floor, then sprang to her feet and headed into the shadows.

Seconds later, Zeetha followed. She had leapt from floor to floor in a tightly controlled acrobatic fall. As she stood, she heard a cracking thump and spun to see Airman Higgs straightening up from a small impact crater. She smiled. His positioning made it look as if the airshipman had simply leapt down from several stories—her smile faltered. How *had* he—

"Where did she go?"

Zeetha's thoughts were derailed and she pointed to the dusty floor where footprints could be seen. "That way." But all too quickly, the trail disappeared. The two stood back-to-back and scrutinized the shadowy room. It was large and full of nooks and crannies. At least seven empty doorways led from it. Zeetha's shoulders slumped. "I think we lost her."

Higgs was peering up at a crenellated ledge that encircled the room. He pulled his pipe from his pocket and stuck it, unlit, into his mouth. "Think you're right," he sighed. Moving silently, while still speaking conversationally, he began looking under tables and behind tapestries. "I don't know what she was doing upstairs, but I doubt she'll be back."

Zeetha kicked over a suspiciously fallen chair and studied where it had lain. "Probably, but that doesn't help. While she's alive, Agatha's in danger." With a shrug, she slid her swords back into their scabbards. "I'm going after her." She looked Higgs in the face. "I . . . can't order you to come with, but I'd like it if you did."

Higgs looked at her and moved his pipe from one side of his mouth to the other. He nodded. "It seems like she's out to get young Wulfenbach, too, so I don't think he'll mind." He gave her arm a brief pat. "Let's ship out."

Back upstairs, the two minions and Krosp were cautiously peering around the doorway. The room was in shambles, although, Moloch had to admit, with three sparks working this was a perfectly normal state of affairs. Even so, there were signs that things had gotten out of hand.

Several racks of equipment had been overturned, and it appeared that most of the electronic components were smoking. A thick smell of charred insulation and ozone filled the room. Little helper clanks were lying about everywhere, inert.

"Doctor!" Fräulein Snaug called out. "Doctor?"

A groan caught Moloch's attention and he dashed over to a heap of parts and rags that stirred, revealing itself to be Professor Mezzasalma. Moloch knelt beside him and fished a small flask of moonshine out of his apron. A sip and the professor coughed and opened his eyes. "Ah, von Zinzer." He shuddered and his metal legs flexed. "Help me up, my boy." Again his legs spasmed. Mezzasalma swore. "That electromagnetic pulse has shorted out my legs." He waved towards a bench, but Moloch had already fetched a toolbox. The professor grunted in thanks and used a screwdriver to pry open an access panel in the control module.

"What happened?"

The professor was wrenching free a row of fuses. His movements slowed as he remembered. "We . . . yes, we were working, and suddenly—" fury filled his face "—that's right! And that blasted adventuress, the one claiming to be the Heterodyne! She popped up out of nowhere, waving a great huge marshmallow gun![11] She killed Diaz—"

"Wait . . . with a marshmallow gun?"

"She clubbed him to death with it."

"Okay. That would work."

"Obviously, she meant to kill us all—"

A heartfelt keening arose. Moloch saw Fräulein Snaug on her knees, cradling the still form of Doctor Mittelmind in her arms. "No," she sobbed softly, "Noooo . . . " Moloch noticed the machinery within the late doctor's chest was also smoking.

"Luckily, Mittelmind has a pulse cannon built into that contraption of his." Mezzasalma shrugged. "It killed him, of course, but her gun blew up."

Moloch looked back at the late doctor with new eyes. "That . . . that was really brave."

Mezzasalma rolled his eyes. "Oh, please. Don't start. He'll be smug enough about it as it is."

Moloch blinked. "What?"

"Oh. You didn't know?" Mezzasalma sighed as he slid a final fuse in and snapped the cover closed. Green running lights began to bloom along his legs. "Mittelmind is part machine." He waved a hand to indicate the rest of the Castle. "He's died several times in here. Claims we're just interacting with his ghost. He's made sure that Fräulein Snaug is very well trained in his personal repair and revivification routine."

Moloch now saw the girl had the old scientist hooked up to a battered-looking metal box. She had slipped on a pair of thick rubber

---

[11] Marshmallow guns (or other similarly useless weapons) are actually fairly common accessories in your typical spark laboratory. No one knows why. They just sort of accumulate.

gloves. With a shout of "CLEAR!" she threw a small knife switch, sending a jolt of power through Mittelmind's inert frame, causing it to jerk and twitch. By the time she had powered down the device and removed the cables, the old man was slowly sitting up, his inevitable grin reestablishing itself upon his lined face. With a squeal, Fräulein Snaug hugged him, relief suffusing her features.

Mittelmind reached up and gently patted her arm. "Thank you, my child. That was exhilarating, as always."

Moloch offered him a hand up, and the old scientist gingerly climbed to his feet.

"Do you do this a lot?" Moloch asked him. "Don't you get memory loss?"[12]

Mittelmind grinned and pulled a small battery out from the recesses of his chest. "As long as I maintain a small emergency power source while I'm dead, I manage to keep my original personality quite intact."

Moloch peered at the battery. "Wait—see that corrosion at the tip? This battery's been dead for ages."

Mittelmind examined it and frowned. "Whoops," he muttered.

Krosp waved them over to the last body. "What about Professor Diaz?"

Mezzasalma, who was now back on his feet, daintily stepped over to them, shaking his head. "His head is totally smashed in, I'm afraid. Dead as a doornail."[13]

Mittelmind shrugged philosophically. "*Sans appel.*"

Krosp frowned. "But I thought sparks . . . "

---

[12] Death-trauma-induced memory loss and the subsequent inevitable personality shift (usually resulting in deranged, murderous, fire-phobic dullards) are the biggest reason why sparks, as a rule, do not attempt to transform themselves into superior constructs.

[13] Many sparks are perfectly willing to experiment on their fellow sparks when the occasion demands. Nevertheless, if one wishes to resurrect a specific person, one must have a functioning brain. While many people are accused of "thinking" with assorted other body parts, this does not actually work.

Mezzasalma shrugged. "Well, I could turn him into an undead mechanical spider."

Mittelmind perked up. "Ooh! Now that I could work with! I could condition it to obey our every command!"

Mezzasalma's eyes began to shine. "Ah, but if we make it a *giant* undead mechanical spider . . . "

"Big enough to inspire fear in the general populace?"

"My dear sir. You think too small! Big enough that it could construct webs that would trap airships!"

"Inspired! Never again will we lack for research subjects!"

Moloch rubbed a weary hand against his temples. "I cannot *wait* to get out of here."

Krosp snorted. "Good luck with that." He continued. "I mean, listen to these guys. Did they do *any* work on that clank?"

This drew an indignant squawk from Professor Mezzasalma. "You impertinent construct! We most certainly did! In fact, I'd venture to say it is complete!"

Moloch looked at him skeptically. "Really. I know sparks work fast, but—"

Mezzasalma shrugged. "Well, we *were* ably assisted by the Lady's little clanks. A pity none of them survived."

Moloch had noticed drifts of the little mechanisms scattered about the room. Victims of Mittlemind's pulse cannon. *Good to know that there's something that can keep them in check,* he mused. He realized Mezzasalma was still talking.

"And, well, you know how it goes when one is caught up in the grip of the spark . . . "

Moloch interrupted him. "Just for the sake of clarity, assume I'm *not* barking mad."

To Snaug's astonishment, Mezzasalma didn't even look offended at this, but merely dipped his head in acknowledgement. "Very well, when you build on another spark's work, you get little flashes of inspiration. You see . . . possibilities you wouldn't have if you had tackled the problem on your own."

Moloch remembered Theo's reaction to the notes he'd found downstairs and nodded in understanding.

Mezzasalma continued. "Now combine that with these marvelous little clanks; they were so useful. We merely had to explain what needed to be done, and they attacked it on a dozen different fronts simultaneously. Plus they allowed us to implement any number of extemporaneous ideas . . . "

Again Moloch held up a hand. "Yeah, yeah. So it's done."

A giant metal paw crashed to the ground behind him. Mezzasalma grinned. "And we made *improvements!*"

Agatha stepped through a doorway and her breath caught in wonder. Even in ruins, the room before them was magnificent. A large airy chamber, capped with a dome that had once been painted in a riot of colors. It was shattered in places, and small shafts of outside light shone in. Two stories tall, it was surrounded by a set of chambers fronted by decoratively carved screens, a surprising number of which were still intact. The floor, though covered in dust and dead leaves, was made of inlaid marble, and in the center, a magnificently salacious statue held primacy.

Gilgamesh stepped into the room and whistled in appreciation. "Wow. It's the seraglio of Satyricus Heterodyne!"

Agatha looked at her map. The area they were in was simply labeled "Bedrooms."

Gil continued, "Yes, I've seen pictures. There's no mistaking it. The first edition of François Mansart's *Les Abominations Dangereuses de L'Architecture* has an extensive collection of plates, and of course here is Alphonse Ennui's masterpiece *The Temptation of Saint Vulcania*, which has the most amazing—oh. I see they've removed those."

To Agatha's eyes it was obvious that, indeed, things had been removed from the original statue. There was no way to tell what exactly had been so outrageous that even some past Heterodyne had felt the need to remove it, but there was still plenty left to tempt the hapless saint, who looked like she was having a very difficult time resisting. Especially the thing with the feather duster. Agatha considered the possibilities and felt her face getting red.

Gil plowed on. "It's still a fantastic piece. It really gives you a feel for the excesses of the early Heterodynes, and . . . "

Belatedly, he recognized Agatha might not be the most appreciative of audiences. "Of course," he rallied gamely, "these books were commissioned for the Storm King, so I'm sure it's all totally exaggerated." He glanced back at the statue. "Mostly."

A chilly silence was broken by Tarvek's barely smothered snort of laughter.

Agatha turned on him. "Oh, do you have something to add?"

Tarvek nodded. "Yup. When you get this place back up and running, I'll take that room over there. It has a nice view."

Agatha stared at him and then, to Gil's astonishment, dissolved into a fit of giggles.

Tarvek saw Gil's face and companionably slung an arm over his shoulder. "Don't worry, old man, when the harem gets too crowded you can bunk with me."

"Tarvek!" Agatha looked shocked. "Don't be mean." She leaned in close and whispered to Gil, "I promise, no matter how crowded it gets, you'll *always* have your own room."

Gil blinked, and then grinned. "At least I'll have someplace to go after Zola topples the empire with her marshmallow gun." This was possibly the most diverting thing anyone had ever said in the history of the world. Even Violetta joined in the uproarious laughter.

Finally, Agatha raised a hand. "Of course there'll be no rooms for *either* of you unless we get this castle working." She giggled at the thought. "Let's go."

"Hee hee," Tarvek snickered at Gil. "I will totally crush you."

Gil slapped him on the back, "Ho *ho!* You just *try* it, sir!"

Violetta grinned. "Well, you're all cheerful all of a sudden!"

"Yeah!" Agatha gave a leaping skip. "I feel great!"

Violetta hugged herself in glee. "Me too! I'm having the best time!"

Gil looked like he was about to burst into song. "That's 'cause this is fun!" He paused, but no invisible orchestra obliged. He shrugged. "I haven't been adventuring in ages! I feel fantastic!"

Tarvek nodded. "Yes! Me too!" He paused. Tarvek was one of those people who had tolerated the "romance of adventuring" right up until he had discovered hotels that served breakfast in bed. "In fact," he giggled, "I'm *unnaturally* happy."

Violetta chucked him under his chin. "Good for you! It's not that surprising, you're just not used to being out of your cage!"

Tarvek stared at Violetta's hand like it was a snake that had given him a kiss. "Violetta. I'm . . . *never* this happy. I'm not *allowed* to be happy." He looked ahead and saw Agatha and Gil skipping down the corridor hand-in-hand. "And it's *all* of us. Why are we all like this?" An idea struck him and he chortled. "Agatha, can I see your map?"

Agatha grinned and handed it over. "Here you go, sweetie!"

Tarvek felt an upwelling of sheer joy and viciously pinched his cheek as he scanned the map. "Focus," he hissed to himself. Things suddenly dropped into place. "Hey, Wulfenbach! Go check out that smashed wall over there."

Gil ambled over, chuckling. "Sure! If it'll make you happy!"

Without warning several huge, green tendrils looped down from the hole in the ceiling, encircled Gil, and then effortlessly hauled him up and out of sight. "Yeek!" He screamed joyfully.

Tarvek did a little dance. "Yes! I was right! Hee hee!"

Agatha whooped with laughter. "Wow! Was that a plant?"

"Ha! Ha! Yes! *Nepenthes dulces*! It incapacitates prey by inducing feelings of extreme happiness! Smoke Knights use a modified form of its pollen, so at first I thought Zola was sneaking up on us." Tarvek gave a solid kick to the shattered wall, causing a section to collapse. A much larger room was revealed beyond. "But then I saw on the map that we were near a conservatory. Of course the Heterodynes would have a specimen. The plants must have multiplied like crazy to have so pervasive an effect."

They stepped through the opening into a riot of greenery. Overhead were the remains of a glass-paneled ceiling, now shattered, allowing light and rain free entry. The results were startlingly impressive. At one time the conservatory had been meticulously laid out. There had once been automatic feeding systems, but they had long ago succumbed to the ruin. Stretches of the beds were choked with brown and rotting bracken, while others had dissolved into evil-smelling swamps. Even so, there were plants in abundance. A few stunted trees, whose seeds had blown in with the wind or been dropped by birds, struggled upward. There were weeds, but the majority of the plants were descendants of the odd and unusual foliage that the Heterodynes had developed or collected on their wanderings. Hundreds of varieties of fungi thrived amidst the decay, many of them phosphorescent in the dim light. Several varieties twitched at their approach, and a few tempting-looking blooms unfolded as they drew near. Prudently, these were avoided.

The crown jewel of this riot of growth loomed in the center of it all. It was a gigantic, fleshy-looking plant, easily towering three meters high. It currently had Gilgamesh secure within its prehensile tendrils. The plant was in the process of dragging him, thrashing, towards a large maw-like blossom that gaped to reveal hundreds of thorns lining its interior.

Gil saw Tarvek and Agatha as they entered. "Sturmvoraus," he called, still struggling violently. "I'm still happy, *but not with you!*"

Tarvek nodded. "Or it could be a single, monstrous hybrid with greatly enhanced capabilities—" At the sound of Tarvek's voice, a cluster of smaller blooms swiveled and released their own clouds of pollen. Tendrils shivered to life and whipped out, ensnaring all three of them. "—that is viable enough to put out cultivars!" Tarvek laughed as he pulled a knife out of his sleeve and attacked the vine holding his other arm. "This just gets better and better," he shouted joyfully. "Oh, by the way, I'm being sarcastic!"

"I think we're going to have some trouble rescuing Gil," Agatha sang out cheerfully. "I'm having trouble rescuing myself! Hee hee!"

By this time Gil had been dragged to the mouth of the central blossom. "Hey guys! Getting rescued would make me really happy! Just sayin'!"

Agatha, still held fast by the vines that wound from her ankles and up her legs, had grabbed several small, crab-like clanks from a stone garden bench. "Hold on! I've almost got these old pruning clanks working!"

"Then we'd better tell Wulfenbach not to act so wooden," said Tarvek, a man who obviously didn't tell a lot of jokes. Everyone giggled anyway.

"Gil!" A new voice called.

At the sound, everyone froze and looked about frantically. It was Zola, hanging from a rope and dangling about a meter above Gil, who was now completely immobilized. "Omi*gosh*," she beamed. "I thought you were *dead!*"

Gil glanced at his waist that was now enveloped by the plant's maw. The plant seemed to pulse and he slid several centimeters deeper. "Well . . ."

Zola laughed in delight. "And this time, *I* get to rescue *you!* I'm so happy!"

Another peristaltic surge and Gil was buried up to his chest. "Oh dear, it's really got you." Zola looked like she was listening to someone behind her shoulder. "Hmm. Auntie Lucrezia says that if I try to pull you out, you'll get all ripped up on the thorns." She rolled her eyes. "And they're *poisoned*, of course, which is kind of adorable." Again she listened. "Okay, all you've got to do is wait until it's eaten you all the way."

Gil's façade of cheerfulness cracked slightly. "What?"

Zola waved a hand reassuringly. "Then I'll cut you out through the soft part."

"I don't think—"

"Oh, don't be modest. You do that kind of thing all the time. Relax. These rascals take over a year to fully absorb live prey, so you should be fine for a few minutes." She considered him. "Though you might get a bit of a rash." She simpered. "But I have some *delightfully* soothing ointment that I'll be happy to apply to all of those hard to reach places—"

"You keep your greasy hands off of him," Agatha yelled.

Zola looked down at Agatha and her smile became sharper. "You're just annoyed that they won't be *your* greedy, beau-hogging hands, you hussy! That's because you'll be dead, which will make me very, very happy!"

Gil struggled to keep his mouth free. "Zola! Don't—"

She silenced him by gently placing a knife in his mouth. "Here. You might have to do this yourself, Gil. Remember to watch out for those thorns."

With that she pulled out another blade as she allowed herself to slide further down the rope towards Agatha, who was still tangled in vines. "I'm afraid *I've* got to go prune the family tree!"

Agatha twisted frantically. "Hurry! I'm stuck!"

"Oh," Zola crowed, "I'm coming as fast as I can!" She suddenly realized Agatha hadn't been talking to her. Instinctively, she twisted in midair and the blade that Zeetha had thrown missed her by centimeters.

Higgs—observing the scene below him from the balcony on which he, Violetta, and Zeetha had just arrived—raised an eyebrow in surprise. "You missed."

Zeetha grinned at him, "Nah. I didn't miss."

Zola dropped to the ground and grinned. "You most certainly—"

"HA!"

Zola spun about in time to see Agatha finish using the sword to free herself. "That's much better," she declared happily.

Despite her drug-fueled bravado, Agatha was feeling nervous. She'd only been allowed to practice with actual blades a handful of times. Zeetha had hammered into her that she wasn't really ready to use swords in any sort of combat. But Zeetha's training had been merciless and Agatha discovered that swinging the meter of steel to be easier than she had anticipated.

Zola watched her and snorted in amusement. "Please. Have you had *any* training with that thing?" Effortlessly she shimmied up her rope until she was out of reach. "You sparks really can be so stupid sometimes. After all—" she languidly produced a small pistol "—bringing a knife to a gun fight doesn't seem very smart, now does it?" She squeezed off a shot, barely missing as Agatha stumbled sideways.

"Well, I suppose it isn't that much worse than bringing a gun to a clank fight."

Zola smirked. "A *clank* fight is it? Pity you don't have any—" A vibration on the rope was her only warning. Zola looked up in time to see the crab-like pruning clank cut through her rope, dropping her to the floor two stories below.

She smashed into an overgrown mound of brambles and large meaty fungi and her gun went spinning off into the weeds. Gamely, she shook her head. "I'm going to feel that tomorrow," she muttered.

Agatha found herself separated from Zola by a wall of poisonous-looking daffodils. "You'd better hope you do," she said menacingly. "Why are you even still here? Your plans are ruined! If you stay here, you'll be lucky to even *see* tomorrow."

Zola snarled. "Maybe I'm just determined to make sure that you don't." With that, she pulled a softly glowing violet-glass ampoule from her belt pouch, bit it hard enough to break the glass, and then poured the contents into her mouth before spitting out bits of broken glass from her now-bleeding mouth.

Watching from the balcony, Violetta blanched, then frantically checked her own pockets. "Aah! She took some of my Movit[14] Number Eleven!"

---

[14]   The Smoke Knights have developed a rather potent line of motivational drugs, all gathered under the family name of "Movit." They range in strength from Movit Number One, which has an effect much like several very strong cups of coffee seasoned with horseradish

Tarvek looked surprised. "Eleven? I thought it only went up to six! That's what you gave me."

"Eleven would have killed you! It'd kill almost anyone!"

Zola's maniacal peal of laughter caused even the sparks in the room to flinch.

"Oh, but I'm not just *anyone*," she howled. "And even if it does kill me, I won't go alone!"

Tarvek swiveled to Zeetha and Higgs who were running towards the combatants. "Don't mess around! Kill her!"

Higgs nodded in acknowledgement, but Zeetha waved a hand. She was also being affected by the plant's miasma. "Hee hee, don't be scared. We won't let Gil's Parisian tart get to you. Agatha can use my sword to cut you out—"

Suddenly Zola was there. A quick foot to his solar plexus sent Higgs into a grasping mass of thorny foliage. A stunning right cross caught Zeetha completely off guard. Her sword flew free and directly into Zola's waiting hand. "*Merci, mademoiselle*," Zola cried exuberantly. "What an excellent idea! I shall use your *other* sword—" She pivoted and, with a graceful lunge, buried the sword in Zeetha's chest. "—to cut you out entirely!"

Zeetha stared at her and silently toppled backwards. Zola stood aside and cleaned the blade with a flick of her wrist. "See? So elegant that even a Parisian tart can do it!" She swung about until she found Agatha. "Let's do it again!"

"ZEETHA!" Agatha screamed in terror. "Zeetha! I'm coming!"

"Agatha! NO!" Agatha, to her surprise, found Tarvek and Violetta holding her tightly. "Stay away from her! She'll slice you to ribbons!"

Furiously, Agatha struggled. "Let go of me!"

---

poured directly into your sinuses, up to the until-now-unknown Number Eleven. Your humble professors, while advocating against unnecessary pharmaceuticals—especially in the work place—must confess it usually takes a dose of Movit Number Three to get them out of bed in the morning. It's all right for us, you see, because it is research; as in fact, are most of the recreational excesses we indulge in. A finding reluctantly confirmed by several Faculty Review Boards.

"No," Violetta snarled. "Tarvek is right. She'll kill you!" Her palm swiftly snaked out and smacked the side of Agatha's head. Agatha slumped into Tarvek's arms. "And that is *not* going to happen while I'm here!" She dashed towards the fray, yelling out over her shoulder, "Get her out of here!"

Tarvek stared after her, appalled. "Violetta! You can't—"

"Go!" she ordered. Tarvek went.

Higgs held Zeetha cradled in his arms. His normally taciturn face was a study in anguish. Zeetha's had gone pale with shock and blood loss; her breathing was becoming irregular. She stared at Higgs with an expression that was full of guilt and regret. "Agatha . . ." she barely whispered. "Protect . . . " With a final sigh she passed out.

Higgs face went blank.

Panting, Zola grinned in triumph. "Aw . . . too bad, sailor boy. She just wasn't as good as she thought she was."

Higgs carefully laid Zeetha out and then slowly stood up. When he turned to face her, his expression caused Zola, even in the grip of her drug-fueled high, to step back.

"Yes," he growled. "But I vas starting to like her."

With a brittle laugh, Zola raised her sword. "Please. I don't have time for you. I've got to go kill that Heterodyne cow. If you're smart, you'll have scurried off by the time I—"

"No." Higgs's punch came from nowhere and lifted Zola off of her feet.

She landed and flowed into a defensive crouch. "I warned you!"

Two more hits and a kick to her midriff staggered her. *I can't even see him moving,* she grasped. "Oh, that's it! Just die!" The sword sliced sideways and caught the grim airman across the chest. A spatter of blood sprayed onto the floor.

"Ha!" Zola spun to face him. "Got you! Now—"

A solid hammer blow struck the side of her head. The fight went on.

Several rooms away, Agatha swam back to consciousness to find herself slung over Tarvek's shoulder. "Wha—?" She mumbled.

Tarvek stumbled slightly in surprise. "What are you doing awake? Violetta must be slipping." He gently set Agatha onto her feet. "At least you've stopped giggling."

Agatha blinked at him as a confused swirl of memories coalesced inside her head. "What did I miss?"

Tarvek took a few seconds to check her pulse, temperature, and eyes. He nodded in satisfaction. "We missed getting killed—so far. And the best way to keep us alive is to get you to the library so we can fix up the Castle." He peered at her again. "You do remember the Castle?"

Agatha nodded and then her face froze. "Zeetha! She's—"

Tarvek had been expecting this and had a firm grip on her arm. "Agatha! Zola is after *you*. She wants to kill *you*. And *you* are the only chance everyone has got. Running back there won't help *anyone*. You can't outfight her. I don't think any of us *can*." A mental image of Mister Higgs smashing the Muse in half with a spanner flitted through his mind. "Probably."

Agatha still hesitated. He grabbed her shoulders and glared at her. "This is not a time to be pointlessly heroic. This is a time to be smart. You can *beat* her with smart."

Agatha glared at him, then nodded. "Right. Gotta fix the Castle, let *it* squash her."

Tarvek picked up the head of Otilia that he had set down on a table. "I think that's what it will take."

Agatha took a step and then stopped. "Wait. Did we leave Gil . . . is he still in that plant?"

Tarvek rolled his eyes. "Don't worry, he'll figure out where we're going."

"But if he doesn't get out . . . "

"Oh, he'll get out and somehow make me look bad while doing it."

Agatha looked at him and frowned. "You have issues."

Tarvek sighed. "I don't want to talk about it." He studied her critically. "You're still staggering a bit. Here." So saying, he pushed the clank head into Agatha's hands and then scooped her up in his arms.

"No!" Agatha protested. "If you're too slow she'll kill you too."

Tarvek grinned at her sardonically. "Well, Lady Heterodyne, don't *let* her."

Agatha paused, and her jaw firmed. "I won't. Fine. Let's go." She pointed up a long flight of stairs. "The library should be right up there."

Tarvek grunted and took a step. "Your wish is my command, O princess." He looked up the long set of stairs and groaned inwardly as he shifted Agatha's solid weight. *This looked a lot easier on the book covers.*

Agatha smacked his shoulder. "*Faster!*"

In the conservatory, Zola staggered back, her face swollen from repeated blows. "I can't *believe* this," she growled. "How many times do I have to *hit* you?"

Higgs frowned at the latest gash on his arm and resumed his determined stride towards her. He checked his movement, and her blade hummed scant millimeters from his face. He gave a small, tight smile. He was learning the rhythms of Zola's fighting style. *Soon.*

From where she was kneeling next to Zeetha, Violetta called out. "Don't even try to knock her out, you hear me? She's had a whole vial of Movit Eleven. She'll be *unstoppable* until it wears off."

"I hear you," Higgs muttered.

But Zola could feel the effects of the drug beginning to fade. *Thank goodness a boost like that isn't sustainable for too long—* Her rumination was cut off by yet another blow to her face. "I have other people to kill," she screamed. "More important people than you! I've got to get Gil out of the plant and hunt down my inconvenient cousin, and *you are getting in my way!*" With that, she pivoted, but instead of moving *away,* she gracefully lunged *towards* the startled airman, dropping to one knee, and driving the sword up through his abdomen. "*So stay down!*"

Zola had only microseconds to revel in the astonished look that crossed the airman's face. She was pummeled, in quick succession, by one punishing blow after another. Finally, Higgs's fist approached her face dead on and everything seemed to slow down. *This must be it,* Zola thought. The fist connected and she recognized that *time* hadn't slowed; her attacker's fist had. It bounced off of her swollen nose with a gentle *bonk*. She stared as the airman's face slowly clenched in pain. Then, through clenched teeth, she heard a puzzled, "Ouch?"

The implications of this terrified her. She scrambled back as the man slowly doubled over and dropped to his knees, a look of intense concentration on his face.

"Ha!" Zola yelled. It felt so good that she yelled it again and shook her sword at him. "*Ha!* Take that!" He slowly swiveled his head towards her and glared.

Zola stepped back. A distant part of her mind, the part occupied by Lucrezia, was shrieking at her: *There was nowhere near enough blood.* Zola hefted her blade, determined to finish this monster off, when a sharp jab in her exposed arm spun her about. But there was no one near. A quick search revealed the tiny dart of a Smoke Knight. She swore and pulled it free. She looked up to see Violetta reloading a trim little blowgun.

"Ha!" she said yet again. "You pathetic loser! Did you just try to *poison* me?" She threw her head back and cackled manically. "As if that could stop me now!"

Violetta smiled. "Oh, I know that. That wasn't poison. That was another dose of Movit Number Eleven." She finished loading her blowgun. "I wonder how much more you can take before you combust?"

A tidal wave of ice-cold clarity and energy burst through Zola's mind. *Not much at all,* it told her. She spun and used the sword to swat Violetta's latest dart out of the air. "I just have to move fast enough to burn it off." But instead of leaping forward, she crashed to the ground. Twisting about, she saw the airman—impossibly still alive—holding her ankle in a grip of iron. Pinpricks of fire bloomed throughout Zola's body. *I cannot let him keep me from moving,* she thought with a jolt of terror. Screaming, she lashed out with her free leg, kicking desperately at the hand that held her. She might as well have been kicking at a steel manacle.

She rolled onto her back and swung the sword on high. "Chop head tiny bits!" she shrieked, bringing down—not a sword, but a long flower stalk that splatted harmlessly on the surprised airman's hat.

Behind her, Violetta chuckled as she examined the sword now in her hand. "Wow! You *must* be messed up! That never would've worked before."

Zola scrabbled at the ground and flung a handful of rocks and broken stones at Violetta, who stumbled backwards and fell against a large ornamental pot. This gave Zola time to twist her foot, slide it free of her boot, and leap to her feet. For an instant she considered staying—trying to finish them off—but inside her head Lucrezia was howling at her to *run.* She needed little convincing. "Fine!" Zola bolted from the room, shouting defiance. "I don't have to stay here! I can kill people *anywhere!*"

Cursing, Violetta wiped at the blood and dirt on her forehead and rolled to her feet. "Oh no you won't, 'cause I'm going to make sure you—"

"No."

Violetta turned and stared as Higgs slowly rose to his feet. *Impossible,* she thought.

"Miss Zeetha is still alive. You stay here and make sure she *stays* that way." He stood straight and rolled his shoulders. "This imposter is *mine.*"

Violetta stepped back. "You got it."

CHAPTER 3

The encyclopedia is the only place in the world where
World Domination comes before Work!
 —The last words of Joaquin the Illiterate, just before
he hit that big red button labeled *Do Not Touch*

The room was immense. A circular cavern easily nine stories
tall. It was capped with a thick dome of green glass, ornately
embossed and etched. Years of accumulated debris on the
outside blocked much of the light that would once have filled the
room, but the dome remained whole, unlike many of the Castle's other
glass windows. Even from the ground, Agatha could see evidence of
automatic hydraulic braces. Someone had taken a great deal of trouble
to ensure that time and the elements would not touch this place.

Wan chemical lights flickered from lanterns hanging from the
ceiling or resting in alcoves. Agatha's eye was drawn to a small
reading room: a steel-lacework gazebo suspended from a cyclopean
chain dangling halfway between dome and floor. Agatha realized her
eyes had been avoiding the walls lined with ornately carved shelves
of books for the simple reason that they were overwhelming.

There were a stupefying number of books. Shelf upon shelf of
them: neatly arrayed, stretching all the way up to the base of the great
dome. Many were behind glass case doors. An entire section was
carefully tucked into what appeared to be an atmospheric chamber
filled with clouds of softly swirling green gas.

Books bound in a thousand kinds of leather, in inlaid wood, in
polished metal, and several other substances she couldn't identify.

They ranged in size from pamphlets so tiny they seemed to be made by insects, to enormous tomes that were surely created for studious giants. Titles picked out in gold and silver glinted from the semidarkness.

And there were other things, there among the books. Scrolls, stelae, and stone tablets inscribed with languages dead or unknown. Enigmatic artifacts from every corner of the Earth. Strange, silent clock-like devices, and globes with odd markings.

A mismatched collection of display cases was scattered throughout. Tantalizing shapes lay obscured by a thick layer of dust coating the glass lids. A row of gigantic oak flat mapmaker files held a multitude of drawers, each labeled with names out of history or, in some cases, what Agatha had assumed was mythology. Clusters of small devices and exotic statuary covered every flat surface. The most mundane object was a frayed, but still opulent, oriental carpet that covered the only open spot on the room's floor.

Agatha and Tarvek stared at it all in wonder.

"Oh my," Agatha whispered.

"Oh yes!" Tarvek conceded. "One of the most infamous libraries in Europa." He gestured expansively. "And it's all yours."

"That's all very well," Agatha replied, "but where do we *start?*" She turned slowly in place. "I don't see *anything* that looks like a control panel."

"Oh, I haven't got a clue," Tarvek admitted. "But while we're searching, we won't be bored." He snapped his fingers. "The Castle should know." He gently rapped on the clank head tucked under Agatha's arm. "Hello?"

Agatha shook her head. "I think it's shut down. Probably to preserve the memory cores."

Tarvek sighed. "That makes sense, but it certainly makes our job more difficult."

"That's true, but . . . " Agatha stopped and looked about. "Wait. The supplies we sent ahead. They aren't here yet."

"The stuff you sent with your little helper clanks? Something must have happened to them. That's bad. They were carrying a lot of important equipment."

"We couldn't have carried it ourselves." Agatha frowned. "But with the Castle shut down, I wouldn't have thought there was anything here that could give them that much trouble."

"I am perfectly willing to believe there are dangerous things besides the Castle itself running around this place."

Agatha shook her head. "Something like that might incapacitate a *few* of them. Maybe. But *all* of them? Maybe they just got lost. In which case they'll find us eventually. We still have the head; that's the only irreplaceable bit."

"But how do we hook it up without any equipment?"

"At this point we don't know what we have to hook it up *to*." Agatha blew a lock of hair out of her face. "I guess I was expecting some kind of obvious interface, like we found down in the crypts.[15] But there's nothing. Nothing here at all."

"But this is where it told you to come."

"Yes. It said that when I got here, it would give me a map of where it needed to be repaired." She paused and looked at the map cases. Then she shook her head. "No, that makes no sense. How could an old map made before the Castle was damaged show where it needs to be repaired *now*?" Agatha began walking in a tight circle. "Down in the crypt, the Castle I spoke to prided itself on the strength of its defenses. It was *meant* to be inaccessible. Even to me. Considering that, I'd think the existence of a permanent, detailed map of its interior and its defenses would be seen as an unacceptable weakness."

She slowly sank to the floor and rubbed her fingers over her

---

[15] The crypt in question held the Throne of Faustus Heterodyne, an ancient interface dating from before the Castle was actually finished. It allowed the Castle to speak through anyone foolhardy enough to allow specialized sockets to be implanted into his or her skull. This was an honor reserved, in recent generations, solely for the seneschals of Castle Heterodyne. It was a creepy and horrible system and thus pretty hard to circumvent.

temples. "If only we could get it to talk again. Just for a minute or two."

"Damage . . . sustained."

Agatha blinked. "What?"

Tarvek looked at her blankly. "*What* what?"

She held up a hand.

"Damage sustained." The words were muffled.

"Can you hear that?"

"No," Tarvek whispered.

"I can," Agatha muttered, "so it's closer to me, but what . . . "

"Damage sustained."

Agatha slowly smiled, and hopped to her feet. "Help me roll up this rug."

Tarvek had questions, but he kept them for later. He began rolling the carpet along with Agatha. The floor underneath was not stone, but a thick slab of dark glass. As the carpet was removed, small lights began to appear in the depths below.

"There's something still active down there," he said in surprise.

"I think I understand now," Agatha said. "The Castle is strong. And one of the reasons is because it doesn't have a centralized brain, per se. I think the whole Castle is the brain."

Tarvek considered this. "Yes, that does make sense. It explains why it fragmented the way it did."

"Uh-huh." She allowed Tarvek to proceed with the carpet while she stared down at what was being revealed. "Did you see this room? The way it's built? I think the Heterodynes thought the library was the most important part of the Castle. It seems like the most reinforced and secure place in the entire building. Which means that when I used the Lion,[16] I didn't kill everything."

---

[16] Fra Pelagatti's Lion was a device capable of generating a low-pulse ætheric "roar." It was constructed by prisoners using parts smuggled in by Zola's organization. It was designed to completely eradicate the artificial intelligence that operated the Castle. When activated, it astonished everyone by working perfectly.

Tarvek finished rolling up the carpet, turned, and gasped in wonder. A ghostly outline of Castle Heterodyne flickered to life in the air before them. As they watched, more and more details were added until a complete wireframe rendering of the entire Castle appeared. Red lights wobbled on within the sketch. Then, starting in what Agatha recognized as the Great Movement Chamber, waves of disruption slowly began radiating upwards and outwards, scrambling the delicate lines as it grew. Agatha grabbed Tarvek's arm and pointed to a floating set of numbers that slowly advanced as they watched. "That's a date and time signature," she said with excitement. "The date that Castle Heterodyne was attacked!"

The numbers clicked forward, each advancement accompanied by growing waves of destruction sweeping over the model before them. "It's a recording of the actual event," Tarvek said, awe filling his voice. He glanced down. Within the glass-covered pit was a large sphere, its surface bejeweled with ever-changing lights. "*That's* your map. One that can be updated on the fly. During attacks it would be *invaluable*."

Agatha was staring at the model. "But it *wasn't* attacked." She pointed to the epicenter of the largest disruption. "If these were explosions, and they certainly *behave* like mathematical models of explosions, they all started *inside* Castle Heterodyne."

They paused as the great central tower began slowly leaning sideways. They found themselves unconsciously holding their breaths until it came to rest in the position the real tower occupied today.

Tarvek nodded slowly. "Everyone always said that the attack on Castle Heterodyne was the first attack by the Other. But every subsequent attack on a Great House was completely different. There was an initial aerial bombardment followed by ground attacks by revenants and slaver wasps." He turned to Agatha, a troubled look in his eye. "My family, and a few other inner members of the Council, *knew* Lucrezia was the Other, but she always claimed *her* attacks were *retribution*. She claimed other sparks had attacked Castle Heterodyne first." He turned back to the model and studied it closely. "There were inconsistencies with her story, even from the beginning, but she was eliminating dozens of powerful, upstart spark families, so they were all too happy to aid her."

He glanced back at the model Castle, in time to see the great northern tower crack apart from the main structure and slide down the hillside. Once it came to rest the structure and lights within it faded and eventually vanished. A few seconds later it again flickered into existence and the cycle repeated. "Now I'm wondering: if the Heterodyne Boys hadn't stopped her, would there have come a day when even the Order would have found themselves on the receiving end of those bombardments?"

Agatha touched the locket at her throat. Tarvek guessed at her thoughts and put his hand atop hers. "Don't even think about letting Lucrezia out. She lied about this for so long, I doubt that I could get her to recant just because I could show her I knew she was lying. She'd just take it as a challenge"

"So . . . " Agatha stared at the shimmering Castle. Glowing red spots were beginning to appear again throughout the structure. She had a sinking feeling every one of them was something important. "So Lucrezia is the one who damaged the Castle? But she was one of its masters. It was the main thing protecting her and her . . . " Agatha remembered the tiny tombstone she had seen in the crypts. The one that purportedly held the bones of her infant brother.[17] She stared at Tarvek. "She wouldn't have killed her own child, would she?"

Tarvek gently placed a hand on Agatha's shoulder. "It certainly hasn't slowed her down as far as *you're* concerned." He glanced back at the still glowing model. "But I wonder what really happened there?"

---

[17] Klaus Barry Heterodyne: child of Bill Heterodyne and Lucrezia Mongfish. He was a little over a year old when he was killed in the destruction of Castle Heterodyne.

Sleipnir stared at Theo in annoyance. "Theo! Please! You have to move Von Pinn!"

"Impossible!" Theo briefly stepped back from the jumble of equipment and snagged a hypodermic needle. "She is prepped and ready! I can't just disconnect her and then hook her back up like a set of toy trains! It shouldn't be much longer." He glanced up at the ceiling as a few small bits of debris pattered down about him. "The others will be back soon, and then we can complete the transfer."

Sleipnir stamped her foot. "But I'm telling you, the ceiling is unstable! It could collapse at any moment!"

Theo nodded. "*That* is why *you* are over there. Out of harm's way."

Sleipnir furiously jerked at the shackle that bound her wrist to the wall. She couldn't believe how easily Theo had suckered her into it. "If you die, I'll hate you forever you selfish pig!"

A larger shard fell and shattered at Theo's feet. "Good," he growled. "Hate me for years and years and years!"

A faint rolling rumble sounded from somewhere distant and began to grow. Sleipnir felt panic slice through her. "NO! THEO! Get away!"

The rumbling grew louder and a faint vibration could be felt. Theo stared upwards. "It-it's not the ceiling," he yelled back. "What could cause—?"

Sleipnir screamed. "It's over here! It's coming for *me!*" She stared up into the blackness of the secret stairwell. The noise was growing louder by the second. It sounded like an avalanche of ironmongery. "It's coming down the stairs!"

"Sleipnir!" In a flash, Theo was at her side. Frantically he jammed the key into the shackle's lock and tried to turn it, but the vibration and the noise was stronger here, washing over them. He enveloped Sleipnir in his arms and slammed her against the wall as the great mechanical security clank roared past them like a golden locomotive, steam pouring out as it spun about to a gentle halt.

Fräulein Snaug rode on its back, squealing with delight and squeezing its other occupant, von Zinzer, tightly from behind. When the great clank had stopped, she bounced down to the ground and took in a great lungful of air before whooping: "That was so much *fun!*"

A faint wheeze from von Zinzer was the only indication the frozen man was actually still alive.

No longer panicking, Theo quickly freed Sleipnir and they stared at the great metal construct with awe. It looked like a giant cat over two meters tall. A cat covered in decorative metal plates with wicked-looking spikes on all its joints. A pair of huge red eyes glowed above a mouth of dagger teeth. The great head swiveled towards them and grinned to show them off.

Theo and Sleipnir stepped back. "Agatha really wants us to load Von Pinn into this?'

Snaug patted the great clank's head. "Yeah!"

"Has she seen it? Now that it's moving around, it seems . . . bigger?"

"Oh, it is," Snaug admitted cheerfully. "And they gave it more teeth. It's all ready to go." She banged the side of the clank's head again, and it tipped forward. Now they could see that—where a small cognitive enginette would normally reside—a gang of Agatha's helper clanks crowded together, operating a makeshift control panel. They waved at Theo who, in response, looked bemused.

Snaug continued. "All you have to do is disconnect this external control panel, hook your patient into the blank enginette inside, and presto!" She waved her hand, airily dismissing several technical hurdles and one outright Abomination of Science[18] with the blithe

---

[18] Everyone had *heard* about Abominations of Science but, like unicorns, they didn't actually believe they existed. Thus everyone was rather grateful when the third Madrid Conference of Scientific Inquiry and Philosophical Horrors—Unleashed! released a codified list of things that constituted actual Abominations of Science. Over the years, this useful list has been updated and curated by our own Transylvanian Polygnostic University and has proven of great use to teachers, courts, and record books. The only downside was that one of the conference members—a Herr Doktor Spanakopita—was so embarrassed that none of his previous efforts met the requirements that he, in a fit of pique, bred a race of unicorns, who went about stabbing people while quoting the parts of the list that covered biological abominations. Before he was stabbed to death, he was graciously acknowledged as a genuine Tamperer in Things Man Was Not Meant to Know and his oft-desecrated gravestone lists his accomplishments in full.

casualness of one who associates with sparks far more than is good for them.

Theo nodded slowly and then, with more enthusiasm: "Yes, I see. Well done! Very elegant!" He clapped his hands. "Let's get started!" A slight whimper caught his attention and he glanced up. "Um, Herr von Zinzer? You can let go now."

The man slowly looked at him. "Nyrrrrg," he growled through clenched teeth.

Theo nodded amicably. "Ooorrr not."

Snaug tapped Sleipnir on the shoulder. "How do you think the patient will handle the change?"

Sleipnir looked at her blankly.

"Psychologically, I mean," Snaug said patiently. She gestured towards the recumbent Von Pinn. "She's been in her current form all these years and now you're putting her mind inside a giant tiger clank with steel claws instead of hands."

Sleipnir considered this. "An interesting consideration, but given the similarities, I think it quite likely that Mistress Von Pinn won't notice much of a difference."

Snaug blinked, then looked at Von Pinn askance. "Ooh, you people *are* fun." She grinned.

Her reverie was broken by the entrance of Mittelmind and Mezzasalma, who had chosen a statelier method of descending the stairs. "My, my!" Mittelmind said approvingly. "This does look like an interesting setup."

Mezzasalma sniffed. "Rather modest, as secret lairs go."[19]

Theo hurried up. "Ah! Herr Doktor! Professor! I wondered where you were."

---

[19]   A secret lab is considered by many to be the physical manifestation of a spark's mind. Thus they tend to be rather individualistic. Some are spotlessly clean; some are filled with dangerous trash. Some are ruthlessly efficient; some are filled with suicidal deathtraps. Needless to say, sparks are usually vocally dismissive of the labs of others, while surreptitiously making notes about things they'd wished they'd thought of themselves.

"We *did* have to see to poor Professor Diaz. That adventuress killed him."

Theo paused. "Oh . . . I'm so sorry. The loss of your friend must be—"

Mittelmind waved a hand. "He helped make us the men we are today."

Mezzasalma nodded. "He'd have done the same to us."

Theo paused. "Wait—*to*?"

Mittelmind grinned at his colleague. "He *did* do the same to you. Remember? That time you were knocked out?"

"And now it's *back*," Mezzasalma huffed righteously. "The nerve of the man! That was my favorite pancreas!"

Theo sighed. "Come, gentlemen, we have a delicate procedure to undertake and I require your assistance. Let us focus on the matter to hand."

Agatha removed a jeweler's loupe from her eye and sat back with a satisfied "ah-ha!" The map shimmered before her.

Tarvek looked up from where he lay face down, peering down through the glass at the mechanism below. "Found something?"

"I hope so. You know those lines we think represent the Castle's nervous system analog?"

"I know the lines you mean. It would be easier to be sure if the thing wasn't so blurry."

"After sixteen-some-odd years without maintenance, you'd be a bit blurry too. That's why we're here to fix it. Anyway, one of the main ones runs right through this library."

"That certainly makes sense. So where is it in actuality?"

Agatha got up and headed towards one of the book-covered walls. "If I'm reading it correctly, there's a hidden room. Several of them, actually, but the one we want now is here." She waved her hands. "—ish."

Tarvek rolled his eyes. "Great. All we have to do is figure out where an evil, paranoid genius would put the access to a secret room that protects his family's greatest secrets."

"True. Let's try to think like a diabolical, amoral megalomaniac." Agatha thought for a second, then turned to Tarvek and smiled at him engagingly. "Where would *you* put it?"

Caught in the light of her smile, Tarvek grinned back and tapped an unassuming book. "Oh, *I'd* put it right *here!*" Instantly a section of the bookshelf swung aside on smooth pivots.

"I *knew* it!" She patted him on the cheek. "Thank you, Tarvek."

Realization of the implications of this played across Tarvek's face and he glared at Agatha. "Now just a minute . . . "

"And here's all our equipment!"

The space was filled with little clanks, each carrying a component or tool. They bounced about and waved. "Fascinating. They didn't get lost, they just continued on to where they were supposed to go."

"Makes sense," Tarvek admitted grudgingly. "They have access to smaller conduits. And secret passageways must run all through the place. That's what we paranoid megalomaniacs would do."

Agatha nodded as she looked at a wall of machinery. It was definitely some sort of monitoring-and-control station. If any place housed the soul of the Castle personality, it would be here. "Really. Now where would you put an access panel?"

Tarvek looked offended, paused, and then pointed towards an inconspicuous set of switches. "There."

Immediately, Agatha looked on the wall directly opposite of where Tarvek had pointed. She found a screw that seemed out of place and, with a deft twist, the false front swung aside revealing a much more complicated array. "Amazing! Well done!"

Tarvek stared at her. "Hey! I said over *there!*"

Agatha waved a hand dismissively. "Oh, I knew you were lying."

As she mentally analyzed the set-up before her, she searched for a rheostat that controlled "insanity." She wasn't surprised it was absent, but a girl could hope. The layout before her abruptly clicked into place. *Yes! This will work!* "Let's get this head hooked in and . . . " A silent seething from beside her gave her pause. "Aw, now you're mad."

"Am *not*."

"Hee. And now you're lying again."

Tarvek, whose pride—not to mention continued existence—had long depended on an ability to lie convincingly, grit his teeth. Suddenly, a cool hand touched his cheek and drew his face back towards Agatha's. Her eyes were wells of sympathy. "Oh Tarvek, I understand you're just using the experience you gained—at great personal pain—from life with your family. I know that deep down, in your heart of hearts, you have a noble soul."

Tarvek's breath caught and his heart clenched. "Agatha— I . . . you . . . " His face went cold. "You're messing with me on purpose."

Agatha's eyebrows rose. "Ooh. You can tell."

With a snort, Tarvek shouldered her aside and studied the panel. "Hand me Otilia's head," he said brusquely. Several tense minutes followed as Tarvek began testing circuits and slowly began constructing a transfer shunt. He threw down a pair of wire-strippers and faced Agatha. "Okay, fine. You know what? I admit it. I'm totally one of the 'bad guys,' okay? I'm a great big devious weasel. But it's not like that should be some kind of great big surprise! And I won't apologize for it either, because I'm with you now and I'm *exactly* the kind of person you're going to need on your side now that you've been revealed as the Heterodyne."

Agatha *tch*ed. "Oh dear, you really *are* mad." She giggled, "And not in a good way."

Tarvek's eyes narrowed. "And *you* are acting very strange." He paused. "You're acting . . . " He recoiled. "You're acting like Lucrezia!"

"How *dare* you," Agatha flared, then stopped, appalled. Her head began to roar, almost sending her to her knees. She took a deep breath and marshaled her thoughts. The pressure receded.

She opened her eyes to see Tarvek watching her warily, a heavy spanner in his hand. When he saw Agatha looking at it, he hastened to hide it behind his back. Agatha held up a hand. "It's okay. She's not in control."

Tarvek kept his distance. "But?"

"*But,*" Agatha replied, "You're right. She *is* here." Gently she massaged her temples. "She's always . . . *pushing*. And well, frankly, I'm exhausted. When this is all over, I want to sleep for a week." She looked at Tarvek with tired eyes. "She can't take control. Not fully. Not while I wear the locket, but she's trying to *influence* me and she's had a lot of experience in doing that to people." A faint wisp of smug malice flickered briefly through Agatha's thoughts. She shuddered. "It's horrible! I can't even trust my own emotions! Tarvek, what am I going to do?"

Several schemes that could utilize this situation arrayed themselves in Tarvek's mind before he viciously crushed all but two of them, which he guiltily filed away for future consideration. He took a deep breath. "You can't trust your own emotions? Fine." He patted his chest. "You can trust mine. I know how you act and I know how Lucrezia acts." He stepped in and placed his hands on Agatha's shoulders. "And yes, there is a difference. A huge one and it's a difference worth fighting for. We'll beat her. You'll see. I'm going to stay by your side until we completely eradicate all traces of her personality from your mind."

Agatha looked skeptical. Tarvek continued, "Between what I already know from my father, and what Lucrezia taught me herself while in Sturmhalten, and what I can learn from her own lab here, I believe that I can remove her rather easily, once I get a chance."

A jolt of fear echoed through Agatha's mind, causing her to actually smile. "I think she believes you can." Agatha took a deep breath and released it in a rattling sigh. She impulsively leaned in and gave Tarvek what she had planned as a brief hug. But once she had her arms around him, she found herself unwilling to let go. Tarvek stared at the top of her head and then gingerly, as if unwilling to allow himself to believe what was actually happening, enfolded her in his arms and held her tightly.

"Thank you, Tarvek," she whispered. "And . . . I'm sorry for teasing you."

"As long as it's *you* doing it, you can tease me all you want."

Agatha felt a delicious shiver at his words, which brought her up short. "Wait. Are these *my* feelings or *hers?*"

Tarvek gave her a tentative squeeze. "Probably yours. I can't see Lucrezia worrying about anything, let alone feel the need to apologize." With a regretful sigh, he released her from his arms. "Now let's finish setting up that transfer."

Theo was living in the moment. He could feel it. That glorious sensation that only came when he surrendered to the power of the spark and let it use his hands and brain to reshape reality. "Hit the first switch," he cried.

Off to the side, Moloch heaved a sigh and grasped a knife switch that was almost larger than he was. "Yeah, yeah, here it goes."

Beside him, Fräulein Snaug looked scandalized. "It's 'yes, *Master.*' " she whispered.

Moloch gave her a sour look. "Not even if it would get me out of here *today.*" Then he drove the switch home. Instantly, halos of electricity blossomed around the laboratory, the largest centered on Von Pinn and the great cat clank.

"The generators are coming up to speed," reported Mezzasalma. He checked some readings, put a hand against an engine cowling, and swore as he jerked it back. "This equipment is too old! I'm getting huge amounts of excessive vibration!"

"Keep them together just a bit longer, old fellow," Mittelmind called out cheerfully. His hands danced across a series of consoles, delicately adjusting current flow intuitively. "The neural translators are almost finished!" He shook his head in admiration. "Ha! That Lucrezia—what a *beautifully* twisted mind! Her system makes it all so *simple!*"

Standing amidst a cluster of power pylons, Sleipnir reported, "Power's holding steady . . . " With a start, she realized she actually had nothing to do. She stared at the pylon above her as a swarm of little mechanisms crawled over its surface. Left behind by Agatha, they had been diligently repairing the equipment even before the others had returned. *They're patching potential shorts before they happen*, she thought with admiration.

Moloch was straining to hold down the lid of a battered soup pot. Faint hammering could be heard from within. "Okay," he called out, "we've disengaged the driver clanks from the security clank."

Snaug sealed up the cranial cover. "The clank should now be fully autonomous."

The clank gave a shudder and its eyes began to glow.

"A possible problem," Mittelmind called out. "The neural interfaces are synchronized, but we're fighting signal degradation on the organic side."

Theo swore as he confirmed the problem. "The strain on the organic body is too much for its damaged state. It is almost spent! We *must* do this correctly the first time!"

A row of lights in front of Sleipnir switched one-by-one from orange to green. "We're getting full signal transfer," she reported. "All circuits are engaged!"

"What we are getting is dangerous levels of oscillation." Mezzasalma scuttled away as one of the generators began visibly shuddering. "The shock mounts are starting to crumble! Cut the power!"

"We're experiencing a resonance disaster," Mittelmind said calmly. "We must shut it down before—"

"No! Not yet!"

A thunderous boom shook the room. Sleipnir stared upwards in horror as cracks began to spread in the already-unstable ceiling. "Theo!"

"Stay where it's safe," Theo yelled back. "You promised!"

"I will! But you've all got to move! The ceiling is going to collapse!"

"Just a few more seconds . . . "

"No!" she screamed as the ceiling seemed to slip sideways. "Now! You've got to move—"

Her voice was lost in a grinding roar of stone and dust that seemed to shake the world—

And then—

There was silence punctuated by the occasional rattle of debris. A particular mound shifted aside, revealing the dusty form of Moloch von Zinzer. He spat out a mouthful of grit, then looked anxiously down at the girl cradled in his arms. "Hexalina? Are you . . . ?"

Snaug blinked and looked up at him. "I'm fine," she whispered, and then allowed herself to relish the situation. "Oh yes," she purred, "mighty fine indeed."

Another pile shifted to reveal Theo, battered but whole. "Sleipnir? Are you okay?"

In an instant, she was next to him pushing rocks aside. "I'm here. Are you all right?"

"I am." Theo freed a leg and examined it in wonder. "Amazing. I really am." He glanced upwards and recoiled when he saw solid metal less than a meter above him. His cry of surprise made them all look up. The great metal cat was standing over them all, legs wide to shield them from the collapse. It shrugged; rocks and support beams slid to the floor. It gave a rumbling rattle, which Theo realized was actually a deep mechanical chuckle. "But of course, children. Am I not Otilia, the Muse of Protection?"[20]

With a groan and a clatter, Professor Mezzasalma extracted himself from under a semi-collapsed table. He sighed, pulled an oily rag from a pocket, and began wiping down his mechanical legs. "I see that if it were not for you . . . ah . . . madam, we would have been crushed."

"Indeed you would have been, were I still imprisoned within that frail sheath of dying meat."

By this time they had all crawled free. The cat clank gave a great rattling shake that sent dust and gravel flying. Theo turned to look,

---

[20] The Muses were a set of nine clanks built long ago for the Storm King. Most people thought them lost, destroyed, or even mythical. But as we see here, this was not the case. Otilia was the Muse of Protection—a job she took very seriously.

but the apparatus—and the remains of the construct they had known as Von Pinn—were entombed under several tons of rock.

The mechanical cat gnashed its jaws and bowed to the assembled people. "Well done, children." It lifted a large paw and regarded it critically. "While this body cannot compare with the work of my creator,[21] I find it—" It flexed its paw and gleaming claws slid forth, and then, with a hiss, smoothly retracted. "—acceptable." It then glanced up and casually shoved Doctor Mittelmind a meter to its left. A chunk of stone crashed to the floor where he had been standing. "But now, children, the Castle continues to crumble and this room is dangerously unstable. We must leave this place immediately."

"Actually," Sleipnir said, "we can't. The ceiling also collapsed inside the stairwell. We're trapped down here."

Everyone considered this. Doctor Mittelmind sighed and clapped his hands together. "Cannibalism it is, then," he said brightly. "Herr von Zinzer, which leg would you like us to start with?"

"My leg?!"

Professor Mezzasalma nodded. "Of course. A minion as talented as yourself, well, it would be foolish to eat you all at once."

At that moment the great clank interrupted. "The collapse appears to have cleared and reopened the shaft made by that troublesome Heterodyne girl."

Everyone glanced up at the ceiling that was easily six meters above them. It continued, "We shall simply go up."

A few minutes later, Professor Mezzasalma finished spinning an efficient web of rope around the body of the clank. Clutching this while astride the broad back was Moloch, looking resigned.

Theo leaned in towards the great head. "Mistress von Pinn?"

The great clank regarded him and seemed to smile. It was an

---

[21] The wizard Van Rijn appears in most popular stories of the Storm King, usually in his role as the king's trusted friend. Little is known about his life (or death if you want to be paranoid about it), but he was certainly a genius who created scientific wonders that even the sparks of today have trouble duplicating.

unsettling sight. "That is no longer my name, child." It flexed its claws hard enough that the rock floor below them cracked. "I am once again worthy to be called Otilia."

Theo glanced up at the smooth shaft above them. "Are you sure you can do this?"

"Wait!" Moloch waved his hands. "*Now* you ask this?"

Fraulein Snaug gently patted his leg. "Don't worry, you'll be fine."

Moloch looked at her hopefully. "Yeah?"

She nodded encouragingly. "And if you die, I promise I'll bring you back."

Moloch looked into Snaug's shining eyes and made an effort to smile. He really did. "Great."

Snaug bit her lip and went slightly glassy-eyed. Moloch looked at her with concern. *Poor kid, she's actually worried.* This was true. Snaug was envisioning the things she wanted to do to Moloch once he was strapped onto a revivification table and was concerned he wouldn't last long enough for her to be able to get around to them all. But no. She shook her head and looked at Moloch fiercely. "You're strong. You'll make it."

At that moment, Otilia crouched down with a pneumatic hiss. "Prepare," she said.

Moloch clenched his hands tightly. "You have *got* to be—"

The great clank leapt. It cleared the rim of the shaft, but just barely. *We're far too short of the top,* Moloch realized. He braced himself for the inevitable fall. The clank beneath him snapped its legs out, connected with the smooth wall before them, dug its claws into the fused stone, pivoted with a speed that almost caused Moloch to black out from the force of the turn, and then again leapt upwards. Three more times it performed this maneuver, until, to his amazement, Moloch saw they had risen above the lip of the hole. Otilia slammed onto the ledge, which began to crack. The great clank scrabbled frantically at the crumbling edge. "*Jump* little minion," it howled. "Jump while you can!"

With a superhuman effort, Moloch rose to his feet and danced across the quaking and rattling cat clank beneath him. He hesitated and then felt the clank beginning to slip. This prompted him to hurl himself, screaming, towards the edge—which, he saw, he was going to miss. As he grasped this, a firm blow struck him from below, propelling him upwards and over the edge. As he flew, he glanced down in time to see Otilia falling back out of sight. *It must have smacked me to get me over the edge and lost its grip,* he marveled as he slammed onto the floor of the Great Movement Chamber.

Faintly, far below, he heard a great booming crash. He crawled back and peered down, hoping everyone was okay.

Theo coughed. A great cloud of dust rolled from the small crater Otilia had made when she hit the ground. With a shudder of relief, he realized there was no sign of von Zinzer, and if he had fallen from that height there would have been a great deal of evidence. "Are you all right, Madam Otilia?"

The great clank stirred and shook its head. "Tricky," it rumbled as it smoothly rose to its feet. "But I think I now have the hang of it." It shook itself again and regarded the rest of those before it with a toothy grin. "Who wants to go next?"

Several minutes later, with a triumphant metal scream, Otilia clambered out of the great hole. "HA! I *knew* I'd get it *eventually!*" The clank then gently lowered itself to allow Sleipnir to slide bonelessly, wide-eyed and shivering, into Theo's waiting arms.

From the side, Fräulein Snaug nodded in satisfaction and turned to Moloch. He was gazing upwards, a frown of concentration on his face. "That's the last of them. They're all up and everyone's still alive," she said and shrugged philosophically. Moloch grunted.

Snaug followed his gaze. "Whacha doin'?"

"Working." He gestured upwards. Over them towered a giant waterwheel. A piece of the ceiling had been dislodged and, falling, had smashed the great wheel's shaft. The wheel itself lay to one side, where it shuddered uselessly in the water that rushed past its motionless blades. "Look. Even once our madgirl gets the Castle's mind sorted out—we'll still be in trouble. All the batteries are almost dead.[22] There's no new power being generated, not with this thing broken."

Snaug stared upwards. "Well . . . sure. But that thing's got to be almost thirty meters tall. What can *we* do?"

The little mechanic nodded. "We can fix it."

"What!" Snaug stared at him. "Us? Fix *that*? It's impossible! Even with the sparks it would—"

Moloch interrupted her. "We don't even need the sparks for this." The audacity of this statement rendered Snaug mute with astonishment. Moloch continued. "Sure, this is tough, but it's not *brains* tough. It's just *hard work* tough." There was a soft chiming from near his feet and Moloch gently scooped up one of the small helper clanks, which handed him a series of measurements on a scrap of paper. He nodded in satisfaction and with a tilt of his head indicated the little clank. Snaug now realized there were hundreds of the little devices clustered around them in the darkness, waiting.

"I think I've got us some help," Moloch finished.

Tarvek stood up and surveyed the intricate web of cables and components that now filled the small chamber. The severed clank head was nestled at its center. "How does it look?"

Agatha carefully tweaked a final dial and then nodded in satisfaction. "I think it's as good as it's going to get."

Tarvek rubbed his hands. "Then it's time to throw the switch!" In the next second their hands collided above the large knife switch. They stared at each other.

"*Excuse* me?" Agatha arched an eyebrow. "It's *my* castle. *I* should throw the switch."

Tarvek goggled at her. "But . . . "

---

[22]   Castle Heterodyne only remained operational at all due to a vast cavern full of Baghdad salamanders, a type of voltaic pile.

"But what?"

Tarvek opened and closed his mouth a few times and then stepped aside. Throwing the switch was the *fun* part. "Nothing. You go ahead."

The corner of Agatha's mouth quirked upwards. "You don't like a girl throwing the switch?"

Tarvek went red. "Don't be ridiculous," he muttered. "These are modern times."

Agatha nodded in understanding. "I promise I'll throw it in a very *manly* way."

Tarvek rolled his eyes. "I don't think that's necessary—" The corner of his mouth went up. *If she could tease him—.* He gave her a wicked look: "—or even *possible.*"

"Then I'll do it *my* way."

The switch slammed home and a storm of applied energy swept through the apparatus around them. The head vibrated and its eyes flared impossibly bright—brighter—and then suddenly went dark. The electrical activity around them stopped with a solid, final *thunk.*

Tarvek released his breath and checked a readout. "That's it. The system is in shut-down mode. The transfer should be complete."

Agatha poked her head out into the main library. Everything was as silent and dark as when they had entered. Her chest felt cold. *What if it hadn't worked?* She took a deep, steadying breath and called out to the still air of the Library. "Castle?"

A vast slow sound, like a mechanically created wind, arose from all around. Agatha waited, tense. The sound faded and swelled from different spots until, out of nowhere, there was a voice. "I am here." It was the Castle's voice, but . . . different. There was a richness and hint of subtlety to it that Agatha had never heard before. Her heart swelled with love and relief. *It had worked!* She felt a bit faint. It was only then she realized how frightened she had been. How much she had worried that shutting down the Castle would kill it for good and just how desperately terrible that would be, for so many reasons.

"Please wait . . . " it continued. "I am still adjusting my parameters."

"Is something wrong?"

The voice contained a sense of wonder now and it slowly began to grow in strength. "Ah. No, nothing is wrong, Mistress. Quite the contrary. However, my prison—" Agatha glanced at the inert Muse head. "—was so *confining*. Now I am home again . . . but it is so *large*. So many routines . . . so many codes that must be run simultaneously . . . so glorious!" The voice was definitely hitting its stride now. "I feel . . . like a raindrop given control over an ocean. And it feels *good!*" It paused. "We spoke in the crypts, and . . . and you have already passed the test of blood. I *remember* that now. I remember *everything*. But . . . "

Tarvek stepped up to Agatha's side. "But—?"

The Castle sounded a bit embarrassed. "But collating and assimilating all of these separate memory streams . . . this will take some time, I'm afraid."

Agatha swallowed and held out her hands. "Is there anything I should do?" *What wouldn't she do, for this terrible, wonderful home of her ancestors?*

The Castle paused. "Duck."

Tarvek dragged Agatha aside just as Zola's blade sliced through the air where she'd been standing. With a snarl, Zola stepped out fully from behind the false door and pointed the tip of the weapon at Tarvek. "If you know what's good for you, you'll stay out of this! I have all of Auntie Lucrezia's secrets! Once this fool is dead, I can't lose! Be nice and I'll let you play out the original plan. Ha! You can even be my Storm King!"

Tarvek lashed out with a foot, catching Zola in the chest by surprise and tumbling her to the floor. "I am not your Storm King!" He leapt towards her, clutching a screwdriver like a knife. "And *my* plan was *much* better!"

To his astonishment, she batted his hand away, grabbed his hair, and slammed his head to the floor all in one swift, effortless motion. "Better? Did you plan on dying like a pig? Because that's where any plan you have now is going unless you do as I say and stay *down!*"

She moved to slam his head into the floor again and Agatha plowed into her from the side, bowling them both over and sending Zola's knife spinning away. "Your plan is *over*," Agatha said. "You've *failed*! I *am* the Heterodyne!" She called out, "Castle?"

"I am sorry, Mistress . . . " the Castle groaned. "*Soon . . .* "

Zola laughed and shot out a leg to flip Agatha head over heels and down a short flight of stairs. Agatha's squawk of surprise and pain ended in a loud shattering of glass. "There! Your stupid wind-up Castle is still grinding its gears!" Zola rolled to her feet, scooping up her blade. "And that gives me all the time I need to kill you, kill you, KILL YO—" a loud shot interrupted her as her left shoulder exploded in a spatter of blood and fabric.

Next to a smashed case, Tarvek swore as he broke open the antique gun that had been displayed inside and slammed in another of its delicately engraved shells. "Confounded thing pulls to the left," he muttered. "Easy enough to compensate—"

Zola's flying kick cracked the stock as she drove it into his chest, knocking Tarvek back into the case, tipping it over and sending a small armory of decorative weapons and ammunition clattering across the floor. "What kind of idiot *are* you," Zola screamed. "I told you to *stay down!*"

Tarvek rolled to his feet. He was astonished. Zola looked like she had been lightly run through a meat grinder, and yet—"How are you even still *moving?*" he wondered aloud.

"*HATE*," Zola shrieked triumphantly. "Hate and drugs! Lovely, *lovely* drugs! *I am a beautiful chemical killing machine!*" She spun like a dancer, the edge of her boot connecting to Tarvek's jaw. He fell to his knees. Zola landed on his back like a gargoyle and began to pound him relentlessly about the head, babbling in a disturbing singsong voice. "But don't worry! I'm not going to kill you! No! Oh no! I mean, I *was* going to! But then I had! A really! Really! Good idea!"

Tarvek had gone so limp there was no more fun to be had by hitting him, so Zola gracefully rolled to her feet and started kicking him instead. "You see, I'm thinking I'll just core your stupid brain and make you my zombie slave! You will be *so* in love with me and you'll positively hate yourself for having chosen her over me! You'll spend the rest of your pathetic so-called 'life' dancing attendance on me and begging forgiveness and telling me how *lovely* and *wonderful* I am and—"

This fascinating and psychologically revealing diatribe was cut off when Agatha brutally bashed Zola in the head with a large book.

Zola rolled and rose to her feet, grinning at them with fever-bright eyes. "Aren't you *listening*? It will take more than *that* to stop me!"

From behind her, Airman Higgs grunted. "*I* was listening." He lashed out with his foot and expertly dislocated her knee.

Zola gasped. Then, balancing on her good leg, she pivoted and delivered a solid punch to the place she'd stabbed him earlier. Higgs gasped in pain.

Zola nodded. "My! If it weren't for dear little Violetta's Movit Eleven, that would've *really* slowed me down!" She began a lightning-fast series of punches, landing them on his injury. "How about you? Still feeling that wound?" With a faint gasp, Higgs fell backwards to the ground. "I guess so," she said triumphantly. Then she grasped her knee and, with a meaty *crunch*, reset it, screaming in a hellish combination of pain and exultation.

Tarvek stared in horror. "That Movit stuff must be really strong," he muttered.

Agatha tried to pull him to his feet. "But look how fast she's moving! It's worse than a P. R. R.[23] She *can't* sustain that. It'll kill her!"

Zola was on them. She kicked Tarvek aside and slapped Agatha

---

[23]   A P. P. R., or Post Revivification Rush, is experienced by constructs and humans that have been brought back from what those of a pedantic turn insist upon calling "death." All of the senses are greatly enhanced and all of the governing mechanisms to be found in the human body are temporarily suspended. This means those experiencing a P. R. R. are filled with a great euphoria and a feeling of invulnerability. This is unfortunate for those around them as while they are mentally unstable, they are capable of great speed, strength, and endurance. However, once this effect wears off they tend to crash and they crash hard.

across the face. "No! Wait—is *that* your plan? Wait me out?" She laughed in cracked delight. "*Pathetic!*" Agatha gasped as Zola grabbed her in a headlock. She felt a sharp tightness around her throat. "I'm going to win!" Zola practically squealed with glee. "And I'm going to kill you first! Right—"

A block of stone a meter square dropped from the ceiling and crashed to the floor less than a hand's length from Zola's foot. She froze. "*Release her!*" The Castle's voice was strong and menacing. "NOW!"

"The Castle!" Zola whispered. She shook Agatha in fury. "You really managed to repair it." Suddenly she relaxed slightly. "But wait . . . " She thought furiously. "You! Castle!" she stepped away from the walls. "You're still not in complete control, are you? If you were, you wouldn't warn me, you'd just kill me! You don't have the delicate control you need yet!" A whisper of sound behind her made her spin, raising Agatha before her like a shield. Tarvek froze, and lowered the weapon he had been aiming at Zola's back. Zola grinned. "And you! I've got a microgarrote[24] around her neck!" Tarvek grimaced. "That's right! You've had enough training that you know what I can do, *right*?" Tarvek swallowed and nodded. Zola grinned. "Then stay back, and I won't kill her . . . yet"

For several seconds the room was silent except for the sound of deep breathing. "Stalemate," Agatha whispered. Zola shook her roughly. Agatha gasped. "But only until the Castle is fully operational."

Zola made a decision. "Come along, dear cousin, it's time for us to leave."

---

[24] A microgarrote is a very thin wire that can easily slice through flesh. It is a staple of pfennig dreadfuls as an assassin's weapon, where it is routinely strung inside doorways, slicing unsuspecting people, constructs, and clanks into messy chunks by their own momentum. This is absurd, as anyone who has ever leapt back from encountering a similarly strung spider's web will tell you. To further disillusion our more bloodthirsty readers, we must point out that bone and metal are quite resistant to it when it is used by hand. Make no mistake: it can still do a fatal amount of damage very quickly, but there is no need to exaggerate.

"How?"

Zola jerked Agatha's head back so that she was forced to look upwards. "We'll go through the dome." She began to drag Agatha along. "You see, I know *everything* Auntie knew, and there is so much more in here than just dry old books." They came to a small cage elevator. Zola hauled Agatha in after her, making sure to keep her between herself and Tarvek. As he watched, fuming, she hit the "Up" button with her hip and, with a jerk and a squeal, they slowly began to rise. "Your family collected all *sorts* of useful little toys."

Agatha watched as Tarvek dashed up the stairs, trying to keep even with the ascending elevator, but quickly falling behind. They finally came to the top floor and the cage wheezed to a stop. Zola pushed Agatha forward until they were before a large wood-and-glass display case that contained an elaborate coat. It appeared to be made of tubes and small fans and seemed to be in remarkably good shape.

"Look at that," Zola said. "The Flight Raiment of King Darius the Incandescent![25] And it's as good as new!" She heaved Agatha to one side and spun a small combination lock. With a screech, the door swung open. "Thank you, Auntie," Zola murmured. She examined the outfit and nodded. She then gave Agatha a sharp smack behind her right ear. Agatha dropped to her knees, stars spinning across her field of vision. Within seconds, Zola was back—now enveloped by the bulky garment—yanking Agatha to her feet. "Designed for quick escapes," she said with approval. "Now this should take us both up and out of here." She strode over to the wall and threw a switch. With a squawk of protest, a section of the overhead dome began to slide open.

"NO!" Tarvek stood before them panting slightly, his weapon

---

[25] This particular King Darius was presented with a "Magic Coat" that let him fly. It worked perfectly for almost fifteen years, in which time he used it to quell rebellions, rescue princesses, assassinate rivals, and awe the general population by correctly asserting that he could see their houses. Unfortunately, he neglected to carefully read the attached *Magic Owner's Manual*—especially the chapter titled "Maintenance"—and thus subsequently earned the sobriquet "The Incandescent."

leveled at them unwaveringly. "You've got the coat. Leave Agatha here and I *swear* I won't stop you."

Zola stuck her tongue out at him. "Ooh, you are such a liar! I am giving you some credit for smarts, you know. There is no way you're the kind of noble fool who would actually *keep* a promise like that." She glanced upwards. "And even if you were, I'm sure the Castle wouldn't."

A deep, architectural grumble was the only response.

Zola laughed. "You see? She leaves with me. But rest assured, once I'm away, I'll release her *immediately!*" She giggled and then paused with a frown. "Oh dear, did I say that out loud?" She swayed slightly. "Definitely time to go."

She slapped a button on her lapel, allowing herself to fall backwards off of the walkway, dragging Agatha along. "Farewell, O Mighty Storm King!" As they fell through space, the tubes on the coat gave a cough, then began to roar. Agatha reflexively grabbed hold of Zola—

—And they were no longer falling. They hung in midair, bobbing slightly in place. Zola rolled her eyes. "I can't *believe* it! It won't carry *two people?*" She glared at Agatha, "Although it's hardly surprising really, with your great big butt."

Agatha snarled, "Oh, you are one to talk, Pinky Miss Fatty-Pants!" She viciously punched Zola's sternum with her elbow. "*And* you've dropped your garrote!"

Zola drove a knee into Agatha's back. "It looks like I'll have to drop you off sooner than I'd planned!"

Agatha felt her hands start to slip. Tarvek launched himself off of the walkway and into the empty space beyond. He slammed into them both, one hand firmly clutching Zola's raiment, the other gripping Agatha. "Hold on!" he growled. The three of them began to spiral downward, while Zola screamed and lashed out furiously.

"Agatha," Tarvek yelled, "When we're low enough, jump!"

"Oh no you *won't*," Zola snarled as she fumbled in her hair. She came up with one of her trilobite brooches, the pin of the clasp extended. With a viper-like jab, she sank the point into Agatha's breast. "You'll let go—*now!*" Agatha gasped in shock. Her hands slipped free. Tarvek watched in horror as she plummeted—

—About a meter and a half, before she slammed into a tabletop, which collapsed under her.

Zola rolled her eyes. "Oh, for pity's sake," she howled. "That probably didn't kill her at *all!* At least it will slow her down long enough for the coup de grâce after I take care of—"

Tarvek's fist shattered her nose. He kept slugging rhythmically at the same spot. As he hammered away, he notice he was ranting in a low, monotonous voice that felt really *satisfying* when he used his fists as punctuation. "You vicious. Poisonous. Remnant of my stupid. Family's stupid. Plan! Your interference. With your stupid. Schemes and your stupid. Backstabbing. Plots. I have lost my castle! My Muses! My sister! My town! My hand is revealed. To those blasted. Upstart. Wulfenbachs! You and Lucrezia. Have done nothing. But destroy. My life. And interfere. With my plans. And now. You're trying to destroy. The one bright. Spot. Left? That. I will. Not. Permit!" He took in a deep breath and realized Zola had stopped moving quite some time before. He focused and saw she was covered with blood and bruises.

Her lips moved. "All right," she whispered, "I give up."

Tarvek stared at her in amazement, then shook his head. "Oooh, nonono, *nooo—you* do not *give up—*" He tightened his hands on Zola's throat. "You *DIE!*"

"Help," Zola whispered. Tarvek gripped tighter. Without warning, he was tumbling across the floor, tackled by an enemy he couldn't see clearly. Did Zola have an ally nearby? Then he realized it was Gil. Gil with his stupid *stupid* soft spot for Zola. They landed hard against a map case. A globe of the moon toppled to the floor and bounced into the shadows. Tarvek thrashed frantically, trying to get his feet under him as Gil continued to hold him down.

Released, Zola was slowly sitting up, moving like a sleeping ghost.

Her face was bloody and blank. Soon she was standing. Then, all at once, her toes cleared the floor and she was rising upwards towards the opening in the dome, gathering speed. The coat left little trails of vapor and dust in her wake that reflected an eerie light. The effect was ghastly and Zola, as a devotee of the Paris Opera, would have been delighted.

Tarvek and Gil stopped struggling and stared up at her in astonishment. "*Stop* her," Tarvek screamed in frustration. But was too late. She soared upwards through the great dome and sailed, still unconscious, into the sky.

"You *idiot!*" Tarvek flung Gil aside, pulled a small pistol from his waistcoat, and fired up after her. Gil grabbed his arm.

"What are you *doing?*"

"Well, I'm sorry," Tarvek shouted, "but it's the biggest gun I could find!"

The Castle roared. "That's better! Gentlemen, allow me!" The entire room shook once, then every metal object in sight spiraled upwards, fountaining up through the hole in the dome.

"Yes!" Tarvek shouted.

"NO!" Gil countered, "I want her alive!"

Tarvek stared at him. "WHY?"

"Well, for one thing—" But Gil realized he was now talking to empty air. He turned and gasped. Tarvek was holding Agatha, helping her to a sitting position. She was covered in blood and bruises.

Instantly Gil, too, was kneeling by her side. She looked up at him and gave a tight-lipped smile. "Tarvek said you'd get out. I'm glad you're all right." She closed her eyes and slumped back against Tarvek. "Sorry," she whispered. "This really hurts."

"Don't worry about Zola," Tarvek muttered as he glared at Gil, "I'm sure the Castle will get her."

When it spoke, the Castle was positively subdued. "Oh, is my façade red. Forgive me, Mistress, but she is already out of my currently limited range."

"Well." Agatha sighed. "At least she's gone."

Tarvek snorted as he examined Agatha's bruises. "For now," he said, resentment coloring the words.

Gil bit his lip and changed the subject. "Agatha. Let me look at you."

Tarvek sniffed. "Already *doing* it."

"Hey, I *am* a doctor, you know."

"Who *isn't?*"

Agatha grimaced. "They wouldn't let *me* take the exams . . . " She pulled aside her shirt and examined her chest. "But I'm pretty sure this wound is superficial."

Gil and Tarvek glanced at each other. Both were decidedly red in the face. They cleared their throats simultaneously.

Gil spoke first. "Ah. Nevertheless, you should still let me . . . us . . . take a look. At the wound."

Agatha colored. "But it's—"

Tarvek broke in. "Zola did it. We need to make sure it isn't poisoned."

Agatha bit her lip. "She uses poison?"

Gil angrily opened his mouth, then paused. "Well," he said slowly, "*I* always thought she just couldn't make coffee, but now I'm not so sure."

Wordlessly, Agatha undid a few buttons. Both Gil and Tarvek scrutinized the wound. Both nodded. "In my opinion," Gil conceded, his ears flaming, "everything looks great . . . I mean good."

Tarvek announced, "Smoke Knight poisons are supposed to be hard to detect, but the fact that you're not already dead is a very good sign. I know it's almost impossible in here, but try to keep it clean."

"I assure you," Agatha said as she buttoned herself back up, "that when this is all over, I will be having a bath for a week at *least.*"

"Violetta will have some stuff we should get on that wound as soon as possible, just in case."

Just then a rattling groan caught them by surprise. Gil looked around and saw a battered form slumped behind a case of fossils. It was beginning to thrash feebly. "Ah, Airman Higgs."

Tarvek looked like he'd just seen a heretofore unnoticed timer click down to "zero." "He's *alive?*"

Gil squatted down next to the injured man and delicately probed the holes in Higgs's shirt. The airman's hand shot out to bat him away, but Gil deflected it absentmindedly. A look of disbelief broke through the mask of pain on Higgs's face. "If even just *half* this blood is yours," Gil muttered, "you shouldn't move. At all."

"Looks worse than it is, sir."

"That's evident. You're still alive."

Higgs grunted in amusement. He rolled to his feet, assuming a swaying semblance of the position of attention. "There. See? Fit as a fiddle, sir."

Gil stared up at him and nodded slowly. "Apparently so."

"How are you folks, sir?"

The question caught Gil by surprise. "What?"

Higgs fished his pipe out of his pocket and indicated the others with a slightly shaky hand. "You lot okay, sir? I mean, last I saw, you were bein' chomped on by a plant and the Lady Heterodyne was knocked out." He glanced over at Tarvek and his eyes narrowed. "That fella was doin' fine."

Gil nodded. "We're all fine, Mister Higgs."

"Well, that's a relief." He took a deep breath. "Permission to leave the Castle, sir."

Gil looked surprised. "Well, not that I blame you for wanting to, but—"

Higgs interrupted him. "I think you missed that part of the fight, sir. Miss Zeetha got stabbed. Pretty bad."

Tarvek opened his mouth. Higgs looked at him. Tarvek closed his mouth and looked away. Higgs continued, "I want to take her—"

"Ah! To the Great Hospital in Mechanicsburg." Gil interrupted. "I'll give you a note. Give it to Doctor Sun and—"

"Uh . . . no, sir."

"No?"

Higgs shook his head. "Not the hospital. Too public. Miss Zeetha, she's been seen with you. With the Lady Heterodyne. People will remember her. I'll take her to—"

Gil snapped his fingers. "Mamma Gkika's."

Higgs nodded. "Yessir."

Agatha looked confused. "Mamma what?"

Tarvek looked confused. "It's a degenerate . . . " He paused. "It's *supposed* to be a . . . bar. For tourists." It was clear he was reconsidering this.

Agatha stepped up to Gil and Higgs. "Zeetha is still back with those plants. We shouldn't be standing around here, we've got to—"

Higgs cut her off. "With all respect, Lady, *I've* got to. You lot still need to get this place back in fighting trim. That Zola girl got out. Someone's gonna find her, and she'll tell them that the Castle is down. Then it'll be a race between the Baron or her people to see who can flatten this place first. I can't fix the Castle, but I can give you one less thing to worry about by getting Miss Zeetha to safety." He nodded towards Agatha. "By y'r leave, of course, m'Lady."

Agatha looked at Gil. "And the people at this 'tourist bar'? They can do a better job of keeping her alive than the Great Hospital?"

Gil considered this. "All things considered? Yes. They have access to techniques the hospital doesn't."

Agatha bit her lip. "All right, I'll trust your judgment." She turned to Higgs. "But are you sure that you can get out of here and get her there safely?"

"It's *your* Castle, Lady. If you tell it to let us go . . . "

"Castle?"

The Castle hesitated. "If you so wish it, it shall be so."

Higgs smiled. "There you go."

Tarvek looked at him. "I don't think he's going to have any trouble at all."

Higgs nodded genially. "You should listen to your friend here, m'Lady. He's a smart guy."

Higgs started off and Tarvek stepped along with him. "You didn't mention Violetta."

Higgs nodded. "That Smoke Knight gal?"

Tarvek nodded. "Well spotted. Yes, is she all right?"

"Yessir. Last I saw, she was lookin' after Miss Zeetha. If she's still alive, it'll be because of your Miss Violetta."

"Mine no longer," Tarvek replied. "She serves the Lady Heterodyne now."

Higgs considered this. "By your order?"

"Yes."

"And you can do that?"

"I can." Higgs absorbed this in silence. Tarvek continued, "And, in her own way, she is very good. Your Miss Zeetha will probably be okay."

Higgs actually stumbled. "Uh, she—she ain't *my* Miss Zeetha, sir."

"Oh." Tarvek waved the suggestion away. "Heaven forbid. I'm sure you'd desert your duties and hare off to save *any* green-haired Amazon."

Under the bruises, it was clear that Higgs' face was getting red. "Ain't *desertin'*, sir. Got *permission*."

"Oh yes," Tarvek granted, "so you did." Under his breath he muttered, "From the Lady Heterodyne, too, I noticed." Instantly Higgs swung towards him, his eyes as cold as death. Tarvek stepped back—

"Tarvek!" Agatha called. "Come and see!"

The two men stared at each other for another second, then Tarvek took off running. He dashed up to the map display and stopped in surprise. The display was much clearer now. It was easier to identify actual architectural features. Within the edifice of light, several red spots bloomed. "*That's* looking better," he said.

"Yes," the Castle boomed. "With the other fragments of my personality eliminated, I am no longer in conflict. However, I am still not yet fully integrated. The places in red are where I still require repairs."

Agatha nodded in satisfaction. "Now *that's* useful! Let's go!"

Within the Great Hospital a particular patch of darkness wavered and resolved itself into a giant but indistinct man. He opened its mouth and slurred sounds came out. Rudolf Selnikov realized something was seriously wrong and gave a scream that, even to his own ears, sounded garbled.

The man reached forward and made some sort of adjustment.

The view clicked into perfect focus. Better than perfect, actually. Rudolf had noticed an annoying blurring of vision over the last year or two. He had accepted that spectacles were an inevitable part of his future, but now—

"How is that?" the fellow, an elderly Chinese man in a medical uniform asked.

"Um . . . better" Rudolf realized something still sounded very odd. "Is . . . is that my voice?"

The old man gave a tight smile of satisfaction. "Indeed it is. And you're lucky to have it."

A few more things snapped swiftly into place. "Wait a minute. I *know* you. You're Herr Doktor Sun! Am I in the Great Hospital?"

Sun looked pleased. "Cognition seems good. Excellent. Yes, you are."

"But why . . . Uh-oh . . . "

"Ah, coming back, is it?"

"Young Wulfenbach! He . . . " Rudolf paused. "I can't actually remember."

Sun nodded as he made an elegant calligraphic note on a chart. "Interesting, but hardly surprising. Typical death trauma." [26]

---

[26] It is the rare person who manages to actually remember their death after they have been revived. There is an amusing theory making the rounds that people would remember their *death* just fine. Death is natural. One goes through their entire life coming to grips with its inevitability. But resurrection—ah, *that* is incredibly *unnatural*, countermanding, as it does, the laws of gods and men and forcibly dragging a person back from the Undiscovered Country, regardless of whether or not that person actually wishes to return. *That* experience,

"DEATH?"

Sun frowned. "Tsk. Look at those readings. Calm down before you break something. Yes, yes, you died. Don't be a baby about it."

"Dead," Rudolf whispered.

Sun waggled a hand back and forth. "Well, obviously not *dead* dead . . . "

"Ah! Yes! Of course! The Baron *needs* me! He's made me a new body!" This idea obviously perked Rudolf up a bit. "Why, that's wonderful. My original was no great shakes, after all."

Sun pursed his lips and looked down at the tank that contained the revivified head. "Well, my Lord Selnikov, I wouldn't get *too* excited about that new body just *yet*."

He turned Rudolf's container about so it was facing a small mirror. Rudolf swore. "Oh, now this is absurd! How am I supposed to shave?"

Sun was impressed. This was usually when these "extreme patients" tended to break down. "Your lordship actually shaves himself?"

"As if I'd trust anyone I know to put a razor to my throat."[27]

Sun observed Rudolf's jawbone was directly attached to the nutrient recirculation mechanisms. "Technically? No longer a problem."

Rudolf glared at him sourly. "Ah yes, that '*Sunny* bedside manner' everyone goes on about."[28]

"In your case, the whole bedside thing is also no longer applicable." Sun paused. "Do they *really* talk about my—"

"What's the price," Rudolf snarled.

"I beg your pardon?"

---

being summarily wrenched apart from the natural order of things and crammed back intro one's meaty little shell, *that* is the trauma so great that sanity demands its erasure. Unfortunately, this is a theory that will only be proved once science has made substantial breakthroughs in ouija technology.

27   Rudolf Selnikov was part of the extended family that contained both the Sturmvoraus and the Von Blitzengaard branches. Murder, deceit, blackmail, and betrayal were everyday considerations, and that was before people got together for the holidays.

28   Doctor Sun did not coddle his patients.

"Don't be disingenuous. Why am I still alive?"

Sun nodded in approval. "You were plucked from the wreckage of an army of unregistered war clanks. You had a lovely big fancy hat. The Baron believes you know *many* things. When he also knows them, *then* you will get your fine strong new body."

Rudolf mulled this over. "And the freedom to enjoy it?"

Sun spread his hands and sighed knowledgeably. "Freedom is such a *relative* term. If you know as much about these 'Knights of Jove' and their machinations as the Baron believes, then, when you are wrung dry, a great many powerful people will hate you very much. So while you would *certainly* be 'free' to leave the Baron's service and protection, well . . . "

Rudolf looked ill. "Zott. He's good at this."

Sun beamed. "He occasionally does his teachers proud!"

"The depressing thing? Twisted and ruthless as you people are, throwing in with you is a step up."

Sun nodded. "For your safety, we released your name as one of the dead."

Rudolf grimaced in distress. "Everyone is going to *know* I died?"[29]

Sun shrugged. "Confound it, that means my lands and titles will go to that insufferable nephew of mine.[30] I'll be ruined socially . . . barred from my clubs . . . none of my old friends will be in if I call, the wretched snobs, even the ones who were eager to call when I wasn't in." He gave a great sigh, which sent a few bubbles up past his nose. "Why, even my wife . . . " He paused as the implications began to percolate through his mind. He glanced at Doctor Sun.

---

[29]   The Fifty Families, who hewed to traditional monarchical practices, were loath to deal with the philosophical ramifications of resurrection, if only because it played hob with the laws of inheritance. Therefore, when you died you were treated as if you were permanently dead, regardless of whether or not you were revivified by mad science a minute later.

[30]   While this appellation could be applied to any number of Rudolf Selnikov's nephews, it is generally assumed he is referring to Aaronev Tarvek Sturmvoraus, who was, within the family, universally admired and personally disliked.

"Can I get a brass plate that says *Reanimated Abomination of Science* bolted to my forehead?"[31]

"Er . . . I suppose?"

Suddenly, Sun Ming Daiyu[32] appeared, in a state of agitation. "Grandfather! Come quickly!" She saw Rudolph and paused. "Ah. Pardon me, you're with a patient." She bowed slightly to Rudolph's jar. "Hello, sir. You are looking much better." The niceties observed, she again turned to Doctor Sun. "Grandfather, if we could step outside?"

Once in the hallway, Doctor Sun turned towards his granddaughter, an expectant look on his face. "The Heterodyne girl—the one from the pink airship—she's out of the Castle! They're bringing her in to Emergency." Without another word, the two began running towards the admitting wing. The staff made sure the hallway before them was cleared as they sped by. Daiyu continued: "She was using some kind of flight suit and the gargoyle sweepers shot her down."[33] She paused. "I haven't seen her yet, but apparently she was flying rather

---

[31] At this time, Rudolf Selnikov was married to the Lady Margarella Oklazavich Selnikov, an adventuress he met in his days as an explorer. She was known for her intense physical appetites. Her flying visits to Sturmhalten were tiring for the entire staff who were expected to keep up with her assorted itineraries which covered her philanthropic and charitable enterprises, her political and entertainment events, and her lectures and general meddling in the affairs of the people of Balan's Gap. It is said there were further excesses she reserved for Lord Selnikov alone. This helped to explain both his physical fitness and his perpetually hunted look.

[32] Sun Ming Daiyu was Doctor Sun's granddaughter. While not a spark herself at this time, she was expected to breakthrough at any moment. Her younger twin, Sun Ming Mei, was one of the students on Castle Wulfenbach and had been present when Agatha's true identity was revealed.

[33] The gargoyle sweepers were not part of the Castle Heterodyne systems, but were actually a part of the Great Hospital's protective array. The Great Hospital prided itself on admitting anybody (though they might very well be arrested as soon as they were wheeled out of Recovery). However, this meant, as a matter of course, people who had enemies were lying around helpless. Needless to say, there was the occasional attack by people who just couldn't resist the opportunity. Quite frequently, these attackers wound up next to their intended victims in adjoining beds, which actually had an astonishing recuperative effect on all concerned, as no one wanted to be the "last man down."

erratically and the reported extent of her injuries suggest that she was seriously injured even before she was brought down."

"Prep Theater Three," Sun called out as they hurried on. "And I want a double contingent of guards!"

They paused as a line of gurneys temporarily blocked the hall. A door opened. "Oh, Doctor Sun! What is it? Are we in danger?"

Sun waved a hand. "Nothing to fear, princess. Someone will be by to see to you soon."

The mechanical figure nodded and bestowed a charming smile on the doctor and his granddaughter and even on the two armed guards who stood outside her door. "Thank you, Doctor," the clank that had once been the Princess Anevka said. "That is so reassuring."

CHAPTER 4

The Heterodyne he built a house, of stones and bones
and screams.

If you've ever been to Mechanicsburg, you've seen
it in your dreams.

Oh, folks go in, but don't come out, and no one
says a word,

For if they do, they go in themselves, at least
that's what I've heard.

The walls and doors they move about, like
the windows and the floors,

And there are deathtraps everywhere, with
spikes and carnivores.

So the Heterodynes are a jolly folk, they
love to dance and sing.

They have a murderous evil house that
gives them everything.

—Balen's Gap/Sturmhalten
children's rhyming song

೬ᎧᏩ

Through a hallway of Castle Heterodyne, Airman Higgs strode purposefully. His Wulfenbach airshipman's uniform was tattered and so was he. Bruises, cuts, grime, and blood covered every exposed surface, but he stood tall, moving without any signs of infirmity. He carried Zeetha like the princess she was, carefully cradled in his arms. A massive, oozing bandage was wound around her midsection. Her color and irregular breathing warned she was terribly close to death.

He walked in silence. A heavy, palpable feeling of very purposefully *not* saying anything filled the air.

Finally, the airshipman stopped. Checking to see if girl in his arms was still unconscious, he addressed the empty air: "You got somethin' to say, you better say it, before you bust a window or somethin'."

The Castle's usual tone of amused malice was gone, replaced with a cold anger. "You are *abandoning* the Heterodyne."

Higgs considered this and checked the girl in his arms again. *It would be close.* He squared his shoulders and continued onwards. "You think Klaus Wulfenbach's kid, the Storm King, a Smoke Knight, and all those others ain't enough?"

"They are not *you*." The Castle continued, "Until there is an *heir*—"

"Oh, not *that* again," Higgs groaned. "I swear," he muttered, "every twenty years . . . it's like some kind of echo or somethin'."

"*I* still have my priorities. The Heterodyne needs her strongest protectors—"

"She needs this girl!"

"She *is* a very good fighter," the Castle acknowledged, "but obviously not as good as she *thought* she was. She'll be no good at *all* in her current state."

Higgs nodded, "Which is why I'm taking her to Mamma . . . General Gkika[34]." He paused, "Besides, it ain't the fightin' the Lady will need her for."

The Castle paused. "I think it will be a while before the Lady will require experimental subjects—"

Higgs sighed. "No."

---

[34] Despite the prohibition of all Jägers in town, General Gkika had chosen to stay in Mechanicsburg. This was part of the deal when they accepted service with the Wulfenbach Empire. As far as can be determined, in the sixteen years the deal was in play, she never left the premises of her tavern, which was merely a façade that hid a much larger subterranean establishment. This served as a hospital and hospice for those Jägers that were too ill or damaged to continue to fight. Jägers refuse to let any medical personnel treat them, except for a Heterodyne, so here they had a place where they could wait until a Heterodyne was actually found.

"Monster fodder?"

"I'm talking about *friends*, you mud hut. How many of the masters have *had* friends. Not alliances, I mean real friends. People they could trust? People who actually *liked* them?"

"Now you're being unrealistic. You're talking about the Heterodynes," the Castle huffed. "The Family *has* no 'friends.' "

Higgs nodded. "And look where the Family is now."

When the Castle spoke next, it sounded uncertain. "But . . . it . . . it all sounds so . . . *messy*." It grew more accusatory. "I think *you're* the one who 'actually likes' this girl."

"An overconfident, optimistic fool like this?" Higgs snorted as he held Zeetha slightly tighter. "You think what you like."

The huge jack-in-the-box clank slumped, releasing a final gout of steam. "Playtime is over, young masters," it hissed. Gil and Tarvek realized they were no longer under attack, and began extricating themselves from the oversized toy's clutches.

Agatha hurried over. "I got the circuits reattached, so everything should be fine now."

"Yes, indeed," the Castle added with a jocular tone to its voice. "Why, I had forgotten I even *had* an impluvium!"

She looked at the two panting men. "Are you two okay?"

Tarvek waved a hand. "I'm good." He looked over to Gil. "You good?" Gil, looking slightly purple, nodded as he pried a mechanical hand from his throat. Tarvek nodded. "We're good."

Agatha looked relieved. "You guys should take a break. I have to figure out where to go next."

Tarvek leaned back and examined the gaudy furnishings of the room. "So this was the nursery," he sighed.

Gil threw the hand across the room. "It explains *so much*." The two sat side by side and watched Agatha move about, appreciating both her and their continued ability to breathe. Finally, Tarvek pulled a sheaf of notes from his coat pocket. He crossed out an entry and examined the rest. "That's two down and two more to go. Unless these repairs uncover even *more* breaks . . . "

He looked at Gil, who had fixed him with a cold stare. "What now?" he asked.

"What are you playing at?" Gil sounded angry.

Tarvek looked at him blankly. "Pardon?"

"You're up to something."

Tarvek squirmed. "What makes you think—"

"You're breathing!"

"You'll have to be a bit more descriptive."

"Zola got away because of me, and you haven't said a word. What are you up to?"

Comprehension dawned in Tarvek's eyes. "Ah. I see. You're waiting for me to twit you about letting Zola escape. In front of Agatha, of course, in order to make you look bad."

Gil frowned. "Pretty much."

Tarvek rolled his eyes. "Tsk. You really do think everyone around you is mentally deficient, don't you? I'm not an idiot. Consider— you've known Zola for *years.* You're used to protecting her. You had no idea that she'd just hurt Agatha. How could you have? Plus, you were all messed up from that plant. So you came running in, saw someone you hate and fear trying to kill her. Of *course* you reacted."

Gil glowered at him. "I do not fear you."

Tarvek looked surprised. "Really? You should. Anyway, there's also no way you could have known that once I let go of her she'd fly away. It startled me, I'll admit. As for Agatha, she's one of the smartest people we'll ever meet. Give her some credit for logical thought. She'd think I was a fool if I gave you a hard time about this, and she'd be right. No, no, she will have to *see* you act poorly for it to make an impression."

Gil looked chastised. "Wow. I . . . I guess I misjudged you."

Tarvek stamped his foot. "No, no, no! You haven't *misjudged* me, you've *underestimated* me! Mark my words. Even if I never break your illegitimate empire, even if I cannot reclaim the Crown of Lightning, I can and will force you to reveal yourself to Agatha as the base scoundrel you really are."

A red curtain slid over Gil's vision. He grabbed Tarvek by the front of his shirt and pulled him in until his rival's face was centimeters from his own. Tarvek looked unconcerned. "You backstabbing sneak," Gil growled. "I will break—"

"GIL!" Agatha stood over them, scandalized. "What are you *doing?* Put him down!"

Tarvek was so pleased that he hardly flinched at all when Violetta's shout caught him from behind. "There you are!"

He turned, grinning. "Ah, Violetta, my little cloud of doom. Even you cannot dampen my spirits right now."

A sisterly sock to the gut wiped the smile off his face. "Did you have to keep moving around so much? I can't believe how long it took to find you idiots."

"I helped," the Castle said cheerfully.

Violetta snarled. "Helped?"

"Oh, come now. We had fun! Alerting you to every *other* trap was more than fair."

Agatha waved an accusatory finger upwards. "We're going to talk about this." She turned to Violetta. "Zeetha. Is she . . . ?"

Violetta bit her lip. "She's tough as nails. It was a clean wound, and I packed her full with half my pharmacopoeia to stop the bleeding and reduce the shock, but . . . " She looked at Agatha apologetically. "I'm not a doctor, but it looked pretty bad. Mister Higgs seemed to think she'll be okay."

She didn't mention that the normally dour airshipman had examined Zeetha in a way that made her think he had seen his share of battlefield injuries. He'd finally rested back on his heels, looked at Violetta, and nodded. "Mighty good job," he'd said, before hoisting

Zeetha into his arms and striding off. Violetta had felt like she'd passed an exam she hadn't even known she'd been taking.[35]

Tarvek strode up with a cushion held strategically over his midsection. "Did they tell you that Zola stuck Agatha with one of her hairpins?"

Seconds later, he was clutching an eye while Violetta was unbuttoning Agatha's undershirt. "I can't believe it! You two let her get hurt *again*? Why do I even let you out of my sight?" She turned to Tarvek, who rolled into a ball. "Didn't you even run any tests?"

"With what," he bleated. "I came in here in a bed sheet!"

"And whose fault was that?" As she was speaking, she pulled out several small packets and ampules. With a deft series of movements, she swabbed the wound and took a small blood sample, which she poured from one vial to another. "That's it, my Lady," she said conversationally. "I'm not letting you marry either one of these useless—ARRGH!"

She spun about in fury and even Gil took a step back at her expression. "Of *course* there's poison. It looks like it's 'Auntie Mehitabel's Natural Causes.'"[36]

Gil bit his lip. "I've never heard of it."

Tarvek shrugged. "I'm not surprised. It's subtle."

"Oh, thank you very much."

"Also slow-acting."

"Uh-huh."

"And really hard to detect."

"Wait. What? I don't even know where you're going with that one."

Tarvek sighed. "I'm not going *anywhere*. It really is a subtle, slow, hard-to-detect poison."

---

[35] Not an unusual feeling for a Smoke Knight, actually. A significant amount of the training seems to consist of going about one's daily business while an instructor secretly watches to see how soon you notice the poison.

[36] One of the subtler of the many fine Smoke Knight poisons that you'll now find available in the Castle Heterodyne gift shop, "Auntie Mehitabel's Natural Causes" makes it look like the victim died of perfectly natural causes. Right on schedule.

"The good news," Violetta said, "is that it's easy to get rid of if you know it's there and if you have the antidote. So usually? Yeah, deadly. Smoke Knights carry that particular antitoxin, as well as some others, of course. You're lucky you've got a Smoke Knight on your side, but you're really going to need some sleep as soon as you can get it."

Agatha nodded in agreement. Neither Gil nor Tarvek disagreed. Antidote taken, the group reformed and continued their trek.

"What's next?" Violetta asked.

"You are now entering what I think is a major problem area," the Castle informed them. "But I am not sure. Because of the damage, I cannot see it."

They stopped short just outside a massive pair of iron doors. The blast of heat from beyond made them turn their faces away and wince.

"Now, I don't remember what is *supposed* to be here, but I remember that it's important. Does it look bad?"

"Well," Gil ventured, staring into the inferno before them. "This is Castle Heterodyne. Maybe it's *supposed* to be on fire."

"FIRE?" the Castle screamed. "I am draining the cistern!" They just had time to look up before the wall of water hit.

In the Great Hospital, Zola lay cocooned in bandages and surrounded by a web of tubes, wires, and monitors. Doctor Sun snapped the lid of his instrument case shut as he finished his running diagnosis. He'd been talking for some time and was desperately wishing for a cup of tea. "Summary?" he asked.

Daiyu made a final notation and nodded. "Zola has multiple injuries, but no life-threatening physical trauma. Her metabolism has stabilized thanks to treatment, but she was already crashing hard from whatever cartload of drugs she got dosed with. We found a lot of interesting things on her when we got her undressed—a fair number of little portable containers that still had drugs or at least residue in them. We should be getting a report on them back in the next few hours.

"She also had a surprising number of weapons secreted about her person. Some of them—" She winced. "Well, I certainly hope we got them all. But I'm very curious to find out what a number of them actually do."

Sun nodded. "I expect Klaus and Mistress Spüdna[37] will be very interested in talking to this one."

"I hope they get the chance. She's still appallingly toxic, and the aftereffects of some of this stuff . . . It's going to take some slow, careful work to flush this mess out of her system without killing her."

Doctor Sun looked intrigued. "I have some interesting new ideas on how to proceed with that."

Daiyu bit her lip. "As long as it keeps her alive." She looked at the still woman on the bed before them. "You know, Grandfather, it might sound crazy, considering her condition, but I'd feel better if we had her in restraints. You know, just in case."

Doctor Sun smiled. "It does not sound crazy, my dear. It sounds prudent." He paused. "Extra guards, as well."

As they left, Zola ever so slightly opened one eye. "And yet they still underestimate me," she muttered. One corner of her mouth twitched into a sly smile that became a wince of pain. "Still . . . Restraints. Guards. Not good. Obviously, the time to leave is *now*!"

With a terrific effort, Zola dramatically raised her head several centimeters from her pillow and passed out.

She awoke hours later. The sky outside her window was dark. The room was dimly lit. Mechanisms hummed, clicked, and gurgled quietly all around her. She felt much better and tried to move, but found herself strapped down. She strained against the restraints and gasped from the pain this awoke all over her body. "Curse this wretched, weak body," she hissed.

After a few minutes of silent fuming, she heard a muffled *thump*

---

[37]   Oglavia Spüdna was the head of the empire's espionage division. She is best known for the quote, "If you can't say something nice about someone, you're not very good at the whole spying thing."

from the other side of the door, which, after a few seconds, swung slightly open. A pair of mechanical eyes peered in. "Now *that* sounds like someone I know," the clank girl trilled as she skipped into the room, but she paused when she saw who was on the bed. Her expression became contrite. "Oh!" Suddenly the clank's voice changed, becoming a vapid parody of itself. "Please excuse me! I must have the wrong room! The guards here seem to have fallen asleep and—" She edged out and began to close the door.

"Lucrezia," Zola hissed. "Wait! Don't go!"

Instantly, the door closed, and the clank was at her side, eyes narrowed, a palpable air of menace gathering around her. "Who are you?" she asked, her voice now intelligent and deadly.

Zola grinned insouciantly. "Why, you silly girl! I'm Lucrezia!"

The clank stared at her, blinking her eyes, apparently in confusion. *No!* Zola realized, sifting through the mind trapped within her own. A code. A blinking code. Designed so Lucrezia could always recognize herself, no matter what shape she wore. Zola swore inwardly, dear Auntie had hidden this knowledge deep. There was now a roaring of contradictory instructions, but there was one sequence that kept repeating through the mind. Zola trusted to luck and relayed the sequence. There was an interminable pause as they stared into each other's eyes, then the clank girl gave her a dazzling smile and stood back. Zola allowed herself to breathe again.

The clank tipped her head to one side and looked Zola up and down. "What unexpected fun. Another me!" She reached out and ran a silver finger along Zola's jaw. "But I'm dying to know, dear . . . who *is* this you're wearing? When I heard the staff talking about a 'Heterodyne girl,' I *naturally* assumed I'd find the me I left wearing our darling daughter."

Zola considered what exactly to tell. *Always tell as much of the truth as you can,* she reminded herself. *It's always so much easier to remember.* She then shuddered when she realized when and where she'd heard that advice. She took a deep breath. "You probably can't tell, since the silly thing got herself frightfully bashed up, but this is Zola. Dear Demonica's daughter."

The clank looked startled. "Demonica? Really?"

"Yes! And she's as gullible as her dear mama! She's part of some scheme the Knights of Jove have got up to, and the darling girl decided to *rescue* me! There we were in the old secret laboratory, so I just copied myself right over her, neat as you please."

"Rescue you? You were in the Castle? Whatever were you doing there, of all places?"

Zola pouted. "Our daughter has regained control."

"*What*?" Lucrezia was genuinely shocked. "How?"

"She's got a device around her neck. A locket. It's keeping me locked down inside her. Another annoying trinket courtesy of dear meddling *Barry*."

The clank froze. "He's *here*?"

Zola closed her eyes. "No. No, he made it years ago, to keep her from breaking through.[38] But no, he himself has been missing for years. He's no threat." The stab of sheer panic that burst from the mind trapped within her mirrored the expression on Lucrezia's clank face. They both looked about frantically before they caught themselves.

The clank glared at Zola. "Do you *want* him to show up?" she hissed.

Zola was apologetic. "I'm *so* sorry, dear. I can't think what came over me."

Lucrezia closed her eyes. It was obvious that if she'd been human, she'd have been taking a deep, calming breath. "But, dear, this explains so much. I barely had time to seal the secret passages under

---

[38] *Breaking through* (or *breakthrough*) is the informal term used to describe the moment when a heretofore "normal" person becomes a spark. This is usually accompanied by excessive histrionics, life-changing trauma, and vast amounts of property damage. It is almost universally accepted the reason the Lady Heterodyne is as well-adjusted and sane as she is, is that she was able to ease into the physiological changes that the spark engenders in the human body without having to weather the inevitable brainstorms *at the same time*.

Sturmhalten Castle before Klaus's troops overran the place. They completely swallowed the tale of 'my treacherous brother,' but the next I heard, he was here in the hospital. There were not one, but *two* new Heterodyne girls in Castle Heterodyne. Since you and Tarvek were supposed to have gone with our priestesses, I had to assume that any number of things had gone terribly wrong."

Zola skimmed the memories of the Lucrezia within her, and sighed. "We were captured before we could join them. Neatly ambushed by dear Klaus himself."

Lucrezia leaned in, a yearning look on her face. "How does he look?"

The emotions and scraps of memory that roared through Zola's mind made her shiver and blush. "Better," she whispered.

"No."

"Oh yes. You know that annoying, softhearted romantic streak he always had? *Gone!* Someone's burned it right *out* of him!"

Lucrezia bit her lip. "Mmm. *That* sounds promising. Is he smarter?"

Zola sighed again. "Maybe a little *too* smart. He *recognized* me. Even after all this time and even though I was so well-disguised." She looked up at the clank. "And *then* he tried to kill me."

Lucrezia made a moue of displeasure. "That man. He *does* sound smarter. We ought to smother him before he wakes up."

Zola blinked. "He's *here?*"

The metal girl preened and flicked her ear with a fingertip. "Oh yes, these marvelous ears can hear the most amazing things. He's still in Recovery, which is why I, 'Princess Anevka of Sturmhalten,' am still here as well."

In response to Zola's blank look, she continued. "The clank body. It was hers, and now it's mine, but they have no idea. As far as they know, darling, I'm just a poor little lost toy being run by the ghost of the Sturmhalten princess. My case is unusual enough that they are keeping me here so I can actually talk to him."

The memories bubbling up from within Zola made her gasp. "You must get to him as soon as possible!"

"Oh, there's no rush." Lucrezia sighed. "It's not as if I could *actually* smother him. Guards, you know."

Zola gave a devilish grin. "All you have to do is *talk* to him, darling. Dear Klaus is already ours."

Lucrezia looked at her uncertainly. Zola continued. "Do you remember that Professor Snarlantz fellow?"[39]

Lucrezia snapped her fingers. "The one with the unfortunate teeth."

"The very same. He was the one the Council entrusted with overseeing our wasp engines. The impudent fellow actually *examined* the things, and . . . well, he managed to improve them."

Lucrezia gasped. "He must die."

Zola twitched her fingers. "Already taken care of, darling. He managed, however, to create a wasp that can enslave a spark, and *I* used the prototype to capture dear Klaus."

Lucrezia leaned in. "And it works? You're sure?"

"Oh yes. Completely."

The clank squealed, hugged herself, then drooped slightly. "Oh, *curse* this metal body of mine. I shan't be able to take full advantage of this at *all*!" She spun to face Zola. "When you're done with him, you must tell me all about it! Or . . . " she held her face in her hands and peeked out between her fingers. "Even better yet, I shall get *him* to tell me all about it!"

It took every bit of acting ability Zola had to respond with the scandalized grin she knew was expected. "You wicked, wicked girl," she weakly responded.

---

[39] Professor Ullebröt Snarlantz (MD, PhD, University of Vienna) was a member of the Council who worshipped Lucrezia for assorted religious and/or scandalous reasons. A strong spark, he was entrusted with the secrets of her slaver wasps. Over the years, he began to experiment, obsessed with the idea of creating different varieties of revenants. His greatest success came when he developed a breed of slaver wasp that could actually infect sparks, which had heretofore been immune. His greatest failure was when he developed a mindless, feral breed of revenant that overran the town of Passholdt, where he had located his hidden laboratory. These creatures killed or converted everyone they found within a thirty-kilometer radius before the Baron's forces heard about it and sterilized the entire area. Good work, doc.

Instantly, Lucrezia was all business. "I've been wearing you out," she declared. "That won't do at all. I should let you rest." She paused to examine the array of medical devices and said: "*Tch.* I can tweak these just a bit. Nothing that old fool Sun will notice, but it will have you up on your feet sooner than they expect."

"Could you, darling? That would be ever so clever of you."

A few minutes later, Zola gasped as waves of agony washed through her. Lucrezia hovered over her, frowning. "That isn't a bit too much, is it? It's so hard remembering what pain felt like."

"No!" Zola grit her teeth and began running through Smoke Knight pain management mantras. "We need every advantage," she gasped.

"That's very true," Lucrezia admitted. "Good girl."

Zola had had more than enough of the clank and desperately wanted to be by herself. "Now you must go! If they find you here . . . "

"True again! Hang in there, darling!"

But the pain became too much and Zola gave a small scream. "EEEEAARRG!"

Lucrezia frowned and waved a finger in mock severity. "*Quietly*, dear." Humming to herself, she slipped out the door, past the sleeping guards, and into the corridor. She had not gone two meters before a shout from behind her checked her progress.

"*There* you are!"

Lucrezia turned to see her physician stomping towards her, his beard bristling in righteous indignation. "Hello, Herr Doktor," she simpered.

"You were not supposed to leave your room," he thundered. "How did you get past your attendants?"

Lucrezia looked up at him contritely. The alpha wave projectors embedded within her metallic frame were still undiscovered. "Oh, they were asleep and I didn't want to disturb them. I'm *so* sorry! All of these terrible events! I—I just needed to walk and . . . and think. My poor town! My poor people! What will become of them? I'm so worried! Oh, Herr Doktor . . . " And here she used every bit of innocently seductive body language she could. "What will become of me?" As she had calculated, the cognitive dissonance caused by having a clank send such signals derailed all intellectual concerns about her method of evading her guards.

"Yes, yes," he muttered, "That's quite understandable, but the Baron will have it all under control in no time. You'll see."

Lucrezia smiled at him. "Oh, I'm sure I'll feel *ever* so much better once I've talked to him."

In an upper room of Castle Heterodyne, decorated in tastefully arranged bones, two people were resting. One was a girl: slim and well-muscled under her prison coverall. Her elfin face was capped with a shock of lightly tinted pink hair. A slight overbite revealed a noticeable gap in her front teeth. "I dunno, big brother. Something is wrong," she was saying.

Her brother was tall and broad at the shoulder. Although he wore a loose sweater, it failed to hide the muscles that rippled whenever he moved. His hair, as well as his neat beard, was a snowy white, and his ageless face was half-hidden by a pair of snow goggles.

The goggles alone meant he would be recognizable to a significant portion of the population of Europa as none other than Othar Tryggvassen, Gentleman Adventurer.[40] The girl was his sister, Saana.[41]

---

[40]　By this point, even the most lackadaisical, just-skimming-to-pass-the-test reader of these textbooks will be familiar with Othar Tryggvassen, one of many colorful threads winding through the life of the Lady Heterodyne. A powerful spark in his own right, Othar specialized in battling sparks, foiling their schemes, and exterminating them. He had decided that since sparks were the source of what, for lack of a better term, we shall call "all evil," then the world would be a better place if they were all eradicated. This he has pledged to do, promising to kill himself when the final spark falls dead at his feet.

[41]　Sanaa was not a spark herself, but had inherited the part of the Tryggvassen make-up that resulted in wandering accidentally into a never-ending series of calamitous (for others) adventures. One of these was responsible for her being sentenced to Castle Heterodyne, where she found love and . . . Oh, I'm sorry, I'm getting a bit ahead of myself.

He considered her words. "We're in Castle Heterodyne," he pointed out. "With exploding collars around our necks, caught between a fake Heterodyne and a real one (as well as assorted criminals, maniacs, and various monsters). I suspect—even if we found any beer in here—it would be evil,[42] or at the very least, flat. Try to be a bit more specific."

Sanaa threw her arms wide. "Where *is* everybody?"

"If I knew where young Wulfenbach was, I'd finish the job, and we could leave this infernal place."

"Not just him. I mean *anybody*. There's a whole bunch of prisoners in here."

Othar considered this as he rose to his feet. "Hmm. Yes, we've certainly covered enough ground. We should have found more people."

"Maybe if you stopped shouting 'Othar Tryggvassen, Gentleman Adventurer, has *arrived!*' every time we walk into a room—"

Othar frowned. "But . . . that's my thing."

Suddenly the entire castle rumbled. The floor tilted slightly beneath them. Reflexively, Othar scooped his sister into his arms, but nothing more happened.

"What was that?" he asked.

"I don't know," Sanaa replied in a low voice. "I've never felt *anything* like that."

"Maybe it was something good?"

Sanaa looked at him bleakly. "You haven't been here very long."

Suddenly a roar filled the room, quickly coalescing into the all-too-familiar voice of Castle Heterodyne itself. "Well, well! Who do we have *here?*"

Othar looked up. "*That* doesn't sound good."

---

[42]   Evil beer is an actual thing. Beer is supposed to make a person feel good about themselves and the world in general. If this is not your experience, then you are drinking evil beer and should switch to something else immediately. The professoressa recommends a nice Benedictine.

Sanaa shivered. "No, no, we're not dead. I'm encouraged."

"Ah, you are Sanaa Wilhelm.[43] The clever one who works with Professor Tiktoffen!"

"Um . . . yes. We were trying to repair you."

"I remember. And who is this?" The Castle asked.

Sanaa spun about and frantically waved her hands, but of course, it was too late. "I am Othar Tryggvassen," her brother boomed. "Gentleman Adventurer!"

"Gentleman . . . great heavens, are you a *hero?*"

"Indeed I am! You've heard of me?" The floor opened beneath him and Othar vanished into the depths, a faint cry of "Foul!" ringing up from the darkness.

"Othar!" Sanaa cried as she peered down into the pitiless blackness. Furious, she glared upward.[44] "What did you do *that* for?"

"Eh. He was a hero. I don't need much more of a reason than that."

"But . . . the Heterodyne Boys were heroes."

The Castle sounded distant. "Yes, but they didn't come home much."[45]

"No, really?"

"Oh, but we had such fun when they did! Well . . . I had fun." It

---

[43] When she was sentenced to Castle Heterodyne, Sanaa realized letting people know she was the sister of one of Europa's most prominent do-gooders was a spectacularly bad idea. Especially since Othar was, in fact, responsible for a significant number of them being in the Castle in the first place. In the cause of self-preservation, she adopted the *nom de detention* of Wilhelm.

[44] Behaviorists find it interesting that, whenever people enter into a discussion with a disembodied entity such as Castle Heterodyne, they invariably assume the entity is hovering somewhere above them. Some have speculated this is a throwback to ancient concepts of unseen entities being some sort of god or spirit. A slightly more sophisticated take is that if you are going to *pretend* to be a god or spirit, you hide somewhere near the ceiling. Proper researchers, such as your professors, who actually bothered to interview the few survivors of Castle Heterodyne, learned it was because the Castle is very fond of dropping things on people.

[45] Bill and Barry's oft-neglected mother, the Lady Teodora Vodenicharova, insisted on raising her children away from the Castle. As a result, the Heterodyne Boys never really warmed up to the Castle. This goes a long way towards explaining their constant adventuring away from Mechanicsburg.

sighed deeply enough that the ceiling fixtures rattled. "I rather miss having a hero about."

"Well, if you drop them down bottomless pits—"

"Oh tosh. If he'd been a real hero—"

Othar stomped in, brushing at his sweater. "This *is* an annoying place, isn't it?"

"Heavens," the Castle tittered in pleasure. "A real hero indeed! Why, I haven't squashed one in years!"

"NO!" Sanaa yelled as a stone block dropped from the ceiling.

Othar languidly slapped it and the block crashed off to one side. "I can see that I shall have to speak to Agatha about making some serious home repairs."

The Castle paused. "Ah . . . you know the mistress?"

Othar beamed, "Why, she's going to be my spunky girl sidekick!"

Sanaa looked amazed. "Really?"

Othar shrugged. "Well . . . we're still haggling over the details, vacation days, dental insurance, you know . . . "

"Hmm . . . " the Castle mused. "The mistress might not *like* it if I squashed you."

Sanaa's eyes went round in astonishment. "Wow."

"No," it continued, "I believe she will want to squash you herself. So . . . to the Torture Room with you!" Again the floor opened up. This time, both Tryggvassens fell. They slid down a winding series of chutes and slides until a vent swung up before them and, with a *thump*, they found themselves in a small, well-lit room furnished entirely in nauseatingly cheerful shades of pink. They sat up and looked around.

"Wilhelm!" came a surprised voice. Approaching them was the avuncular figure of Professor Hristo Tiktoffen.[46] "Look at you! You're not dead!"

---

[46]   Professor Hristo Tiktoffen (MFA, PhD, MAR, Rupert-Karls-Universität, Heisenberg) was the Chief Prisoner within Castle Heterodyne at the time of our story. He had a genuine appreciation of the Castle and served as the main facilitator between it and the other prisoners.

"I'm glad you're all right, Professor."

Meanwhile Othar was looking about, a puzzled look on his face. "This is a torture room?"

Tiktoffen shrugged. "It's more of a *psychological* torture chamber."

Sanaa looked puzzled. "Does that even work?"

Othar stood defiantly in the center of the room and shook his fist at the unresponsive ceiling. "Take me seriously, you fiend!"

Tiktoffen smiled. "On some better than others."

At Mamma Gkika's, Airshipman Higgs turned the lights up a bit brighter and selected another needle preloaded with surgical catgut. He clenched his pipe a bit tighter between his teeth and, with a resigned sigh, drove it into the flesh of his arm, stitching up the last of the slices that Zola had inflicted on him. He worked quickly and methodically, using an airman's cross-herringbone stitch, typically used to repair gasbags. It left a distinctive scar after healing, and if Higgs' skin was to be believed, it was a ritual he had performed often. He tied off the end and clipped the thread free with his teeth just as a ragged moan rose from the bed beside him. When he heard it, he closed his eyes briefly and took a deep breath. When he turned, his face was its usual mask of imperturbability.

Zeetha stirred. She had several hoses and tubes hooked up to her arms. Higgs examined the smallest hanging bottle. It was empty, except for a faint purple residue. He nodded and closed the drip valve. *For good or ill, it was a done thing now.*

Zeetha's eyelids fluttered slowly. Her color was still wan and the whites of her eyes were actually a faint yellow. Her long green hair had been braided up and draped over the back of the pillow. She ran her tongue across her dry lips. Higgs held out a cup of water and, wordlessly, she took it. She sipped carefully until it was empty.

Higgs leaned in. "How d'you feel?"

Zeetha seemed to see him for the first time. She gave a start and snarled. Then she blinked in astonishment, but Higgs merely nodded. "That's good."

She tried again. "Agatha . . . " she growled.

This time, Higgs actually smiled. "Good priorities," he whispered. He reached over and delicately pushed a lock of hair from her face. "But don't you worry about her at the moment. She'll be just fine. At least for a while."

Memories came crashing down on Zeetha and she twisted away from Higgs's hand. To her alarm, she discovered that every muscle ached as if she'd been beaten. "No thanks to me. I've completely failed her—"

Higgs tapped her nose. "Now you *stop* that." She looked at him. "Near as I can tell, one of the reasons she's still *alive* is because of what you taught her." Zeetha opened her mouth, but Higgs interrupted her. "You're good, but you're what—early twenties? And that Sturmvoraus fella called you 'Princess.'" He leaned back and hoisted one of Zeetha's swords. Her eyes bugged out at this assumed familiarity, but he ignored her as he scrutinized the handle, then slid the sword out of its scabbard slightly and examined the steel. He nodded as if it confirmed something he'd already suspected.

"Probably from some cut-off backwater, yes? Where, I'm guessin', you were used to bein' one of the toughest things around." He looked at her face and nodded again. "And that overconfidence . . . "

Zeetha could take no more. "Don't talk to me like you're my wise old grandma, you—"

Higgs cut her off by taking her hand. "You died."

During her travels with Master Payne's Circus of Adventure, Zeetha had become convinced that when sparks were talking, there were always jokes flying somewhere high over her head. She felt like that now, but if this was a joke, it was more abstruse than usual.

She tried to pull her hand free and discovered she couldn't—even though Higgs's grip appeared to be a casual one.

"But I don't feel . . . " The words ground to a halt.

Higgs reached towards the space between her breasts, where she had *felt* the stolen sword punch through. Without hesitation, he gave it a solid thump with his fingers.

Zeetha tried to jerk back and prepared to mentally block the pain, but there was only a faint twinge.

She stared at the bandaged spot, and then suddenly drew in a great gasping lungful of air, feeling her heart pounding within her chest. Higgs released her hand and prepared to sit back, but Zeetha reached out with both hands and clasped him tightly before he could move. "No," she whispered.

"Yes," he said pitilessly. "You were drugged. The plants in that room were making everybody stupid and reckless. Consequently, you didn't take the fight seriously. Even that fake Heterodyne was affected, but she still took you out with one thrust. You seriously underestimated her."

Zeetha shuddered. Death—it was always there, but to be killed by someone like Zola—the shame. "Wait a minute. I don't feel dead." She looked around the room. "And this isn't some resurrectionist's.[47] This is Mamma Gkika's."

Higgs nodded. "The old Heterodynes were dab hands at life and death. They didn't share their secrets with *many* people, but they gave some of 'em to the Jägers. You weren't dead for long, you weren't too messed up, and you died fighting for a Heterodyne. It was a long shot, but the general thought it was worth tryin."

"General? What general?"

"The Jägers have generals. They're Jägers that have lived long

---

[47]   As a rule, sparks have an intrinsic fascination with learning the secrets of life and death. Considering that thousands of mad scientists have been tinkering in this particular field for several centuries, it should come as no surprise there is an astonishingly diverse body of work on the subject. Resurrectionists are specialists. They tend to be relatively minor sparks who have collected dozens, if not hundreds, of different techniques for raising the dead, and are conversant on which method is suitable for the occasion. Despite this, their track record is actually pretty dismal. Someone considered a top-notch resurrectionist usually succeeds in only one out of fifty attempts. The industry also has one of the best written "no refunds" policy in the western world.

enough they actually have learned to think. They dictate what the rest of the Jägers do. Mamma is a general."[48]

Zeetha looked at him shrewdly. "And she brought me back to life because you asked her to. What did you do for her?"

Higgs looked at her and shrugged. "Saved her life, along with a bunch of Jägers, and some other people she cared about." He looked off into a distant memory that only he could see. "It was a long time ago, but Gkika's got a long memory."

Zeetha stared at him and licked her lips again. "I feel . . . strange."

Higgs glanced at the empty bag. "Not surprised. Comin' back from the dead ain't easy." His gaze sharpened. "You ain't sorry I did it, are you?"

Zeetha considered this. Traditionally, in Skifander, if you were careless enough to get killed in battle, it was generally agreed you were better off dead. But . . . "My grandmother always said that death comes to us soon enough. We shouldn't welcome it."

Higgs looked at her shrewdly. "That's twice you've mentioned her. I'm guessin' your old grandma's one of the few back home who could take you on, and I'll bet she'd say the same." He leaned back in. "If you stay here, there's old folks who could teach you plenty if you're smart enough to realize you still have stuff to learn."

Any lingering despair evaporated under the heat of Zeetha's rising anger. To be lectured like this, by one who didn't even wield a weapon. Who—what did he think he was? Oh sure, he'd somehow held off the Otilia Muse and hadn't been killed by Zola, and the Jägers

---

[48]   Every army in history has included women who disguised themselves as men: to be near a loved one, to escape something so onerous that army life was an improvement, or simply because they wanted to loot and pillage in the company of like-minded companions while seeing the world. Usually, these women hid their sex from their companions and superiors. Sometimes for decades, because they would be drummed out if discovered. The big difference with the Heterodynes was that if one of their warriors was discovered to be female, they simply didn't *care*.

had failed to touch him during their bar fight. From out of nowhere a jolt of clarity shot through Zeetha and she gasped. "Omeetza."[49]

Higgs looked at her quizzically, his pipe drooping comically. She immediately dismissed the idea. For one thing, he was too young. For another, there was no evidence of the drive and burning single-mindedness that was the legendary hallmark of the true Omeetza. But still, he had a point.

"I . . . I will learn whatever it takes to protect Agatha and then I will kick your smug butt."

Higgs blinked and then smiled. "That's a date."

The Valley of the Heterodynes sits high in the mountains and contains not only the walled town of Mechanicsburg, but large swaths of farmland and managed forest. Here and there, a farmhouse, private villa, or military outpost adds interest to the landscape.

In an observation tower set some distance to the west of town, an unusual amount of activity was taking place. Uniformed figures were everywhere. Some were running through marching drills, many were sparring—wielding fearsome weapons—and some sprawled about, apparently doing nothing at all.

The uniforms of easily half-a-hundred armies were represented, including several that had been eradicated over a century ago. The faces of the troops were even more of a collection of oddities than the outfits they sported. This was a Jägermonster[50] outpost.

---

[49] Skifandrians take weapons very seriously. A member of the warrior class spends her entire life getting better and better at wielding bigger and progressively more destructive weapons. However, there *is* a theoretical limit to how big and nasty a weapon one can carry without rupturing something. At that point, a supreme warrior will often aim for Omeetza, an advanced level of skill which requires no weapons at all.

[50] The Jägermonsters were the core of the army of the Heterodynes. They were monstrous reavers and pillagers, who became more physically warped as they grew older. While Bill and Barry redeemed the Heterodyne name, the deeds of the Jägers had remained fixed within the lore of Europa, and they continued to be shunned and killed when possible, which was not very often. Because of this, after the Heterodyne Boys had disappeared, the Jägers had taken service with Baron Wulfenbach who, in return for gaining an already feared army, granted

Outside what had once been a modest feast hall, a dark blue Jäger in a sharp uniform (it had taken over eighty years to properly accessorize), led a small, disheveled group to a low wooden doorway. He rapped twice, threw the door open, and growled, "Hoy! Sirs, dey iz here."

Dimo, Maxim, and Ognian stepped forward. Facing them were the Jägergenerals.

The largest, General Goomblast, gave a slow smile when he saw them. Considering the size of his head and the great mouth that almost bisected it, this procedure took an alarming amount of time.

General Zog, the oldest, fixed them with a glare that could make even innocent soldiers worry. Since the word "innocent" was one that most Jägers had to have explained to them several times, it was doubly effective.

The third, General Khrizhan, observed them from the comfort of a folding brass and canvas campaign chair. Compared to the other two, he looked positively welcoming.

All in all, Dimo considered it a very well done tableau.

"Com in, my boyz," General Khrizhan purred. "Iz goot to see hyu!"

Zog glared even harder. "Und heff hyu forgotten how to salute?"

The three paused. Ognian looked worried. "Um . . . yez?"

Maxim leaned over. "No, no. Hy tink dis iz vun ov dose *trick* qvestions, brodder."

Dimo deliberately placed his hand on his hip. "Ve vos *detached*."[51]

Khrizhan nodded, as if this was a minor detail that had slipped his mind. "Ah, yez, so hyu vos. Und den hyu vent and found us a Heterodyne gurl."

---

them the protection of the empire. It was a deal that had worked out well for everybody.

51   After the Heterodynes disappeared, the Jägers were absorbed into the forces of Baron Wulfenbach. However, they had pledged undying loyalty to the House of Heterodyne. In order to resolve this conflict, a group of Jägers volunteered to leave the Baron's service and dedicate their lives to searching the world for a Heterodyne heir. Everyone was sure there was no such thing and that this was, in effect, a suicide mission. But honor would be served and the Jägers, as a whole, would survive. Then Agatha appeared.

At this point Maxim tentatively raised a hand. "Vell, ektually, *she* kinda found *us*. Doz dot still count?"

Khrizhan made a show of considering this, then nodded again. "Yez."

Maxim relaxed. It was apparent this question had been bothering him for a while.

Goomblast clapped his tiny hands together. "Hyu dun goot, boys! Ve iz gun haff a beeg party vit drinks, und fightink, und vimmen in hats, und lotsa fightink! Hoo, yez!" Oggie nudged Maxim in the ribs and the two grinned at each other. This was more like it.

Dimo waited.

Zog stared at him and casually scratched his beard. "Oh. Vun *leedle* ting: dis Agatha gurl. She vouldn't be de *Odder*—vould she?"

Ognian's jaw dropped. "*Vot?*"

Maxim shook his head. "Dot's *krezy!*"

Dimo sighed and rubbed his temples. "Um . . . " He stood a little taller and hooked a thumb towards the window. "But mebbe hyu dun vant me to giff my report vit dot guy hidink behind de curtain?"

There was an embarrassed pause, and then the curtain was swept aside, revealing Boris Dolokhov, the Baron's second-in-command. "How about if I'm *not* behind the curtain?"

Khrizhan looked at Dimo appraisingly. "Ho," he said softly. "Iz hokay, Dimo. But, how did hyu know he vos dere?"

Dimo shrugged. "Schmelled soap."

Boris frowned. "But that could have been anyone . . . " He glanced at the generals. "Ah. Never mind. Go on."

Dimo took a deep breath. "Hokay. De Lady Agatha iz not de Odder. But her mama, de Lady Lucrezia, vos. *Iz.*" There was a sudden hiss of indrawn breath from General Goomblast. He had the look of someone who was finally connecting things that had been bothering him for some time.

"In Sturmhalten, she somehow gots shoved inside de Lady Agatha's head. She is like a . . . a dybbuk, I tink. Sumtimes she iz in control— sumtimes not. De Lady Agatha, she fights her, but de Odder is verra stronk. Now Meez Agatha gots a leedle device dot keeps her mama qviet in her head. It vos built by Master Barry."

All of the generals went still at this. Zog licked his lips, but Dimo forestalled his questions. "He vos last seen eleven years ago.[52] Hy haff heard nozzink of Master Villiam.

"Vitout her mama in her head, hy tink de Lady vill be kinda borink, like her papa.[53] Bot she *iz* a Heterodyne, und a pretty stronk vun."

Boris and the generals mulled this over. Finally, General Khrizhan leaned forward. "Und how does hyu know all dis?"

Dimo squirmed slightly. "Der Lady gots dis varrior gurl trainink her. She's doink a pretty goot job ov it, as far as ve ken tell." Both Ognian and Maxim nodded in agreement. "Anyvay, dey iz goot friends. At Mamma Gkika's, dis Mizz Zeetha told all ov dis to hyu Master Gilgamesh."

Boris nodded slowly. "So that's why he went into the Castle."

Dimo smirked. "Dot's *vun* reason, yez." He turned back to the generals. "Ennyvay, dot's all verra hush-hush."

Khrizhan's eyes narrowed. "But how does *hyu* know—"

Dimo threw his hands up. "Hy vos listening at de door! Like a great beeg *sneaky pants! Hokay?*"

The generals all looked at each other with raised eyebrows. Zog shook his head. "Dimo! Hy iz *shocked* at dis behavior!"

Boris shrugged. "Still, it *was* rather clever of him."

Zog nodded, pleased. "Hy *said* hy vos shocked."

Khrizhan looked at Boris shrewdly. "Bot hyu dun look too heppy."

"I'm not," Boris sighed as he used two of his hands to clean his pince-nez. "With this girl installed as the Heterodyne, the Jägers would very likely wind up as tools in the Other's war of conquest—"

---

[52] For a while, Barry and Agatha lived incognito, in the town of Beetleburg, with the constructs Adam and Lilith Clay. Adam and Lilith were themselves hiding their past identities as "Punch" and "Judy," the famous assistants of the Heterodyne Boys. Barry disappeared shortly after he constructed the locket for Agatha.

[53] For the record, Dimo means Agatha probably would not venture forth on extended campaigns of conquest, carnage, and pillage. Proving that you just can't please everybody.

Goomblast's hand smacked down on a table so hard that it broke. "*Dot vould neffer heppen,*" he growled.

Boris carefully replaced his glasses. "Really. There was certainly a time when the Jägers had no qualms about helping the *old* Heterodynes lay waste to Europa. So now, if the Other, as the new Heterodyne, were to *order* you, wouldn't you be *forced to—*"

"No!" Goomblast snarled. "Hyu gots it all wronk! Hyu know *vy* Jägers hates der Odder's bogs? Iz becawze dey sqveeze pipple's *minds!* *Force* dem to obey! Ve Jägers iz not *compelled* to serve. Effry vun uv uz reached out our hands und *took* de Jägerdraught[54] by *choice.* Und ve got de goot end ov de deal, hyu bet ve did! Ve serve de Heterodynes *freely,* out ov luff und loyalty, und de Heterodynes haff always *earned* dot, yez dey haff." He turned and slowly poured himself a glass of wine, then made no move to drink it.

"But dot Lucrezia, she vos *alvays* bad krezy, und not in a *fun* vay. She treated efferyvun like dey vos her servants. Treated de Jägerkin like leedle pets— No, like dey vos *property.* Ve put op vit her only becawze ve iz *patient . . .* and becawze Master Bill vos in lurv."

He stared moodily into the depths of time and then furiously smashed the untouched wine onto the floor. "But Jägers iz not leedle petz!" he roared. "Hy iz not surprised at *all* to hear dot krezy lady is de Odder! She *alvays* vanted to make efferyvun obey her! But the Jägers vill *not* be forced! Ve vill *neffer* submit to soch a ting!" He stood panting like a spent warhorse, his hands clenching and opening spasmodically. Khrizhan and Zog came up beside him and each gripped one of his shoulders fiercely.

Khrizhan turned to Boris and spoke quietly. "Und now she tinks she vill tek control ov our Heterodyne? Ov a leedle gurl who has

---

[54] Little is known about the process by which a normal human was transformed into a Jäger, but we do have tantalizing clues. It involved a ritual which cumulated with the ingestion of the famous Jägerdraught. The formula is unknown, but one of its ingredients was almost certainly untreated water from the River Dyne. Odds of surviving the process were only slightly below fifty percent, and those who did survive recall it as being "the worst thing they ever experienced, and yes, completely worth it."

not yet had de chance to find out vhat kind ov Heterodyne *she* vill be? No!" He shook his head. "Dot iz too much!"

Zog roared in agreement. "Ho! But our Heterodyne fights! She fights for her life! It iz a battle worth fightink! As goot as de old days! Ve vill support her, and keep her safe, until she kin get her krezy mama out ov her head!" He paused. The energy seemed to drain from him and he slumped, rubbing his shaggy brow.

"A *lovely* Heterodyne story, I'm sure," Boris said icily, "but how will she *do* that?"

The three generals looked at each other. Finally, Goomblast shrugged. "How should *ve* know? *She* iz de Heterodyne, und she looks like a stronk vun too." He nodded. "She vill vork it out somehow, dey alvays do."

Before Boris could make a retort, Ognian gave him what he no doubt considered a friendly punch to the arm. "Or mebbe," he said with an impudent grin, "dot young Wulfenbach vill find a vay, hey? He iz vun schmot guy! *Und* he iz already in *lurv* vit her, jah?"

Boris ignored the pain in his arm and waved his hands (which made for an impressive display when he really got going), "What? *No!* We *can't* let them get together! It would be the same as handing the empire to the Other without a fight!"

Khrizhan gave a derisive snort that a hippopotamus would have envied. "Eediot," he said witheringly. "Dey iz *already* togedder in de Castle, vhere ve couldn't touch dem effen if ve *vanted* to, vich ve don't, becawze dot iz der *best* ting dot could haff heppened!"

"How can you *say* that?"

"Becawze hy knows pipple![55] *Tink!* De Lady Agatha and hyu Prince

---

[55]   As hard as it is to credit, this statement is actually quite true. As we mentioned in an earlier textbook, all the Jägers took up little hobbies to stay in touch with their slowly-receding humanity. This extended even to the generals. General Goomblast was a historian, specializing in the Jägerkin. Zog studied the arts of war and, despite actually remembering what it was like to live as a horse-warrior, was adept at seeing the benefits of new technology—especially as to how it could be used to kill people. In his spare time, he was a frequent contributor to the *Mechanicsburg Consumer Safety Bulletin*. Khrizhan studied

Wulfenbach, dey iz *young!* Dey iz in *lurv!* Dey iz gun get de Kestle fixed up and den dere dey iz, nize und safe.

"Dey vill *start* vit der talkink, und der Kestle vill make sure dat der iz vine, und a beeg cozy fire, und sudden death to ennyvun who tries to disturb dem." All of the other Jägers gave a wistful sigh at the romantic picture Khrizhan's words painted.

He continued in a low, confidential voice that had all the others leaning in with rapt attention, "Den dey starts vit der keessing—"

He smacked his great hand down onto a table top, causing the others to jump. "—und *den* dey realize dot her *mama* gun be right der, vatchink *efferyting* de whole time!" He paused to let this sink in, then chuckled knowingly. "Dey vill haff de Odder out ov dere in less den a veek!"

Boris stared at him and his eye twitched slightly. "And that's your answer. You're going to risk everything to follow a new Heterodyne on the off chance that this—this young woman can defeat the Other. Just like that."

Khrizhan nodded, all bluster gone. "Hy tink she gots a goot chance. De Heterodynes haff faced *lots* ov bad tings und dey haz alvays come out pretty moch hokay."

Boris, who was not particularly concerned about the fate of the Heterodynes, preoccupied as he was by worrying about the fate of everything else, gave a small sigh. "I see." He straightened up and spackled a look of pleasant affirmation over his face. "Well, this has been *most* informative." Boris deftly fished several pocket watches out of several watch pockets and made a show of studying each of them in turn. "But now, I must return to my duties." His hands swirled and returned the watches to their various pockets. "If you would *please* advise your new mistress: the threat that the Other presents, not only to her, but to all of Europa, is very grave. The Baron has studied the Other. She can and must come to him peacefully for assistance." He

people and, thus, was very good at manipulating them.

turned to go, but paused at the doorway. "I wish I could believe she will do so, but sparks can be . . . well . . . " All of the Jägers in the room nodded in understanding. "Good day, gentlemen, and good luck." And he was gone.

Ognian tapped a fang. "Dot . . . dot did not go verra well. Did it?"

Dimo sighed. "No, brodder, it did not." He grabbed a bottle of wine and had it halfway to his mouth before he realized where he was. He paused and looked guiltily at General Zog, who swiped the bottle from his hand, took a deep swallow, and handed it back to him.

Khrizhan had been staring at the door. He turned back. "Hyu gots dot right," he rumbled. "Meester Boris must know dot *ve* know that *he* knows dot de Lady *cannot* go to de Baron."

Goomblast deftly shortstopped the wine as it was being passed to Maxim and emptied the last of it into his great maw. When he was done, he selected a fresh, wicker-wrapped carboy of fortified wine, bit the top off, and graciously offered it to Maxim. "Yez," he said judiciously. "Even if Meez Agatha destroys de Odder inside her head, she vill neffer be able to prove dis to de Baron's satisfaction. No! he vill vant her locked op! Studied! Und, effentually, *destroyed*. He vill not take de *risk*."

General Khrizhan cleared his throat. "Hy must concur." He bowed formally to Zog. "Dis iz your time now."

Zog gravely returned the bow. "Dis hy accept."[56] He straightened and faced the others. "De House ov Heterodyne must now prepare for var!"

---

[56]   This exchange presents a tantalizing glimpse into the command structure of the Jägergeneral hierarchy. While the Jägers did seem to possess assorted levels of rank, it's believed that up to a certain point these were acquired along with their hats since the ranks didn't really seem to mean anything until they got to the rank of general. There were seven known generals and, as far as we can tell, they were all of equal rank. This could cause obvious problems, however, as we mentioned earlier, each general had a field of expertise. This exchange seems to indicate that when certain categories of situation presented themselves, the general with the closest field of expertise would assume a temporary command position.

Within the Castle, Agatha only had time to scream, "Hold on!" before a torrent of water descended.

Both Gil and Tarvek responded instantly, shouting, "I've got you, Agatha!" as the deluge hit. When the water subsided, Agatha realized she was actually being held tightly by Violetta.

"Is the fire out?" the Castle asked.

Gil and Tarvek opened their eyes to see that each of them was desperately clutching, not Agatha, but a thick metallic tentacle. A huge mechanical squid had been washed in along with water from the cistern and now lay, inert and dripping, in a puddle of receding water.

Although the squid was old, it turned out to still be functional, and indeed, quite useful. It had been designed to be operated by two drivers, so Gil and Tarvek found themselves wedged together in the cockpit, each trying to master the controls before the other. Agatha, one sturdy tentacle wrapped around her waist, was being hoisted here and there towards hard-to-reach parts of the Castle with the rest of the tentacles handing her tools as needed. Tarvek, at least, could not let well enough alone.

"*Why* are there mechanical squid in the water cistern?"

The Castle sighed. "Why is everyone so surprised about that? Where else would we keep them?"

"Well," Tarvek conceded, "I suppose when you put it like that . . ." Agatha signaled, and he pushed a lever, swinging her slightly to the left. "At this rate, we might actually get this section repaired before nightfall."

He was answered by silence and Tarvek realized he was doing all of the work in this supposed conversation. He turned to Gil, who was sitting hunched forward, an intense look on his face. He saw Tarvek staring at him. "I've been thinking," he began.

Tarvek confined his response to a simple, "Really."

Gil ignored the tone and continued. "Yes, when we get the Castle fixed, *then* what? We're counting on it still being functional enough to defend the town. Maybe even the pass. But even if we can, my father still thinks Agatha's the Other." He glanced at Tarvek. "And he isn't entirely wrong. I don't think I'll ever be able to convince him that she isn't a threat. We're going to be under siege. Probably for the rest of our lives."

Tarvek ground his teeth together. "I can't believe this," he snarled. "I'm actually going to have to *explain* things to you, just to shut off your endless moaning." He glared at Gil. "Just listening to you is killing me already."

"You don't think this is serious? We've never even found a cure for traditional revenants, and this new type is much worse. You have no idea—"

Tarvek cut him off. "As a matter of fact I *do* have an idea. I have *several*, because I've been thinking about this for *years*."

Gil blinked. "Years?"

Tarvek paused and then took a deep breath. "My father. He worked with Lucrezia Mongfish before she became the Other. Before she was married to Bill Heterodyne. She was tinkering with something like the slaver wasps even back then. Those we call the 'classic revenant'—the ones created by the wasps, the shambling monsters—they were a *mistake*. An 'unfortunate statistical extreme,' according to her notes.

"She later recognized they were actually very useful. When the slaver wasps were deployed in an actual human population, the appearance of the shamblers obfuscated the fact there was a larger population that was *just* as infected, *just* as controllable, but without any obvious signs. Nobody noticed they were infected because nobody ever actually *tried* to control them. It was just thought that most people attacked by wasps got off without suffering any ill-effects."

Gil stared at him. "My father just discovered this when we took Balan's Gap. You're saying you knew this was happening *years* ago?" His released the controls and gripped the front of Tarvek's coat, yanking him forward until their noses nearly touched. Tarvek met the fury on Gil's face with a silent glare. "You." Gil continued: "Your family. Your Knights of Jove. Your stupid 'Storm King' plotting. You were working with the Mongfishes—with *Lucrezia*—and you *knew* she was the Other? *Knew* about slaver wasps? No *wonder* Sturmhalten was crawling with revenants! I thought at least you would stop at that. But here you are, practically her successor! Is *that* how you planned to 'reclaim the throne'? By enslaving everyone?" He gave Tarvek a vicious shake.

Above them, Agatha cleared her throat. Startled, they looked up to see her hanging by her ankles from the unresponsive squid tentacles. The look on her face was one of remarkable patience considering how much effort she was putting into keeping her tools from falling out of her belt and pockets. "Could you two put off killing each other long enough to mind the controls?" she asked sweetly.

Gil looked guilty. He was still clutching the front of Tarvek's coat. "Oh. But—well—" Gil began.

"Help," Agatha commanded.

"Right." Gil released Tarvek.

"Sorry." *Why am I apologizing?* Tarvek wondered. *I'm the one about to get throttled.* He industriously bent over his side of the control panel, and Gil did the same, guiding Agatha back up to spot where a stone gargoyle had been moved aside to expose a nest of wiring.

They worked in silence for a few minutes. Gil was tense and clearly furious. Finally, he could stand it no longer. "I'll see to it that you're publicly flogged for a *week* before your execution," he growled.

What would Agatha think of you then, eh? Tarvek wondered silently. Still, he had a nagging worry that if all she heard was Gil's point of view, she might actually get over it. *It was so unfair.* "That," he said aloud, "is *just* what I'd expect from a despot's spoiled brat. Already planning my torture and execution? Who needs a trial?"

Gil glowered and Tarvek continued: "After all, it doesn't matter it was my father and his friends who did all that. I was, what, three years old at the time? Obviously, I have some culpability." He could see Gil relax and begin to look thoughtful. *Keep talking.* "Imagine being raised in that snake pit. My father, in thrall to the memory of a lunatic who had her own fanatical order of warrior priestesses living in our *actual basement* enforcing her vaguest dictates.

"Do you know *why* female sparks have been statistically underrepresented in our generation? Because the Geisterdamen collected all of the ones they could find, hoping one of them was their lost Holy Child—that's Agatha, by the way—and they were very good at finding them. Once found, they brought them to my father. One-by-one he strapped them into a machine and tried to infuse them with the mind of Lucrezia. Since they *weren't* Agatha, they *died.* Every single one of them."

Gil stared at him in horror. "Why didn't you tell my father?"

"Because I didn't *know!* I only found out when he tried it on my sister Anevka after she broke through! I had to build her an entirely new *body!* By that time, I had long been exiled from Castle Wulfenbach and any loyalty I might have to your father's unjust and capricious regime had long evaporated." Gil frowned and hit a switch. "But—" and here Tarvek was the one to look away, years of inner conflict roiling through his memory. "But I was sickened by the waste. All of those sparks. All of those women who might have done something *amazing.*"

He shrugged. "By this time, it had been years. Even my father was beginning to flag in his fanaticism." Tarvek sighed. "Or so I thought. I tried to—subtly, of course—steer him away from his obsession, but he surprised me. Despite any outward dithering, he remained Lucrezia's slave to the core. He must have said something to the Geisterdamen because they began to turn against me. Lady Vrin was convinced I was working against Lucrezia's interests, which, to be fair, I *was.*

"The Storm King's plan was my ticket out of there. Once I was established, it would have been simple to clean house. Naturally, *their* plan was a mess, but I could have worked with it. I could have used them to further my *own* plan, and it would have all gone *perfectly!*

"Then Agatha showed up, and it was like fate! It was as if the heavens themselves were saying 'Yes! This will work!' Instead of a *fake* Heterodyne girl, here was a *real* one and she was *wonderful!* It was all going so well . . . *That* should have warned me, but no . . .

"Then my father was killed. When I tried to get Agatha out of Sturmhalten, the Geisterdamen caught her, put her in the machine, and installed Lucrezia."

He wound down and stared blankly ahead for long enough that Gil had to prompt him. "Then what?"

Tarvek sighed. "I thought Agatha was dead. That Lucrezia was in control permanently. I . . . I didn't think of her as I do now. Not quite. I mean, she was too perfect. Together we could have . . . " He paused again. "But like I said, I thought she was gone.

"The Geisters still didn't trust me. If I hadn't moved quickly, they would have killed me. I sucked up to Lucrezia *outrageously.* It's what she expects people to do. She loves it. *Needs* it. She let me live while I flattered her, but I knew that wouldn't last forever. I had to actually make myself *useful* if I was going to survive.

"So I assisted her. Because of my knowledge of my father's work, I already had enough of the basic principles. As we worked, I learned a lot more; certainly more than she thought she was teaching me. She's insanely proprietary about her secrets, but she was in a hurry and incredibly fatigued. Even so, I have no doubt she would have killed me when she was more secure. She did try to, in Balan's Gap when your father attacked." Tarvek paused. "That was very well done, by the way. I knew something like it would happen, but *still* . . . "

"Lucrezia," Gil prompted.

"Yes. As I said, she was very tired. She knew she didn't have a lot of time and she pushed herself to extreme limits. I . . . I really got the impression she had forgotten what limits there *are* to a human body. Things she said . . . " He waved that line of speculation aside. "The *important* thing was that when she had pushed things too far, she collapsed, and Agatha resurfaced.

"I was astonished. I had no idea Agatha was still in existence. She couldn't maintain control for long, but whenever her personality manifested, we worked together to try to get a message to the Baron. That giant image over Sturmhalten? That was *her* idea."

"I didn't get to see that," Gil said with regret. "I heard she was wearing this outfit . . . "

Tarvek grinned. "She was *beautiful*."

"I also heard she accused my father of being the Other."

The smile slid off of Tarvek's face. "Ah. Yes. Well, That wasn't actually *Agatha*, you know."

Gil's eyes narrowed. "Of course not. *You* did that. You must have tampered somehow. Agatha would have told the truth, and Lucrezia would have destroyed any message that mentioned the Other."

Tarvek thought about lying, but the first rule of lying was in knowing when you had a shot at getting away with it. "Yes."

Gil regarded him silently. Tarvek half expected him to lunge for him again. *And I can't say he isn't entitled,* he thought to himself. Instead, Gil sat back slightly, staring at the console.

"And you say you can free Agatha?"

Tarvek nodded slowly. "Not . . . not immediately. But with what I already knew of Lucrezia's work, plus what I learned from her in Sturmhalten, and with access to the lab we saw downstairs, I'm confident I can remove Lucrezia from Agatha's mind." Gil looked up and opened his mouth to speak, but Tarvek interrupted. "And be able to provide enough evidence that I can prove it to your father." He thought for a minute. "Actually, I don't see any reason why we couldn't have him present for the procedure." He glanced at Gil. "If we could trust him to not try to blow everything up."

Gil looked thoughtful. "I *think* I can guarantee that. He'd be more interested in verifying the procedures and learning as much as he can about what Lucrezia's done. After all, he is a known connoisseur of spark styles.[57] Or is that too villainous?"

Tarvek refused to take the bait. "There you are," he said primly. "I'm not saying Lucrezia isn't a terrifying lunatic or that her wasps are anything less than horrific. It's simply that I, as a scientist, can appreciate the elegance of her designs"

Gil nodded reluctantly. "True. And I guess even *you* wouldn't want that to happen to *Agatha*."

A shudder went through Tarvek. Memories coursed through him: the terrible sense of loss when he had thought Agatha was gone. And his father's laboratory, the work his family had spent their lives on. How many people had they destroyed over all that time? How much of that was he, personally, responsible for? He felt ill. "No," he said slowly. "Of course not! It shouldn't happen to . . . well, to *anybody*."

He went silent, lost in thought. Gil looked solemn, watching his controls, but not actually seeing them. A shout from above reminded them they had, once again, forgotten what they were doing, and could they please move the squid about eight meters down the hallway to the next spot that needed repairs?

They scrambled to obey.

Outside the Castle, evening was falling across Mechanicsburg. Inside the Great Hospital lights were being dimmed and the few visitors who had been allowed, even with the Baron's residency, were being gently but firmly shooed out. In one of the intensive care wards, a long double row of patients, many of them connected to gently

---

[57] Klaus always claimed that sparks were like artists with recognizable styles. One of his talents was in being able to differentiate and recognize them. This proved useful on more than one occasion. When someone sends a giant mechanical echidna to ravage a rival's vineyards, for example, they don't necessarily sign it. (Although it is not unheard of for a spark to do exactly that.) Klaus claimed there were other similarities between sparks and artists, such as an inability to deal with certain realities and the associated ability to construct a reality more to their liking. Plus, they tend to be terrible with money.

whispering devices, were completely failing to appreciate the gift of entertainment that had been offered to them.

Standing on a chair in the center of the room, a humble storyteller concluded an enthralling narrative that had taken a great deal of time and effort to uncover. " . . . and thus, the evil princess was defeated and the foolish wizard was saved!"[58]

Gentle snores were the only response. That and a soft clapping from a smiling nurse. "Thank you so much," she said, removing something from her ears. "It's always best for the patients if they can sleep drug-free." She pulled a small envelope from her apron and handed it over. "Doctor Sun said if you'd like a residency—"

The storyteller sighed. "Thank you, but—"

At that moment Captain Bangladesh DuPree peeped around the corner. Anyone who knew her would have been astonished. Captain DuPree seldom entered a room unaccompanied by an excessive amount of decibels. As it happened, a serene, avuncular chat with Doctor Sun about the need for quiet around patients, delivered while he was casually paring down a block of marble with his fingertips, seemed to have gotten the point across. Seeing the storyteller, she snapped her fingers. "Hey! Is that the boring guy?"

The nurse nodded. "Oh yes."

"Fantastic! Hey, boring guy! I got a job for you!" She beckoned the storyteller to follow her.

The storyteller was a patient man who was used to this sort of treatment. He sighed and adjusted his hat. They strode down hushed

---

[58] Spoiler alert! This is the thrilling conclusion to "The Foolish Wizard Who Dared to Love A Non-Wizard," one of the many stories to be found in *The Collected, Vouchsafed, and Completely Uncursed Tales of the Wizard Folk of Finland* (Foglio & Foglio/Transylvania Polygnostic Press). The Finns have an interesting reputation among the rest of Europa that they do not go out of their way to debunk. Although the intelligentsia of Europa scoff at this obvious canard, there is no denying it is aided by the Finns seeming ability to control the weather, the actions of plants and animals, ice and fire, as well as time and space. These are, no doubt, all simple parlor tricks used to terrify outsiders and make potential invaders think twice and will surely, someday, be revealed as such by science.

hallways softly lit except around the occasional nurse station or guard post. To his surprise, they turned into an unfamiliar corridor. He attempted to make conversation. "I don't think I've ever been in this part of the hospital before."

"Don't act stupid and we'll let you leave it."

Ordinarily, this would be what we in the storytelling business call a "conversation stopper," but the storyteller caught a strange note in her voice. The captain was worried about something. This, given what rumor had told him of her character, was astonishing. He also knew, instinctively, that mentioning this would be unwise in the extreme.

They turned a corner and came to a fully staffed checkpoint. No less than six guards and two towering Wulfenbach military clanks stood before them. The captain stepped up. A password and countersign were exchanged sotto voce. A cloaked officer in a cap fashioned from a slaver wasp skull stepped up and presented a fuzzy cat-sized animal with an unusual amount of legs. Its back was orange and its belly was fluffy and white, it looked like something between a weasel and a caterpillar. It snuffled at the captain for a moment, then chirped happily. The officer swiveled it to face the storyteller. The beast wuffled at his coat and snorted, then wrinkled its pointy snout and retched, before disappearing into the officer's cloak. The officer scratched his head. "Clean, I guess."

The captain nodded and jerked a thumb. The storyteller followed her. "Now, he never sleeps much anyway," she said, breaking the quiet. "And he's in a funny mood, so do the best you can or I'll slice your liver out."

They had stopped in front of another door that was again flanked by a pair of guards. A nagging suspicion gripped the storyteller's gut. "Wait. Who is it you're taking me to?"

The captain looked at him and sighed in exasperation. "The Baron, you fool. Make him get some *sleep*." She gently opened the door.

From within, the Baron's voice emerged. Commanding as it was, it held undertones of exhaustion. "DuPree, if you come in here, I will kill you WITH THE POWER OF MY MIND!"

Captain DuPree froze, her hand still on the door handle. She glanced at the storyteller and nervously licked her lips. "I . . . " she whispered, "I'm pretty sure he can't really *do* that." Faster than his eye could follow, she darted out her hand, grabbed the storyteller's coat lapel, and slung him into the room. "So get in there!" She slammed the door behind him.

Within, ensconced in an astonishing nest of burbling medical apparatus, the ruler of the Wulfenbach Empire glowered like a caged animal. He was swathed in bandages. Assorted tubes and catheters festooned the hospital bed. The eyes in his relatively undamaged face followed the storyteller's every move.

Behind him, a nurse sat in the shadows, a small book on her lap.

After gawping for several seconds, the storyteller whipped off his hat and executed a formal courtier's bow. "Good evening, Herr Baron."

"Is it? Tell me what they are saying in town."

"Me? But—"

"You are a man of the streets. You have to know when to tell another story and when to cut and run."

There was a great deal of truth to this, but there were also numerous proverbs about telling truth to power. The storyteller hesitated. The Baron frowned. "I've had reports of you. Flatter me or lie, and I'll *know.*"

The storyteller sighed. "Everyone *knows* there is a new Heterodyne. They're just waiting to see if it's the coffee one or the pink one."

"What is Burgermeister Zuken[59] saying?"

The storyteller blinked. "Um . . . I don't know, but . . . why would anyone care?"

---

[59]   When Klaus had absorbed the Valley of the Heterodynes and Mechanicsburg into the empire, he was told that the area's leading family, the Von Mekkhans, were extinct. This left a power vacuum, so the Baron appointed a town council, which was headed at this time by one Stanislaus Zuken. He was, by all accounts, a very nice fellow who spent most of his time collecting butterflies and trying to stay out of everybody's way.

The Baron nodded. "Very good. And what are they saying about *me?*"

The storyteller considered this, then shrugged. "You're sick. You're dying. You're dead. You're going to destroy the Castle. You're going to marry the Heterodyne. She's your daughter. You built her. You're here to support her. She's a trap to draw out your enemies. You're here to kill her. You're here to turn over the empire. You're actually Barry Heterodyne. You're a construct. You're the Other. You're bankrolling one of the Heterodyne girls. You're bankrolling *both* of the Heterodyne girls because you want to see who wins. The winner will marry your son. You really like waffles. You . . . "

The storyteller's voice was growing faint. "Breathe *in*," the Baron commanded sharply.

The storyteller sucked in a huge lungful of air and wiped his forehead. "Thank you, Herr Baron."

Klaus rolled his eyes. "And the mood on the street?"

"Tense. Waiting."

"For something good or something bad?"

The storyteller shrugged. "That depends on who you talk to."

Klaus' eyes narrowed. "And you?"

"There is a reason I'm hiding here in the hospital, Herr Baron."

The Baron nodded slowly. "Yes . . . " He thought for a second. "Now, as to why you're here . . . "

"Ah! A story! Of course! So, listen, this duck walks into a bar—"

The Baron peremptorily held up a hand. "Wait. I had something else in mind. A story of the Storm King."

The storyteller rubbed the stubble on his chin as he ran through the catalog in his head. "Oh. Of course. Let's see . . . There's the one about how the Muses were stolen—and the king won them back in a pie-eating contest?"

The Baron blinked. "What? No."

The storyteller waved a hand. "No, of course not. That's for children, really . . . and the Baker's Guild . . . " He drew himself up. "You, uh . . . you can't mean the one where he seduces the Thousand

Wives of the Moon. 'Cause that's Harvest Festival stuff, and whereas I know we're both men of the world, as it were, it doesn't seem appropriate . . . "

"Of course not!"

The storyteller's breath caught, and he furtively looked over his shoulder before leaning in. "You . . . " He dropped his voice to a whisper. "You don't mean the one about how he was brought down by the Heterodyne Girl?"

Klaus actually smiled. "No."

"Good! I could get into real trouble telling that one in this town."

The Baron nodded sympathetically. "I imagine so. No, do you know the one about how he *became* king?"

"Of course! *The Queen of the Mines and the Lamp That Summoned the Night!*" The storyteller rubbed his hands together. "Good summer solstice story."

The Baron shook his head. "No, not that one. The other one."

The storyteller paused. "Ah, yes, the other one. The *other* one . . . " He frowned. "Huh. Why I haven't told that one in . . . " A look of surprise crossed his face. "Never. I don't *know* another one."

The Baron raised his brows. "Really? Well, you should. Let me tell it to you."

And so he did:

"In those days. There was no shortage of evil wizards. The worst of them all was Prince Clemethious, patriarch of the dreaded Heterodynes, a family of monsters so fearsome they were only spoken of in whispers. Clemethious was known for his wicked sense of humor. It was said that he always smiled, even as he slept, because he dreamed each night of new horrors to unleash upon his hapless enemies.

"After years of villainy, he was challenged by a good and noble king, who drove the Heterodynes and their monsters back to their dark lair. For the first time, Clemethious did not smile, for he was dead at last!

"But the eldest daughter of Clemethious was a witch and, by forgotten magics and arcane science, she seduced and then cursed the good king. He became a gigantic madwolf under her control. Lightning leapt from his jaws and he ran wild, despoiling the countryside as the witch rode upon his back, laughing in triumph. She was queen at last!

"The good king's family was killed and his castle became a ruin inhabited only by monsters. Things were worse than ever and the people despaired. But the king's young son had not been killed. He had been secretly stolen away by his nurse who was a giantess. Under the cover of night, she brought him to a cave high in the mountains and there she raised him in secret. The boy grew strong and he grew fast, but the giantess would never allow him to leave the mountain. Only when he could take the copper pin from her hair, said the giantess, would he be ready to venture into the world of men.

"So the boy tried and tried and tried to overcome the giantess by force. Every time he failed. Then one day he realized that although he would never be strong enough, he could be smart enough. Through trickery he easily managed to pluck the pin from her head. The hairpin of a giantess is large enough to be a fine sword for a prince. So the prince, now well-armed, left the safety of the cave to find his fortune.

"Meanwhile, the kingdom was still suffering in fear of the witch and her terrible wolf, but the witch had grown dissatisfied with her games. The people still remembered it was the wolf who was their ruler, not the witch. The crown stayed tightly affixed to the wolf's head, crackling with the stuff of lightning and, try as she might, the witch could not remove it. She could only rule through him. This ate away at her terrible pride, driving her mad with envy. In petty revenge against this perceived injustice, she used the madwolf's power to make the people's lives a misery.

"Seeing this, the prince realized that, although his father was truly lost, the people of the kingdom could still be saved. Not through strength, because the madwolf was power incarnate, but through intelligence and trickery. He disguised himself as a fortune teller. Due to his superior understanding of meteorology, human psychology, and statistical probability, he had become famous throughout the land. Soon enough he was brought before the witch. Through flattery and blatant use of false equivalency, he convinced her the crown could be removed from the madwolf, but only by the magic of his copper sword.

"The witch accepted the sword with delight. She wasted no time in attempting to use it to slay the lightning wolf, but she was woefully ignorant of the science of conductivity. Consequently, when she used the copper weapon, she was instantly struck down by her own enchanted lightning and slain. The madwolf, too, died of the blow and wept tears of joy at his release.

"And thus, the Kingdom was freed. The prince took the throne, and as the Storm King, he ruled wisely and well for the rest of his days."

Klaus took a deep breath and allowed his head to sink back onto his pillow. "The end," he whispered. He glanced at the storyteller. "You really haven't heard that one before?"

"Um . . . no. It's got no basis in actual history and it doesn't even fit in with any of the other stories about Valois. No, I've never even heard one like that before. Not about the Storm King."

Klaus closed his eyes. "Amazing. And you're such a collector too."

The storyteller was intrigued. "You know my work?"

"Tales of the Despot: Portrayals of the Baron in Tavern Jokes and Songs. That was yours, yes?"

"Erk. A . . . a minor work, Herr Baron, of no real importance.[60] I was drinking—"

"Ah, well, I hoped that *you* might be able to remember the name of the book."

"The . . . the book?"

"Oh yes, it was a large one, and very old . . . red binding . . . all

---

[60] Be that as it may, it *is* still available from Transylvania Polygnostic University Press.

stories of the Storm King. They were great favorites of my son when he was young. Now, who was the author? He was a Hungarian . . . was it Masat?"

"Masat? The master storyteller? But all his work was lost!"[61]

Klaus waved this away. "Oh, surely not *all* of it. Well, never mind. My son does still have the book—"

"He *does?*"

"Oh yes, I'm sure he'll be able to tell me its name."

The storyteller was frantic. "But . . . but I must—"

Klaus yawned, and his eyelids drooped closed. "Ah. And I am tired now. Tell DuPree I said 'good job.'"

"But . . . " The storyteller flapped his arms in frustration. Klaus opened one eye and fixed him with a hard, questioning look and

---

[61] Gaspard Masat was a contemporary of the Storm King and, indeed, was a member of his court, traveling the length of the king's realm and reporting on what was happening. He was known for having an eye for significant details and an insightful knowledge of how people thought. Many of his reports were, for espionage purposes, written as stories. These were so popular that they were told long after the rulers he had written about had been conquered. After the fall of Valois, he found himself without a patron. To make ends meet, he produced a magnificent poetic cycle chronicling the rise, reign, and ultimate fall of the Storm King: *A Villám a Korona.* He folded the definitive versions of all of his stories into this work. This proved successful. *Too* successful, actually, as instead of writing *new* material, he spent the rest of his life rewriting it, changing the facts with every iteration in order to cater to the changing tastes of the public. Unfortunately, as your professors are all too aware, the public's taste for the dramatic is a hole that can never be filled. It is said that in the final version, the climactic battle at Balan's Gap had Andronicous leading warriors from the moon—mounted upon all the animals of the Earth—fighting an army of flaming Heterodynes that were each thirty meters tall, and that, after their defeat, their corpses formed the Transylvanian Alps. Good stuff, to be sure, but he tried to pass it off as history witnessed firsthand. Skalds may be able to get away with foolishness like that, but the universities of Europa and their various historical societies have no patience with out-and-out fiction. To make things worse, he insisted that all editions of *A Villám a Korona* retain the same title, marginalia, appendices, indexes, and bibliographies. This meant it was very easy to confuse the later, fabulist versions with the factual original—which was actually a unique, first-person chronicle of the Storm King's reign. Eventually, out of sheer annoyance, *all* editions of his books were ordered destroyed. Thus today, while Masat is known as a great storyteller, none of his actual stories have survived. The irony!

the storyteller gave up. "Thank you, Herr Baron." Without another word, he turned and left.

As the door shut, there was a metallic *pop* from the shadows. "Well, *I* thought it was a load of nonsense."

The shadow of a satisfied smile ghosted across the Baron's face. "Really? Well, it wasn't for you."

The clank that had once been Anevka Sturmvoraus and now held its own version of the consciousness of Lucrezia Mongfish, tossed her head in amused irritation. "Oh, you're impossible. Just go to sleep." Instantly, as he'd been ordered to, the Master of Europa slept.

CHAPTER 5

History is one of the world's great soporifics, if only because it mostly consists of perfectly ordinary people doing the logical thing in order to get home in time for dinner. But it does not have to be! What readers want are stories! Tales of evil, or possibly just absurdity, people going to great lengths to ensure nobody gets to enjoy dinner but themselves. An instructor must, of course, chronicle the same dry events and long-dead personalities that have bored untold generations of students. But with the addition of a mad queen who occasionally storms through the narrative torturing kings and seducing monsters, I can solidly guarantee those same students' undivided attention!

—Gaspard Masat, in a letter to the Board or Regents of the University of Wittenberg, applying for the position of History Master[62]

❦

On the streets of Mechanicsburg, Vanamonde von Mekkhan,[63] seneschal to the Heterodynes and de facto leader of the town of Mechanicsburg, awoke to realize he was being led through a street of small shops by the gentle pressure of a hand tucked inside the crook of his arm. Moreover, someone was *talking* to him. "So even though the Baron has the town officially sealed, the Smuggler's Guild has been bringing in food. They hope to stockpile enough to last an additional six months."

---

[62] He did not get the job.

There was a pause and Van realized he was expected to contribute something. "Thass good," he mumbled.

"Ah. You're awake again. Good." The hand on his arm gave a slight squeeze. "They said we could discuss terms later."

"Thass *bad*."

"I agree. So I demanded a bulk discount of an additional twenty percent off now or they could discuss terms later with the Jägers."

"Thass . . . " Van ran the statement back through his head. "Wait. Is that good?" He opened his eyes and peered at the small figure resolutely dragging him along. She was at least twenty centimeters shorter than he, so all he could really see was the top of her head. Her hair was a rich chestnut and cut in a wavy bob that bounced gently as she strode along.

"Well, I admit it wasn't very *nice*," she was saying. "I also told them that we'd been approached by the Wulfenbach Dark Fleet,[64] so they took it."

Val pondered this. "Thought the Dark Fleet was a . . . whatchamacallit . . . rumor."

"Oh yes, but it's one they've heard."

This actually got Van's eyes open all the way and he leaned forward to examine the girl a little more closely. She glanced his way with large, blue eyes, then went back to watching the street. The rest of her face was delicate with a snub nose and a small, thin-lipped mouth. She was dressed in a white traveling half-cloak and dress.

---

[64] The Wulfenbach Dark Fleet was supposedly a band of smugglers that operated from within the admittedly already-extensive airship fleet of the empire. They were legendary for being able to circumvent blockades, because they already had all the empires' codes and passwords. They were, according to the numerous stories, ballads, and epic poems told about them, good-hearted philanthropists and crusaders for the justice that occasionally fell between the empire's cracks. They were also completely fictitious and, at this point in our story, the Baron was getting rather impatient waiting for someone to fill this obvious ecological and sociological niche. He was beginning to think that, like so many other seemingly obvious things, he would have to do it himself.

Initially Van registered her as a tourist, but the ease with which she was navigating the streets spoke otherwise.

Van licked dry lips. "Who *are* you?"

The girl glanced at him again and Van saw that she was tired as well. "Oh, not *this* again."

Van looked worried. She took pity on him and sighed, "I am Vidonia Orkaleena. I am the one who is putting you to bed. For the first time in days."

Van considered this. Orkaleena *was* the name of a prominent Mechanicsburg family of snail traders, but this young lady was completely unknown to him. This, in of itself, was very odd, as both his mother and grandfather had contrived increasingly outlandish situations where he had found himself spending time alone with every suitable bachelorette Mechanicsburg possessed. Thus, he was conflicted. He certainly *wanted* to go to bed, but would be damned if he let an outsider dictate his actions. He opened his mouth and Vidonia turned to face him.

"You've already done everything you possibly can, and you need to sleep now or you will be of no use whatsoever to the town when the attack comes!"

Well, Van thought, if she is an outsider, she's a remarkably sensible one.

Technically, Vidonia was not an outsider, though Vanamonde could be excused for not knowing who she was. The Merchant House of Orkaleena had been a rather modest importer of glassware and exporter of Snezek—the famous Mechanicsburg liqueur[65]—when,

---

[65] Mechanicsburg, as has been mentioned elsewhere, was a town not traditionally known for engaging in much commerce. Historically, they obtained their vast wealth by plunder and tribute. When they needed something they could not grow, produce, or build themselves they, as often as not, went out and stole it.

Still, even among brigands, one will find artisans and so, in the unique crucible that bubbled within the shadow of the Heterodynes, the people of Mechanicsburg occasionally brought forth things that other, ostensibly sane, people actually wanted. For example: about four hundred and seventy-five years ago, one Simaeous von Uúrsk brewed up "a rather amusing

about twenty years ago, the Mechanicsburg snail had begun to make major inroads onto the tables of the rest of Europa.[66] The patriarch of the family at that time, Opa Orkaleena, saw an opportunity and went after it with gusto. Under his direction, Mechanicsburg snails appeared in London, Istanbul, Khartoum, Moscow, and just about everywhere in between.

As a result, his eldest daughter, Vidonia, had grown up on the road with the occasional flying visit home. Her education had been an exotic blend of foreign politics, languages, mercantile stratagems, and an exhaustive knowledge of the care and feeding of vast herds of snails. All through this, she had clung to the idea of Mechanicsburg as a place of refuge and security. She had endeavored to learn as much as she could about it, which proved useful as her family's clients were always interested in hearing more about it.

Two months ago, her father had died and she had turned over the running of the family business to her equally gastropod-infatuated brother, Opa Junior. And now—young, unencumbered, tired of a life on the road, and modestly wealthy—she had returned to Mechanicsburg only to discover it to be one of the most boring places on Earth.

She had been sitting in a coffee shop, deciding what to do with herself when a strange girl had walked in, built a coffee machine, and

---

little herbal digestive" that relied on local ingredients, including assorted vegetation and insects that had originally been mutated into existence by imbibing the toxic waters of the Dyne. It quickly became the Other Thing the town was known for: Snezek. Snezek (the name came from the noise that a person invariably made the first time they tasted it) was soon being served at late-night dinner parties across three continents. Its presence at a gathering indicated the hosts were madcap bohemians who dared to dance along the edges of propriety and that, pretty soon, those present could expect someone to be tossed into the fountain wearing naught but their unmentionables.

[66] The story of the commercialization of the Mechanicsburg snail is a fascinating one in its own right and deserves its own book. But, in brief, it started when a merchant from Mechanicsburg discovered that a colony of hometown snails had bred within the bedding of leaf mulch he had used to cushion a fragile load of machinery he was delivering to Amsterdam. By the time he arrived, he had enough snails that he could prepare a respectable feast for his buyer, who was so impressed that he ordered more. The rest is history.

completely changed her life. From that moment on, she had been delightfully busy. Also from that moment, she had been one of the people telling other people what to do. She had really missed that.

Vidonia also discovered she was drawn to the only person here who seemed to be working harder than she was and, increasingly, she found herself helping to facilitate his orders. A short while ago she had discovered him blearily trying to convince a gas cylinder that it needed to paint the street, which was when she had led him off.

They turned the corner onto the Street of Schemers and Van halted. Vidonia ran into him. "Wake up," she said.

"Wait. Stop." Vidonia paused. Van sounded more awake now. He pointed. "That's my house."

Vidonia nodded encouragingly. "And a very pretty house it is. Let's—"

"Look!" With a shock, Vidonia noticed the front door at the top of the stairs was hanging slightly to one side. Someone had smashed the door open and then tried to prop it back up so it wouldn't be noticeable. "Something's wrong," Van growled. He went up the stairs at a run.

A slight push and the door crashed to the floor. They stepped inside. There was no one to be seen. "Mother?" Van called. He was answered by silence. Vidonia looked around. There was evidence of a fight. Nothing extreme, but a turned over table with a shattered vase and scattered books spoke volumes. Van ran deeper into the apartment. "Grandfather?"

He stepped into his grandfather's bedroom and came to a halt. Here they were. His grandfather, Carson von Mekkhan, propped up stiffly in bed; his mother, Arella, sitting upright at its foot. Van blinked. His mother looked injured. Her face was bruised. Why were they *glaring* at him like . . .

A sudden gasp from behind caused him to spin about. There was Vidonia, in the no-nonsense grasp of a squat, aging man with an evil grin. The man held a short, businesslike knife pressed delicately to

Vidonia's throat. "Indeed, indeed!" he said in a jocular tone. "Here they are, and here you are and here we all are! And now, I have *you*—the most important man in Mechanicsburg, yes?"

How does he know? Vanamonde wondered. I've tried to keep such a low profile.

The little man smiled even wider. "Vanamonde Heliotrope:[67] the Ringer of the Doom Bell!"

Van blinked. "The what?"

The man with the knife rolled his eyes. "The Doom Bell? Big bell? Middle of town? *Surely* you've seen it?

"Of course I've—" Van took a deep breath. *He doesn't know.* "What do you want?"

"Why, I want you to do your *job*, sir! I want you to ring the Doom Bell!"

Van licked his lips. "My job—"

The man tutted and flicked a card towards Van, who managed to catch it in midflight. He was surprised to see it was one of his grandfather's Official Doom Bell Ringer cards.

"That *is* your family's *job*. Is it not?" He allowed himself to look about the room and nod approvingly, although his grip on Vidonia remained rock solid. "A nice soft place, sir, yes? A familial reward for services rendered to Heterodynes past, no doubt. Live on the payroll of the town but never do the work?" He shook his head in mock severity. "Tsk. No, that will never do." He became deadly serious in the space of an instant. "I *will* have you ring that bell."

---

67   When Baron Wulfenbach took over Mechanicsburg, the van Mekkhan family resolved to not give the Heterodyne secrets to an outsider. Therefore, the Baron was informed that all of the Heterodyne's seneschals were dead and their knowledge lost. As an additional subterfuge, the family adopted the name of "Heliotrope." Of course everyone in town knew who they really were. Now, an outsider might say that a secret of this magnitude being kept from Baron Wulfenbach (of all people) for over fifteen years strains credulity, which is fair, considering the Baron's reputation for ferreting out secrets. Mechanicsburg, however, is a very insular place, and telling Klaus the van Mekkhans were still around would have gone against the best wishes of the Heterodynes. This was something that any Mechanicsburg native would have been almost incapable of doing. Besides, "putting on over" on outsiders is considered a fine sport.

Van glanced at Vidonia. He could see she was furious. She was swiveling her eyes about, trying to figure out something to do, which caused his heart to seize up, as the man holding her was obviously well-versed in this sort of business. The knife was positioned to be driven home in an instant, and despite the man's ebullient bonhomie, Van knew he would do so in a heartbeat. Van felt his exhaustion ebbing. He took pride in his role as the de facto ruler of Mechanicsburg. He still wasn't sure who this girl was but, as he felt a certain responsibility for both the locals and tourists of the area, he wasn't about to let her get murdered right in front of him.

He made soothing motions with his hands. Ostensibly for the man, but really for Vidonia, who seemed to get the message. "But—" Van tried to wrap his head around the situation. "But *why* are you doing this? You're Baron Krasimir Oublenmach, right?" The man's start of surprise confirmed his identity to Van's satisfaction. "You're one of the people who brought in that false Heterodyne girl. Why are you even still here? Your plan is *ruined*! Your 'Heterodyne' was severely injured while fleeing the Castle! She's under heavy guard at the Great Hospital—*if* she isn't already being interrogated."

Surprisingly, this just made the little man grin even wider. "Indeed, indeed! Routed by a genuine Heterodyne, no less! Even *you* must be surprised at the turn of events, eh? *Astonishing* times, are they not, sir?" He sighed the sigh of a man who tried not to be surprised by life's surprises. "Yet real or fake, it makes no difference to an old pirate like myself!"

Van shook his head. "But, your fake Heterodyne! Your plan . . . "

Oublenmach chuckled in what looked like genuine delight. "What a *glorious* plan it was! A magnificent edifice of dreams and iron." Here he gave Van a knowing grin. "Those aristocratic fools did love it so!" He shrugged. "But I am a lesser man, alas, and I am simply in it for the treasure!"

"Treasure?" Van's eyes went wide. "You're talking about the *Treasure of the Heterodynes*? Are you *serious*?"

Oublenmach laughed like a man sharing a secret-but-delicious shame. "Oh, I know. I *know*! The fabled treasure, accumulated by *generations* of brigands too mad to actually *pay* for anything! Absurd, yes?" He waved a hand dismissively. "It's a fairy story treasure hunters have told each other for a hundred years![68] Right down to the loyal guardians, who would rather die than betray their masters.

"More level heads, of course, know there is no treasure. A castle, a town, a monstrous fighting force—all of these must be maintained— paid—fed—and no doubt the old seneschals, at least, were *practical* men. They must have been devilishly good at it, for in the thousand years this town has existed, never—not *once*—has there ever been a record of the place experiencing hard times, no matter the current state of the actual Heterodyne. An *extraordinary* thing in and of itself. Yes? And the stories say the main vault only opens when the Doom Bell rings! Why, it is the final fillip that declares the whole thing naught but a fanciful embroidery on a dreamer's tale!"

Oublenmach sighed wistfully, then tightened his grip on Vidonia. He pressed the knife slightly deeper into the flesh of her throat, causing her to give a small gasp. "Ah, but still . . . I think we shall ring it *anyway*, yes?"

Van shared a glance with his grandfather, then straightened up. "You *do* realize the bell is only to be rung at the Heterodyne's command?"

Oublenmach's face settled in a moue of disappointment. "Sir, we *both* know that, *technically*, you are incorrect. It is *also* rung when a new Heterodyne is *declared*, yes? And is there not a *new* Heterodyne? Why, yes sir, I believe there is! So, gentlemen, I believe the bell *should* ring! Tradition demands it!"

"No!" Carson interrupted. "Not yet! The bell *can't* be rung until the Castle accepts her!"

Van nodded slowly. "It's true. We can't just—"

---

[68] Longer than that, actually. People began to do the math regarding the House of Heterodyne's lopsided balance sheets as early as the 1300s.

A squeak from Vidonia cut him off. Oublenmach ostentatiously relaxed his hand. "Ah, what is *this*?" he mused. "It seems there is a grain of truth to even the most outlandish story. Loyal guardians indeed. You see, *I* would think that given the *present* circumstances, a small excess of enthusiasm on your part would be seen as quite *natural*. What else about the story is true, I wonder?" He chuckled. "Ah, curse this insatiable curiosity of mine." He stared at the family von Mekkhan and shook his head. "Would you truly sacrifice your lives? Quite possibly, quite possibly. You are noble men and women of a family with a long tradition of service and sacrifice, I have no doubt, yes? But, as I said before, I am made of lesser stuff."

He pointed his chin towards Arella, who sat seething at the end of Carson's bed. "As you can see, I have no scruples about striking a woman—even your dear old mother—and I'll do it again, if I must. But I will admit, sir, my heart wouldn't be in it. Motherhood and all that." He then pressed down gently and Van saw a small bead of blood form where the point of the blade touched Vidonia's throat. The girl closed her eyes and refused to make another sound. "Ah, but I *can* cut the throat of this innocent young lady, sir. *That* I can do as easy as pie."

Van felt sheer rage fill him, blowing the last vestiges of fatigue from his mind. He nodded once. "Grandfather," he said, never taking his eyes off of Oublenmach. "Where are the keys to the bell tower?"

Carson blinked. "But . . . "

Van cut him off. "Agatha is the Heterodyne. *You* know it. *I* know it. I should have started repairing the bell *yesterday!*"

"*Repair?*" Oublenmach growled. "Talk fast, sir."

Van sneered at him. "Do you think you're the *first* to hear of the treasure? The *hundredth*? 'Ring the bell and gold will fall out of the sky.' Minstrels have been bleating that drivel for *centuries!*"

He pointed at Oublenmach. "Have you *looked* at the bell? I mean, really *examined* it? Because if you have, you'll have seen that striker mechanism has no hammer! We had a steady stream of treasure hunters stomping in here for years after the Heterodyne Boys vanished. Before the Baron took over, we had to deal with them ourselves. So we disabled the bell by removing the hammer." Van shrugged. "It *can't* ring."

Oublenmach smiled coldly. "Ingenious, as a short term solution, sir. But I will not believe that anyone in this town seriously thought the Heterodynes were extinct. You have prepared for your master's return, so do not expect me to believe that you cannot repair the bell easily, when you must."

Van smiled at him, and a touch of unease slid across Oublenmach's brain. "Of *course* it can be repaired," Van said quietly. "And yes, I know where the hammer is. I'll even tell you where to find it; It's hanging in a bar in town."

Aboard Castle Wulfenbach, Boris strode into the main war room. He paused a moment, admiring the work of the mapmakers. The paint on the scenery before him was still fresh. The master strategists of the empire had many cities and traditional battlegrounds models kept in permanent storage, but no one had ever seriously thought Mechanicsburg would be the site of an engagement. The scene before him had been built very quickly and entirely from scratch.

The tabletop was almost thirty meters square. The mapmakers had lovingly recreated the Valley of the Heterodynes. Girt by its famous mountains, the town itself huddled within its walls in exquisite detail. It was surrounded by painstakingly reproduced defenses that had (thankfully) been deactivated decades ago, but still remained a part of the landscape and thus had to be taken into consideration when planning ground operations.

Sprinkled throughout the valley, with more crowding the loading tables off to the side, were representations of the empire forces that were being deployed. Boris frowned. In his opinion, there were too many. The Baron was devoting an excessive amount of men and material to this.

Overhead, he heard the hiss of pneumatic servos. Kleegon the

Battlemaster glided down in his powered observer pulpit to hover beside him.

Kleegon was a construct who had helped free himself from the Count of the Iron Ski[69] and risen quickly within the empire's command structure. His brain had been augmented so much that it now had to be contained within a glass dome; his eyes had been replaced with a single ruby orb that never blinked. "As usual, our forces are in red. Despite the fact we have had to restrict ourselves to ground troops, we have almost finished containing Mechanicsburg." He glided over to one of the maps showing the surrounding area and indicated a main road. "However, we have several *outside* forces approaching. Their stated goals are irrelevant, as their actual purpose is, in many cases, painfully obvious.

"The first is a loose coalition of the old Smatterburg Duchies, led by the Philosopher King of the University of Aalborg. He believes the Baron and the Heterodyne will destroy each other and is determined to pick up the pieces. Not a unique situation by any means, but I mention him because of his primacy, and because he has managed to put about two thousand men and four medium airships into the field. They're moving slowly as there has been a bit of rain east of the Duchies and they are encumbered with two shock cannons they are hauling overland, which they refuse to abandon.

"Then there are the forces loyal to the House of Valois—"

Boris interrupted. "You mean the walkers? Master Gilgamesh destroyed them."

Kleegon sighed and gave a Gallic shrug. "Ah, but this is a *different* group. Mostly cavalry, some foot soldiers, and a unit of Drakken horses.[70] Mostly the dregs of the Fifty Families. They seem caught

---

[69]   Kleegon had been in charge of the count's forces and had choreographed a battle against the Baron that, while appearing formidable, had allowed the Wulfenbach forces to win handily. What had caught the Baron's eye was that, when the battle was over, the defeated enemy lines spelled out: "HELP. I AM A PRISONER IN THE CASTLE. SECOND FLOOR, THIRD DOOR FROM THE LEFT."

[70]   Drakken horses were an unusually successful cross between regular horses and lizards,

up with the whole idea of pillaging, which is why they are still over a hundred kilometers away.

"The last group *seems* to be a genuine popular uprising, but they are suspiciously well-supplied on such short notice. They claim to be marching to Mechanicsburg to defend the Heterodyne girl, though the plan seems to be to keep her captive until their own Storm King arrives to take over."

Boris bit his lip. "Their own . . . ? Not the *same* Storm King as the other groups?"

Kleegon shook his head. "There are at least three claimants being hailed by assorted groups. I'm sure more will emerge as time goes on."

"They already have." Captain Smoza stepped up and consulted the report in her hand. "The majority of our forces not here or at Sturmhalten are reporting waves of rebellions, mutinies, and outbreaks." She looked up, a hurt look on her face. "It's as if the whole empire was just waiting for a reason to revolt."

Boris looked like someone had struck him. "I . . . I didn't think it was this bad . . . "

"It isn't!" Kleegon delivered this judgment in a ringing tone. "These may be genuine rebellions, but the incidents causing them have clearly been exaggerated and overblown. Those involved have been manipulated into erupting simultaneously. The purpose is clear: weaken the perception of the empire's strength, and so convince the populace it needs a new strong, central leader. If the Baron does not re-establish himself as that leader, I calculate a seventy-eight percent chance the empire will suffer an outright collapse before one of these pretenders can establish sufficient control."

Smoza considered this and voiced what everyone in the room was thinking: "This doesn't sound like a very well thought out plan."

---

with the added "benefit" of breathing fire if properly coaxed. Unlike regular horses they grew torpid in the cold and could only move quickly in short bursts. Like regular horses they tended to explode if allowed to eat clover, which they will bite through concrete barriers to get at. This campaign was one of the few on record where they were actually deployed.

"IT IS MADNESS!" The speaker was a huge man with a magnificent mane of bright orange hair. A pair of thick cables ran from just above his ears to a stout staff that supported a brass skull encrusted with tubes and lights: Herr Doktor Eeliocentric Chouté.[71] "THE JACKALS GATHER WHILE THE WOLF LIES WOUNDED!"

Boris felt mixed emotions. Chouté's bluster was an affront to his tidy sense of propriety, and yet, when he was around, all other problems seemed to retreat in importance. "Thank you for our requisite daily dose of high drama, Herr Doktor, but I am told that the Baron will be back in the morning."

This was news to everyone. "BUT AFTER HIS DISASTROUSLY QUIXOTIC BATTLE WITH DOCTOR SUN, HE STILL LIES INSENSATE WITHIN THE FULL BODY HEALING ENGINE, YES?"

"Well, he was *placed* there," Boris conceded. "But as soon as he deemed himself sufficiently healed, he forcibly removed himself. I thought Sun was going to kill him. Eventually he was made to see reason by Sun and the Princess Anevka, of all people."

Smoza looked blank for a moment, then brightened. "Anevka. That's the clank that thinks it's the Sturmvoraus Princess, yes?"

"AN ABOMINATION THAT CURDLES THE MILK OF ALL HONEST MEN!"

Boris shrugged. "Well, aren't we all?"

"OH, I *SAY*, SIR!"

---

[71] Herr Doktor Eeliocentric Chouté (MD, MEN, Cambridge) was often accused of not having a brain in his head. This was technically true, as it was located in a fortified container atop the staff he carried with him at all times. This had two noticeable effects: On the one hand, he now had a brain that could be tuned so it could ignore the thousand-and-one distractions a messy organic body produces that interrupt one's thinking. As a result, Chouté was a brilliant intellectual, capable of clear and fast insights that easily propelled him into the Baron's inner circle. On the other hand, he was a man desperately afraid of losing his humanity and, thus, he allowed himself to thoroughly embrace his emotional responses. This made him overly loud at times, but Klaus liked the fact that he was entirely incapable of subterfuge.

"But she's strong, she can't be wasped, she doesn't need sleep, and he *listens* to her. *That's* an abomination we can use."

Suddenly Castle Wulfenbach rocked, causing everyone to stagger slightly.

"What was that?" Smoza gasped. The jolt had knocked her hat off, revealing a small furry green creature nestled in the tidy nest of her hair. "That was not good," it grumbled, shielding its eyes from the light.

Boris handed Smoza her hat. "We're under attack, of course. I was afraid of this."

"UNDER ATTACK? SHEER PERFIDY! WHO WOULD *DARE?*"

Boris shrugged. "Only every spark within five hundred kilometers. What I want to know is *how?*" He strode over to a large circular window. "I've had all our defenses armed and ready for—"

With a *THUMP*, an enormous ape with brightly colored wings slammed into the glass, stared at the startled people inside, and screamed defiance before dropping off.

"Was that a flying monkey?" Smoza asked. The creature in her hair shivered. "Giant monkey," it whispered. Smoza reached up and stroked it comfortingly. "I always thought they were smaller than that." She agreed.

Boris and Chouté glanced at each other and nodded. "Professor Senear.[72] I thought he'd been awfully quiet lately."

Smoza gently settled her hat on her head. "So which army is he associated with?"

"Boris snorted. "None of them. This man is a spark! A blasted, lunatic, scheming, unpredictable spark! *They've* been chafing under

---

[72]   Professor Julius Senear [Litore Aquilonaris Elementary (advanced program), ScD, DVM] specialized in creating flying anthropoids. Many sparks have a favorite field of study, to be sure, but few were as dedicated to a central concept as Professor Senear. He wanted viable flying apes, did everything he could to make this dream come true, and succeed he did. It is thanks to his tireless efforts that at least three separate and distinct species of Aeroapes* can be found today, infesting the towers and roofs of Europa's cathedrals, castles, and opera houses.

the Baron's heel even worse than the governments! Now that they know that he's incapacitated—"

A unicycle messenger careened into the room. When he saw Boris, he waved his hands frantically. "Sir! Mechanicsburg is under attack and not by us! Spotters report unknown clanks, airships, and artillery strikes!" He skidded to a halt before Boris, panting. "Sir, the Great Hospital has taken a direct hit!"

Boris's face went white. "The Baron!"

The hospital room shuddered and, alarmingly, began to list to one side like the deck of a ship at sea. The clank that was now Lucrezia leapt up and dashed towards the door just as it burst open. A squad of Wulfenbach troops and doctors poured in. "We're under attack," the chief doctor shouted. "The Baron must be moved to safety immediately!"

Lucrezia paused. Klaus would no doubt be moved to the safest location possible. She pirouetted smoothly on one perfect mechanical foot and began to give orders. "That entire bank of monitors can be disconnected," she said, "as well as these emergency pumps. The Baron is in no danger of needing them."

The doctor opened his mouth, then glanced at the elaborate setup around the patient. To his surprise, the clank's suggestions were all sound and would make moving the Baron significantly easier.

"You heard the lady," he declared. "Get moving!"

Lucrezia smiled graciously. "*Princess*, actually."

Back in Castle Heterodyne, Agatha slapped a final solenoid into place. A row of switches flexed like a prisoner who, after breaking free of his restraints, takes a deep, unfettered breath. "Yesss," the Castle sighed. "I am once again in full control of this section. Well done, Mistress." It paused. "I remember . . . Oh dear. I *am* sorry about that *unfortunate* incident in the kitchen."

Agatha was encouraged. The Castle was beginning to stitch together memories and control functions from more and more of its far-flung sections. "Glad to hear it," Agatha said. "Did that fire do much damage?"

"Oh. Yes. Let me see. Ah . . . " There was a roaring sound from the next room, an electric snap, and a great whoosh as the fires once again ignited. "It is *supposed* to be like that. Part of my heating system, you know."

Gil glanced at Tarvek. "Told you so."

Tarvek grit his teeth. "You were guessing."

Agatha stared back into the blue-flamed inferno. "All of that," she asked incredulously, "just to heat this place?"

"It is a vent of coalbed methane your ancestors harnessed. And a good thing too. I'm told some of the towers get a bit chilly in deep winter, even with all this."

Agatha made a face. "Well, thank you for the lovely surprise shower, then. And . . . my ancestors . . . did they *ever* build anything *small?*"

The Castle considered this. "The master's bed only sleeps six . . . "

Agatha nodded wearily. "Sorry I asked."

Soon, the group was resting in a suite of maintenance halls near the furnace room. Agatha examined a wall of pipes and gauges while debating with the Castle as to which of several new problem spots was closer. Violetta disappeared into the adjoining rooms on some mission of her own. Tarvek sat with his back to a stone wall, head resting on one cupped hand, feeling miserable. Gil stood by watching Agatha pace, then looked down at Tarvek. "What's with you?"

"Shut up. I am unhappy and I wish to brood in peace."

Gil nodded. "Oh, I *know* what's bugging you."

Tarvek focused his glare on Gil. "Really?"

Gil nodded. "Sure. Because Agatha is involved, it's finally hitting you that—just maybe—using the Other's tech to control other people might be considered—oh, I don't know—kind of *wrong?*"

Tarvek sighed. "No, not that." He seemed to consider what Gil had just said and waved a hand vaguely. "Look, just leave me alone, okay?"

Gil crossed his arms. "No, I get it. It must be tough realizing that you're a slimy toad who failed 'Ethics in Government 101.' "[73]

Tarvek glared at Gil. "Well, I never got to *finish* that class, now did I? Why, I didn't get to finish *any* of them, I recall, as I was thrown off your high-and-mighty airship." Gil bit his lip as Tarvek continued. "I had to get *my* lessons by surviving amongst a bunch of evil-minded, cynical, backstabbing old fools, who, I might add, were *still* smart enough to hide an entire *army* from the great Baron Wulfenbach. Who, I will delicately point out, took over Europa by force and used guns and worse to control people—so how are you any better?" Tarvek held up a hand. "But, you know—even at a distance—I learned a lot from your father. If someone can't handle an unpleasant truth? Lie to them. If someone won't listen to reason? Show them the unhappy alternative. If people don't choose to live peaceably? Don't give them a choice. If you don't like the rules—"

"What is this?" Violetta had returned, a crate of supplies resting on her shoulder. "I leave to get you guys something to eat and you light the place back on fire?" She glared at Tarvek. "This is somehow your fault, isn't it!"

"NO!" Tarvek said, even as Violetta sent a quick punch towards his stomach. However, even as Gil winced in sympathy, Violetta let out a squeal of surprise and clutched her fist in pain.

Tarvek turned to Gil, smirking. "As I was saying, if you don't like the rules—" He hoisted up his shirt to reveal a slightly dented steel plate tucked into his belt. "Change the game."

He then turned to Violetta and drew himself up. "I'm sorry, Violetta, but as my days of needing the family to underestimate me appear to be over, I will no longer require your assistance in that particular charade."

---

[73]   Ethics in Government was one of the groundbreaking classes students on Castle Wulfenbach, many of whom were destined to be rulers or the advisors to rulers, were required to take. Sometimes over and over again until they could pass it or at least fake it convincingly.

Violetta stared up at him. "You . . . you're implying that all this time, you've been *letting* me beat on you?"

Tarvek nodded gently. "You'll just have to find someone else to vent your frustrations out on. Maybe that von Zinzer fellow."

Violetta's face went scarlet. "Shut up!" she lashed out. "There's no way I'll ever believe you're anything but a worthless fool!"

However, when her blow landed, Tarvek was no longer there. Violetta felt a gentle slap to the back of her head. "Well, yes," Tarvek said in a cool voice from behind her, "that was the idea, now wasn't it?"

Violetta spun and prepared to strike. Tarvek stood there, watching her. He looked completely open. Violetta paused and slowly lowered her hands. One of Tarvek's eyebrows quirked upwards in approval, which just made Violetta angrier. "You and your stupid games," she hissed between clenched teeth.

Tarvek shrugged. "Those 'stupid games,' dear cousin, are what kept both of us alive. But enough of that." He turned to face Gil. "I'm starting to think someone else here is playing his own game." He studied Gil for a moment. "You're really smart. I know this, but sometimes you act . . . so shallow. You got all that information out of me just now, by simply mooning about like a drunken poet. I should've noticed it earlier, but between finding out who you really are, and the echoes of the you I can still feel from the *si vales valeo* . . . well, I'm beginning to realize you might be just as much of a manipulative, sneaky weasel as I am." He considered Gil's stony countenance. "Well, maybe not as much as I am myself, but I'll put that down to a lack of inclination, as I'm sure you had reasons similar to my own. I'm all right with that. You're of more use if you're smart." He took a deep breath and suddenly was within a centimeter of Gil's face. "But if I find out you're lying about being here to help Agatha, then we shall have to see if you're as deadly as I am."

Gil stared at him and then nodded once.

Violetta had not just brought food. She had also found more tools and a stout leather work apron-and-tool-belt combination, which she was busy helping Agatha into. Agatha was busy examining the new tools, choosing the most useful and tucking them here and there within easy reach. As she worked, she watched the two men across the room thoughtfully. "You say Tarvek's been playing the fool?" she asked Violetta. "I can't really say I've seen it."

Violetta wasn't impressed. "Huh. Well, not around *you*, so much."

Agatha nodded thoughtfully. "Ah, but around his family? I can understand that."

"Yeah, but now we know we can't believe what either of them are really up to. I mean, what about Wulfenbach? If *he's* so much smarter than he lets on, then what is he *really* in here for?"

Agatha gazed at Gil and sighed. "I have to assume it's what he says. But since he's the one who *has* been playing the idiot around me, I can't be sure."

The science of acoustics is a funny thing. A conversation flowing in one direction can be indistinct, but words flowing in the other direction can bounce off surfaces that deliver it crisp and clear to those nearby. Which is why, although Agatha and Violetta could not hear Gil and Tarvek's discussion, those two heard Agatha's statement loud and clear, as indicated by the slow reddening of Gil's face. Tarvek stared at him and a grin of understanding bubbled up across his face. "You weren't actually playing the idiot with her, were you?"

"Shut up!" Gil muttered. "I *am* here to help her—but it's like I do everything I can to make myself look bad around her!" He gave Tarvek a shrug. "I must have inherited my father's natural ability to infuriate women."

He then poked Tarvek with a finger. "But *you*—all that stuff you told me about your work with Lucrezia? I wasn't actually fishing for information—you spilled that all by yourself. From what I hear, you don't make mistakes like that. Maybe *you're* not at your best at the moment either. Has that occurred to you?"

Tarvek bit his lip and looked away. Gil nodded. "Still, you are right. I *do* play games. I'm good at them. Definitely better than you . . . if only because I don't go on about them to my enemies." He grinned. "And you know what? I am Gilgamesh Wulfenbach. Heir to the Empire and Defender of the Pax Transylvania. I will crush this whole Knights of Jove/Storm King mess of yours." He leaned in. "Don't worry—I'll let you escape so you can go skulking around with your perfect little plans. After all, I'll *always* need someone to take the blame."

At that moment, Agatha strode up, map in hand. "You guys ready?"

Gil nodded. "Oh, I'm ready." He looked at Tarvek and smiled. "Are *you* ready?"

Tarvek smiled back. "I am *so* ready."

At Mamma Gkika's Bar, Baron Krasimir Oublenmach spat out a small mouthful of blood and whispered, "Ladies are delicate creatures who should never be struck or awakened too early in the morning." Then he paused and thought as hard as he could. *This next part. It was very important.* "Ninety-nine."

The hand around his throat flexed slightly, and Oublenmach continued. "Ladies are delicate creatures who should never be struck or awakened too early in the morning." He licked his lips. "One hundred."

At the other end of the monstrous arm pinning him to the wall, the face of Mamma Gkika broke into a sharp-toothed grin. "See? Dot vos not so hard."

She then turned to Arella von Mekkhan, who was seated in a comfortable chair with a cup of tea in her hand. She had several bandages artistically arranged on her face. "Okay, sveetie, hyu vants hy should keel heem now?"

Oublenmach stirred feebly. "Yes, please," he moaned.

He was casually pulled forward and then slammed back into the wall. "Shot op, hyu."

Arella sighed contentedly and sipped from her cup. "No," she said thoughtfully, "I believe he will be . . . useful."

Mamma looked at the hanging man skeptically. She sniffed. "Hyu tink so? Ve need rude pipple schtupid enuf to valk into my place vit a gon? Hy already *gots* clowns, sweetie." She sighed. "Lots ov dem."

"Ah, but *he* wants to ring the Doom Bell. He wants the Hammer."

Mamma was astonished. She hauled Oublenmach close to her face and stared into his eyes. "Vot? Hyu vants de *Hammer?*" Each question was accompanied by its own tooth-jarring shake. "De Hammer ve *guard?* De Hammer vot rings de *Doom Bell?* De Bell vot iz only rung to announce to de vorld dot de *Heterodyne* iz here?"

Krasimir realized there was a conversational gap he was actually expected to fill. He tried to think what answer would get him killed quickest and chose—"Yes?"

Less than thirty seconds later he found himself sprawled on the early morning street, a gigantic bronze hammer tossed into his lap. Behind him, the doors to Mamma Gkika's slammed shut as the proprietress' resounding laugh echoed from within.

The command center, such as it was, had been established atop one of Mechanicsburg's taller warehouses. Van surveyed the town with a pair of elaborate night vision binoculars. Near his feet, people came and went. To one side, Herr Diamant smacked his hand to his head in disbelief. "But how the devil could you *lose* him?" He asked incredulously. "He's dragging a hammer bigger than he is!"

The hapless man before him shrugged. "Well, the rescue gongs rang and—"

"You did the right thing, Ozker," Van said without lowering the binoculars. "Besides, we *know* where he's going. Now we need people to clear the streets for the firefighters." Everyone nodded glumly. The great brass fire dragons of Mechanicsburg were capable of navigating rubble and ordinary congestion, but they did poorly when actually being shot at.

One of the town's sewer workers appeared at the top of the stairs. "Van! We've got some crazy mole machines coming up in the hospital grounds!"

"Good. That'll give Doctor Lazar's golems something to hit." He turned to another man, who looked exhausted, as he gratefully gulped the mug of coffee that had been thrust into his hands. "Gregor?"

"My boys are doing what they can, but a lot of the automated defenses are still dead." Everyone glanced upwards to the ruined castle that perched on the high pinnacle of stone at the center of town.

Van bit his lip. "Well, keep trying or we'll all be dead."

Within Castle Heterodyne, a doorway blocked with shattered stone quivered. Rocks were then knocked aside by several steel tentacles. Quickly, a hole began to widen and, within minutes, a giant mechanical squid pulled itself through. Agatha and Violetta were piloting it with Gil and Tarvek enmeshed within its coils. Tarvek consulted a map. "Looks like we're almost there."

Gil looked down as the squid reached several tentacles out and began the tricky procedure of hauling itself across a dark chasm. "That's okay," he called up to Agatha, "take your time."

"Oh, relax," the Castle chuckled. "It's not *that* deep."

Agatha smiled. "Castle. You're active here?"

"Yes, Mistress, the dead area is still up ahead."

Agatha looked about. This particular part of the Castle was severely damaged. "If you're active here, why is this area still so messed up? I thought you could self-repair?"

There was silence for a moment. "Well, normally, yes," the Castle admitted. "But I am still . . . weak. I lack the *mechanica vitæ*[74] I require."

---

[74]   There is some argument as to what *mechanica vitæ* actually *is*. At first glance, most engineers assume it is an antiquated term of the Heterodyne's devising for simple electricity. However, one must remember that, when dealing with the Heterodynes and their creations, nothing is ever simple. The Castle has intimated that several of its more arcane mechanisms

Agatha paused. "All of those drained batteries in the power room . . ."

"Yes, exactly. It has been quite the strain to do all I have."

Violetta blinked. "Wait. In that case, isn't all of this just a huge waste of time? The whole *point* of repairing you was so you could help defend the town."

"It was most certainly *not*! I will do what I can for Mechanicsburg, of course, but I am *Castle Heterodyne*. My purpose is the recognition and subsequent protection of the Heterodyne and their family. All of Europa believes I have failed and they will not believe otherwise until you are publicly recognized by me. And you *will* be—even if it is my final act!"

Agatha blew a lock of hair out of her face. "Let's hope it doesn't come to that."

They trundled into a larger room and stopped in astonishment. An enormous machine stood in the center of the room, all huge curved blades and gigantic feet. Clustered around its base was a large group of Castle prisoners, who turned to look at them as they entered. One of them pointed to Agatha. "Oy! It's one of the Heterodyne girls!"

"I hope you don't mind, Mistress, but I have taken the liberty of gathering some potential minions to aid you."

An overly muscled man wearing a disturbing green hood that hid everything but a perpetually manic grin spat on the floor in annoyance. "Just our luck. That's the wrong one."

The massive construct R-79 levered itself to its feet. "Maybe not. That is the one we were supposed to kill."

Instantly, slabs of stone shot from the floor. They encapsulated

---

are powered by the mysterious energies it extracts from the River Dyne. These are the same energies that mutated wild animals, served as a component of the Jägerdraught, and killed almost anyone who dares to drink the water. It was also instrumental in the Lady Heterodyne briefly achieving a state of being that no one *really* wants to call "Godhood," but there you are. From this we are forced to conclude that there *might* be something more in the water than can be understood by conventional science. Since all of this mysterious energy is extracted by the Castle before it is allowed to proceed out into the world, examination is impossible at this time.

the front row of prisoners and began slowly crushing them. Agatha rolled her eyes. "You didn't explain who I am?"

"Trust me, Mistress, they'll be *much* more willing to listen once you properly get their attention."

A terrified eye peered out from a shrinking stone compartment. If its movement was any indication, its owner was nodding frantically. "I am willing to be convinced we were misinformed!" The stones stopped moving and crumbled back into the floor. In quick succession, the remaining captives expressed a heartfelt willingness to display an open mind.

Agatha felt the weight of expectations settle on her and, with a sigh, clambered up until she stood atop the mechanical squid, staring down at the assembled prisoners. "Yes. You have been misinformed. Let me set you straight. *I* am the rightful Heterodyne! Your pink fake fled from my castle in bloody shreds! This is my castle! I am the one who killed it—and I am the one who brought it back! *I* am the one who will restore it to full strength, and *you* are going to help me—or you will feel that strength on the backs of your necks! Do you understand?"

Below, several dozen of the most hardened criminals and minions in the empire stared upwards and mentally revised their place in the pecking order. "Yes, Mistress," they muttered.

In the back, one brave soul spoke up: "But won't Wulfenbach—?"

Gil stepped forward. "I am *Gilgamesh* Wulfenbach! The House of Wulfenbach will honor its word! When this castle is repaired, you will all be free to leave!"

There was a skeptical silence, into which Tarvek stepped up. "And *I'll* make sure he *keeps* that promise," he declared.

The prisoners stared at him blankly. One, who held a large multi-wrench slung comfortably over his shoulder, spoke for them all. "Who the Hell are *you*?"

Gil stared at Tarvek. "What are you *doing*?" he hissed.

Tarvek smiled genially at him. "Go ahead. Tell them who I am."

"You can't be serious."

"It'll impress them," he leaned in and dropped his voice, "and help Agatha." He smiled winningly. "Which is what we both want, yes?"

Gil stared at him sourly. "This," he indicated Tarvek, "is Prince Aaronev Tarvek Sturmvoraus. Heir to the throne of the Storm King." The crowd drew in a collective gasp. Gil continued, "And a loyal *vassal* of the House of Wulfenbach." Tarvek blinked and looked at him. Gil smiled wider and spoke without moving his lips. "Or else."

Any protest Tarvek might have made was cut off as the man with the wrench made a wide gesture towards him, unfortunately with the hand that held the wrench. Tarvek dodged backward, but the tool caught him lightly on the forehead anyway.

The man didn't even notice. He yelled at the assembled crowd. "What is the *matter* with you lot? The Castle says that she's the Heterodyne?" He glanced up into the shadows and flinched. "Fine! But you idiots can't really believe that *these* two clowns are—"

A dark woman dressed in once-pristine white—down to an elegantly worked eye patch—cleared her throat. "Um. Herr Doktor, that *is* Prince Sturmvoraus."

The wrench swung round again. Tarvek ducked. "Really?"

The woman nodded. "Yeah. A guy I did knife work for had a portrait. Said he was gonna be the Storm King."

The man known as Doctor Wrench[75] considered Gil and Tarvek with a fresh eye. "Huh."

She continued. "And Wulfenbach's kid *is* in town. So that really *could* be him."

The crowd looked to Wrench and held its collective breath. He

---

[75] Doktor Thanos Wrenchetkya, (PhD, MAE, MTE, Krakow University of Dangerous and Ungainly Concepts)—known as Doctor Wrench—was a respected spark in his own right, but as a person, lacked any interest in telling other people what to do. This unique skill set made him one of the most prized assistants in Europa. Within Castle Heterodyne, he quickly became one of the community leaders amongst the prisoners, and later became one of the Lady Heterodyne's most valuable assistants.

looked at Agatha now with new respect. "And you've got them both on your string, eh?" After a moment of consideration, he knelt before Agatha and presented the enormous combination wrench to her in supplication. "Well done, my Lady." Silently, the remaining prisoners dropped to one knee and bowed their heads.

"Loyal vassal?" Tarvek growled softly.

Gil nodded. "*And* we're both on Agatha's string."

Tarvek continued to glare for moment, then gave a resigned smile. "Well. That I can live with."

Gil nodded. "You and me both—"

Then they simultaneously added: "—for the moment."

The hospital hoist descended smoothly, despite the rumbling and booming that shook the walls. The lighting had gone out and, seconds later, green emergency lights had flickered on to replace them. Aside from the Baron, only two doctors and Lucrezia had been able to cram aboard, but the others had actually seemed grateful they had an excuse to go bounding back into the collapsing hospital to rescue more patients. Lucrezia just shook her head. Everybody wanted to be a hero. This place was a bad influence.

The chief doctor finished his examination of the Baron and sighed in relief. "I don't know what Sun's been doing to him, but some of these modifications are amazing." He glanced up at the other doctor. "You have to look at this. He's healing faster than anyone I've ever seen!"

Lucrezia was no stranger to pride. It was one of the things that kept her going. But this had an unfamiliar flavor. Watching dear Klaus snore was nostalgic, of course, but it got boring after a while. She had amused herself by tweaking the medical equipment in an effort to get them out of this dreary place as quickly as possible. Now, here was this doctor, whom she knew was as knowledgeable as any on Sun's staff, marveling over it honestly, without trying to flatter her or curry favor or anything. She allowed herself to relish the feeling as the lift continued to move downwards.

The only fly in the ointment was that if she were to speak up and actually let the doctors know that she—not Sun—was responsible for these paltry improvements, their resulting adulation would be gratifying, of course, but it would be pathetically short-lived. She would have to kill them almost immediately.

And really, darling, she thought to herself, just how needy are we?

Wrench had been filling Agatha in on the events of the last few days: " . . . weirder than usual and then it ordered everyone here. "

Agatha nodded. "Well, supposedly the very last break I have to repair is in the next room."

R-79 cleared its throat. "Yeah, okay, we seen that. It is pretty obvious."

"That's a relief. We could use an easy one."

Wrench shook his head as he led her through a doorway. "Um . . . he said 'obvious.' Not 'easy.' "

Agatha stopped dead. "Oh."

"Do you *really* like it," Lucrezia asked the doctor coyly. "That makes me very happy. I want you to know that."

Before Agatha was a large room filled with what she identified as boilers, rows of them, stacked atop one another for several stories. On the far wall she could see an immense crack that ran in a jagged line through the masonry. Where the crack intersected a fat electrical cable, the cable had been sheared apart, and a perpetual display of sparks snapped and crackled around the break. Between Agatha and the cable was a sunken concrete floor, occupied by at least twenty of the autonomous security clanks. They moved slowly back and forth, occasionally colliding softly with each other. At each collision, there would be a brief flurry of metal teeth and claws before the creatures turned aside and ambled off in a new direction.

Easily a dozen of the nearest turned towards the people who entered the room. After a few tense seconds, they swung their heads away in disinterest.

"They're not attacking?" Agatha asked.

Wrench looked at her askance. "You're *complaining*?"

"Well, no, but . . . "

Wrench waved a hand. "No, no, I get it. They're as haywire as the rest of this place, I guess, but they'll still snag you quick enough if you're in the wrong area."

"Ah. And where's that?"

Wrench pointed. "See that dark smear at the bottom of the ladder? Doctor Ott figured that was where it started."

"Did he say why?"

"Nope. All he said was 'AAIEEEE!!' "

Agatha stared at him. "I . . . see."

Wrench shrugged. "Hey, that was *his* idea. If you know how to take those things out from over here, I'm all for it."

Tarvek stepped into the room. "So, what's the—" He saw the security clanks and stopped in his tracks. "AAAAHH! *Those* things again!"

Agatha nodded. "Yes." She glanced up at the machinery around them. "I suspect that this might be their control center." As she continued to examine the room, a calculating look entered her eyes.

Tarvek slumped. "Oh perfect."

Gil stepped in. "So what's the . . . " He paused. "Ah. More of those is it? Could be useful."

Tarvek looked at him. "That's all you have to say?"

Gil shrugged. "I've fought lots of clanks. I know the only other one I saw was already being controlled by Agatha, but they don't look *too* tough."

Tarvek grinned at him. "I will renounce my *crown* if you walk down there right now."

Gil stopped dead. "That bad?"

Tarvek nodded. "Oh yes, but I don't expect you to take the word of a lowly vassal."

Gil patted Tarvek on the shoulder. "I will, actually. So, do you have any *useful* ideas?"

Tarvek considered this. "If we threw in every minion we have, we might take out *one* of them."

Gil waved a hand. "That's a *terrible* plan."

Wrench looked pleasantly surprised. "*Thank* you, sir!"

"I mean, there's got to be close to twenty of them. We don't have *near* enough minions."

Wrench sighed.

Tarvek nodded. "What do you think, Agatha?"

But Agatha was nowhere in sight. "Where did she go?" Gil asked, raising his voice due to the machine roar rising behind them. "She was right here . . . " The three men looked at each other, then scattered, just as the gigantic device they had seen in the anteroom smashed through the wall behind them. It tottered into the room, great metal scythes creaking outwards, and then it began to topple forward. The security clanks on the ground stared upwards, uncomprehending, as it rushed down towards them until, with a great rolling boom, it slammed to the ground, cracking the floor and throwing up dust and loose debris.

Anti-aircraft fire filled the sky, but the projectile screamed along unscathed, striking the last few undamaged walls of the Great Hospital. The detonation was pitched so low that it was hard to hear and was accompanied by a burst of purple lightning. The remaining structure shuddered and began to collapse in an unnatural fashion. It appeared that the brick, steel, and glass had been transformed into some sort of liquid. The building dropped with a rolling roar and began to spread outwards in huge waves. Shrieking soldiers, patients, and staff dashed to avoid the onrushing mass. Those stuck by it were quickly engulfed in flowing stone.

The crowd quickly separated into two groups, each with a different purpose. One group was moving evacuated patients into the surrounding, undamaged buildings, though there were distressingly few of these. The other half was frantically trying to extricate those still trapped inside.

The liquid stone stayed liquid, which made freeing these victims easier, but the rescuers soon realized, to their horror, that the slurry was now draining away through stairways, shafts, and vents. It was making its way down into the hospital's lower levels, where—no doubt—hundreds had sought shelter. A trooper dug at a pool of stone slurry with an entrenching tool and saw his effort was like trying to shovel out a pool of mercury. There was smoke and grit everywhere. Hundreds of Wulfenbach troopers toiled trying to clear the debris.

Occasionally, they would raise their heads and realize they were being aided by the same townspeople they had been fighting less than an hour before. At the moment, it simply wasn't important. People were being found and many of them were even still alive—tucked within pockets of collapsed brick or huddled within sealed rooms. Cheers went up whenever this happened, and the sound gave strength to the remaining workers.

Doctor Sun moved among the survivors, an oasis of calm professionalism that steadied all around him. Another cheer went up, but it was cut off. Sun glanced up and saw a trooper hauling a clank out of a pit. The clank was formed to look like a young woman and its remaining clothing was in tatters. Ah, yes. It was the clank that believed itself to be the Princess Anevka. She had been at the Baron's side, the last time he had looked in. The troopers talking to her seemed to be gesturing oddly, then several of them moved off while the others took up guard positions. He hurriedly finished his instructions and headed towards her. She saw him approaching and drew herself up.

"Herr Doktor Sun." She indicated the tunnel from which she had emerged, and which the troopers were now guarding. "We must establish some sort of perimeter to keep people back. I'm afraid there is some sort of gas leak. I don't know what it is, but I'm afraid it is very toxic." She drew herself up and her voice seemed to ring out. "I am afraid that Baron Wulfenbach is dead. Along with the brave doctors who stayed by his side."

Sun closed his eyes and swore. The stupid machine had blared out the news like a town crier. Everyone within three hundred meters must have heard it, and there would be no way to contain the information. He glanced towards the looming castle. Young Gilgamesh's task would be even harder now. He glared at the clank. The foolish thing meant well, and guarding the shaft *was* the correct thing to do, but he had quite enough of helpful clanks.

He flagged down an orderly. "Find an engineer," he ordered. "I want that clank deactivated and off site. Then put together a team with breathing apparatus. They are to go down and retrieve the bodies of the Baron and anyone else present." The man nodded and took off. Sun considered the matter closed and turned his mind to trying to deal with the news that was even now sweeping through the air: *the Baron was dead.*

Word spread through the people present and continued unchecked faster than one would have thought possible. It was relayed in tones of shock, of amazement, of joy and horror. Via radio and hastily scribbled message. By official communiqués and by voices screaming it from the top of shattered buildings. It roared through Mechanicsburg and then began to spread through the forces of the empire like the waves in a pond caused by a stone dropped from three kilometers high.

Many disbelieved it. Many wanted to believe it. Many more did not, but *everyone* had an opinion about it. The news continued to spread throughout the known world.

CHAPTER 6

Life is nothing but a constant series of choices. What to eat, where to go, with whom to mate? This ability to choose is a universal constant that defines life and differentiates it from inert matter. What further separates humanity from base Animalia is this: the choices available to us can increase exponentially, and can even begin to include abstract, counterintuitive choices that would never even occur to any other animal, *exempli gratia*: Should I even continue to live at all?

—The introduction to *How to Buy Comfortable Shoes*
(Mechanicsburg Cobblers Association)

(Note: In 1792, because of falling sales, the Mechanicsburg Cobblers Association commissioned the production of a give-away pamphlet entitled *How to Buy Comfortable Shoes*. In a move that, in retrospect, seems obviously flawed, they thought to save money by hiring an out-of-work philosopher named Rabelais Van Zowkensteen to write it. The resulting six-hundred-page "pamphlet" is rightly regarded as *the* definitive work on human cognitive behavior *vis-à-vis* choice versus predeterminism.

Numerous accolades and awards followed, none of which Van Zowkensteen was able to appreciate as he was kicked to death by the officers of the Mechanicsburg Cobblers Association, who had seen their organization bankrupted by an excessive printer's bill.

The Heterodyne of the time, Yog Heterodyne, was so impressed by the efficacy of the boots used in Van

Zowkensteen's execution (Model # 4711 All Leather Wingtip Stompers), he ordered that all Heterodyne forces be equipped with the same from then on.

This order completely revitalized the Mechanicsburg shoe and boot industry. As a result, a commemorative statue of Van Zowkensteen was commissioned by the now-grateful association. This stands today in the Square of the Four Ironies (of which he is the second).

This sort of thing happens a lot in Mechanicsburg, and a wise traveler should take pains to see that it does not happen to them.)
—An excerpt from "Chapter 5: Things Happen Here: How to Prepare Oneself For the Oddities of Mechanicsburg," *Pontexeter's Guide to Transylvania, Moldavia, Wallachia, & Croatia*, 10th Edition

ᴄᴖᴖᴄᴖ

Within Castle Heterodyne, things had stopped falling. The giant machine and its scythes had come to a stop. A door near the top of the device swung open, and Agatha popped out, grinning. "Ta—daah!" she gestured with a showman's flourish. Gil and Tarvek, crawling out from beneath some strategically placed steel slabs, saw the machine had fallen, blades extended, so that the top of the longest would serve as a bridge directly to the damaged cable. "There we go! Now we can travel *above* the security clanks!"

As the dust settled, Gil saw several of the security clanks, undamaged, continuing their endless shuffling paths across the floor, the steel arc curving gracefully over their heads.

"But . . . " He took a deep breath. "They could still attack us. If you're going to haul that huge thing in here, why not just smash them?"

Agatha shook her head. "Oh no. The Castle wouldn't like it if I broke them."

"Aw, come on. The Castle isn't even active in here. We won't tell." Gil looked to Tarvek for assistance.

"Oh yes," Tarvek continued sincerely. "They were totally smashed up when we found them."

Agatha put her hands on her hips. "Excuse me? Those are *my* fun-sized mobile agony and death dispensers. They're works of art! You can break your own stuff, thank you very much." Gil and Tarvek both opened their mouths to protest, but Agatha cut them off. "You just head over there. I'll be there in a minute."

Violetta took the lead, dancing along the length of the long blade. "Come on!" She laughed. "We're almost done!" She executed a series of hand flips. "Look at this! It's perfect! An *elephant* could waltz down this thing." Violetta smirked, "And Tarvek? This time, don't jump on one, okay?"

The two men looked at each other, sighed, hoisted up their satchels of tools, and looked at the top of the blade. It was flat and even, slightly curved, and wide enough that, had it spanned, say, a lovely chattering brook in a beautiful forest somewhere, it would have been no trouble to cross. Using it to cross over a pit of mechanical tiger clanks, on the other hand . . .

They eyed each other dubiously, then Tarvek offered Gil his arm. Gil nodded. They hooked arms and stepped out together. Instantly the heads of the clanks below snapped to attention, tracking their progress and grinding their metal teeth in an unnerving susurrus.

"You *jumped* on one?" Gil considered this. "I'll bet *that* went well."

Tarvek didn't bother to shrug. "It seemed like a good idea at the time."

"Because he was stupid," Violetta sang out from before them. She paused and spun about on one toe. "Hey, *I've* got an idea! Maybe you should each jump in! I'll bet they'll lock up trying to decide who to shred first!"

She twirled back and froze. When the huge machine had fallen, the security clanks had been scattered, and one had been thrown atop the wide maintenance platform that ran halfway across the room. The makeshift bridge passed nearby, close enough the tiger clank was now daintily stepping onto the top of the blade, glowing eyes fixed on Violetta "I'd start with this one," she whispered, "because *I'm* not riding it."

"Aunt Terella's garmhounds!" Tarvek snapped.

Violetta blinked. "Ah!" She caught the rail of the platform in both hands. With an acrobatic kick, she straightened into a handstand and stiffened into immobility. The clank padded towards her.

"Okay, we can do this!" Violetta growled through clenched teeth. "There's only the one up here, and it can't see me as long as I hold still."

"Right. Now *we'll* lure it past you." Tarvek called out, waving his arms, "Yoo hoo! Here, kitty kitty!" The clank had paused briefly near Violetta, who was having trouble keeping her arms from trembling. "Just hurry up!" she muttered as the clank gave an inquiring growl and continued towards the two men.

"Why are we doing this exactly?" Gil asked as he tried to compensate for Tarvek's gyrations.

"We're using our wits. Don't try to take notes, just work with us."

As the clank moved past her, Violetta took a shallow breath. "Okay, let it get a little closer, then I'll lure it off of this thing. Somehow . . ." She looked around. There was nothing she could use to lure the clank anywhere. They were at least five meters above the ground, which was a seething mass of other tiger clanks. The only other thing she could see that could be of any conceivable use was a nearby cage-like lantern that hung at the end of a rusty chain.

"Violetta, it's getting close." A quick glance showed the clank was less than two meters from the now-frozen pair. A jolt of terror went through Violetta as she noticed a draft of air was gently ruffling both men's hair.

Tarvek's face was set in a wide, sickly grin. "Eeoletta?" He called without moving his mouth. "Oo ken attract its attention anytime now."

Violetta gazed out over the empty room and swallowed. "Okay, okay! I'm working up to it!" With that, she pulled a knife from her belt and tossed it at the clank. It smacked into the back of its head with a solid *clunk* and dropped to the ground. Instantly, the great machine whirled in place and roared directly towards her, screaming in triumph. With a shriek of her own, Violetta launched herself into open space, the clank behind her, claws extended and jaws agape. Violetta sailed through the air and smashed into the light fixture, which rocked wildly as she scrambled to hang on. With a startled "Graah?" The great security clank continued downwards and crashed into a stone pillar.

"Ha *ha!*" Violetta screamed down at the clank as it pulled itself back to its feet. "Take that, you giant tin toy!" She glanced back at Tarvek. "I can't believe this stupid plan actually *worked.*"

"Look out!" Gil shouted, as a fusillade of bullets screamed through the air. They hit the chain holding Violetta's perch aloft. The rusty metal gave way, dropping the lantern into the pit of clanks below. Violetta leapt just in time, barely catching hold of a railing that overlooked the floor.

"Those were shots," Tarvek said, looking about wildly. "Where did they come from?"

Gil stared up at the great engine. "Agatha?"

Near the control cupola stood Professor Tiktoffen, holding Agatha slumped in his arms. "She's here," he cried. "The Lady Heterodyne is hurt! Hurry!"

Gil and Tarvek stared. "Tiktoffen!" Tarvek called out. "Where have you been? We'll be right there."

Gil stopped him. "No. Wait. Agatha looks . . . odd."

It was true, Tarvek thought. Agatha lay in Tiktoffen's arms in a very peculiar fashion. It looked . . . wrong. Drugged? Her eyes fluttered open and she muttered something unintelligible. Then, suddenly, her eyes went wide as she lashed back with one foot, smashing it down onto Professor Tiktoffen's shin. He shrieked, and dropped the ends of—

"A garrote!" Tarvek shouted in surprise.

In the few seconds she had, Agatha tore the loop of wire from around her neck and yelled "RUN!" She then vaulted down the side of the great machine, heading for the gap in the wall.

"*Damn* it," Tiktoffen swore. He straightened up and yelled, "Stop! I *want* you alive, but I don't *need* you alive!" Unsurprisingly, this appeal did not check Agatha's progress. She slipped past the shattered wall and vanished. Tiktoffen threw up his hands. "Fine. So much for tricks and foolishness. I'll catch the girl—" From behind an engine casing, Captain Vole[76] and a pair of prisoners, armed with small Wulfenbach-issue machine cannons, appeared. "—You kill those fools."

Vole grinned. "Yez, master!"

By this time Gil and Tarvek had reached the base of the great claw. Gil stopped in astonishment. "Vole? What are you doing here?"

With a laugh, Vole raised the gun and fired off a burst. Gil was yanked behind a cowling by Tarvek, who hissed, "Have you no survival instincts at all?"

"But how did he even get in here? He's supposed to be working for my father!"

"Iz true!" Vole cried gleefully as he began to leap downwards towards them. "Ov cauze, de Kestle ain't gun keep a *Jäger* out! Ve iz praktikally *family*, hey?" He slammed to the ground and carefully adjusted his hat. "Und yez, hy did vork for de Baron, yah, iz de truth!

---

[76]   Captain Vole was once a Jägermonster, but renounced the Jägertroth or the Jägermonsters renounced him. Either way, he now holds loyal Jägermonsters in utter contempt.

But now, de Baron is dead!" Both Gil and Tarvek were stunned. Vole continued. "De Great Hozpital haz been destroyed. Lots uv pipple killed. Herr Doktor Sun haz seen all de survivors . . . " He shrugged. "Sorry, leedle Prinz, but hyu poppa iz *gone*." Vole now grinned. "Chust like his wretched nicey-play empire." Vole sighed happily and turned to his two companions who had just joined him. "Vell," he conceded, "*Almost* gone. But ve gun fix dot *right now*. Come on, boyz, iz a goot day for *regicide*!"

Agatha dashed up a stairway and around a corner to a long gallery. Windows opened along one side, looking out at the smoke and fire of the battle raging outside. If she could lure Tiktoffen to a place where the Castle was active . . .

She heard him pounding up the stairway after her. She came to a closed door and frantically began trying to pull it open. Professor Tiktoffen saw her and nodded in satisfaction. A burst of gunfire from behind them caused him to ruefully shake his head. "Tsk. Captain Vole is a man of simple tastes. Still, he *is* useful."

Agatha answered him angrily as the door began to move on groaning hinges. "Useful *how*? What are you *doing*? I was almost done!"

"Indeed you were," the professor said admiringly. "As for me, why, I am filling a vacuum! Sparks! Hard to believe it but, really, they have no imagination. Every fool with a minion and an oversized farm animal thinks they can replace Klaus." He patted his chest. "I, on the other hand, simply want to replace the *Heterodyne*." He threw his hands out. "A town full of minions! This magnificent castle—I must thank you for the repairs, by the way—all it needs is a master to get everything rolling again. And that will be *me*!"

Agatha snorted. "Ridiculous. Even if I wasn't here—which I am— the Baron would never allow it!"

"Of course he would have! I already worked for him! I worked for *all* of them! Wulfenbach, the Order, the Silent Librarians, Albia's Intelligence, the Downunders, Sons of Franklin, the Master of Paris, All of the Vaticans—hard to keep them all straight, sometimes! But I—*I* was *everyone's* inside man!"

Agatha, meanwhile, had gotten the door open far enough that she could begin to squeeze through. Tiktoffen casually fished a small, weighty tool from a coat pocket and threw it, striking Agatha directly in the back of the head, bringing her to her knees. "But I never lost sight of the fact that I was always working for *myself!*"

Agatha shook her head desperately attempting to clear it and realized she was sprawled over a corpse. With a gasp, she rolled aside smack into another body. She tried to get to her knees while looking around wildly. She saw most of the prisoners who had been sentenced to the Castle. They had been shot, often at close range. Against a wall stood two dead-eyed men who tracked her movements with their rifles, even as Tiktoffen strolled into the room. "Now it's all in danger of falling apart," he continued blithely while shaking his head. "A real *Heterodyne*, for pity's sake." He paused and gave a small, self-deprecating smile. "Ah, but I imagine you get that a lot."

He stepped to the center of the room, put his hands on his hips, and slowly swiveled about to take in the full extent of the slaughter. There were easily three dozen bodies strewn about in slowly expanding pools of blood. He nodded in satisfaction. "Well, perhaps it's actually just all coming together. It's how you look at it, I suppose."

Agatha stared at him. "But . . . " She looked about at the dead people around her. "But they were *with* you. Why are you killing the other prisoners?"

Tiktoffen snorted. "Because I *knew* them. Why do you think they were in here to begin with?" His boot nudged a genial-looking man with a curly mustache. "Franz here liked turning people into beetles. Zonia believed orphan blood had medicinal properties. Krag insisted on putting his feet on my bed. Trust me, I'm doing the world at large a favor. With the Castle repaired they would have been released back into society."

"And you think you're *better*?"

Tiktoffen rolled his eyes. "And here I thought you were a smart girl."

"Smarter than *you*," she shot back. "Smart enough to know where I am. This is one of the sections I've already fixed."

The men by the wall tensed and shot a worried look at Tiktoffen. He waved them down and merely appeared interested.

"Castle!" Agatha called, "Are you there?"

"Yes, Mistress."

Agatha hesitated. There was *something* about the Castle's voice. "Catch these insects for me!"

Nothing happened.

"I-I am sorry, Mistress," the Castle whispered. "I . . . I *cannot*!"

Tiktoffen released the breath he'd been holding and smiled. "Oh. Didn't I *mention* that?" He spun, spreading his hands to encompass the entire structure. "I *love* this place!" he shouted exuberantly. "Old Faustus[77] created something *extraordinary*! Nothing less than a new form of *life*! Beautiful! I read everything I could before I came here, but it was all rubbish and hysteria. I was still unprepared for the reality. The Castle was broken. Insane. Like everything else in this valley, it needed a master. *Me*!

"Repairing it, learning how it worked, how it thought . . . it was *exhilarating*! But it was also dangerous! Like a feral child with a doomsday device. I worked on the Lion, but I doubt I would have ever used it. You saw more clearly than I did there, I'll give you that.

---

[77] Faustus Heterodyne was one of the most brilliant of the old Heterodynes, but not in a good way. He was the one who learned how to leach the poisonous energies from the Dyne and was the one who actually created the intelligence that animated Castle Heterodyne. He based its mind upon his own, naturally, which explains quite a bit about the Castle's predilections and temperament.

A brilliant solution! I'll also freely admit that mine was nowhere near as *elegant*."

He rolled up his righthand sleeve, and Agatha saw a device had actually been grafted into his arm. The place where it met his flesh was red and tender-looking. Lights blinked slowly, and the needle on a small dial flicked even as Agatha watched. Tiktoffen chuckled, "No, *I* simply learned to *tame* the poor creature." He strutted over and bowed slightly. "So I must beg your pardon, Lady Heterodyne, but your house belongs to *me* now."

Agatha had palmed a spanner and used it now to backhand Tiktoffen across the face. "Belongs to you?" She snarled, "You? You talk too much and you got too close!"

Tiktoffen glared at her, pure hate in his eyes. "How dare you, you ungrateful trollop! I was *going* to let you live!" He called out to the two men, "KILL HER!" Instantly the two rifles swung up, but never finished their arcs. Holes opened beneath them both and they dropped screaming into the darkness.

Agatha smiled a smile her ancestors would have been proud of. "Just as I thought."

"Castle!" A shaken Tiktoffen demanded. "I *order* you—"

The Castle cut him off. "Really, Professor. I may not be able to hurt *you*, but no one else may hurt my Heterodyne."

Agatha strode towards him, smacking the wrench into the palm of her hand. Her voice was taking on an odd, unsettling tone. "Well, well. It appears that I can hurt *you* without any consequences at all. How terribly unfair! Try to steal my beautiful castle, will you?"

"Steal? *Me?*" Tiktoffen's hand rippled and a homemade knife appeared there. "You arrogant upstart. Let us find out who can hurt whom." He came in low and fast. There was no initial testing of Agatha's abilities, it was obvious Tiktoffen wanted this fight over and done with as quickly as possible. Agatha remembered Zeetha's lessons and pivoted, allowing him to slip past, while blocking a last-second swipe with her wrench.

"Give up, girl," Tiktoffen snarled. "It is not too late. You couldn't manage this without me, anyway!"

Agatha stayed on the balls of her feet and watched the arm holding the knife. "By 'this,' I assume you mean 'kill people and bluster.' I'll cope without your experience."

"No." Suddenly the knife was in Tiktoffen's *other* hand slicing a shallow cut into Agatha's leg. "I mean juggle the thousand enemies who will come to try and take this place now that the Baron is dead!"

This declaration brought Agatha up short. "*Dead!*" Tiktoffen leapt in and sliced one of the straps of her leather apron, leaving a light scratch under her collarbone.

In a fury, Agatha lashed out with the wrench, delivering several well-placed blows. "I cannot believe I fell for such a cheap bluff!"

Tiktoffen staggered back, wiping blood from his nose. "It's no bluff," he cried. "The Baron died when the Great Hospital collapsed! The empire will go up in flames!" He again darted in. Faster than the eye could follow, he jabbed the back of Agatha's hand, sending her wrench spinning away.

He grinned in triumph. "And *I* will be the master of the strongest castle in the most impregnable town in all Europa! Blissfully unencumbered, I might add, with a chit of a girl *stupid* enough to bring a spanner to a *knife* fight!"

Agatha pulled back and smiled nastily. "It's harder to *break* things with a knife."

Tiktoffen looked at her blankly, then stared at the device in his arm, now shattered and giving off small trails of smoke. With a last small patter of flashes, its sensors went dark. "AARGH! What have you done? What have you *done?*"

"I've freed my castle," Agatha replied. "It's off your leash, now."

"You think it's that simple?" Tiktoffen snarled as he cradled his arm. "You think you've won? The Heterodyne Boys *hated* this place! Your family *abandoned* it! The Castle is mine now! It *wants* to be mine! It's been working with me for years!" He was screaming up towards the ceiling. "Castle! Do you hear me? I came here *willingly*! I've spent *years* repairing you! Helping you! You *must* choose me! You know I'm your ally! I'm the one who *loves* you!"

There was a terrible silence, then the Castle spoke slowly. "And I am fond of you, Professor. You were a much-needed point of sanity when that was something I myself could not supply. And you never gave up."

A marble column two meters in diameter and easily five meters tall dropped from the shadows of the ceiling and crushed the professor flat. "Which is why I shall end this quickly."

The Castle continued to speak, although its audience was no longer listening. "But, you did not repair me. I don't believe you ever could have. I am not complete without a Heterodyne."

Agatha coughed, choking on the cloud of dust that had been thrown into the air. She wondered if she were imagining the slight tinge of sadness in the Castle's voice. "Thank you," she said. "I . . . was a little worried you might not choose me, after all."

"Nonsense, my Lady. The professor was amusing, but I have no need of clever outsiders who, as you say, put me on a leash." The Castle's voice now carried oceans of disdain.

Agatha tapped her chin thoughtfully. "Glad to hear it. Now let's take a look at this device of his."

"What?" The Castle sounded shocked. "Oh, you don't want that. I'm sure it's totally destroyed." A few more stone blocks hammered into the top of the pillar.

"I'll be the judge of that," Agatha said, tapping her foot.

"But why? Here we are getting along so well."

"Well, A: Because I want to see how it works so I can defend you against anything similar. And B: While I am becoming weirdly fond of you, I still don't actually *trust* you."

"Hmph. Clever girl. You *will* be a fun one. But no matter the depths of his megalomania, the professor was not family. You most certainly are. Therefore I would not crush *you*."

"That leaves a lot of leeway."

"Oh, now you're just being suspicious."

"*You're* the one who told me that exact wording is important."

"Indeed I did. But switching gears, if I may . . . In my current state of repair I cannot see the details, nevertheless I must report that the professor was correct: the Great Hospital *has* been destroyed."

"What? How?"

"I do not know. There were multiple attackers. It is quite likely that the Baron truly *is* dead. A pity. He was a loyal ally of the family. Ah well, it comes to all of you eventually, even the devious ones."

"Oh." Realization hit Agatha all of a sudden. "Then, Gil . . . "

"Ah. Unfortunately, you probably won't need to worry about him for much longer. From what I can hear, Vole is intent on killing him—and they are currently out of my reach. I am sorry, my Lady. I would do something if I could." Without a word, Agatha turned and dashed back the way she had come.

The Castle's voice followed her as she ran: "Now, don't cry," it sounded jovial. "When this is all over, I shall find you some lovely *new* consorts. *Lots* of them!"

Agatha ran faster. "No!"

"Nonsense, my Lady. You still have a spare—" It paused. "Oh. Perhaps not. It sounds like Vole intends to kill both of them. Ah, well. Back to square one."

"First of all," Agatha shouted as she ran, "they are not replaceable!"

"Ah. Of course not, my Lady," the Castle purred.

"Second of all, I sincerely doubt that thug can actually beat them, unless he sneaks up on them somehow."

"Yet, you drop everything and rush to their rescue?"

"I still have work to do back there, remember? Anyway, if I let all that other stuff distract me, what would happen to *you*? Have you thought about *that*? Do you really want Mechanicsburg to fall because I was too boy crazy to think about anything useful?"

"Hmm." the Castle pondered this. "True, once or twice, some of the more *romantically minded* of the family *have* caused problems . . .

and I still have structural damage from the great Saint Valentine's Day Riot, but that was such fun . . . even so, in your hurry to get back to work, you have completely forgotten Professor Tiktoffen's nasty little device."

Agatha blinked. "Ah. Oh. Yes . . . can you keep it somewhere safe for now?"

"Well, it is under a large, heavy pillar, so, yes."

"Good. Just remember that I want it back later. No dumping it into a furnace or something."

"Perish the thought," the Castle said primly. "And I am *so* glad that you are not one to let romantic concerns distract you—"

"Of course not." Agatha answered, matching its tone. "That would just be silly."

"—because more enemies have arrived. The battle is about to begin in earnest."

A dozen tiger clanks padded along, staring up at the trio that walked along the top of the great blade. Vole, in the lead, moved with much greater surety than the two men who followed him. They shuffled their feet, determinedly not looking down at the metal-fanged faces peering up at them.

Vole waved them forward impatiently. "Hokay, dis gun be simple-peezy, yez? No fancy schtuff, just *shoot* dem, hokay?"

The two men grunted assent just as Gil and Tarvek jumped out from behind a furnace, threw a pair of hammers, and darted back under cover. Each hammer found its target and, with matching shrieks, the men following Vole toppled off the blade and vanished into a red-tinged flurry of metal below.

"Idiot! You missed Vole!"

"So did you!"

"Quick! Throw something else!"

Two more tools shot out. One slammed into the side of Vole's head, the other knocked off his tall, white hat. Vole watched it fall out of sight, then turned to face them. His face was an inhuman mask of rage. "Hyu die now," he proclaimed.

"You call that *throwing*?"

"Hey, at least *I* got his *hat*."

Vole lunged around the corner of the furnace, only to discover no one there. "Schtupid brats," he growled. "Hyu iz already dead. Hyu just needs to hold schtill so hy ken finish de job. Hyu schtupid empire iz over. Vunce hyu iz dead, de Pax Transylvania will fail! Europa vill crumble to her knees!"

From atop a storage tank, Gil shouted down at him, "And you *want* that?"

Vole answered with a burst of gunfire. "Ov cawze," he roared, "Death and destruction *efferyvere*! Keel or be keeled! De rule ov de most vicious! Eet vill be glorious! De Jägers vill vunce again be de *schtuff of nightmares!*"

From somewhere behind him, Gil yelled again, "I thought you weren't a Jäger anymore. You said so yourself!"

Vole laughed. "Dose oldt fools who served hyu poppa—dey vos an *embarrassment* to de very name. Dey vill die! Professor Teektoffen, he sez dot hy vill lead a *new* pack of Jägers! Strong, *ruthless* Jägers! Harvested from de strongest ov dose who come to serve de new masters ov Mechanicsburg! Ve vill burn Europa to de ground und gnaw her bonz!"

Gil glanced at Tarvek. "This guy's nuts."

"You *think*?" Tarvek shrugged. "It's why the Jägers disowned him. He tried to kill Bill and Barry. Said they were too *weak* to be Heterodynes." Tarvek sighed. "The idiots forgave him, of course."

Gil frowned. "I could take him if it wasn't for that gun."

Tarvek perked up. "Really? Allow me!"

Seconds later, Tarvek appeared, capering atop a bank of exhaust valves. "Give it up, you elephantine kitchen goblin! Even when the Pax Transylvania falls, *I* will maintain the peace as the Storm King!"

Vole spun about, screaming. "No hyu von't! Hyu gonna die!" He swept up the broom in his hands . . . and stared at it in astonishment. "Vot der dumboozle?" he gasped.

From a catwalk, Violetta popped up, cradling Vole's rifle. "You royal fool," she screamed at Tarvek. "What are you *doing*? You are not my responsibility anymore! Don't just jump in and expect me to save your blue-blooded butt!"

"Like you could resist such a beautiful opportunity to show off," Tarvek smirked. "Besides, I knew—"

The broom, thrown with the force of a javelin, cracked into his jaw, sending Tarvek to the ground.

"SHODDOP!" Vole screamed. "Hyu annoyink schmot guy! Hy vos gonna keel hyu anyvay, bot now Hy iz gonna keel hyu *dead!*"

"No." A voice spoke from behind Vole, who spun in time to receive a solid smack to the jaw from Gilgamesh, "*You* shut up!"

The ex-Jäger fell to his knees. Gil wearily cracked his knuckles. "Do we really have to do this again, Captain?" Gil sighed. "I would have thought that thrashing you once would have been more than enough."

Vole nodded reasonably. "Hokay—funny ting about dot." Faster than the eye could see, he lashed out, catching Gil squarely in the gut, sending him flying into a bank of meters. At the same time, he snatched up a bit of shattered pipe and fired it over his shoulder, catching Violetta squarely on the forehead. She dropped from sight. He then strolled over and addressed the gasping man. "*Dis* time, hy dun gots to vorry about hyu poppa." With the ease of long practice, his boot snapped out and smashed into Gil's jaw. "*Dis* time, hy dun haff to vorry about schtupid leedle details like keepink hyu *alive!*"

He grabbed Gil and slammed him back into the wall of instruments so that Gil was looking straight into his inhuman eyes. "Und *dis* time," he hissed, "hyu *knocked my hat off.* So *dis* time—"

—SLAM—

"*Hy* iz gunna vin, und hy iz gunna do it by keelink hyu—"

—SLAM—

"Into leetle bits!"

—SLAM—

Vole looked into Gil's dazed face and smiled. "Iz dot *different* euff for hyu, brat? Hy mean, hy dun vant it to be *borink*, yah?"

"Excuse me . . ." Tarvek, a crowbar slung over one shoulder, waved a hand. Vole and Gil stared at him.

"So, Wulfenbach—just checking—is this going to be some kind of macho exercise where you insist on battling a potentially superior opponent alone in some kind of misguided attempt to 'prove' your intrinsic worth?"

Gil frantically shook his head. "No," he gasped, "I'm only that stupid in front of Agatha."

"Drat."

Further conversation was cut off by Vole using Gil as a flail to smash Tarvek across the face. The prince regained awareness as Vole, his hand around his throat, slammed him up against the wall next to Gil. Vole was grinning and shaking his head. "Ho, ho," he chuckled, "vot a *joke!*" He rapped Tarvek against the wall. "*Hyu* vos gonna be de *Storm King?* And *hyu*—" It was now Gil's turn to be slammed. "Hyu poppa seriously thought *hyu* vos vorthy ov hiz empire?"

He shook his head in disgust. "Hyu haz been hangink around vit dose *losers* dot allowed demselves to be *domesticated* by hyu poppa. Hyu haz never ektually fought a Jäger for real, vich iz vhy neider vun ov hyu vos taking me seriously, vich is *insultink!* Important lesson, cheeldren, when hyu iz supozzed to *fight*—" He slammed their heads together. "—*FIGHT!* Dun *play* at fightink while stendink around beink all schmartarse."

He started to slam their heads together again, but stopped halfway to their pates, a look of disgust on his face. "Hyu iz a disgrace. Dere ain't even any spawt in killink hyu pampered clowns." He sighed. "But hit gots to be done. Thenk goodness neither ov hyu losers gots a hat." He considered this and smiled. "Ennyvay, it vill be fun to tell dot Heterodyne sow all about how hyu died, yah?"

He tightened his grip around their throats until their eyes bulged slightly. He then leaned in and lowered his voice conspiratorially. "Und hey, dun feel *too* bad. Hy tink de two ov hyu vould haff been dem dangerous hiffen you'd had a chence to grow op a leedle." He squeezed—

—and howled as a bullet tore through his chest. His hands spasmed, Gil and Tarvek dropped and bonelessly slid off the ledge to the ground below. All around them, the security clanks paused in their endless prowling and stared at their supine bodies.

Violetta frowned. "Oh come *on*, that was a sweet shot."

Her irritation was justified. Vole, obviously not dead, had dodged behind a conduit. "Dot *voz* a nize shot, sveethot," he called out gaily. "Bot dey iz schtill gun be dead guyz!" Once out of Violetta's sight, he touched the wound on his chest and grimaced. Then he leaned over the edge and called out, "Hoy, heroes! Hy gots a fun idea! Hif *vun* ov hyu jumps up now for der kittehs, de odder might be able to get avay in time to vatch me keel hyu gurrrl friend!"

Tarvek and Gil, surrounded by a ring of curious clanks, stared at each other. At the exact same moment they exploded into action, both screaming: "*Don't screw this up!*"

The clanks lunged. Gil and Tarvek were only saved because the giant clanks got in each other's way. The two found themselves facing each other as they clambered atop the same clank.

"You know," Tarvek shouted, "perhaps we should have *discussed* this!"

"Too late, now!" This appeared to be the case. Steel claws pulled them down. Fang-lined jaws opened all around them—

"GRRAAAARGH!!" A tearing metallic shriek filled the room and the tiger clanks froze. After the briefest of pauses, the clanks retreated, leaving Gil and Tarvek in the middle of a slowly growing circle of clear floor. Before them stood Krosp, arms behind his back, a smug grin on his bewhiskered face. "Looks like I arrived just in time."

Gil blinked. "Krosp! You mean . . . you—?"

"Hurr hurr hurr . . . " The security clanks parted and a larger version strolled forward. "You are very amusing, little emperor," it growled.

"Give me the moment," Krosp snarled, tail lashing.

Theo and Professor Mittelmind stood at the clank's shoulders. Theo waved at Gil. "We brought Von Pinn—" he hastily corrected himself. "Madame Otilia! We fixed her up just like your notes said! She's going to be just fine!"

Mittelmind rubbed his hands together. "Lucky for you, we've made *improvements*!" He indicated the docile ring of clanks around them. "I was able to analyze the command circuits and, as a result, all of these wretched things will now obey her!"

Tarvek and Gil staggered to their feet. "Good job," they chorused.

At that moment, a great explosion was heard in the distance. Several seconds later, the entire castle shuddered like an angry lizard in aspic.

"What was *that*?" Sleipnir cried.

"Our time's run out," Tarvek replied. "The Castle is under direct attack!"

Theo showed an assured grin. "If we can signal Castle Wulfenbach—" He was interrupted by the loud crack of a gun, and a spurt of blood from his shoulder.

Everyone took cover behind the great clanks. Mezzasalma dragged Theo, clutching his shattered shoulder. On the walkway above, a fierce battle was taking place. Vole had managed to catch Violetta and wrest the gun out of her hands.

Now, one might think this would be a short fight but, in fact, Violetta was scrambling over Vole like a monkey on a tree, jabbing him everywhere with an apparently endless supply of small daggers that she would have *sworn* were poisoned—but so far, they were having no effect.

For his part, Vole had spent several fruitless minutes trying to dislodge her, even slamming himself back into the rough, instrument-covered walls, all to no avail. Eventually he had sighed in exasperation and concentrated on the important task of killing people. This was proving equally difficult, as Violetta kept slapping the gun and spoiling his aim.

"Knives und sand!" He snarled. "Betveen hyu und de dam kestle rattlink, how iz a guy supposed to shoot somevun?"

"Give that back, you thief!" Violetta returned. "I stole that gun off you fair and square!"

"Ho! Grow op, sveethot! Hyu iz just mad 'cause hy stole it back!" Violetta yanked his hair and stuck another knife into his scalp. Vole roared. "Finders keepers, losers bleeders!" He howled. Vole wasn't often impressed by "normal pipple," but with every knife thrust, Violetta was dangerously close to earning his respect.

Onto this display of Grand Guignol[78] themed acrobatics burst Agatha. When she saw the scene before her, she stopped dead. "Seriously? You guys haven't gotten rid of *him* yet?"

Violetta looked offended. "Hey! Be fair—this guy is pretty tough."

When he saw Agatha, Vole's face twisted from petulance into a mask of rage. "*Hyu*? So hyu heff keeled Professor Teektoffen, den, hey?" He sighed. "Vy iz hy not sooprized?" He raised his gun and pointed it towards Agatha, allowed Violetta to get a firm grip on it, then casually flung it—and her—away.

He grinned reproachfully. "Diz iz just vunna doze days. Hy svear, sumtimes, if hyu vants an atrocity dun right, hyu gots to do it hyuself. But I come in here to keel sparks, und dots vot hy iz gonna do!" He lunged towards Agatha, but was unprepared for the impact of Gil landing on his back.

---

[78] Grand Guignol is a form of decadent "theatre" where the performers pretend to maim, torture, and messily kill each other for the edification of a jaded public. It flourished briefly in Paris, where it was officially frowned upon, but was not *actually* illegal because it *did* fall under the heading of "Art." Impresarios kept trying to outdo each other with more and more horrifying spectacles, until Professor Charnel and His Demented Death Clanks booked Le Théâtre du Grand-Guignol for one night. He promised *A Show to End All Shows* and, in this, he proved himself amazingly prophetic. He had neglected to explain to the aforementioned death clanks that it was, in fact, merely a show.

Vole rolled his eyes and flexed his claws. "Hyu schtupid brat. Hyu dun' learn too goot, do—"

Four sledgehammer blows hit various parts of his face within seconds. Vole staggered and just had time to realize that the thing he felt pressing into his throat was the barrel of the gun, and that the terrifying face centimeters from his own was Gil's, when he heard the sound of the trigger snapping home. Nothing happened. Twice more Gil pulled the trigger and then stared at the gun in disgust. "So it's one of *those* days," he growled.

Vole stared at him. "Hokay," he admitted weakly. "Hy tink dot maybe hyu learns pretty dem goot, ecktually."

Another far-off explosion caused the building to roll in place. Small stones rattled down from the ceiling. This made Vole shake off his bemusement and grin. "Ho-ho! Sounds like Count Nikolaba's Thunder Hogs haff arrived! It von't be lonk now! All ov hyu iz gonna die! Starting vit hyu, brat!"

Gil nodded once and then snapped Vole's face to one side with the force of his sudden punch. "Okay, change of plan." Even in Vole's battered state, he could hear Gil's voice had entered registers that were usually only reached by the most crazed sparks. This was worrying, as Vole, an experienced reader of sparks, had the definite impression the young Wulfenbach was just warming up. An uppercut to his jaw derailed this train of thought while splintering several of his favorite teeth.

Gil continued. "I've been thinking about your earlier lesson, Captain, and you're absolutely right." A heavy boot was driven into what, on a human, would have been the solar plexus. Gil made a mental note of the effect (minimal) and continued, "I *must* take you seriously. If my father *is* truly dead, then the empire is in danger. And if the empire falls now, with the Castle still weak, then this *town* will fall and everything we've done here will have been pointless." A leg sweep sent Vole's head back into the stone wall hard enough that a block cracked. "I will have to hold it all together." There was an obvious note of regret in his voice echoing amidst the madness. He shrugged at Agatha. "I'm the only one who can." He spun towards Vole, who flinched as Gil considered him. "You'll come with me. You're big and menacing . . . in your own way. You'll make a fine lackey."

His pride stung, Vole screamed as he attacked. "Hyu iz *krezy*! Hy vill rip hyu *heart* out!" But his headlong rush only added to the impact of Gil's boot heel impacting on his nose.

"Oh, you'll certainly *try*. You'll try again and again and again! Won't you?" Gil grinned. "At least, I'm counting on you to try."

Vole stared at him in confusion. "Hyu . . . hyu iz krezy! And not in de goot vay! Hyu iz talkink like hyu *vants* me to keel hyu!"

Gil laughed merrily. "Nooo! I *want* you to *try*! After all, I have to show the world that I'm strong enough to hold the empire! We'll make it a game: Who's the scariest monster?"

Vole stared at Gil and a shudder ran through him as he sagged within Gil's grip. "Mebee hyu could just keel me, instead?"

Again Gil laughed and ruffled Vole's hair. "Oh no! Just think how *impressive* it will be when word gets out that I keep a pet Jäger around to *attack* me—just to keep me *sharp*!"

Watching Gil's display of bravado and his mastery of Vole, Agatha was torn. She didn't want him to go. She wanted him to stay here by her side where she could listen to him talk in his beautiful intense voice forever.

The other possibility was simply giving up. Going with him now. Abandoning the Castle and the town and everything involved in being the Heterodyne, just so she could remain by him where he'd protect her . . .

When she realized the nature of her inner conflict, she snarled at herself in disgust and slapped her face hard. There was an amused giggle within her head and she felt Lucrezia retreat.

She's getting better at this, Agatha reflected.

She took a deep breath and saw that everyone, including Gil and Tarvek, was staring at her in sudden concern. She held up a reassuring hand. "Gil. There's no time for—! You . . . you've got to go! Now!"

Gil was in a heightened state of awareness. He saw the way Agatha was looking at him and the rest of the world fell away. He wanted nothing more than to take her into his arms and never let her go, and he knew—he *knew* that if he did, she would hold onto him just as fiercely. But even in this state, he was all too aware of the reality of the situation. "Yes . . . " He bit out. "I *know*. But . . . I will be back."

Agatha took another deep breath. "You'd better."

Tarvek stepped in and genially slung an arm around Agatha's shoulders. "Oh *yes*," he said cheerfully, "*Do* drop in sometime! We'll bake a cake!"

Gil felt a genuine flash of gratitude to Tarvek. The explosive action required to twist his arm up behind Tarvek's head before slamming him into a headlock relieved quite a lot of tension. The thrashing and squealing from under his arm was a happy bonus. He focused on Agatha and squeezed Tarvek's arm tight enough that there was a slight *crack*. "Listen to *everything* this duplicitous snake says. His tail is on the line here, too, so he'll give you good advice."

Agatha looked at him with eyes he could stare into forever. "I know."

With herculean effort, Gil turned on his heel and strode off. After several steps he paused, turned, and came back. Only then did he unclench his arm and let Tarvek burst free. He stared longingly at Agatha for a second, then nodded and again turned. "Right. I'm off."

Agatha watched him go, leaning slightly forward. Behind her, Tarvek rolled his eyes. "Oh, for pity's sake," he said irritably. "Go give him something to fight for."

In a flash, Gil spun about. "GET WOUND, STURMVORAUS! I DO *NOT* NEED *YOUR* HELP—"

And then Agatha's lips were on his and her arms were around his neck, pulling him tightly against her in an embrace that held months of desperate longing. With a shudder, Gil swept her up in his arms and returned her kiss with an ardor that easily matched her own. One hand tangled itself in her hair. As he pulled her closer, she began to feel as though she had once again drunk the water of the River Dyne, as though the whole world contained nothing but the two of them in this moment with infinity stretching out around them.

The others watched as the air above them began to waver from the heat. Krosp nodded and gave Tarvek's arm an impressed punch. "Wow. I wish she took *my* advice so readily."

Tarvek looked down at the big white cat from the crumbling battlements of all his glorious, romantic plans, and a great weariness filled him. "Just shut up." He indicated Gil. "He's right. If the empire falls into chaos now, we're *all* finished."

Agatha and Gil broke apart, panting. They almost kissed again, but both raised their hands to each other's faces at the same time and their fingers entwined.

"Okay," Gil said.

"Right," Agatha agreed.

"Gotta go."

"I know."

"Gotta . . . save the empire. And stuff."

"I'll just . . . you know . . . fix my castle . . . " Agatha blinked. "Speaking of which, I'd better tell it not to kill you on the way out."

Gil smiled. "I'd appreciate that." He snapped his fingers. "Vole! Let's go!" The tall Jäger, who had retrieved his hat, sighed and stepped out behind them.

Violetta walked beside Vole. "And here I was expecting you to attack them while they were kissing."

Vole shook his head, one warrior to another. "Dun be schtupid. She vould rip my fangs out."

As they walked away, Agatha tried to review what had just happened. That kiss and the feelings behind it. Had that been her? Or Lucrezia? She looked at Gil, tried to look at him analytically, and failed spectacularly. Then she caught a faint smirking echo: *His father was better.*

Her temper flared white hot. *I will burn you out with fire*, she vowed. The thing inside her head snickered and retreated.

Agatha realized Lucrezia was using her desires. That was how she was so good at manipulating people. *I can't allow myself to feel anything until this monster in my head is gone.* She looked up and saw Gil and Tarvek arguing about something. The sight brought a rueful smile to her face. *This was going to be difficult.*

Soon enough they came to a part of the Castle that Agatha recognized. "Castle? Can you hear me in here?"

When it answered, it was obvious the great intelligence was distracted. "Ah. Yes, my Lady, I can hear you."

"I need you to get Gilgamesh Wulfenbach and Captain Vole to the nearest outer gate as quickly as possible. And no killing them along the way, got it?"

"What? Oh, of course not," it muttered. "Work now, play later."

"And no maiming them either." Agatha was starting to get a little worried. Usually, by this time, the Castle would be merrily implying it would utilize all sorts of creative workarounds to an order like that. "I want them completely unharmed, both mentally and physically. Do you understand?"

"Yes, yes, fine," the Castle said testily. The floor opened beneath Gil and Vole and they silently dropped from sight. "Off they go."

"What have you done?" Agatha screamed.

"What? Oh yes. This chute will take them directly to the Gate of Chimes."

Agatha peered into the darkness of the pit and nodded slowly. "Oh. Well. Good then. Once they're out of the building—"

"Once they are out they will serve as an excellent distraction, I'm sure."

Agatha stared upwards, grabbed a convenient sledgehammer and hauled off before a particularly nice bit of wainscoting. "I *told* you . . . "

"*Not in the facing!*" the Castle squealed. "What did I do? They are completely unharmed as you ordered! They are being escorted outside as you ordered! It's not *my* fault that once they leave my protection, they will directly face all of your attackers. I thought that was your plan! I barely have enough strength to maintain the integrity of the inner keep!"

"Well, stop them! Don't let them leave!"

"Erm," the Castle sounded somewhat sheepish. "The Gate of Chimes is still one of my dead areas. I am sorry, my Lady, but I am running out of power. I have to use everything I have for defense. Soon I will not even be able to . . . oh bother," it said wearily. "There goes the Tower of Green Bone."

Agatha turned to the others with a fierce gleam in her eye. "This is it. We fix the Castle now or not at all."

Another shudder shook the building as they dashed off. They piled back into the room and found the remaining great security clanks clustered around Theo and Sleipnir. Theo was grimacing as Sleipnir wound a bandage around his upper arm.

Agatha paused, and then joined them. "What happened?"

"That crazy Jäger shot him. He was aiming for Gil."

Theo grit his teeth as Sleipnir tied the ends of the bandage around his bicep. "Glad to help," he muttered.

Sleipnir looked around. "Where is Gil? Is he okay? He didn't leave without us, did he?"

Agatha rolled her eyes. "I told the Castle to get him out quickly, but now he's about to be dumped right into the middle of invading army. It isn't safe out there."

Another rumble shook the building and a small block smashed to the floor. Sleipnir glanced at Agatha. "Unlike in here."

Agatha looked around. "I see you've fixed the final break. Maybe we can use these fun-sized death dispensers to catch up to him, and—"

Sleipnir raised a hand. "We didn't fix any break."

Agatha's eyes swiveled over to the end of the room. Obligingly, the sheared conduit gave a gratuitous burst of sparks. Her gaze swiveled the other way and she found herself staring into the eyes of the great tiger clank upon whose nose her hand rested. "You didn't?" She swallowed. "Then how—?"

The great machine gave a cough of laughter. "Their central control system remains damaged. They are somewhat weak and slow. They cannot hear your castle, but they do obey *me*."

Understanding lit Agatha's eyes. "Madame von Pinn?"

The great head nodded. "Otilia now, but yes."

Agatha clapped her hands. "Excellent! Then Gil will be fine! Mobilize as many of these things as you can control! I'd like to see the army that can stand up to you!"

"We'll have to hurry if we're going to catch him," Sleipnir said.

"That's true!" Agatha thumped the side of the great tiger clank, which growled softly. "Okay. I'm going to get this right this time." She cleared her throat. "Castle! I want to send these clanks to help Gil get back to Castle Wulfenbach safely. What is going to go wrong and how can I prevent it?"

"Ah. Mistress. Hello." The Castle's voice was vague and it spoke with long pauses in between words. "Um . . . well, until that break is repaired, the, ah, they will not function outside of my walls."

"That's all right." Agatha said. "I'll be staying here to fix the break. It shouldn't take long. If Madame Otilia can catch Gil before he leaves, they'll be all set."

Otilia cut her off with a raised paw. "If *you* remain in the Castle, Lady Heterodyne, then I must also stay." She growled.

"What? No! Gil needs you!"

Gears could be heard grinding within the great clank. "No, my duty, now that I have found you, is to stay beside you, the Heterodyne girl. That is my sacred trust!" Her voice reflected her inner turmoil. "To do otherwise would betray my king."

Tarvek stepped forward. "Now *that*, at least, I can do something about!" He strode forward until he was nose-to-nose with the great clank. It towered above him.

"Otilia, Muse of Protection: I, the true heir to the Storm King, release you from your guardianship of the Heterodyne girl. You will assume your place at my side."

Otilia's head reared back in surprise. "You? The Storm King? Do not play games, child."

"This is no game," Tarvek said calmly. "I am Valois's direct descendant. Supported by the Knights of Jove. Even Wulfenbach acknowledged it."

Otilia's eyes flickered and looked to Agatha. "Great heavens—did he really?"

Agatha looked at Tarvek with a growing respect. "He *did*, actually."

Tarvek examined his nails. "In front of witnesses and everything."

Otilia's massive head began to swing from side to side. "But . . . my task . . . it was set by my *original* master. But . . . if the power *is* properly invested in a legitimate heir . . . but the Wulfenbachs do not have the authority to legitimize a king."

"At the moment, I am a vassal of the empire," Tarvek explained patiently. "And the empire has long demonstrated the de facto power to legitimize regional governments that operate within its sphere of influence. This has been recognized and accepted by other independent governments within (such as Hofnung-Borzoi) and outside of its borders."

The great mouth opened and closed several times. "But you have not been *crowned* . . . "

Tarvek leaned in towards the tiger's snout. "Do you *want* to save Wulfenbach or do you want to *argue* with me? I offer you purpose and a resolution of your logic conflicts."

"I do, but . . . I . . . you . . . "

"No, no," Tarvek said icily. "Do take your time. Perhaps you no longer wish to be my Muse."

The great head shuddered and then dipped in supplication. "Forgive me, sire."

Tarvek gently laid a hand on the steam cat's brow. "It is done." He clapped his hands together in glee. "This will be great! I can't wait to see Wulfenbach's face—"

He was interrupted by a shove from behind as one of the vast metal paws gently eased him to the ground. Otilia's voice was amused now. "You and young Master Wulfenbach. Such a *troublesome* pair. No. You will stay here, where you will be safe."

Tarvek thrashed furiously. "No! I swear—I'll come right back! Just as soon as Gil sees that I saved his bacon, okay?"

The paw pressed down. "No! I am the Muse of Protection! My king will not go haring off into a war unprepared!"

Tarvek opened his mouth, but Otilia overrode him: "*That* is the price of my acknowledgement."

Tarvek bit his lip, then sighed in exasperation. "Very well."

"The wisest path is often the most difficult," she said archly.

Tarvek glowered up at her. "Yeah, I'm beginning to see why old Andronicus wrote about you lot the way he did."

The clank nodded. "And, as I did with your ancestor, I will leave you with something to ensure that you behave."

One of the smaller tiger clanks padded forward and, with a low chuffing sound, took up a position behind Tarvek's right shoulder. "I will now go," Otilia said. "Do not attempt to follow. Your guardian is not as *sophisticated* as I. Your clever words will most likely only annoy it."

With that, she turned, and the rest of the clanks fell into formation behind her. Sleipnir and Theo had clambered aboard one of the smaller ones waved goodbye as the entire pack thundered out of the chamber and down the hall.

Tarvek, Agatha, and Violetta watched them go. "Right," Tarvek sulked. "I'll just sit here on my useless, royal butt." He turned to Agatha. "Come on, let's fix that last break."

He was surprised at Agatha's expression. "Tarvek," she began—

He turned away. His heart felt sick and he badly wanted a distraction. "We've still got work to do if they're going to get past the Castle gate."

Agatha tried again. "Tarvek, you're not—"

He waved her aside. "Now, it looks like a simple break, so you probably don't even need me to—"

Suddenly Agatha grabbed his arm and spun him around. "Shut up and *listen* to me!"

Tarvek blinked. Agatha continued. "Tarvek, I'm sure Gil will be all right. That reprogramming you did on Madame Otilia was *brilliant*. She'll get him through to Castle Wulfenbach and he'll . . . he'll take over the empire and we'll have time to fully repair the Castle. I know this is all . . . difficult for you, and yet you've still done everything you can for him. Without you, well—you've been *wonderful*."

Tarvek had trouble meeting her eyes. "That . . . that's nonsense. I haven't done anything for *him*." He looked at her. "Obviously, it's all been for you. Everything. That, at least, isn't going to change."

Agatha looked flustered. "Tarvek . . . I . . . "

He waved his hands and gently took her shoulders. "Agatha, no matter what happens, I'll . . . I'll always be your ally! I'll always do everything I can do to help you. Even if you don't—I mean . . . " Tarvek suddenly realized his face was scant centimeters away from Agatha's and that her hands were now clasped atop his own. "Even if you and . . . and . . . "

He realized where his traitorous mouth was taking the conversation and clamped it shut.

Agatha found herself drawn closer as she stared into his eyes. "Oh—thank you . . . " she managed. "I . . . um . . . "

They gazed at each other for a long moment and both began to blush feverishly for no reason whatsoever. Tarvek jerked his hands back. "Oh. Ah, hey! Listen to me blather! We'd better get to work!"

"Yes!" Agatha took a step back and had to refrain from reaching out to him again. "Yes! Yes, we certainly should!"

Tarvek's hands flexed and he deliberately turned away. "You go ahead and get started," he said faintly. "I'll get the rest of the tools and stuff out of the squid and be right back."

"You do that," Agatha said. "And . . . and we'll get this placed fixed."

She turned and walked, her head aswirl with conflicting emotions. *How about that kiss with Gil?* a distant part of herself was shouting, a delirious subsection of her brain that had been replaying it over and over and over again, but . . . she was *also* all too aware of the feeling of Tarvek's hands on her shoulders. The way she had wanted to listen to him talk forever. The way she felt with his face so very close to hers . . .

Tarvek, meanwhile, was listlessly tossing tools into the leather satchel he'd been hauling through the Castle. He paused and examined a particularly worn-out screwdriver. *Well,* he thought with a bitter sigh, *at least I know what to get them as a wedding present.*

Suddenly Violetta was there. Her face was a study in outraged wonder. "I can't *believe* it," she said.

Tarvek sighed. There was nothing like family to twist a knife in a broken heart. "Ah, Violetta, here to play 'taunt the loser'?"

She ignored this. "What the heck was that back there?" she demanded. "You're all set to get the girl, so you try to run off and get yourself *killed*?"

Tarvek slammed a steel file into the bag with a satisfying clang. "I was not going to . . . " The part of his mind that continually parsed Violetta's dialogue for content and humorous mistakes delivered its message, and he paused. "Wait. All set to *what*?"

He turned to see his cousin slumped against the wall, a look of amazement on her face. "I'm totally going to win that bet with von Zinzer." She looked at Tarvek. "I never win *anything*."

Tarvek felt a touch of concern. "Violetta, have you been licking your knives again?"

Violetta shook her head. "No! Seriously!" She pointed back towards Agatha. "You've won! The way things are going? *You're* going to be the one she keeps!"

"Don't be insulting. When she kissed Wulfenbach, my glasses started to melt. There's no way I can compete with—"

"She was kissing him *goodbye!*"

"Explain."

Violetta stared at him. "You're joking. I really have to explain this to you? You live for this stuff."

Tarvek put a hand on hers. "Violetta, please."

A look of surprise widened her eyes. "You're not joking!" She massaged her temples. "Argh. It must be love," she muttered. She looked Tarvek in the eye. "Power balance! Think! The Baron is dead . . . "

Tarvek blinked. "Gil is the heir. He's the new ruler of the empire."

"And my Lady Heterodyne is—?"

Tarvek considered this. "Ah. A powerful spark in charge of a historically troublesome rogue state. Oh dear."

"'Oh dear' is right!"

"But if she can get the Castle repaired and Mechanicsburg's defenses back to their full strength—"

"Then there's even *less* chance she'll want to sign on as his happy vassal, but as ruler of the empire he'll feel like he can't just let a Heterodyne run loose."

"But . . . but surely if she *marries* him . . . "

Violetta looked skeptical. "Oh? And what happens the first time there's a conflict?" Tarvek opened his mouth and she waved a hand peremptorily. "I don't mean something you can fix with a nice bunch of flowers, I mean when Gil cracks down on the smugglers, or any of the hundred-and-one unsavory things this place considers perfectly normal."

Tarvek looked at her inquiringly. Violetta just shook her head. "I told you, I was assigned to the Bürgermeister. There are two calendars here. There's the public one for the tourists with all the market days and feasts and whatnot, and there's the one they take seriously. The one the smugglers and shapeshifters use. The one that tells when things are due to rise from the underground and the townspeople congregate for chanting and secret processions. Rituals the people of this town are convinced are necessary to keep life as we know it safe." She took a deep breath and looked at Tarvek with eyes that had seen too much. "And

I . . . I can't tell you they're wrong," she shook her head. "Let's just say it would be a hard sell. Anyway, with that much of a power imbalance, would he be *asking* her to clean things up? Or *ordering* her?"

"Oh, please. All he has to do is ask her—" He shrugged knowingly. "In a politically respectful yet romantic manner . . . "

The look on Violetta's face stopped him and his eyes widened. "Sweet lightning," he whispered, holding his head in his hands. "This is all going to end in flames."

"Not *necessarily*," Violetta said triumphantly. "That's where *you* come in!"

"Where *I* come in?" A sudden realization hit him. "Wait . . . a bet? *You* bet on *me*? And how is it even *possible* you are on my side?"

Violetta carefully examined a speck on the wall. "You know . . . family . . . "

Tarvek crossed his arms. "*That* means I should be looking for the knife in my back." He paused and then gingerly felt about on his back.

Violetta threw up her arms. "Yeah, yeah, okay. I was brought up to be one of your Smoke Knights. Keeping you alive and out of trouble. Useless junk like that. Then suddenly, I'm reassigned. I'm sent out here to Mechanicsburg—supposedly to spy on the Town Council—who, in less than five minutes, I realize are a bunch of idiots who, half of the time, don't know which end of their pretzel to hold, if you know what I mean. Of course *everybody* knew the real reason I got sent out here was that I wasn't good enough to be anywhere important. Then I found out it was your fault.

"You were the one who weaseled around, pulled a bunch of strings, and got me sent out here. No matter how much I hated you before, I hated you more after that. After *years* when I didn't know if anybody was even bothering to read my reports, I found out you were here. Wounded. In the Great Hospital. They also mentioned I had been lucky. That in the last three years, someone had taken out *twelve* of your assigned knights. Three of them didn't even last a full month."

She glared at Tarvek. "So *something* was going on and you knew! You got me out of the way on *purpose*, didn't you?"

Now it was Tarvek's turn to look evasive. "Violetta, it's not like you ever *liked* being a Smoke Knight. So what if it was boring out here? At least you didn't get killed doing something you hated!"

Violetta looked at him. "Yeah, that's what I thought. And I figure, if you'll do that for *me*, you'll burn down Hell to keep someone you love alive, and I want the Lady Heterodyne kept alive!"

Tarvek considered this. "You think I can do that?"

"That's what I'm betting on. You're a spark, use your brain for something useful for once! Sure, if she marries kissy-boy she'll be happy. Very happy . . . " A faraway look came into Violetta eyes, "Okay, super blissed out in every possible way—"

"Yes, yes!" Tarvek snapped. "I GET it, all right?"

Violetta sighed. "But she'd be giving up a lot of her power and I'm worried about how long she'd live. Now you—you're a total sneak."

"What's that got to do with the price of body parts?"

"You'll weave treaties, build alliances . . . you'll rebuild the Empire of the Storm King from scratch, and you'll do it from a place of strength—right here in Mechanicsburg. And because the two of you are both starting from the same level, you'll have a much better chance of working *together* and being happy for a long, long time!" Violetta sighed, but this time, there was a look of anticipation in her eyes. "And there will be lots of parties," she whispered, "and I'll get to dress up and dance with . . . " She shook her head sharply and looked at Tarvek more seriously. "You'll probably wind up as some sort of evil dark lords or something, but I have a feeling the Lady Heterodyne might be one of those girls who can get into that sort of thing, if you know what I mean."

Oh, Tarvek knew. He started to say something, but Violetta leaned in, "And I think she could make the whole 'Evil Queen' look work for her, you know?"

A look of anticipation filled Tarvek's face and he shivered. "Tricky . . . " he breathed. "She's an Autumn."[79]

"Anyway," Violetta declared, "you just stop trying to be some kind of hero and stick to Plan B: *Be* helpful, *be* patient, and *be* there! Now *I'm* going to go make sure nothing eats her while she's working. *You* snap it up and pull yourself together! Put those royal madboy skills to work and help her win!"

Tarvek shooed her off. "Okay, okay! I'll be right behind you!" He stood staring at the wall for several seconds, his grin fading as he began spooling through possibilities.

The first thing she'll want to do is get as many of those fools in the Order—those who aren't in thrall to Lucrezia—on her side. Weeding her loyalists out will be tricky, but the Smoke Knights will help there . . . they've got a grudge. He allowed himself a quick smile. Or they will, when I've finished explaining things to them. Whom to approach first . . . Von Bulen, I think. He loves a good Heterodyne story . . .

He brought himself up sharp and gave a small, amused snort. "Tsk. I'm plotting like there's a chance this could even happen. Still, whether she wants me or not, it won't be wasted effort. She'll still need strong alliances." He sighed at the images that flickered down his inner runway. "And she really would look lovely in black . . . perhaps with a bit of a bat-wing motif . . . "

He took a deep breath, clapped his hands and stood tall. "Maybe Violetta is right! Maybe I *do* have a chance! Yes! Things are looking . . . "

—and that was when Sanaa plummeted from above, enveloping him in a rough canvas sack.

"Ha!" she crowed. "Gotcha!"

---

[79] There is a design aesthetic amongst certain of the Parisian fashion houses that classify people according to aspects of their physiognomy into various "seasons." Pale, blue-eyed blondes with brittle laughs who like to stake their victims out on ice floes tend to be "Winters," and so on.

Tarvek began to shout and thrash. Reluctantly, she brained him with a pry bar. He went limp. "Sorry about that," she muttered. As she wound him in ropes, she hummed a little ditty about the joys of rescuing royalty: "Rescuing the prince! Rescuing the prince!"

A cacophony of noise burst from the next room and, after a final shriek of rending metal, Othar strolled in, wiping oil from his hands. "Sorry," he said. "One of those steam cat things. What is this?"

Sanaa pointed proudly. "I got him! I got Wulfenbach for you!"

Othar looked impressed. "Indeed you did! Well done!" He pulled the wrapped man to his feet and frowned as he began to slump back down. "You didn't hit him too hard, did you? I am supposed to bring him back alive."

Sanaa waved a hand dismissively. "Nah, he's fine! But you said he was all dangerous and stuff, so I knocked him out quick!"

Othar shrugged. "Oh, you did very well! Good girl!"

Sanaa giggled. "I rescued him good."

Tarvek began failing about and, even though his voice was muffled, it was obvious he was working his way up to a prolonged rant about something. Othar grinned. "Actually, it sounds like you didn't hit him hard enough. Go to sleep, you." He expertly delivered a sharp rabbit punch to the back of Tarvek's head, causing him to again pass out.

Sanaa looked a bit distressed at this. "Not too hard, he *is* awfully cute."

Othar was instantly serious. "Young lady, that is no reason to be soft on a villain! What have I told you about getting romantically involved with evil?"

Sanaa closed her eyes. " 'It's not a bad way to kill time as long as it ultimately results in the total destruction of her lair and the ruination of her nefarious plans.' " She then looked up at Othar innocently.

"Uhh . . . well . . . I *meant* . . . "

Sanaa smiled devilishly and patted her brother on the cheek. "Oh, don't worry. It sounds like he's in love with the Heterodyne girl, anyway. But don't forget to tell him it was me who rescued him!"

She gingerly touched her collar and frowned. "Oooh, I wish I could go with you—it'll be so cool!"

Othar swung the limp body over his shoulder. "Of course you shall have the credit! And fear not! When I deliver him to the Baron, I'll demand that you be released immediately or I shall throw this lout out of the airship!" And with a jaunty laugh, they headed towards the exit.

CHAPTER 7

The Doom Bell is one of the crowning achievements of the science of sound. Audiologists and acoustical researchers go to great lengths to ensure they stay as far away from it as possible.

Long ago, when Mechanicsburg was a much smaller town, the Heterodyne announced important events like his return from abroad or the birth of an heir, by personally running up to everyone in the town and shouting, "Guess what?" Considering the predilections of the Heterodyne family, this was incredibly nerve wracking, especially if you guessed wrong.

Eventually, the town grew to the point where approaching every inhabitant became impractical, and the Heterodyne at the time (Cain Heterodyne) ordered the construction of a bell that "Would have the same effect on the people as my own self!" It is safe to say the engineers who undertook the casting of the bell from his designs fulfilled this mandate.

The actual construction process of the great bell itself, down to the composition of the alloys used in its casting, have long been the subject of speculation among metallurgists, but as the Heterodynes were never free with their secrets, speculation is all that remains to us. Attempts have been made to replicate the bell. These experiments are never officially sanctioned, as even when they "succeed" the results are invariably distressing.

The University of Vienna Music Department once constructed a model that, when struck, caused every animal within five hundred meters to commit suicide.

The Research Department of the Czar's Imperial

Marching Band built a replica that was struck once—*and never stopped ringing,* the sound growing louder and louder by the minute. The noise was perceived over three hundred kilometers away before the bell could be destroyed by cannon fire. Everyone within twenty kilometers remained deaf for the rest of their lives.

Today the Tower of the Doom Bell is one of the enduring symbols of Mechanicsburg and is featured on a wide variety of souvenir items. It is spoken of with pride by the locals and the Official Ringer is a provisional member of the Mechanicsburg City Council.

Unlike every other bell within the empire, it is *not* rung for ceremonial occasions, to commemorate anniversaries, or to mark special days on the Mechanicsburg calendar. In fact, evidence exists that the bell can no longer ring at all, which is just how everyone likes it."

—An excerpt from "Chapter 3: Things of Interest Within Mechanicsburg That Will Not Technically Kill You," *Pontexeter's Guide to Transylvania, Moldavia, Wallachia, & Croatia,* 10ᵗʰ Edition

⟡⊙⟡

Within the Tower of the Doom Bell, Baron Krasimir Oublenmach gave a grunt and, with a *CLUNK* that echoed throughout the stairwell, managed to hoist the great hammer up onto the next step.

He paused, panting, and glanced down at the steps that spiraled away behind him. He'd felt every one of them. He took a deep breath and surveyed the steps ahead of him. They looped around the perimeter of the great tower a soul-crushing number of times, but—*but!* He *was* able to catch a glimpse of a trapdoor that led to the outside.

He gave a small titter of greed-fueled anticipation and, once again, grasped the bronze hammer and *lifted*—

Outside on the streets of Mechanicsburg, foreign troops moved gingerly through the town. Resistance had been sporadic, but when it came, it was terrifying. Unlike most of Europa, the people of Mechanicsburg had never experienced this particular aspect of the fortunes of war and they made it clear in a thousand ways that they did not like it. In this they were aided by many things. The terrain of Mechanicsburg itself is convoluted and quite often vertical. Ambushes were easy and effective. There were also a superabundance of bolt-holes and hiding places. These had been developed through the centuries of living under a string of unstable spark despots.

The Heterodyne family had a well-known tradition of sparing the people of Mechanicsburg from their assorted cruelties, but that's not to say they didn't occasionally snatch unwary people off the streets. It was just that, when they did, they had every sincere intention of *improving* them.

There was also Mechanicsburg's reputation. It was honestly earned, to be sure, and had only grown in the telling. While it was true that much of the city's fabled lethalness was currently disabled, this was not common knowledge. Besides, there was still more than enough oddity in Mechanicsburg to set people from normal urban environments justifiably on edge. Therefore, it was understandable that the forces moving through the streets had quickly adopted a "shoot first, then shoot again" policy.

One such unit served as a microcosm of the larger army. Its mechanical walkers had been supplied by one of the lesser kingdoms tucked away on the border between France and one of the innumerable Germanic states. One of the drivers carefully lifted the walker's right foot over a fallen wall, without breaking his stream of nervous, one-sided conversation. " . . . and anyway, I don't understand why we're doing this."

On a raised seat behind him, his lieutenant rolled his eyes. "Shut up, you pig!"

The other driver, who managed the left foot, and was thus a much more experienced soldier, nodded in agreement. "Yeah, man. Shut up."

"I mean . . . attacking a hospital . . . "

A smack from a riding crop dented his hat. "Imbecile! How dare you question my orders!"

The other driver nodded. "It took out the Baron."

"And now we're attacking a . . . a busted castle? What does that even mean?"

"Stinking poltroon! Your tortures will be exquisite!"

"Hey. Some of us are just tryin' to kill things, here."

Despite himself, the older soldier was drawn into the conversation. "Look. They said that the Baron's kid is in there. So bringing it down is just smart. Kill him, kill the empire."

"Yes, yes." The lieutenant sighed as he settled back in his chair. "But we also have to kill the Heterodyne girl, if you must know."

"Ho-ho," the second driver smiled around his cigar. "A twofer! Sweet!"

"But . . . but I thought we needed her alive so she could marry the Storm King."

"Lackwit! Cretin! Wrong Heterodyne girl! Wrong Storm King! Wrong! Wrong! Wrong!"

"See? I never know what the heck we're doing."

The second driver just grinned. "You gotta enjoy the little things, man. Like the killin'."

The first driver slumped. "Well, I *do* like blowing things up . . . "

"That's it! Start small!"

One story up in a room that deliberately did *not* appear to be the center of Mechanicsburg's government, several eyes watched from behind slightly parted curtains as the soldiers crept past. Van sighed and looked back at the people in the darkened room. "You're sure the Street of the Goldmakers[80] has been evacuated?"

Vidonia checked her notes. "Yes."

"And they—?"

Carson von Mekkhan chuckled. "Left the acid sprayers running? Oh yes. Also the Tunnel Rats are all in place. They say they can collapse any street you want, 'just say the word.' "

Van nodded glumly. "Well, we can only destroy the town once, so we'd better make it count."

Vidonia touched his sleeve. "We should get going too."

"Yes, yes, I know. Have all the children made it to the Red Cathedral?"

A twisted figure lurched into motion. It looked like it was made of stretched leather swathed in rotting bandages and studded with the occasional glowing dial. Lips slowly peeled back from oddly elongated teeth. In a sibilant voice it hissed, "They have, and the Crypt Masters[81] will keep them safe. This we so vow!"

A small girl in a pink frock groaned and slapped her forehead.

The Crypt Master paused. "What?"

The girl looked at him beseechingly. "Oh, come on, great-great-great gran'pa—talk *normal*!"

The creature looked bewildered. "What? But this is the Speech of Vowing, you snotulous child!"

---

[80] It used to be called the Avenue of the Alchemists, then Exploding Row, then the Alley of Odors, then the Corrosive Corridor, then . . . well . . . you get the idea. This latest name was put into place by the Mechanicsburg Chamber of Commerce in a desperate attempt to remove an embarrassment from the town's maps. Surprisingly, within twenty-four hours of the new signs going up, people actually started producing gold. This has provided a rich field of experiment for those who study the power of names and expectations.

[81] In Mechanicsburg, when one is making end of life decisions, one of the options offered is to be reanimated as a Crypt Master. These (let's be honest) hideous creatures are responsible for the general maintenance and caretaking of the subterranean parts of the town where even jaded, lifelong residents are hesitant to go. Even those who have chosen it admit they are now trapped in an endless existence as a twisted mockery of life—but it does give Mechanicsburg's more civic-minded senior citizens something to do.

The girl grabbed the creature's wrist and dragged it towards the door. "Well *I* vow that you are sooo embarrassing!"

"I will smite your allowance!"

Van watched the creature totter from the room, a troubled look on his face. "You don't think that growing up here might make us a little . . . weird, do you?"

"LOOK OUT!"

A projectile smashed through the window. It smacked into the far wall, then dropped to the floor. It was a complicated-looking metal sphere. Van stared at it in horror.

"That was too close." Carson swore. "*Now* can we go?"

"Yes!" Van shouted. "Everyone get out! Quickly! I've heard about these!"

Suddenly, the sphere unwound and a single glass eye snapped open. "Freeze!" A voice shouted from a small speaker, "Stay where you are or die! I can hear you, you know!" The device coiled itself up like a snake and swung about, surveying the room. It saw the people huddled together and stopped. "There you are! Ha! Why this is marvelous! I can see everything!" There was the sound of rustling paper. "Where is that idiot's speech—ah!

"Leaders of Mechanicsburg! Prepare to . . . " Abruptly, the lenses on the eyes spun about. "Wait a minute . . . who the devil are you fools? You're not . . . " The owner of the voice obviously turned away to address someone near them. "I mean look at them. They aren't the City Council! Oh well, I'll just kill them anyway."

Which was when one of the great suits of armor that stood alongside the wall, swung its huge axe down, slicing the device into sparking fragments. In the street below there was a rumble, followed by shouts. At the window, Vidonia yelled, "Hey, come and take a look at this! Something's happening!" The others stared down in wonder. Below, in the street, a wall had collapsed, trapping one of the three-man walkers.

"I didn't order that," Van said.

"You should have. It's bottled up a whole unit."

Carson tapped the glass and pointed down the other direction. "Look. Both ends of the Folding Bridge have gone up. Those soldiers are trapped on Tiny Monster Island."

"What? We have to—"

"They'll be fine as long as they obey the signs and don't leave the path," Carson said as he watched the troopers ignore the signs and climb over the railings. Then they started to dance. Carson smiled. He always loved that part.

Van looked bewildered. "But who . . . ?"

The ornamental fountain in the corner gave a gurgle and then a stream of water spurted out into the bowl. Carson fell to his knees and clapped a hand to his wounded head. "It's back," he moaned.

A dry chuckle filled the room, "Hello, Carson," the Castle said. "I had a bit of trouble finding you, but I did it! Yes, I did! And you're still alive to appreciate it. That's a bit of a bonus. Ah, but we have no time to play. There is work to be done!"

Within Castle Heterodyne, Agatha leaned back and, raising the goggles from her eyes, critically examined the weld that was still fading from red to gray before her. "I think that's the last one. Castle? Can you hear me?"

There was a rumbling that echoed throughout the entire castle, as the structure . . . flexed. "YES!" The voice of the Castle was triumphant, its timbre full and rich with none of the faint notes of emptiness Agatha had noted before. "Well done, Mistress! I am still accessing . . . but I believe I am once again complete." It paused. "Within my main structure at least. My conduits into the surrounding town are damaged, but it appears that most of this is due to accumulated negligence, as opposed to damage from outside forces. Unfortunately, said forces are quite capable of further damage and my energy levels are insufficient to properly defend the town. I must warn you, they are continuing to fall at an alarming rate."

Agatha absorbed this. "Can you ensure that Madame Otilia will be able to reach Gil?"

"That I can do, Mistress, and the security grid is functional enough that the other units with her will be able to operate within the confines of the town."

"Great!" Agatha turned. "Come on. Tarvek, let's . . . " It was then that Agatha and Violetta registered that Tarvek was, in fact, not there.

"Where'd he go?"

Violetta rolled her eyes. "Oh, I cannot believe he missed this! He was supposed to be here by now!" A flicker of uncertainty crossed her face. "He really was—I'll go get him." She dashed off.

"Castle?" Agatha asked, "Is Tarvek all right?"

There was a pause. "I am sorry, Mistress, but I cannot seem to locate him."

In the Mechanicsburg Town Hall, Van finished annotating a map of the town. It now showed all the places in town the Castle insisted needed to be repaired. He handed it off to the Head of Public Works. "Have every mechanic you can find get out to look at these right away."

The man nodded as he examined the map. "Yessir." He glanced out the window. "Gonna need some support so my boys don't get shot," he said glumly.

Van acknowledged this. "I'll see who I can round up." He looked vaguely at the ceiling and addressed the Castle. "What exactly are these repairs that they're so important *right now*?"

"There are secrets that I had . . . forgotten," the Castle replied. "Indeed, I am beginning to remember many things that once were lost."

"That's very cryptic, even for you," Carson said. "The town is under heavy attack, and you want us to risk valuable people to chase vague memories? What kind of 'Things that once were lost?' Socks?"

There was a pointed silence. When the Castle spoke again, it had a more formal cant to its voice. "Carson von Mekkhan, you always were a suspicious old grouch, even when you were young. I, more than any other, appreciate what you did when your son died. No one, in the history of the family, ever assumed the mantle of seneschal twice in one lifetime. Therefore, by my authority, I shall see to it that your pension is doubled."

Carson sat down. "My pension? But—"

"Hear me now: I, Castle Heterodyne, hereby recognize Agatha Heterodyne as the Lady of Mechanicsburg and Vanamonde von Mekkhan as her seneschal. *So stop carping!*"

The Castle continued, "Your young one here has been very well trained. He has already dispatched minions without subjecting me to a string of badgering questions. His naive trust in me gives me great hope for the entertainment value of the young generation." The suit of animated armor reached out and the immense hand tapped Van's head. "We'll get some lovely holes drilled into your head as soon as possible, young man."

"What!"

"Oh yes! What jolly times we'll have!" A faint explosion sounded from somewhere outside. "Assuming that you and the Lady Heterodyne manage to pull this off."

Van started. "The Lady Heterodyne! So she's all right? Where is she?"

"Never fear, she is on her way. Soon the Heterodyne will once again scream defiance from atop the walls of Mechanicsburg. It will be glorious! Now, my power is fading and I have many things to do. Your task is to defend the Lady and the town. I will provide aid where I can." With that, the suit fell apart with a hollow clatter.

Van stared at the pile of scrap metal and unconsciously ran his hand over his head. He then straightened up and faced the others. "Let's get to work."

Gil and Vole stood at a window analyzing the attackers that were throwing themselves at Castle Heterodyne's defenses. Gil shook his head. "Everybody is shooting at everybody else. I don't understand."

Vole grinned. "Hyu poppa iz dead." He shook his head. "And effrybody knows. Dot vos schtupid. Dey should haff vaited for *hyu* before dey announced it. Dey couldn't have caused more chaos if dey had *vanted* to. Efferybody iz determined to grab a piece of sumting, even if it iz filled vit holes." He pointed up at a flotilla of large metal heads equipped with machine guns that dangled beneath cheerful looking gasbags. "See? Perfect example. Dose gunheds iz for fighting infantry. Vhy iz dey not down by de town gates vere dere iz lots of pipple to shoot? Dey ken't do nottink to de Kestle but knock out vindows."

"True," Gil agreed. "But *we* count as 'infantry' at the moment and we're here."

Vole amiably conceded the point. "Und hiffen dey vos after us, dot vould make sense. Killink hyu vould change efferyting. Bot dey izn't. dey iz shootink at dose fency dressers from de Mactovia Duchies dot are comink in over der vall, und dose guys vos allies last hy heard." He paused, "Hy admit dot dey iz going out ov dere vay to be goot targets." There was a rattle of gunfire. "Ho! Nize grouping."

"The trick will be keeping that from happening to us."

Vole waved a hand. "Dot's a bridge ve gots to cross ven ve ken gets to it."

Gil glanced down at their feet, which were still gripped by the stone hands that had, quite unexpectedly, formed out of the floor itself. "Granted." He sighed. "This place is so . . . amazing, you wouldn't think you'd get tired of it, but . . . "

Vole snorted. "Diz iz nottink. Hyu try puttink op vit it for a hunnert und fifty years."

Gil considered this. "I keep forgetting how old you Jägers *are*."

Vole looked surprised. "Old? Hy guess . . . "

"Has the Castle changed much?"

"Nah, it schtill thinks its fonny."

"Oh, come on," the Castle said, "this is hilarious."

They started. "So Agatha did it?" Gil asked. "You're finally repaired?"

The Castle hesitated. "My core systems are now . . . functional, yes . . ."

Vole sniffed deprecatingly. "Hyu iz schtill priddy messy."

A brick thwacked into the side of Vole's head. "Quiet, you! I have no power to spare for superficialities. Plus," it added grudgingly, "My secondary systems are still incapacitated. But I am fundamentally whole."

Gil looked worried. "Still, without power, you'll soon—"

Vole interrupted. "Hyu'll schtill be a useless pile of schmart-arse rocks!"

Another brick thumped into the back of his head. "Quiet! It is true. Until my generators are restored and my power supplies back within operational parameters, I cannot defend the town as I normally would, and I am . . . " The Castle paused. "Sorry, I am inordinately distracted by having to act in many places at once. I must use my remaining power sparingly. Cleverly. With subtlety."

Vole snorted. "Hyu couldn't do subtle vit a ton[82] ov bricks!" And then he flinched. When nothing happened, he looked up and the flying brick caught him squarely on the jaw.

"I am aware of the challenge," the Castle said with some satisfaction. "But now it is time for me to release you. You must go."

"We were on our way when you detained us," Gil pointed out, as the hands of stone melted back into the floor. "What's different now?"

They turned at the sound of a metallic chuckle from behind them and saw Otilia and her small army of tiger clanks clattering up the stairwell. "Now I am here, and the most dangerous things on the field outside will be with you," the Muse announced. "We have been sent to accompany you. The Lady Heterodyne insisted."

---

[82]   A *ton* (or *tonne*) is an outdated unit of measure for weight used throughout most of Europa up until a century or two ago (depending on where you are). It is equivalent to somewhere between 910 kilograms (known as a *short ton*) to one thousand kilograms (known as a *long ton*). It is a variant of the word *tun*, which is still used as the word for the largest barrel commercially made, capable of holding (approximately) 954 liters. The Jägers consider anyone joining their ranks to be a newcomer until they have drunk enough liquor to empty a tun and then spilt enough ichor to fill it back up. They have a rather jolly little song about this, which you really don't want to listen to while you're eating.

"Did she now."

"Oh yes. Now at this time, we can only go as far as the city walls . . . "

"That should be fine." Gil hesitated. "My plan is to first get to the hospital site."

Otilia regarded him. "You are aware it has been almost completely destroyed?"

Gil swallowed. "I . . . yes."

"Your father was an amazing man, Gilgamesh, I owe him a great debt."

"I . . . know he's gone, madam, but there will still be Wulfenbach troops in the area. At least some of them will have seen me take out those war clanks . . . and they'll know my father is . . . is dead. Until I can get to Castle Wulfenbach, they'll be the most likely to accept my authority. I'll need them, assuming I can convince them of who I am, of course."

"Oh ho!" Sleipnir crowed from atop the cat she and Theo were riding. "That we have covered!"

Gil actually broke into a smile at the sight of them. "You're coming with? Excellent!"

Sleipnir waved a hand. "Of course! Sorry we're a little late—but we almost forgot something!" She reached back to Theo and held up the ridiculously magnificent hat that the Jägers of Mamma Gkika's had made for Gil. "Ta-dah! You shouldn't go anywhere without your wonderful hat!"

Gil stared at it and felt the weight of inevitability settling on his soul. "Yesss . . . " He sighed. "With my luck, that will be *exactly* what I need."

Otilia broke in. "If we are to make it out of the Castle courtyard, let alone win the way to the hospital site, we must find a way past those aerial forces."

Gil looked concerned. "But surely, now that the Castle's been repaired—?"

The Castle's voice sounded as though it were under stress. "Ordinarily, yes, and . . . I am doing my best, but under the present circumstances, I have . . . so far . . . only been able to take out a few of them."

"If that's the case, why were you wasting any of your remaining power detaining me?"

The Castle made a sound eerily reminiscent of a sigh. "I did mention that the mistress would prefer you . . . alive, did I not? Ah well, all of the masters had their little quirks . . . "

"She really thinks I'm going to just wander out into the middle of a battlefield?"

Sleipnir snorted. "Didn't you do just that the other day? Big army of war striders? You with a walking stick?" She tapped the side of his head. "Ring any bells?"

"Once," Gil said reasonably. "I did that once!"

"I think maybe you just haven't had another chance."

Gil threw his arms wide in a gesture of exasperation. "Oh, come on! Give me some credit. You were surprised to find us still here, right? What did you think I was doing? There are workshops scattered all through this place. Okay, sure, I *am* going out there—"

Gil reached down and grabbed a device that had been near his feet. He snapped a switch and it began to glow. Lightning danced between a glass tube at its tip and contacts along the barrel. The whole thing began to pulse with a menacing thrum. "But I'm not going unarmed!"

Agatha and Violetta were picking their way through a rubble-strewn hall lined with portraits and partially intact stained glass windows.

"So you're saying that Tarvek is not in the Castle at all? And the security clank that Otilia assigned him—"

"Ah. I am . . . currently fighting battles on many fronts, but . . . one moment . . . " The Castle went quiet for a while, then resumed.

"Yes, that does seem to be the case. As for the fun-sized mobile death dispenser assigned to guard him . . . I am sorry to say it is no longer operational. It has been . . . smashed, and very professionally in my opinion. It must have happened just before you restored me to full operation . . . but you will be happy to know that I have . . . ah . . . I did manage to capture your other consort. I held him until Madame Otilia reached him."

"That *is* good, but—" she glanced at Violetta and felt a touch of guilt "—Tarvek . . . he wouldn't have destroyed that clank himself would he?" She remembered her kiss with Gil. "He's probably pretty mad—"

Violetta shook her head. "No way! That's not it!"

Agatha looked uncertain. "He's not here and whatever happened, he did leave the Castle. That means he'll have to face all those attackers as well—and now he doesn't even have a Mobile Fun Unit to help defend him."

"That is worrying," the Castle acknowledged. "Hm . . . however, he does not appear to be currently engaging the attackers . . . but, my Lady, he . . . struck me as a resourceful young man. Excuse me . . . "

A number of explosions sounded in the distance. "Yes, as I was saying," the Castle continued, "for now, we must trust in his strength and search for him later. I have accepted you as the Lady Heterodyne. Mechanicsburg needs you. There is fighting in the streets. I have informed the town leaders you are on the way. You must go forth to defend your town, as the Heterodyne should."

Violetta broke in, "That's all very mythopoetic, but how are we to get to them alive? All those armies and things are still out there!"

The Castle chuckled. "I still have a few last tricks saved up, and it looks like the Lady's surviving consort should provide you with more than excellent cover. Hurry, though, it is almost time!"

Within the curtain wall of Castle Heterodyne stood numerous small buildings. One particularly nondescript-looking one housed a trapdoor connecting to a tunnel system that, although comprising an excessive number of stairs, had managed to convey Vanamonde and the remnants of the actual City Council[83] to the Castle without

---

[83] When Klaus Wulfenbach assumed command of Mechanicsburg, the actual government, loath to reveal the family secrets, had claimed the Von Mekkhan family was extinct. Klaus had established a City Council, which contained enough of the old movers and shakers of the

coming to the attention of the soldiers battling all around them. Van peered over a windowsill in time to see a squad of troops equipped with shiny brass legs go jogging past.

"Get down, you young fool," the Keeper of Public Records and Secret Histories hissed. "Do you want them to start shooting at us?"

"Well, I have to watch for her, don't I?" Vanamonde waved in the direction of the great front gates.

"Don't worry," the Castle assured them, "you'll know when she is here."

The Minister of Clanks and Dangerous Devices was in the process of tearing his handkerchief into shreds. "But I tell you, she'll be shot instantly if she comes out here! Surely one of the old tunnels—"

Again the Castle chuckled. "I think she'll surprise you."

"She'll have to," the Mistress of Pain and Culture snapped. "We're losing ground everywhere. There are at least seven different factions brawling out there. If this girl can't come up with something pretty amazing, this town is finished!"

"I am aware of that, Lady Vitriox, but you've got to give her a chance. She's a Heterodyne. Don't you old-timers remember what that means?"

"Do not worry, young seneschal, they . . . are about to be *reminded*." A series of explosions erupted outside. The window frames rattled, and the gunhedz drifting above began to explode into flames. "I believe you may all now safely approach the windows. The show is about to begin."

The sight that greeted the Council's wary eyes was a show indeed. The gates swung wide and a wave of the Castle's security clanks poured forth, led by Gilgamesh Wulfenbach riding the largest of them all. He thundered out of the Castle gates shouting, "Ha! And that one's for Agatha!" as he fired crackling bolts of energy from a glowing brass weapon the size of a small cannon. The smaller tiger clanks swept aside any infantry foolish enough to not immediately take to its heels. The

town that there was no trouble at all in maintaining the Von Mekkhan family's secrecy, while still managing to get things done.

soldiers never had a chance. Anyone who stood his ground and tried to shoot was brought down by the huge metal clanks. All hopes of covering fire from the forces overhead were being burst as Gil, roaring through the fray, sent great crackling bolts of energy into the sky, taking out one floating gunhed after another. He was laughing in mad delight and ranting as he rode: "Ha! You idiots missed! You sent those stupid balloon heads against *Castle Heterodyne*? Pathetic! And what are *those*? Siege hammers? Oh no, I don't *think* so!" The siege hammers in question disappeared in an explosion of blue light. "Oooh! You brought wrecking treaders, did you? Nice! I *love* those things!" Another flash of blue light. "*When they explode!*" He paused for a bout of maniacal laughter.

The City Council watched it all, jaws agape. The Treasurer and Smuggler's Liaison turned to Vanamonde, who was regarding the carnage with a remarkable air of sangfroid.

"I . . . I thought you said the new Heterodyne was a girl."

Van nodded. "She is. *That's* just the boyfriend."

"That's—"

"Uh-huh."

They all stared at him now. A series of blasts punctuated by a gale of laughter lit up the room.

The Town Coroner and Master of Recycling swallowed. "We're . . . we're going to have to break out those little iron cages for their children, aren't we?"

"Uh-*huh.*"

Bend. *Lift.* Drop. Breathe . . .

Oublenmach precipitously comprehended he was no longer inside the bell tower. He was in the open air. On the roof. Before him loomed the great immensity that was the Doom Bell of Mechanicsburg. A shell of bronze easily five meters across, hanging before him, cast with a relief of a grinning skull on three sides, each skull bearing the trilobite of the Heterodynes on its forehead. He had done it! He had brought the hammer to the top! He had—

There was a *CRACK* of metal snapping free of a shell of verdigris. Octavo, the towering demonic automaton that for years had lounged, inert, against the bell itself, moved. It rotated its head, then its shoulders. Debris pattered down onto the rooftop. Octavo pulled and, with another *crack*, its mighty arms snapped away from the spots where they had adhered to the bell. It swung them about, testing the joints. It then deigned to notice the man before him. "Aaah . . ." It rumbled (although Oublenmach did not know it) in the voice of Castle Heterodyne, "It certainly took you long enough."

Ponderously, the automaton swung about on its squat legs, its knee joints crunching horribly, until it was directly above the man. To his credit, Oublenmach was so astonished at what he was seeing that he quite forgot to cower. Octavo nodded respectfully and reached out, effortlessly lifting the great hammer. "Thank you, little man. Well done." It began to turn away, paused, and then turned back. "You may want to cover your ears. Not that it will do you any good."

Oublenmach blinked, then truly remembered where he was. *No*, he realized with a growing horror, *running wouldn't do any good either.*

"Mistress, do have everything you will need?"

Agatha looked around. "Probably not, but—"

"Excellent! Because it is time for you to mercilessly crush your enemies beneath your boots like the insects they are! Muhhahaha!" The Castle was not prone to maniacal laughter, but it demonstrated a fine grasp of the essentials.

Agatha rolled her eyes. "Marvelous. Here we go, then."

"Young von Mekkhan!" The Castle sounded almost giddy with excitement. "She is coming! You will all go out to meet her now."

The Council looked even more nervous. "But—isn't it still dangerous—?"

Vanamonde raised a hand in the dismissive manner he had seen his grandfather use a thousand times before when the time for discussion was past. They fell silent. He squared his shoulders and headed towards the door. "Let's go, ladies and gentlemen." That said, Van couldn't help flinching slightly as he stepped outside. He need not have worried. The great mechanical cats had swept the area clean of opposition. Van hopped atop a waist-high wall and peered down the great causeway that led to the rest of the town. Even from here, the effect of Gil's sortie was unmistakable. Military units were shifting, even as he watched, as their commanders understood yet another power was now in play.

"Impressive," he murmured. "Wulfenbach's really tearing through town. He's already reached the Avenue of Oubliettes.[84]"

The Mistress of Finance, Taxes, and Involuntary Servitude started. "Wulfenbach! You mean that's the Baron's son?"

Lady Vitriox sniffed. "His father would've hit the gate and begun another sweep by now."

Van dismissed this as typical ageist hyperbole, but found himself frowning nonetheless. "Hm. Actually, I don't really like that . . . " he admitted thoughtfully. There was no denying that even in the few minutes he had been on the field, Gil was making a difference. In a stroke of good luck, the first few Wulfenbach units he encountered recognized him instantly, and a wave of organization and renewed purpose could be seen spreading outward from his position. Van turned back to the rest of the Council. "It's bad to let the empire steal our thunder right from the start . . . "

The Master of Music and Assorted Dins shook his head. "Oh come, there's hardly any fear of *that*, now, *is* there?"

Van looked at him blankly. "Why not?"

The old people stared back at him in astonishment. Then as one, they all craned to stare at the Tower of the Doom Bell. The master had been examining the tower with a set of opera glasses and offered to pass them around. The Master of Revels and Subsequent Regret

---

[84] A local term for the more prosaically named Street of Dogs, which was where many of Mechanicsburg's cheaper hotels can be found.

snatched them and studied the tower. "Octavo is moving! He . . . yes! He has his hammer!"

Van still looked puzzled. It was Lady Vitriox who realized it first. "You're too young!" She swung back to the others in obvious distress. "He's too young! He's never *heard* it!"

The Master of Death and Afterwards gasped, "None of the young ones have heard it!"

Van broke in. "What am I missing here?"

"Your family! Your official job! When there is a new Heterodyne— the Doom Bell rings!"

Van absently patted the pocket where he kept a stack of business cards. The bell. Yes, he'd rather been looking forward to hearing it.

"Nobody has heard it for ages! They removed the hammer!"

"Even when the Heterodyne Boys were here, they *never* rang it! Not even for the birth of the child!"

Van looked wary. "So?"

The Master of Music and Assorted Dins gripped Van's arms. "So even if you're used to it . . . it has an effect. A *terrible* effect—"

"Oh, so it'll hinder any enemies in the area? That's good."

"But it could cripple our own defenses! Even while there are more invaders incoming!"

Van looked at the agitated elders and a trickle of uncertainty bloomed within his heart. "Oh . . . come on. You're just messing with the new kid again, aren't you?[85] I mean, when all's said and done, it *is* just a bell, right?"

Agatha stepped out of the doorway and gasped. The courtyard before her was filled with rubble and the occasional body. Windows were shattered. Even as she watched, a small gatehouse slumped to the

---

[85]   A reasonable assumption, as the City Council had celebrated Van's first day on the job by telling him he was expected to personally meet and shake hands with every one of the creatures hidden within the town. He only realized this was a joke after his third attempt to "shake hands" with a creature who did not actually possess them.

ground in a shower of blocks. From another structure, Vanamonde appeared leading a dozen old people who were so intent on her that they frequently stumbled on the debris that littered the ground. "Okay," she muttered. "They're all staring at me. You can get started any time."

"You have to *say* it," the Castle demanded. "Just like I told you."

Agatha sighed. "All right." She raised her voice and was astonished when it boomed forth, amplified beyond anything she could have naturally produced. "People of Mechanicsburg! The Castle is mine! I am your Heterodyne!" She hesitated.

"All of it!" the Castle hissed in her ear.

Again she sighed. "TREMBLE BEFORE ME!"

Atop the tower, Octavo slowly wound up, the hammer rising majestically over its shoulder. It glanced down at Oublenmach, who had gone straight through terror and was now philosophically resigned to being terrified at a later date. "I love this part," it said conspiratorially.

Then it *swung—*

And the Doom Bell's awful tolling washed over the town.

Deep under Castle Heterodyne, the air in the Great Movement Chamber was alive with expectancy. Moloch von Zinzer took a deep breath, cupped his hands around his mouth, and roared: "Now for the last time—*PULL!*"

Below him hundreds—no, it had to be thousands—of little clanks tightened their grippers around cables. A sound like an ocean of ticking watches arose and the clanks began to creep forward. Lines tightened, freshly greased pulleys began to groan as they slowly turned, and the great paddlewheel began to sway upwards into position.

Moloch was standing on the newly replaced spindle shaft, guiding it towards its socket by way of signals to the teams of clanks who adjusted the guide ropes accordingly. He was also employing excessive amounts of swearing.[86] The wheel shuddered as it thudded gently—a *bit* too much to the right of the opening. Moloch signaled the clanks to pull back and try again and, this time, as the wheel swung free, he grabbed hold of a rope, kicked off, then slammed his feet onto the side of the shaft as it slid forward, nudging it perfectly into place.

"Release the ropes!" With a series of coordinated tugs, the carefully tied knots unraveled and dropped away.

Atop the wheelhouse, Fräulein Snaug threw her weight onto the great clutch lever, engaging the gears. Far below, the paddles stopped *fighting* the rushing torrent of the River Dyne and, sluggishly, began to move *with* it. Within the tower, gears clunked against each other, resisted for a moment, then engaged. Fresh applications of grease began to spread within hidden surfaces as they were, once again, warmed by friction. More and more of the mechanism ground to life.

Within the Great Movement Chamber itself, there came a flickering of lights. Before Moloch's satisfied eyes, all the telltales began gleaming brighter, successive waves of them switching from red to green. With a whoop, Moloch did an ecstatic hornpipe jig atop the now-turning shaft. He then grabbed the rope anew and, with a quick hand-over-hand pull, hoisted himself to the top of the tower. There, Fräulein Snaug pulled him up and into a spontaneous hug of joy.

"Hey, Castle," Moloch called out. "You feel that, you stupid pile of rocks? It's fixed! Your power's back on!"

"Well done the two of you! And just in time!"

DOOOM!

---

[86]   Scientists have calculated the amount of energy released by a well-educated and erudite cusser. It seems to actually have a positive effect on projects that require physical manipulation of mechanical forces. What's more, the more florid the language the more it helps. Engineers have known this for as long as there have been engineers.

Even here, deep underground, the toll of the Doom Bell overwhelmed all other sounds. Moloch and Snaug screamed and clutched at their ears. Their eyes rolled up into their heads and they fell, senseless, to the top of the juddering tower.

The Castle gave a little *tut* of disapproval. "Well, you'll get used to it. The minions always do."

The Heliolux Airship Fleet swept towards Mechanicsburg from the east. The communication room of the flagship was an organized babble as dozens of operators coordinated the movements of the rest of the empire's army. Or rather . . . *tried* to. One of the operators sat back and stared blankly at her receiver. "It's stopped," she announced in surprise.

Her supervisor looked up from her clipboard. "What? What do you mean it's stopped? They were in mid-sentence."

"I know!" The operator frowned and slammed her fist down on top of the receiver in a practiced manner. This did nothing and she shrugged apologetically. Her supervisor bit her lip and examined her sheet with a growing worry. Similar scenes were taking place across the room. Something was . . .

The supervisor's thoughts were not aided by the bellow of the ship's captain from the doorway. "Lieutenant Hagopia, am I to get *any* confirmations at all today?"

Captain L'Marge was tall and round, everything the manual told you a good airship officer wasn't. She was also the oldest airship officer serving under the Baron, so no one had ever dared to bring this up. Her no-nonsense waddle-strut was often imitated, but never within five hundred kilometers of her last known location. What all the imitators got wrong, though, was how *fast* the woman moved. Lieutenant Hagopia found herself directly under L'Marge's pitiless eye as her precious clipboard was snapped away and examined. "We are *supposed* to be invading Mechanicsburg today. It would be *delightful* if I knew other people from our unit would be *joining* us."

"We're trying, ma'am, but everything's gone higgledy-piggledy."

L'Marge stared at her. "Believe it or not, Lieutenant, I rather pride myself on how well we facilitate communication. You should try it."

Hagopia took a deep breath. "All of the units we're supposed to be coordinating . . . " She indicated her clipboard. "We're losing them."

L'Marge stared at her. "Rumbletoys?"

"No answer."

"Ninth Ætheric?"

"No answer."

"Knifegrinders?"

"No answer!"

"Wind Walkers?"

"They were cut off."

L'Marge pursed her lips. "Too many different units." She glanced out the window. "I'm not seeing any ground action." She reached over and slammed a communicator switch. "Tower maintenance! Are we still on the air?" They stared at the speakers, but all that came through was a rolling hiss of static.

"What the Hell is going on?" L'Marge scowled. "We'll miss the fighting!"

"Wrong!" Everyone jumped as a cheerful voice rang out. In the hatchway stood a Jäger, his uniform crisp and jaunty. L'Marge was the first to grasp what was happening. Her hand darted towards the holster at her side, but the Jäger's hand was already gently closing over it. He gave an apologetic shrug and flipped the gun out and into his own hand.

L'Marge snarled. "How dare you betray—"

The Jäger tapped her lips with a clawed hand and smoothly retracted it before she could bite him. "Hyu iz *confused*, sveethot. De *Heterodyne* iz de vun ve ain't betrayink today. Dot vos de deal und de Baron knew dot."

L'Marge stepped back. "That . . . that girl is a fake."

The Jäger considered her with an arched eyebrow. "Hyu sure about dot?"

"Yes," she lied. "And don't hurt my people! We're noncombatants!"

The Jäger glanced at the gun in his hand and absentmindedly spun it around his finger. "Ho, yez? Iz dot vot hyu calls flyink around melting pipple down below into leedle puddles?"

L'Marge blustered. "We are a communications—"

The Jäger ended the discussion by crushing the gun in his hand. "Und hy iz de Princess Hasenpfeffer ov Spätzle"[87]

Another Jäger popped into the control room. "De rest of de fleet iz secured, Jorgi."

Jorgi nodded and then loomed over the pilots. "Hokay, keeds, hyu can land dis ting." He surveyed the ground and then jovially clapped a hand on each of the pilot's shoulders, causing them to start violently. "Howz about right outside de Monsters' Gate?[88] Ve gots to be ready to march in, yah?"

One of the pilots stared at the hand on her shoulder and said the first thing that came into her head: "But, you can't go into town, can you?"[89]

Jorgi winked at her. "Dot's right, dollink, not yet. But verra soon."

DOOOM!

Everyone in the cabin shrieked and collapsed. Jorgi quickly grabbed the controls, and with a knowledge that would have shocked Captain L'Marge if she had been coherent enough to appreciate it, began to guide the airship smoothly towards the ground.

"Verra soon indeed," he chuckled. "like, *right now!*"

---

87   Just for the record, he wasn't.

88   The Monsters' Gate was the entrance traditionally reserved for the creations of the Heterodyne, many of whom were large, loud, or socially inept.

89   When the Jägermonsters allowed themselves to be absorbed into the armies of the empire, part of the deal was that they could no longer enter Mechanicsburg as it was assumed they would be a bad influence on the townspeople. In the years since the deal had been struck—what with the perennial rumors of smuggling, black markets, and assorted financial hanky-panky amongst the townspeople—compared to the stellar performance of the Jägers, Klaus had often wondered who had been influencing whom.

The streets of Mechanicsburg were burning. Not all of them, of course, but Captain Kepler of the First Smarty-Pants Brigade vowed that, with enough time, he'd make sure he got to them all. He was roused from his murderous contemplation by one of his men stomping up to him, coming to order with a pop and a clank. "Sir!"

Kepler flicked a switch on what looked like a pair of ornately enameled mechanical hip waders and wheeled to face him. "What is it, Spinoza?"

"Got a situation, sir."

"Another one?"

"We've finally taken some prisoners, sir. They're just townspeople, but they were really giving us a hard time."

Kepler looked around and nodded. "How many?"

"Eight, sir."

"Anybody important? Doctors or City Council?"

"No, sir. I think they're bakers."

Kepler shrugged. "Okay, so what's the problem? Shoot them."

Spinoza blinked. "Shoot— but we can't do that!"

"Don't tell me you're out of bullets?"

"No, sir! But . . . but they've *surrendered*. And they're just a bunch of old men! Civilians!"

"So what are we *supposed* to do with them? Give them a kick in the pants and send them home? Who do you think is fighting us? 'Civilians' have wiped out half our squad! I've never *seen* resistance like this. They're shopkeepers, for Ares' sake! They shouldn't care who's in charge! They'll cheat *anybody!*"

The lieutenant trotted along silently, giving his superior time to wind down. "Well, this *is* Mechanicsburg, sir. They're not happy unless a Heterodyne in charge."

"Well then, their Heterodyne can protect them."

Soon they arrived at what indeed proved to be a bakery, though, from the state of its walls it wouldn't be functioning for quite a while.

Indications were the shutdown might be permanent, at least as far as the staff was concerned. They were lined up against a brick wall with ten armed troopers covering them.

Kepler stomped onto the scene and the troops gave him a salute. "Don't look at me when you're covering prisoners," he roared.

"Sir! Sorry, sir!" The soldiers snapped back into position. Kepler shook his head. It was easy to see why they'd allowed themselves to slip. The men against the wall were obviously bakers. Even beneath the battle grime, you could see the flour. But . . . these weren't just bakers. Even now, it was evident these were men just waiting for an excuse to leap back into action. Kepler had been a professional soldier long enough to know the most dangerous thing a career soldier could face was an impassioned amateur. They didn't follow the rules. He stood behind his men now. "You treat those men with respect?"

"Yes, sir!"

"Now, shoot them!"

"Yes—what?"

"Stand to attention!" They snapped into place. *Don't give them time to think,* Kepler thought grimly. "Form a firing line! Ready, aim—"

DOOOM!

The soldiers collapsed to the ground along with several of the younger bakers. The older men along the wall stared for a second before breaking into wild grins. One or two of them looked like they were going to be ill, though whether that was from the bell or the near death experience they would be hard-pressed to say.

The bakers gathered around the twitching soldiers. "That girl," Second Kneader Svenorgi said, "she really is the Heterodyne!"

"Which girl?"

"Time enough for that later," Ovenkeeper Kaspodin snapped. "We have to deal with these guys."

"Tie 'em up," said Master Gorpedi, already hauling a coil of rope out of one of the bakery's sheds. "They're just kids."

"And the one giving the orders?"

Master Pitokya pulled a rolling pin from his apron pocket and slapped it into his hand. "Oh, him we treat with *respect*."

Outside Mamma Gkika's, Gil held up a hand and the herd of tiger clanks came to a stop. "We're here," he announced.

Sleipnir looked at the building in confusion. Even with the shutters closed over the windows and the furniture from the beer garden stacked against the wall, there was no mistaking the nature of the establishment. "Gil? What do you mean, 'we're here'? This is a beer hall."

Gil vaulted off the clank. "It's not just a beer hall."

"I thought we were heading towards the Wulfenbach lines. There aren't any troops here."

Gil thought of Mister Higgs and wondered if he was still with Zeetha. "I wouldn't be too sure about that." He gave a couple of booming knocks on the front door.

"Okay, so why a beer hall?"

"Because it's not *just* a beer hall." He strode over to Theo, who was slumped forward across the back of his clank. When he realized Gil was next to him, he straightened up and gave a very creditable performance of a man in only mild discomfort. "Don't bother," Gil said. "I can see you're in a lot of pain. If only because these cats aren't the smoothest ride."

"It's just my arm," Theo insisted. "I won't hold you back."

"No, you won't," Gil agreed. "Because *you'll* be *here*."

"In a beer hall."

"It is not just a beer hall!"

The front door groaned open and a girl dressed in an abbreviated uniform posed in the entryway. "Sorry, sveethot, ve iz closed."

Suddenly she recognized Gil and her demeanor warmed considerably. "Oooh! It's hyu again! Come on in!"

Sleipnir stared at the girl and then at the few other girls she saw framed in the doorway. She calculated she was wearing more than all the women put together. Theo swiftly became accommodating as they stepped forward to help him down from his clank and into the building.

"It had *better* be just a beer hall," Sleipnir growled.

The doorkeeper smiled, revealing an elaborate set of sharp false teeth. "Ho! Is someone feeling *shy*?"

Theo blinked at the women. Sleipnir ducked under his arm, ostensibly to lend him support. "Jägers? Female Jägers?" He muttered.

"No," Sleipnir answered under her breath. "These are . . . costumes, I think."

"But why would customers want girls to dress as Jägers?"

A pale-skinned girl dressed in strips of black leather giggled saucily. "Hyu vanna find out, cutie pie?"

Theo stared at her. "No," he said slowly. "No, I don't think I do."

Gil recognized the look in Sleipnir's eye and quickly interrupted. "Will you please tell Mamma we're here?"

"Hy iz already here, Master Wulfenbach." Mamma swept into the room, defusing Sleipnir's annoyance with her sheer physical presence. Mamma was well over two meters tall and from her stunning aquamarine hair to her elegantly pointed ears there was no question she was a genuine Jäger. Gil noticed her usual attire— an elaborate gown—had been replaced with a finely decorated set of golden armor. She clapped her hands. "Gorls! Dis gentlemen is vounded! Schtop foolink around!" Instantly, professionalism of a different sort filled the room. Theo was laid on top of an empty table, and one of the girls began cutting away his bandage.

Gil filled Mamma in on what had happened at the Castle while she gave him a military overview of what had been happening in the town. A mug of really fine coffee had somehow appeared in his hand. He took a drink and finished up. "So Agatha should be done any time now."

"Dot's goot," Mamma said with a smile. "Becawze hy gots a cellar full ov ediots who's chust about to burst!"

An involuntary yip of pain caused them to glance over at Theo. "Can I leave the two of them here until the fighting's over," he asked quietly.

"Ov cawze! Ve gets heem fixed op toot sveety! Dot's French," she added helpfully.

Gil nodded. Mamma laid a clawed hand on his arm. "Vait, vun more ting." She took a deep breath. "Hyu poppa. He protected my boyz. Hy . . . all ov de Jägerkin, ve vill not forget dot."

"Memory goes both ways, madam. The Jägers served the empire loyally. It is my hope we will be defending the town together, assuming I can take control of my father's forces quickly. But now I must—"

DOOOM!

The room rocked as people moaned and fell, twitching.

"YEZ!" Gkika was on her feet, roaring in triumph. "De Bell rings! Ve haz a Heterodyne again!" She glanced at the people sprawled across the floor. "Keeds today," she sniffed. "Kent even take a leedle existential despair." She sighed. "Ho vell, s'poze hy gotta . . . "

"Agatha!" With his exclamation, Gkika noticed Gil was still standing beside her. She stared at him, astonished. His face was lit with an unholy glee that gave even her pause. "She did it," he marveled.

Gkika glanced at the others strewn on the floor and frowned. "Iz . . . iz hyu okeh? De sound ov de Doom Bell—"

Gil snapped his head towards her, and she stepped back from the fire in his eyes. "It means she's taken the Castle! She's alive and fighting! It sounds *beautiful!*"

Gkika shivered. "Hokay," she said over a growing roar that could be heard building in the cellars. "My boys iz comink and de Lady Heterodyne's consort iz gonna need an escort!" She grinned. "Let me get mine hat!"

In the courtyard before what today is known as The Lady's Gate, the City Council of Mechanicsburg dropped to one knee and bowed respectfully. Count Roargapotts, the Minister of Snails, hauled a dazed Vanamonde up from the ground with one burly hand, and manually inclined his head along with the rest of them. That done, he gently laid the young man back down. He faced Agatha, who was watching with concern. "He will recover quickly, my Lady. The von Mekkhan family was never one to cultivate philosophical pretensions."[90] He took a deep breath, then exclaimed, "Welcome home, Lady Heterodyne."

At this, all of the elders of the Council looked up at Agatha. She was struck by the *need* that burned within their eyes. She remembered the effect she'd had on the people in the coffee shop. *A whole town of minions waiting for a master.* For several seconds, various possibilities warred with the ethical quandary this presented. Who was she to determine every aspect of these people's lives? Then she looked about the town, the town that her ancestors had built and shaped to

---

[90]   We are all going to die. Maybe tomorrow, maybe a thousand years from now, but in the end Grandfather Death will take each of our hands, and no mistake. Throughout history, nearly everyone has hoped that this particular rule might not apply to them, whether because of blue blood, excessive attention to diet and exercise, money, or simply a refusal to acknowledge such a thing is even possible. The Doom Bell was crafted in such a way that, on hearing it, all this self-delusion is stripped away. The listener is forced to come face-to-face with the complete and total understanding that death—*their* death—is inevitable. Most people do not take it well. Counterintuitively, Mechanicsburg natives, who were almost guaranteed to hear the bell several times throughout their lives, were known as a people with an incredible *joie de vivre*, living their lives to the fullest. This actually makes sense, as the tolling of the bell periodically reminded them that they should enjoy themselves while they could.

serve their every whim. She again noted the obvious signs of decay that had begun to manifest ever since her family had left. Her jaw tightened. Priorities.

"Thank you, sir, but I cannot help but notice my home, as you call it, appears to be on fire. We can't do anything useful about that with you all on bended knee. Please get up."

This pronouncement had a marked effect, and Agatha noticed the people before her looked pleased as they rose to their feet. One of the ladies of the council, a rawboned harridan equipped with a shining pair of brass goggles, positively simpered and stepped forward. "Noticed the fire, have you?" She glanced out at the burning buildings. "And what do you think about that?"

Agatha stared at her. "What do I *think* about it? I think we need to put it out and get busy crushing everyone who's attacking us! The town is being invaded!" At this the entire council sighed in evident relief and a few even clapped their hands in delight.

Van had recovered somewhat. Herr Diamant helped him to his admittedly still shaky feet, then slapped him on the back. "Excellent!"

Agatha frowned. "An invasion is excellent?"

"No, no—" Van raised a hand. "Allow me to explain. What is *excellent* is that you noticed."

"Not just that." The woman leaned in. "But that you care!"

A man with an elaborate beard nodded vigorously. "That's not always the case, you know."

"It is an encouraging sign!"

"We also like the 'crushing' part."

"The Heterodynes have always protected Mechanicsburg, but some of you were better at it than others."

"In the War of Three Winters, your grandfather set the old Town Hall on fire, ostensibly to keep the people warm. He kept it burning for five months."

Agatha looked pensive. "Well, desperate times—"

"He lit it in June."

"Your *great*-grandfather decided that all of the children of the town should be *magnetized*—so we'd never get lost." The old man speaking sank into a pool of memories. "I used to get stuck to the Iron Bridge every time Mother sent me out for cheese," he murmured.

Another lady, a grand dame who reminded Agatha of nothing so much as a preserved dragon she had once seen in the Beetleburg Museum, sighed. "And your great-granduncle Ominox would goad enemies into attacking—and then yell 'surprise' when he released the magma bees!" She tittered at the memory. "Oh, I had such a crush on him!"

Agatha bit her lip. "And here I was worried I wouldn't be any good at this," she muttered.

Vanamonde leaned in and murmured, "You have fifty generations of lowered expectations working for you, my Lady."

One of the council members who had stayed towards the back gasped and waved a large watch on a chain. "Two minutes and she hasn't killed *anyone*! A new record!" The rest of the Council cheered.

What alarmed Agatha the most was that she couldn't tell if they were kidding or not. She turned towards Vanamonde. Aside from a newfound realization that life was transitory and we are all but insects crawling on an insignificant ball of rock hurtling through the cold, pitiless, void of space—he was feeling much better. "What is the situation?" she asked him.

Van considered this. "Well, the Doom Bell will have knocked out a lot of our attackers . . . "

At that moment a trio of spidery mechanisms, each piloted by what appeared to be a mummified pilot, hove into sight over the Castle wall. On sighting Agatha, the loudspeakers atop their central domes began to blare: "Death to the Witch of Mechanicsburg!"

Van sighed. "So it's a safe bet that anything left is going to be a bit tricky."

Agatha swung Gil's lightning cane upwards and sent a bolt crashing into the midst of the invaders. Several of them exploded most satisfactorily, but the third continued to advance, screaming, "DIEEEEEE!" over and over again in a manner everyone was beginning to find rather annoying.

Again Agatha aimed her stick, but this time it brought forth nothing but a faint crackle. This so outraged her that she scarcely noticed when Van grabbed her by her toolbelt's leather straps and dragged her away while the rest of the Town Council pelted the surprised invader with bricks.

"So, about these defenses?"

Van shrugged as he pulled her along. "The empire disabled our *obvious* weapons, but we're working on them. We have sappers in the tunnels and, of course, there are the tunnels themselves. There's a lot you can do with a good tunnel. We also have various tradesmen who use dangerous tools on a daily basis,[91] the Town Watch, and the Town Militia,[92] but they've mostly just got small arms and whistles."

"Whistles?"

"Really loud whistles.[93] Oh, and Frau Hoggle's got a really mean dog."[94]

"That's it? Centuries of mad science and we have *nothing*?"

---

[91]   As someone who had been raised by a construct blacksmith capable of throwing a sledgehammer through a meter-thick wall, Agatha understood this concept instinctively.

[92]   The Junior Heterodyne Society started over a century ago as an informal gang of Mechanicsburg youth. Their antics so amused Machiavelli Heterodyne that he made them the official town militia. Over the years, Machiavelli and subsequent Heterodynes encouraged them by providing uniforms, a barracks, and the power to "keep the peace" (not that there was a lot of trouble when the Heterodyne was in residence). Lest anyone be under the mistaken impression the Heterodynes of old harbored anything remotely resembling philanthropic urges, it should be pointed out that the J. H. S. was regularly supplied with experimental weapons and other devices, and was expected to use them. Opinions differ as to whether this was actually for the purposes of testing or whether it was purely for the entertainment of the Heterodyne.

[93]   By now, any reader of these chronicles should understand that when we say "loud," we're essentially talking about sonic weaponry.

[94]   Frau Hoggle's dog, on the other hand, was a perfectly normal Batavian Ripping Hound, who went into a murderous rage whenever anyone attacked Frau Hoggle by, for instance, breathing her air.

"I didn't say that. We have stuff, but without the Castle we don't know how well it will work."

From around the corner in front of them stepped an elegantly dressed, seven-meter-tall clank, fashioned entirely out of well-polished mahogany. Seeing Agatha, it whipped off its opera hat and bowed. "Lady Heterodyne," it boomed in a voice with a smooth burr to it. "My master demands your hand in marriage at your earliest convenience. Or else—"

The implied threat was cut off by a gigantic, shaggy green creature that leapt down from a rooftop, picked up the clank, and, with a scream of triumph, began hammering it against the cobbles.

Van sighed. "Until we know, we'll just have to rely on the monsters."

Agatha stared. "Monsters." She looked at Van askance. "I would have led with the monsters."

"Oh, well then, yes. We actually have quite a lot of those."

This particular monster, now sporting the opera hat at a rather raffish angle, lumbered over to the two people. It looked a bit nervous. "Herr Von Mekkhan," it said in a bubbling voice. After a bit of confusion, Agatha realized its three eyes were placed below its mouth. "Snoz can be out. They rang the Bell. They did!"

Van held up his hands placatingly. "Indeed they did!" He indicated Agatha. "Lady Heterodyne, this is Snoz. Snoz, this is the new Heterodyne."

Agatha looked up at him. "Hello."

Snoz looked a bit perplexed and gnawed absent-mindedly on an eyebrow. "A . . . girl?"

Agatha rolled her eyes. "Yes."

"Huh. Never seen a girl Heterodyne before."

Agatha crossed her arms. "And?"

Suddenly the creature grinned. "And new Heterodyne is cute!" He turned to Van. "Snoz like." He turned back to Agatha and raised a preemptory finger. "But Snoz is already in a committed relationship."

Agatha stared back. "I . . . I'll keep that in mind," she said faintly.

With a sigh of relief that a potential workplace crisis had been averted, Snoz leaned back, clapped his hands, and rubbed them together. "Snoz must go smash things now." With a last small bow, he launched himself up onto the nearest building, and dashed off over the roofline.

Agatha glanced back at the shattered clank. "How *many* monsters," she asked Van.

"Well," he said calculating, "a couple of hundred, more or less . . . " Just then, a low rolling moan sounded, followed a second later by a slow, lugubrious drumming. The sound caught at Agatha's heart. It spoke of loss and a great sadness brought about by separation. Her eyes began to feel hot and tears welled up. Then, even as she listened, the sounds changed. They became a joyful roar, the roar of a conquering army finally returning home. Oddly, this didn't stop the tears. She wiped them away and glanced at Van. A plethora of emotions chased each other across his face. "But it sounds like there are about to be a whole lot more!" he added.

At Mechanicsburg's eastern gate, a unit of the Mechanicsburg Militia, specifically three generations of the Mitsof family, stood resolutely by the family gun. At the first moaning, they had frozen in place. The youngest clung to her father's coat and stared out over the wall into the mists encircling the town. "What is that, Poppa?"

"I don't know, Baylijacha." her father muttered.

Behind them, her grandfather started like he had seen a ghost.[95] "It's the Jägers," he breathed in astonishment. "They're coming home!"

Now, in the heart of the mist, shapes could be seen moving. Lurching, shuffling ever closer to the gates. Baylijacha leaned over the parapet in fascination. "Real Jägermonsters?" She studied the figures and frowned. "I thought there'd be more of them."

---

[95]   Living in Mechanicsburg, of course, he *had* seen ghosts (or as near to as made no difference), but this was like seeing a ghost *he didn't know*.

Her father shrugged. "Well, it has been a long time . . . " A dry chuckle from behind them broke his chain of thought. "What's so funny, Gramps?" The old man had leaned back against the stone wall and a delighted look filled his face. The younger Mitsof felt a twinge of uncertainty. He'd never seen his father look so . . . mischievous.

"You are," the old man cackled. He turned his back on the advancing figures and looked out over the town. "These are the *Jägers* we are talking about. Right now our enemies are watching them advance, and thinking the same thing *you* are." He swung about and poked his granddaughter in the head. "But don't *you* be fooled." He raised his voice confidentially, "Right boys?"

With a ringing guffaw, Jägers appeared. Popping up from manholes, creeping out from eaves and chimneys. Throwing back shutters and rooftop doors. One burst upwards from where he had been hidden in a peddler's cart, scattering snails and giving the peddler himself a minor heart attack.

"Hyu leesten to hyu grandpoppa, keed!"

"Ve iz beink sobtle az all get owt!"

"Jah! Dot's psykologikal varfare, dot iz!"

A Jäger dropped from the ledge above them and clapped the old man on the back. "Goot to see hyu again, Mitko! Nize lookink keeds."

Tears appeared in the old man's eyes and he pumped the Jäger's hand vigorously. "Thank you, Borislav. Welcome home!"

"Tenk hyu." He tipped his hat to Baylijacha. "Hello, leetle gurl! Later hy vill show hyu how to throw a knife!"

"Ooh . . . really?"

"Uv cawze!" Borislav clapped his hands and roared out over the unsettlingly large pack of Jägers that had assembled below. "Hokay boys, ready to paint de town red? In de *best vay possible*?"

"YEZ!"

That roar, and many like it, was heard all over town. One of the councilmen was fretting as he and Herr Diamont were hurrying down the road. "They'll want to move back into the Jägerhall! But the Butcher's Guild has been using it as a slaughterhouse."

Herr Diamant waved a hand. "Won't be a problem, Itzokk, we won't even have to redecorate."

Aboard Castle Wulfenbach, in the vast Situation Room, Boris stared at the map of Mechanicsburg. With a sinking heart, he watched dozens of units shift color or be plucked from the board entirely. Beside him, a unicycle messenger explained the changes. "—numbers indicate that *all* of the Jägers are there, sir! But it should be impossible, unless they somehow knew about all this *days* ago!" Boris massaged his head with three hands. *At least days ago*, he thought glumly.

"STOP!" The trooper at the door just had time to add, "INTRUDER!" before a solid fist knocked him to the floor. His assailant stepped into the room and immediately raised his arms, a tricky operation as there was a large canvas sack draped over one shoulder.

"I am no intruder," he boomed, "Othar Tryggvassen—Gentleman Adventurer—was *invited!*"

Boris stared at Othar and an uncharacteristic feeling of hope washed through him. "You mean . . . you *found* him? You found Master Gilgamesh?"

Othar laughed as he swung the sack over his shoulder. He dropped it onto the deck with a solid *thump*, then opened the sack with a dramatic flourish, revealing the soles of a pair of shoes. He blinked, then with a graceful flip turned it right side up. "But of course! Allow me to present: *Gilgamesh Wulfenbach!*" With a second showman-like flourish, he whipped the sack upwards. There stood Tarvek Sturmvoraus, grim and seething. Othar stared for a long moment, then made a *ta-dah!* motion with his hands as he smoothly added, "*Master of Disguise!*"

As the last reverberations of the Doom Bell faded away, people inside Castle Heterodyne began to stir. Professor Caractacus Mezzasalma found himself splayed on the floor. With an embarrassed jolt, he began folding himself upwards. "Sweet lightning," he gasped, "what on Earth was *that?*"

To one side, Professor Mittelmind stood enraptured. "Why, that must have been the Doom Bell," he marveled. "Astonishing!" He saw his colleague's distress and hurried over to help him up.

Mezzasalma stared upwards in amazement. The older man seemed perfectly unfazed and, indeed, his usual cheerful smile appeared unforced. Mezzasalma was still trying to decide if he would ever smile again. "Getwin . . . were you unaffected?"

Mittelmind shrugged as he offered a hand. "Oh yes. Already dead, you know." He looked about. "But I *am* worried about Fräulein Snaug." He grasped Mezzasalma's hand and, revealing an unexpected strength, hauled him to his feet. "Come on, up up! Strength of the spider and all that!"

With a final mechanical ripple, Mezzasalma staggered to his feet. He looked about at the Castle. It felt . . . different. He shivered. "So the young lady really *is* the Heterodyne. Well spotted, Tiktoffen."

Mittelmind nodded. "I wonder if any of his machinations paid off?"

Mezzasalma snorted. "My dear fellow, he's so convoluted, how would he know?"

Mittelmind laughed in delight, but stopped as he noticed a prone figure across the room. He hurried over. "Oh dear, it's little Wilhelm!"

The girl was slumped against a gigantic ornamental vase. "I do hope she's alive," Mezzasalma said. "They're no fun when they're dead."

Mittelmind frowned, "Oh, I say, sir."

"Present company excepted, of course." Mezzasalma leaned in and checked Sanaa's neck. "A pulse, and a very healthy one." He gently moved her chin to one side, and the collar around her throat fell apart, the pieces dropping to the floor. Both men gasped in horror, then felt a further wave of panic as their own collars disintegrated into shards that pattered down through their scrabbling fingers. For a timeless moment they stared at each other and then realized they were, in fact, not going to blow up.[96]

"The Castle," Mittelmind whispered in amazement.

"It's repaired," Mezzasalma shouted. "They rang the Doom Bell!" He allowed himself to believe the unbelievable. "Good gracious, old fellow, we're *free!*"

---

[96] Prisoners sentenced to Castle Heterodyne found management to be rather laissez-faire, in that they were free to do pretty much anything they wanted. Antisocial behavior was regulated by the other prisoners, who were themselves no models of patience and rationality. Escape was prevented by collars that exploded if they went beyond the Castle doors. It was a very cold-blooded system, but after even a superficial perusal of the prisoners' list of crimes, no one felt sorry for them at all.

CHAPTER 8

The period of political unrest that subsequently became known as The First Shudder officially began when Baron Klaus Wulfenbach was injured by the Lady Heterodyne at the Battle of Balan's Gap. Up until this point, the Empire of the Pax Transylvania had seemed unstoppable and, indeed, inevitable.

Analysis indicates a great deal of Wulfenbach's initial success was due to the absolute chaos that reigned in the areas he conquered. The power of traditional royalty, as exemplified by the Fifty Families, was on the wane. Ascendant sparks, long kept as servants to royals, were realizing they could sit in the Big Chair themselves. Of course most sparks found it hard to understand that the ability to create carnivorous butterflies did not in fact prepare them for the complexities of good governance. Once they were in charge, things usually deteriorated quickly. The empire, on the other hand, was very well-run indeed, if only because the Baron tended to sweep up sparks and other disruptive elements and find ways to keep them productively occupied, preferably somewhere well-removed from the center of governance. After the first decade, several kingdoms and independent principalities actually petitioned to be absorbed by the empire.

Of course, even in the face of what everyone else considers a universal advancement, there are always those who have something to lose. Aside from the aforementioned Fifty Families, there were sparks, trade guilds, and other religious and fraternal organizations that believed they had been unjustly reduced in power and influence under Wulfenbach rule.

Many of these coalesced in the effort to overthrow

the empire and reestablish the Storm King who, being a more traditional monarch, would theoretically be more willing to recognize the inherent superiority of established authorities.

The original cabal had a fairly well-thought-out long-term plan that analysts today still insist had a very good chance of success. Unfortunately for the plotters, and one could make a good argument for the rest of Europa as well, a series of metaphorical hammer blows shattered this plan into fragments.

Among these were the revelation that the Baron had a son, Gilgamesh Wulfenbach, who looked to be as strong a spark as his sire. Secondly was the appearance of an actual Heterodyne heir who, just to throw a further monkey wrench into well-laid plans, was female. The third was the discovery that the Other, the terrible and mysterious spark who had been the scourge of Europa a generation ago, had managed to infect a significant portion of the population with mind control wasps. Infected individuals were now simply waiting, often without their own knowledge, to be activated as the Other's slaves and soldiers.

When news spread the Baron was seriously injured, the temptation to act quickly proved simply too great. Carefully laid plans were hastily abandoned and easily several dozen factions attempted to be the first to seize the moment. The coalition was shattered.

It was at this point, when the firm hand of the empire was needed most, that the word spread that Baron Klaus Wulfenbach was not injured—but dead.

—An excerpt from Professor Gaspard Van Loon's *A History of the Pax Transylvania: Europa's Golden Age* (Amsterdam Free Press)

❧❧❧

Atop the Tower of the Doom Bell, Baron Krassimir Oublenmach realized his tongue was touching the stones of the roof. They tasted like the snail vinaigrette at his favorite restaurant in Krakow, which he found rather amusing. Then he realized he might possibly be insane. He took some comfort from this and attempted to sit up. He failed miserably and wept at the unfairness of it all.

This small movement brought him to the Castle's attention.

"Heh heh heh," it chuckled. The sound awakened survival instincts Oublenmach had long ago assumed were unnecessary and taken to their primordial bed. Oublenmach swiveled an eye upwards and saw the bell-striker slumped against the bell itself, the great hammer propped up against his knee. "You are still alive, little adventurer?" the Castle boomed. A gigantic finger gently poked him in the side. He twitched. "Extraordinary."

To Oublenmach's astonishment, the great figure then leaned over and rearranged him so that he was lying a bit more comfortably. The striker then continued conversationally, "You wanted the treasure of the Heterodynes, yes?" Oublenmach didn't bother to deny it. He was a man who would work twice as hard on a project if it meant avoiding the terrible *sameness* of "honest labor," and he had found hints of something wonderful behind the hyperbole usually associated with the mythic treasure.

"Well, I don't know if you *care* anymore, but it's here." This statement acted as a tonic on the supine man. His eyes widened as a massive shape clawed its way up and hung effortlessly from the edge of the tower.

It took a few seconds for Oublenmach to understand what exactly he was seeing, but when he did, the breath caught in his throat. It was a dragon. Not your elegant, gracile dragon who dined exclusively on chivalric knights honey-baked in their own armor, no. This was a cobby, coarse, workaday dragon with a hide that could stop a cannonball. Round, green-tinted brass meters were implanted along its length. As it heaved itself to a slightly more comfortable resting place, Oublenmach saw the impossibly small, outstretched wings and the great iron door strapped like an improbable corset across its chest. A porthole in the door's center gave off a yellow glow, hinting at the alchemical energies roiling within.

The great head swung about and glanced at Oublenmach with sleepy eyes. Then the beast gave a great snort of dismissal. It addressed the bell-striker in a voice like boulders grinding together: "You woke me up for *this*?"

Oublenmach thought this a bit unfair. The bell-striker's hand gestured placatingly.

"A Heterodyne has returned to us," the Castle said.

With a grunt, the dragon hauled himself the rest of the way onto the tower. One of the reasons for his clumsiness became evident when he laboriously swung a huge, mildewed canvas sack over the parapet, setting it down hard with a metallic clink that immediately caught Oublenmach's attention. He then rested both clawed hands under his wings and leaned back, producing a series of meaty crackles. He sighed with satisfaction and looked around. Below, a large part of the town was burning or at least smoking. The dragon blinked and looked interested. "Hey, I think we're being attacked."

There was a significant pause before the Castle replied: "You're not really a 'morning person' are you Franz?"

The dragon had begun to breathe faster and a cloud of steam purled from his jaws. "Hold on," he muttered. "Hold on. This means I get to do this the *fun* way!" He waddled across the tower to look over the other side and almost stepped on Oublenmach. He peered down at the man. "So what is this?" He glanced over at Octavo. "You got me breakfast?" He considered Oublenmach critically. "I'd *prefer* a croissant . . . "

"Oh, I'm afraid not," the Castle interjected. "*Technically*, this person has aided us."

Franz swiveled a skeptical eye back down at Oublenmach. "*Technically*, huh?" He sighed. "Fine." The dragon then dug into the great sack, swung his hand out, and opened it, releasing a great handful of gold coins that rained down onto the startled man's head. "LONG LIVE THE NEW HETERODYNE," he bellowed. "REJOICE, YOU."

Franz looked up. "That was unsatisfying," he said. He looked down on the beleaguered town. "What about *your* job, Castle? Doesn't look like you're doing much from up here."

"I am not," the Castle said bitterly, one put-upon employee to another. "I am repaired, but my power is nearly depleted. I am doing what I can. The rest of the Heterodyne's servants are awakening and returning."

"Will that be enough?"

"That depends on the Heterodyne. Everything depends on her now."

Franz's eye ridges rose. "A 'her' is it? *That's* different."

"You're not going to get overly traditional about this, are you?

The Dragon wistfully licked his pebbly lips and sighed as he looked out over the town. "Can't see as the traditional Heterodynes have been terribly effective lately. A change sounds good to me." He sniffed. "Not that the rest of us are chopped liver."

"You might as well be," the Castle sniped back. "As long as you just stand around here jawing!"

"Okay, I'm going, I'm *going!*"

Unnoticed by the two, a wondrous thing had occurred. Whether it was the dragon's voice roaring scant meters from his head or the heap of gold millimeters from his nose, Oublenmach's broken mind had shuddered back into productive operation once again. His hand reached out and grasped a pile of coins, while his mind spun back up to speed. *Gold. The dragon. The Great Guardian. All of the legends were true.* He gave a feeble chuckle that came out as more of a wheeze, but all things considered, it was still impressive. *I can do this,* he realized. *There really is a treasure. Now all I have to do is make it mine, and I'll have won!*[97]

Down on the meaner-than-usual streets of Mechanicsburg, the presumptive ruler thereof was trotting along at a fair pace when she noticed the man beside her was having a rough time keeping up with her. She stopped and Van gratefully stumbled up alongside her, gasping mightily. *I'm not even breathing hard,* Agatha realized. *Thank you, Zeetha.* From behind came the giant tiger clank that was now Otilia. Krosp rode on top, looking about with great interest.

Clamped delicately in its jaws was the scruff of Violetta's tunic. The Smoke Knight had been hit particularly hard by the Doom Bell and had yet to revive. Agatha had thought about leaving her somewhere safe, but looking around she was forced to come to the conclusion that no such place existed within the town walls. "I think we've lost them," she told Van.

"Good," he panted. "I didn't know they even *made* those electric wasps anymore."

"They don't. You can't get the parts."

Van looked interested. "Really? We should sell those."

Agatha rolled her eyes. "I think the *first* thing I should do is get up to the city walls. See what we're facing."

Van sucked in a huge lungful of air and tried to look authoritative. "No way. I'm taking you to the cathedral, where it's safe."

---

[97] Thus began Krassimir Oublenmach's storied career as a loyal servant of the Heterodyne family. This was a categorization he strenuously denied throughout his life, but the results spoke for themselves and they spoke through a solid gold megaphone. However, this is all in the future and so, for now, we must leave him lying on the tower roof, his future before him, as this present chronicle is not his story.

"How am I supposed to get anything done from there?"

"You won't. The Jägers and the other monsters will do the fighting. That's what they were *made* for! *You* are the last Heterodyne. You have to be kept safe until the town is secure. You've *done* your part! You fixed the Castle. The Doom Bell rang. At this point, what else *can* you do?"

Agatha was startled by Van's vehemence and stepped back, only to run into a wall. *No,* she looked around, *not a wall. A statue.* They were in Heterodyne Square, and she found herself staring up at the famous iron statue of the Heterodyne Boys. Her father, personified in metal, standing there so strong and so pleased with himself. Uncle Barry, recognizable to her, but oh so much younger and happier than she had ever seen him in life, confident and ready for anything. Both of them were giving their famous "thumbs up" signal, implying there was nothing they couldn't handle. They were before her larger than life and, as far as the town was concerned, completely useless. *Well, unless I could find a way to drop them onto an attacker,* she thought.

Mechanicsburg has always needed a Heterodyne, Agatha noted to herself. And the Heterodyne it has right now when it needs one more than ever is me.

"Wrong question, Herr von Mekkhan," Agatha said in a voice rich in the harmonics of the spark. Vanamonde stared at her as she went on. "I *am* the Heterodyne. My town is under attack. The question you should be answering is: What *can't* I do?"

Agatha wouldn't have been a spark if she couldn't have continued in this vein for several more minutes, but she was knocked out of the moment by a burst of cheering overridden by a strong female voice. "Ho! Now *dot's* de right attitude, sveethot!" Agatha whirled and saw crowds of Jägers pouring into the square from all different directions. Foremost was Mamma Gkika, clad in her shining golden armor and toting a gigantic battle axe over her shoulder. "Bot effen if hyu *iz* a strong spark, if neffer hurts to half a nize army to back hyu op!"

Before Agatha could move, she was swept up into a fierce hug that lifted her off the ground. "Zo hyu iz de new Heterodyne," the giantess murmured as she gave her another squeeze. "Velcome home, sveetie!"

Agatha struggled to breathe and gasped out, "Who . . . are . . . *you*?"

"Ho!" Agatha found herself gently deposited on the ground, and the Jäger fired off a crisp salute. "Jäger General Gkika at hyu service, m'Lady!" She clapped her hands and continued, "And deez iz my boyz." As one, several hundred slouching Jägers snapped to parade-ground attention while issuing a joyful roar that echoed all over the town. Gkika nodded and smiled proudly. "Hyour boyz, ektually."

"Thank you," Agatha said. She turned to the assembled monster soldiers. "I'm so glad you're here." She couldn't really think of what else to say. Her throat tightened and the tears were threatening to return to her eyes. "I'm . . . sorry it took me so long to return."

It was evidently the *perfect* thing to say. The group simultaneously dropped to one knee and with one voice shouted, "Dot's hokay, ve kept busy!" This was apparently as much formality as they could manage. The shout dissolved into great peals of wild, delighted laughter.

Agatha turned back to General Gkika. "I didn't know there were other generals."

Gkika grinned. "Hyu just met dose three old ogres on Castle Wulfenbach, yez?" She gave Agatha a conspiratorial nudge. "Lucky for hyu dere iz more of us dan dot." She stood up. "Ven dis iz all calmed down, hyu vill get to meet *all* ov us. But for now, my boys tell me dot dere iz more trouble on de vay, und hy haff not seen any decent trouble in ages! Dis iz gonna be *fun!*"

Agatha felt a touch of relief. Here was someone she could ask for advice and probably even get it. "Okay general, what should we do first?"

Gkika nodded. "De first ting ve gots to do iz collect all de invaders dot iz schtill messed op from de Doom Bell. Den ve start pooshink out the vuns dot ain't messed op and mess dem op ourselves. Der townspipple should start shoring op de defenses, although . . . " She looked troubled.

"What?"

"Ve iz unprepared, Mistress. No enemy has effer breached our valls like dis before. De Kestle is supposed to be in charge of de town defenses, but it iz obviously schtill damaged." She looked at Agatha seriously. "Dis iz not goink to be easy."

Agatha took a deep breath. "Well, let's find out just how tough it's going to be."

Gkika nodded. "Hy gots just de place."

Shortly thereafter, Agatha stood atop a precarious-looking tower that rose several stories higher than the buildings around it. The rooftop area was girt with odd observation devices as well as assorted levers Van assured her did nothing ". . . at the moment."

Mamma spread her arms proudly. "De Heterodyne's Observation Tower! Iz de perfect place to direct battles und speet on pipple!" Agatha looked around. It *was* perfect. The Jäger continued, "Und ven hyu iz not fighting, hyu ken bring hyu boyfriend op here. Diz plaze gets hit by lightning all de time. Iz verra romantink!"

The thought brought a flush to Agatha's cheek. She covered it by looking through a massive telescope. The Awful Tower swam into view, lightning crackling along its length.[98] Agatha jerked back in surprise. A quick search found a dial that was currently set to PARIS. She nodded in appreciation and snapped it to LOCAL. The tower shuddered as gears began adjusting the viewer's focal points.

---

[98]   The Awful Tower is the lair of Simone Voltaire, the Master of Paris. At the time of our story, he had been ruling that independent city state for over two centuries. The tower itself is still one of the tallest standalone structures in Europa. It was universally despised by Parisians when it was first erected, but in the last hundred years it has become the international symbol of Paris, even as the locals make a great show of pretending that it doesn't exist.

Agatha turned back to the Jäger. "You say there's trouble coming. What kind?"

"Ve haff a bit ov breathing spaze," Mamma admitted. "Bot ve gots vun beeg army coming up de pass from Sturmhalten. Lotsa nasty monsters," she said with a touch of admiration. "De Baron looks like he's throwing effery ting he's got at us from all sides. Der armies ov de empire iz schtill in control ov de overall area, includink a fair amount ov de valley.[99] At de moment, dey seem to be preoccupied vit dealink vit odder attackers." Gkika smiled. "Vitch iz mighty sportink ov dem, since most of dem are determined to take de town. Ostensibly to support de new Heterodyne."

"Support me?" This was news to Agatha.

Gkika shook her head. "Dun hyu gets hyu hopes op, sveety. Dot's just vot dey iz *sayink*. Most of dem sound like dey iz here for dot pink gurl. Dey iz not hyu friends. Und they gots factions und divisions und fightink among dey own rebellion." Her lip curled in contempt. "Dese guys iz a mess."

Agatha looked hopeful. "So that should make them easy to crush, right?"

Gkika shrugged. "In de old days, yah, hyu betcha. Right now? Vell, all our really *goot* veapons iz out ov commission and de Kestle iz schtill acting all broken-like. Back in hyu grandfodder's time it vould haff already sent dese jokers packink, *yah!*"

"It's not the Castle's fault," Agatha explained. "I *repaired* it, but it was operating on stored power. It can't generate any more at the moment."

"Technically no longer true, Mistress." The Castle's voice seemed to be emanating from a small grill set in a nearby wall. It sounded

---

[99] The town of Mechanicsburg sits within the Valley of the Heterodynes, circled by impassible mountains and steep chasms. It was chosen by the family for its inaccessibility. Strategists over the centuries have declared that a well-equipped invading army could be thwarted by one strategically placed man armed with a few rocks, a lava cannon, a flock of winged, acid-spitting worms, and "those windup things with the mirrors that make horses explode." They spoke from experience.

small and far away. "It was a close call, but I am pleased to report that your chief minion has restored my main generators."

"Dot's goot," Gkika said.

"That's *wonderful*," Van declared.

"To a point. But I am still weak. It will take time to build up sufficient energy to do anything truly useful."

Agatha looked wary. "How long?"

The Castle hesitated. "All nonessential systems are already shut down. With everything shunted to the charging of offensive weapons alone . . . I would say about three years."

Agatha stared. "Three years."

"At the present rate. Give or take a few weeks, yes. Less than ideal I'll admit, but I still have systems—exterior systems—that need repair. Ah, but three years from now, *watch out!*" It paused. "Well, assuming you're still alive, of course."

Agatha rolled her eyes. "This is terrible." Glumly she looked out over the town. "At least it's not just us. Our enemies are also running around like headless constructs. That's unbelievably lucky." She turned to Van and General Gkika. "But, I have to say, I'm not impressed. To let all of the town's major defenses fall into such disrepair—just because you were under the empire's protection—"

"Dot vos not our fault," Gkika objected. "De Baron disarmed all de really goot schtuff."

"Why? If you were part of the empire—?"

"To keep the *rest* of the empire happy," Van interrupted. "Wulfenbach may have been friends with Masters Bill and Barry, but historically the House of Wulfenbach and the House of Heterodyne were adversaries. The old Castle Wulfenbach was part of the system of picket fortresses the Storm King established to keep the Heterodynes contained.[100] The Baron's conquest of Mechanicsburg

---

[100] In addition to Castle Sturmhalten to the west and the original Castle Wulfenbach to the east, the ring was completed by the Refuge of Storms to the north and Castle Von Drakken to the south.

served several purposes. Having the town under his control was great for the Baron's image. Everyone assumed he had full access to the Heterodyne's secrets.

"He didn't, of course. He tried to learn as much as he could, but this town has a *lot* of secrets. He made a great show of dismantling and decommissioning some of the masters' more horrific devices." Van sighed. "But so many of the townspeople believed the masters would someday return, they would just quietly repair what the Baron had destroyed. Then the Baron would send people in to disarm things again and then our people would sneak back and fix things so that they only *looked* broken. Then the Baron's people would come back and break things again in new and more subtle ways . . . " Van spread his hands. "It went on for *years.*"

Keeping you all quite busy, Agatha thought to herself with a touch of admiration. Aloud, she asked, "Why didn't he just haul it all away?"

"Oh, he did take some of it." Van waved a hand towards a bronze statue of a huge, horse-headed pikeman. "But frankly, it would be hard to move everything and, in every other way, we were good subjects of the empire. We never gave them a reason to worry." Van reached up and inserted a finger into the horseman's nose. Its eyes began to glow and it shuddered into a defensive position, pike held forward. "As a result, we've managed to retain a number of things the empire overlooked." He grinned. "Like the Torchmen. A lot of them crashed because we couldn't maintain and test them properly, but they still gave the Baron a nasty surprise."

Agatha regarded Van for a moment, then looked up at the clank beside him. Yes, she thought. The Baron will remember that Mechanicsburg is a place where he can't expect the rules to apply. He'll assume that everything is more dangerous than it appears to be. She felt a wave of exhaustion wash through her. She shook her head and examined the cane in her hands. "How quickly do you think we can get Gil's lightning generators analyzed and replaced?

You know, those things he had all along the town walls? I know most of them melted, but—"

Van waved a hand to cut her off. "Lady Heterodyne, please! We've had people working on duplicating them since we saw them in action! Those things are *amazing!*"[101]

A wave of pure happiness suffused Agatha's being. *I knew there was a reason I liked this town,* she thought.

Gilgamesh marched, scowling, through the halls of Castle Wulfenbach. Atop his head was the magnificent hat that had been the gift of the Jägermonsters at Mamma Gkika's. It was a glorious, handmade creation adorned with wings, spikes, a burner on top that could be set to spout a small burst of flame, and a banner around the band that declared the wearer to be "Gilgamesh Wulfenbach, Schmott Guy!" It was ridiculous in every way, and yet it was astonishingly effective at speeding him through what was supposed to be an iron-tight ring of security. Gil had landed his small air pinnacle at one of the outer loading docks—tense and fearful, not knowing what he would find now that the news of his father's death had spread. The guards had been jumpy and unsure, suspicious even of him. They had slowly and meticulously begun with the proper procedures, until Gil, frustrated, had retrieved the stupid thing from the ship and hefted it onto his head. To his disgust, it was as if a magic switch had been thrown. Their eyes widened and they bowed obsequiously while waving him on. As he moved through the halls of Castle Wulfenbach, similar scenes took place again and again. Guards would initially challenge him, only to defer to the majesty of the hat that proclaimed him their leader. Gil grew more and more furious yet perversely curious: would this

---

[101] The Lady Heterodyne is referring to the ambient electricity accumulators that Gilgamesh Wulfenbach used to great effect against the walking battle fortresses of the Knights of Jove in their attack on Mechanicsburg. This is all chronicled in our previous textbook *Agatha H and the Voice of the Castle.*

phenomenon actually take him all the way to the Command Center of Castle Wulfenbach? Only once did he encounter a no-nonsense captain who had refused to accept "that ridiculous hat" as proof of identity. Gil had knocked him out with a single well-placed blow and continued on, making a guilty mental note to promote the man when time allowed.

And now he strode into Castle Wulfenbach's great hall, making straight for Boris, who seemed incapable of deciding whether to focus on Gil's stormy face or the monstrous hat.

"Boris!"

"Ah—Yes? Master Gilgamesh?"

"Yes! That is in fact who I am. Who else could ever wear so majestic and commanding a hat?"

Boris stared. "Um. Surely no one, sir."

"Good. So we're all agreed I am, in fact, me?"

"What? Yes! Of course!"

"Good!" Gil turned on his heel and stepped towards the nearest soldier. "You!" He snatched off the great hat and bundled it into the startled man's arms. "Take this, hide it in a safe place, and never speak of it again."

The soldier opened his mouth, saw the look in Gil's eye, and swallowed. "Yessir!" He barked before scuttling away.[102]

As soon as the hat disappeared around the far corner, Gil allowed himself to relax. This lasted all of three seconds until Bangladesh DuPree charged into the room, eyes wide with excitement. "I heard there was a hat!" She called.

Gil fixed her with a sideways frown. "You're delusional." Then he turned fully to face her. His serious expression made her stop short.

---

[102]   Where this nameless soldier took the infamous hat has been a subject of speculation for years. However, it was recently discovered in an abandoned Wulfenbach outpost on one of the Azores islands. It currently occupies a place of honor in the *Musée de la Mode et du Textile* in Paris.

"Weren't you supposed to be with my father?" He asked, "What *happened*?"

"He sent me out of the hospital!"

Gil stared at her. "And you *went*?"

"Well, yes! Because doing what he says is my job!"

"Oh, and you always follow orders."

"Hey! I followed *his* orders! Even when I thought they were stupid! He says go do this stupid thing—I go do it! And when the attack came, I had to run all the way back to the hospital! But I couldn't . . . I couldn't *find* him! I couldn't find him *anywhere*! And . . . and—" To Gil's horror and amazement, tears started to appear in her eyes. "—and then the whole place came down and I couldn't save him," she sobbed. "And I really, really tried."

Automatically Gil folded her into his arms and held tightly as her body shook. "I know," he murmured. "And if *you* couldn't do it, no one could."

He felt fingers dig into his spine. "You have made me cry." The muffled voice came faintly from somewhere near his dampened waistcoat. "For this I will kill you."

"Yes, yes," Gil murmured as he gently stroked her hair, "you do that."

It was the silence that made him look up. Ranged around the two of them were all the powers of the empire, not just the leaders of its military forces or Klaus's inner coterie of sparks, monsters, and adventurers. Ranged behind the great figure of Captain Patel[103] stood the crew bosses and chief technicians who spoke for the huge staff that ran Castle Wulfenbach. Also present were representatives of the vast trading houses that kept the empire supplied, as well as

---

103   Amit Patel was the authentic captain in command of the Castle Wulfenbach airship. He had been an air pirate until he had been recruited by Klaus. He, thereafter, served from Castle Wulfenbach's launch until its destruction. Klaus hired a lot of air pirates. On the whole, they proved to be superior flyers, knew the importance of taking orders, and were good in a fight.

functionaries from the foreign services. With them, Gil noted with a rising wave of panic, were the ambassadors of the empire's most important neighbors.

Gil looked back to Boris, who met his eyes and slowly bowed before him. The crowd behind solemnly followed his lead. Boris straightened and said the words that had haunted Gil's nightmares for over a decade: "Everyone is waiting . . . Herr Baron."

Gil felt Bangladesh freeze. He gently released her and saw that, although she was still wiping away tears, her eyes now held an expression of deep amusement. She was back to laughing at him. *Good.* He squared his shoulders, prepared to issue his first command . . . then hesitated. "No." He shook his head. "This doesn't feel right."

Boris stepped forward and gave him a look that any parent would recognize as a variation of *Not in Front of the Children,* while surreptitiously indicating the assembled onlookers.

Gil lowered his voice. "Calling me *Baron,*" he chided. "Surely you have more faith in my father than *that.*" A thought 'struck him. "Unless . . . have you found his body?"

Boris waved a hand quickly. "No, sir, but I *am* acting on his direct orders."

"What?"

Boris took a deep breath. "Your father gave me *very* clear instructions regarding the actions I am to take if there is ever any cause to believe him dead. I am to publicly recognize you as the new baron without delay. I believe his intention was to ensure an orderly transition and preserve the peace throughout Europa. *Especially* since there would undoubtedly be some sort of trouble going on if he were to be killed in the first place."

Gil could feel the unassailable walls of his father's logic slamming into place around his future. "I . . . see. Very well. But I will not be so quick to assume his title."

Boris smiled. "That should be no trouble. Your father left orders that if this was your response, then I should use one of your other legitimate titles: Your Highness."

Gasps echoed throughout the room.[104]

Gil stared at Boris sourly. "I can't even imagine what *that* is about. Just one more thing he never bothered telling me, I suppose." He became aware of Bangladesh staring at him. "What?"

She shook her head in admiration. "I always wondered how Klaus planned to run off and leave you holding the bag." She waved at the watching assemblage. "Very impressive."

Gil allowed himself a flash of familial pride. *Very impressive indeed.*

Half an hour later, after he had spoken some words that both soothed and inspired, Gil found himself the center of a tight little squad striding along one of the great corridors towards the Map Room. "What is the current situation?"

"We are attempting to control a fifty-kilometer ring around the town, but this is under attack by, at last count, nine different forces," Boris replied. "Several of these enemy forces have actually managed to enter the town. They are concentrated in a wedge to the south. The imperial forces within the town are scattered throughout. Communications were disrupted by the Doom Bell and we lost contact with many units.

---

[104] The title of "Highness" is generally considered the exclusive property of traditional monarchy, which the Wulfenbach Empire was most definitely not. The inference, therefore, is that Gilgamesh Wulfenbach claimed this title by relation to his as-yet-unidentified mother. This was, in retrospect, a masterful political stroke on the Baron's part, doubly effective because it was unexpected. A great deal of the longstanding friction between the Baron and the Fifty Families—the loose cabal of royal houses united by intricate bloodlines and a growing realization they were being replaced by the ascendant spark meritocracy—was the result of the Baron's unwillingness to acknowledge that the innate property of royalty was a thing worth considering. Although he had sufficient temporal power to easily have declared himself "Emperor" and suffer few, if any, dissenters, Klaus Wulfenbach would never bother to call himself, nor allow anyone else to proclaim him, anything other than his legitimately inherited title of "Baron." Thus, when he revealed his son and heir theoretically occupied an acceptable position within the Fifty Families established hierarchal structure, it immediately swung several influential Houses from detractors to actual supporters.

"The remaining forces are now regrouping on the grounds of the Great Hospital. Many of them are now being used for relief efforts and to clear rubble. There is a very heavy guerrilla presence in the rest of the town. Although they are not attacking any of the troops working at the hospital, they are proving remarkably effective against the enemy forces.

"Reinforcements have been called for, but there have been numerous local rebellions and several outright mutinies have tied up a distressing amount of our armies. We believe these to be coordinated, by the way. Someone wants our forces in Mechanicsburg to be undermanned. The only people with that sort of intercontinental influence are the Fifty Families. We have sent units to search out the known power players, but they have gone to ground. Ironically, the Wulfenbach units we can expect to arrive first are the ones who were stationed the farthest away—on the borders or in the wastelands—but I do not expect the first of them to be here in less than ten hours.

"The most worrying of the outside problems is Sturmhalten. We've lost contact with our people there and we've reports of a horde of monsters emerging from the town's sewers. Those are now approaching Mechanicsburg." Boris sighed and rubbed his eyes. "Every other group they encounter is either killed—or joins them. Including every one we've sent."

Gil nodded grimly. "The Other."

Boris looked harried. "But . . . but *how*? Isn't the Lady Heterodyne the Other? The Jägers told me—"

"No!" Gil paused. "Well, she's *one* of them—a little—but only sometimes. Anyway, she's not the one we have to worry about. At least not at the moment."

"There's more than one of them?"

Gil saw the look on Boris's face. "We're working on it, okay? I'll explain more later."

Boris turned to Bangladesh DuPree. "Am I the only person who's worried about this?"

Bang shook her head. "*I'm* worried."

Boris blinked. "You are?"

"Sure. I'm worried I won't get a chance to shoot her."

To Boris's amazement, he suddenly understood why the Baron had allowed Bangladesh to continue to exist. He leaned in towards her. "If you *must* shoot her," he said *sotto voce*, "don't miss."

Bang's eyebrows rose in surprise and she gave him a delighted punch on the arm. "We're connecting!" Boris felt sick.

Gil clapped his hands. "The first thing is to reestablish communications to all the troops. All attacks on Mechanicsburg are to cease immediately and they are all to proceed to the grounds of the Great Hospital."

Boris looked uncomfortable. "That order has already gone out, sir."

Gil looked surprised as they entered the map room. "Already? But, why—"

"Because *I* told them to!"

Gil stopped and stared. Tarvek was standing in the middle of the room, on top of the actual map table, a set of airship markers in his hand. "We're now focused on defending the town and restoring the peace."

"What are you doing here?" Gil demanded, once his surprise had passed.

"Running your empire," Tarvek snapped. "And *you* left before me! What *took* you so long?"

Gil stared at him. "You're supposed to be with Agatha!" He pointed accusingly at Tarvek and turned. "Boris, he's supposed to be with Agatha. Why is he here?"

Boris threw his hands up. "Your father sent Othar Tryggvassen into the Castle to get you, but he brought this fellow back instead. We were hauling both of them off to the brig and Prince Sturmvarous glanced—*glanced*—at the operations table here as he was dragged past. From that alone he was able to deduce—and argue convincingly—that the 20th Chemical had been subverted. If they'd gone another kilometer, they could have destroyed our entire supply line, as well as the ammunition haulers. Within an hour, most of our units would have been defenseless. It was his idea to contain them with the 43rd Air and the Slow Movers." Boris shrugged. "He's been coordinating the military ever since."

Gil regarded Tarvek sourly. "Who's been assessing his decisions?"

"Myself, Kleegon, the Deep Thinkers, and the rest of the High Command." Boris dropped his voice. "He's actually made several moves that will have great long-term benefits for the empire."

"Really."

"Yes, *really*," Tarvek interrupted. "You think I'm going to mess around with stupid plotting while Agatha's in danger?"

Gil considered him seriously. "No, I think it would be really *good* plotting that would help us *now*, while setting things up to *your* advantage for later."

Tarvek opened his mouth, hesitated, and then mentally switched gears. "Let's concentrate on the now."

Gil gave him a satisfied grin and extended a hand. "Fair enough. Show me what you've done." They clasped hands and Tarvek pulled Gil up onto the table. For a while, they picked their way across the tiny model countryside discussing strategy. Gil paused when they came to a fleet of sleek airships. "I'm worried about this squadron of sky-sharks. They're not flying in a standard Wulfenbach pattern."

Tarvek nodded. "Well spotted. Their officers are loyal to the Knights of Jove. I was waiting to see if any other units joined their formation. A few have—" he indicated two ground units marked with red flags "—but I believe their expected allies have not arrived. They should be very much on edge. If you take out the lead ship, which contains the leaders of the Moglar Alliance, then the Sharks, as well as the Mecha-Schnauzers and the 5th Wheel Guns, will desperately try to pretend they were never disloyal at all."

Gil nodded. "Boris, I want that ship cocooned and dropped right now." Gil looked at Tarvek quizzically. "But hang on, Sturmvarous, don't the Knights of Jove answer to you?"

Tarvek sighed. "They answered to my father and to the heads of the Order. I was probably written off as soon as I was captured at Sturmhalten. I seriously doubt my coming down with something as exotic as Hogfarb's Resplendent Immolation[105] was an accident."

Gil patted him on the shoulder. "Oh well, tough luck about the whole Storm King thing, then."

Tarvek twitched his shoulder away from Gil's hand, and looked serious. "Wulfenbach, I have some rather . . . unpleasant cousins who would *love* to have me out of the line of succession. If one of them becomes the new Storm King, you're going to really wish it had been me."

Atop the walls of Mechanicsburg, Agatha was kneeling on the stones, rooting around inside the workings of one of Gil's lightning accumulators. She sneezed, crawled backwards a bit, and settled herself on her haunches with a scowl. Violetta handed her a clean rag and she wiped her hands. "He insists on using copper," Agatha groused. "No wonder these things melted."

Violetta ignored this. She had always left anything involving the workings of machinery to Tarvek and now she did the same with Agatha. She preferred more interesting topics of conversation. "Did you notice he wrote your name on all the bolts?" She raised her eyebrows as she spoke.

Agatha flushed. "Obviously he has too much time on his hands—" Surreptitiously, she slipped an inscribed hex-bolt into one of her belt pouches. "—but I thought it was very sweet."

General Gkika stepped up, grinning. "Goot news, Lady! De Bone Qvarter haz been cleared."

---

[105]　Hogfarb's Resplendent Immolation is one of the more entertaining of the bioengineered diseases. The sufferer changes color, shifting quicker and quicker through an unnatural palette until they literally go up in an impressive pyrotechnic display fueled by burning fat. It has the distinction of being one of the few very horrible things we discuss in these textbooks that was not created by a member of the Heterodyne family.

Krosp appeared by her side, studying a map. "Yeah, those street cleaning machines you repurposed are really effective." He shrugged, "It's a pity they're corroding the actual streets."

"Picky, picky," Agatha muttered. "What about the group that was giving us trouble in the North Windings?"

Lady Vitriox glanced at a column of smoke. "The Dark Light Guards? They continue to put up a strong resistance, but they are falling back to the east."

Agatha glanced at Krosp's map. "Perfect. With the Dyne to the south, they'll funnel into the Greens—"

Van rubbed his hands. "Where they will have no cover at all!"

Krosp frowned. "You're sure they can't take the cathedral?"

Van smiled beatifically. "Oh, I really hope they try."

Agatha gracefully rose to her feet. "How long do you think we have before the next wave of attackers arrives?"

Krosp and the Jäger glanced at each other. "Vell," Gkika admitted, "most ov de Vulfenbach forces haff ektually broken off. Dey iz all congregating towards de Great Hospital. De vuns dot ain't, hy tink it becawze dey haven't gotten proper orders."

Agatha's eyes narrowed. "You mean the fighting is over?"

"Not at all," Lady Vitriox said primly. Her statement was punctuated by a burst of green lightning that erupted upwards from a northern tower, striking a gigantic bat that appeared to be made out of polished copper. It spiraled down and out of sight.

"There are a lot of different enemies attacking us," Krosp said sourly. "I'm assuming that, at the moment, the imperial forces are more concerned with searching for the Baron."

Suddenly, there came an immense, thunderous booming sound, and the ground itself shuddered. A wall of metal, taller than the ancient stone walls of Mechanicsburg by at least ten meters, had appeared outside of town. Above it, three airships shot into the sky, relieved of their burden. Agatha looked and saw a flotilla of similar ships, each towing a similar burden, and all approaching fast. Even as she processed what she was seeing, the next wall segment slammed to earth, followed by another, and another—each operation, with typical empire efficiency, taking place within seconds of the previous.

Krosp stared in fascination. "Dropwalls!"[106] He waved a paw. "I've seen blueprints." He squinted and then scratched his head as he studied the ever-growing array. "But . . . they're all facing the wrong way. They're not *containing* us, they're *defending* us."

Gkika's jaw sagged in surprise. Then it shut with a snap. "Ho. Hyu iz right." She dashed off, calling over her shoulder, "Hy iz gun get some troops on dem!"

Krosp shook his head. "Weird. The empire doesn't make mistakes like that . . ."

Agatha's heart gave a great thump. "It's Gil! He got through!" She allowed herself a deep breath. "Well, that's a huge load off my mind. With Gil buying us time, we'll be able to get a lot more done on the town defenses . . . but I still I still want everyone working at top speed."

Lady Vitriox looked approving. "My, my. You're a smart one, aren't you?"

Agatha nodded. "I hope so. I won't sit back and rely on the Wulfenbach forces to defend us. Not that long ago they were the ones *attacking* us. An hour from now, they could attack us again. This is *my* town. *I'll* protect it.

"I . . . do trust Gil, but I don't know how much I can trust the ruler of the Wulfenbach Empire. I want us strong enough that nobody can take us. They'll have to *negotiate* with us."

Van gnawed his lower lip. "That's . . . very astute, my Lady."

Krosp swatted at his knee. "Don't sound so surprised, pal. She's been learning from the *best*!"

---

[106] Dropwalls, as their name suggests, are gigantic barriers designed to be dropped from the air to act as containment units and siege towers. One would think that dropping a multi-ton machine would be the best way to surround your enemy with a multi-ton heap of rubble, but no. Dropwalls are designed so that when they impact, not only do they remain intact, but compression devices along the base "harvest" the kinetic energy of the impact, using it to activate and power up the walls' built-in defense mechanisms.

Agatha sighed and pushed her glasses up onto her forehead. She rubbed her eyes. Van looked at her with concern. "Are you all right, Lady?"

Agatha looked up. "I guess. I just wonder how many other girls have to worry about whether or not it's smart to really trust their . . . you know, the guys they—"

Lady Vitriox crossed her arms. "*All* of them," she said flatly.

"But mine has an army!"

The old woman shook her head. "They *all* do, my Lady. It consists of other men."

On the great map aboard Castle Wulfenbach, the last of the dropwall models was slotted into place. Tarvek looked over the field display and nodded in satisfaction. "That should keep your little empire tottering along for a few more months." His voice became condescending: "Say, you're really getting the hang of this!"

"Golly, do you really think so?"

"Well, no, but if flattering you will get me back to Agatha faster, then . . ."

Gil gave him an evil grin. "Oh, I'll get you there fast. *Cannoneers!*"

Boris was impressed. The two young men worked together very well, all the while sniping at each other viciously. They seemed to be having a good time. Boris found himself wondering how many actual friends Gil had managed to have in the course of his unusual upbringing. These thoughts were interrupted by a commotion on the other side of the map.

A guard clank held a scruffy-looking man by the collar. A pair of regular guards escorted them. "We caught him attempting to sneak aboard, hanging from the gondola of a supply ship," one of them explained. He hooked a thumb towards Gil. "Says he's a storyteller. Insists on seeing Master Gi . . . " he corrected himself, "Uh—His Highness. Matter of life and death. Normally I'd just chuck him inna tank, but this whole operation's been so screwy, I . . . Well, I thought I should bring him in."

The men turned towards the guard clank and discovered it stoically holding an empty coat. They whirled in time to see the prisoner eagerly addressing Gil. "You! Young Wulfenbach! I must speak with you! It is of the utmost importance! It's about a book!"

Gil, startled, raised his voice. "Boris? Get this—"

Suddenly Tarvek blinked in recognition. "Wait a minute . . . *You?* How did *you* get here?"

Gil looked at Tarvek. "You know this . . . ?"

Tarvek nodded furiously. "He should be rotting in a cell under Sturmhalten![107] Because of his ridiculous antics,[108] the Deep Library is infested with giant smudge beetles,[109] which happened while he was collecting vile and scurrilous[110] stories about my family!"

Gil regarded the man with interest. "Well, he sounds well informed, anyway." He waved off the squad of clanks arrayed behind him. "What do you have to say?"

Your professor then explained he was seeking the book by Masat with the stories of the Storm King that had been revealed to exist by the Baron. When Gil looked bewildered, he launched into an impassioned recitation of the story the Baron had told him back in the hospital. This only deepened Gilgamesh's confusion.

---

[107] Which, in fact, your dear professor was, until he was fortuitously released from this unjustified incarceration by people searching for the as yet unrevealed Lady Heterodyne. The sordid details of my time in "stir," as we hardened criminals call it, can be found in one of our previous textbooks: *Agatha H. and the Clockwork Princess.*

[108] Those actions which Prince Sturmvarous refers to as "antics," are clearly included in *Transylvania Polygnostic University's Research & Acquisitions Guidelines*:
Method #18: Small conflagrations deemed an acceptable method of determining the location of a secretive libraries' rare and important books, but only if the library in question has a diligent, devoted, and spry staff of sufficient personnel.

[109] Giant eastern European smudge beetles (*Lymexylon lacrimo atramento Europa gigantus*) are filthy animals that feast on wood pulp and have a predilection for libraries. If that was not bad enough, when they eat books, they digest the *paper*, but pass the *ink* through their digestive system almost untouched, leaving large, inky smears wherever they go. Prince Sturmvarous' accusation is therefore particularly hateful and, I assure you, completely false.

[110] Scurrilous, yes—but not untrue.

"I've never heard this moronic story in my life," he said. "And you're claiming that my *father* told it to you?"

"Yes! He said it's in the book! The one in your library! The one by Masat! He said you'd let me see it!"

"There is no such book," Gil said with finality. He pointed towards Your professor. "Get him off the Castle. That story makes no sense."

As the man was unfairly dragged away in what many concur was the young Wulfenbach's first act of tyranny, Prince Tarvek touched his shoulder. "It makes sense to me," he said in a low voice.

"Seriously?"

"Yes, the plan was for a Lucrezia to get close enough to wasp the Baron. She . . . she must have managed it, but I can't imagine how . . ."

Gil was appalled. "My father? Impossible! Sparks can't be wasped!"

Tarvek looked tired. "They've developed a new strain."

"They? They, who?"

Tarvek was thinking. He answered distantly: "Some of Lucrezia's followers within the Order. Mostly a spark named Gottmurg Snarlantz . . ."

Gil stared at him. "And you knew about this!"

"Yes. But I didn't know she had got to your father. We have to—"

Gil grabbed hold of Tarvek's coat and shook him so hard his teeth rattled. "Black fire and slag," he swore. "Just when I start to forget what you are, you reveal another level of corruption!"

"I'm telling you about it now," Tarvek gasped. "Listen to me. We've got to get out of here. Back to Agatha. Right now!"

Gil stared at him coldly. "Why? So you can infect *her* with one of your—"

"NO!" The slap Tarvek delivered was sharp enough that Gil's saw flashes of light.

He leaped forward and slammed Tarvek to the ground, shouting, "Hold your fire!" as shots whistled over their heads.

"Sir! Are you all right?" Guards were rushing towards them.

"I'm fine, Captain." Gil responded. "Leave him alone." He turned back to Tarvek, who was still on the ground. "You idiot!" he shouted. "Are you trying to commit suicide?"

Tarvek glared up at him. "You *know* I wouldn't do that to her." Gil paused. He *did* know that.

Tarvek kept talking: "Besides, Lucrezia has already *got* to Agatha. I'm the only one who knows enough—*because* I allowed myself to work with her—to actually have a chance of breaking her free!"

"All right! I know! Have you already forgotten how much trouble we went through to keep you *alive*?" He smacked the back of Tarvek's head. His anger was fading, but the fool could have got himself killed. "How dare you risk yourself and her by acting so *stupid*!"

"Ow! Let me up!" Tarvek struggled to his feet and rubbed his head. We've got to get you out of here. Quickly!"

Gil snorted. "Don't be absurd. I stay here. I want you to stick close to Agatha. You're an opportunistic serpent up to your ears in treachery and intrigue, and I'm counting on *you* to spot and deal with any hidden threats. And yes, try to find a way to get rid of Lucrezia. I'll use the empire to clear out the obvious attacks. I can't join you until I've got things back under control."

Tarvek looked like he wanted to throttle him. "That's *exactly* what I'm trying to tell you," he said through clenched teeth. "I see a huge threat—to Agatha and to you—*right now*! You're no use to either of us if you stay here and get wasped!"

Gil scowled. "I really don't think—"

Tarvek interrupted. "I *know*, but *try*. Your father's death was announced to the world without *any* warning. Think about it. Your empire isn't run by fools, but no preparations were made to contain the damage that news like that would cause! It just got blurted out to everyone. I'd wondered about it, but . . . hearing that story just now? It's obvious to me there are two intellects working at a level I'm just beginning to see. One is trying to warn you—that's your father—the other is preparing to trap you!"

"Me? How—?"

"*Think*! You were safely ensconced within Castle Heterodyne. No one could touch you there, not without destroying the Castle and everyone in it. But once we heard your father was dead, out you came! I'll bet a lot of people saw you emerge and I'm also betting you made a big deal about returning to Castle Wulfenbach."

"Well, yes. The troops needed to see—"

Tarvek waved his hands. "No, no, I'm not saying you did anything wrong." He grimaced. "I'm saying that someone was counting on you doing the *right* things. Coming here, assuming control." He rubbed his forehead. "But I'm more and more convinced that if you stay here, you'll be wasped. Or worse. The only thing that's missing is—"

A Castle messenger sped in, waving a flimsy wildly above her head. "The Baron is alive!" Her excited shout filled the room, which spontaneously erupted in cheers. "He's returned to Castle Wulfenbach! He's on his way here!"

"Time to go," Tarvek said as he dragged Gil out of the room.

"Wait!" Gil looked back. "If my father *is* really here—"

Tarvek nodded. "An excellent way to put it. You want to argue? Fine! But do it while we move!"

Gil made a snap decision and the two ran down the corridor and headed off into the depths of Castle Wulfenbach. "How do I know you're not just *guessing* about my father?"

Tarvek nodded. "Weren't you *listening* to that idiot's story? It's obvious that your father has used him to get a message to you! If he's been wasped, he wouldn't be able to tell anyone about it directly and shouldn't even be able to hint at it in such a blatant manner." He paused in admiration. "Your father is extraordinary, it's like the usual rules don't apply to him. As if Lucrezia doesn't control his entire brain." Tarvek shook his head. "But she *can* control his actions and, now that he's here, it'll be simple for him to lock you up." He looked at Gil. "There are enough people who'll think it's reasonable, considering you went into the Castle in the first place."

Gil conceded this. "If you're right about this, then what can we do?"

Tarvek grinned. "We stay alive and out of her clutches. We're both dangerous to her in our own way. I *studied* with her! She showed me all *kinds* of things! And I think I've developed a formula to keep a person safe from wasp infection."

"Why haven't you—?"

"*I've been kind of busy lately!*" Gil conceded the point. Tarvek continued. "As far as I know, there was only the one prototype of the spark wasp variety. It should take some time even for Lucrezia to make new ones, but we can't be sure of *anything* when it comes to her. I'll teach you my formula. If we get separated, you get to a lab and dose yourself as soon as you can."

Before he could stop himself, Gil muttered, "How do I know it won't just kill me or something?"

Tarvek stopped and faced him. "Okay, you know what? I never knew what I had done to make you hate me so much, but I've finally figured it out. That time we were caught sneaking into the records vault? I'm betting *that's* when the Baron finally told you he was your father. He probably warned you against me as well—told you all about my family and what treacherous backstabbers we all are."

"And that's not true?"

"Of *course* it's true! But you were—" Tarvek paused. "We both were looking for something exciting about your past. It was just for fun! How was *I* supposed to know how it would look to the Baron? He was giving me a lot more credit than I deserved, but it's no wonder I got thrown off of Castle Wulfenbach."

Gil, who had done his best at the time to get Tarvek sent away, looked embarrassed. Tarvek had another revelation. "And all that time in Paris! When you were wallowing in debauchery with your doxies, tarts, and pirates . . . You were trying to convince *me* you were nothing more than a disgusting, lecherous, drunken sot." He paused and then punched Gil on the shoulder. "I want you to know I bought into that completely. Well done."

Gil twitched his shoulder away. "Fine! I'll . . . I'll trust you . . .

just shut up about it." He started pacing in a different direction. "Assuming you're correct, we've got to be careful and we don't have a lot of time. We can't just run to the nearest dirigible bay."

"Why not?"

"My father is a brilliant strategist. He can outthink *anybody*. He's at least always five steps ahead of his enemies . . . "

"Except possibly Lucrezia."

"Except possibly Lucrezia. So if he's under her control—"

"Neither of them would be stupid enough to let it show."

"Yes. They'll be careful. Subtle." Gil lowered his voice. "I'm saying we don't know how long he's already been aboard."

Tarvek bit his lip. "At least seven key people were called away from the Operations Room while we were talking."

Gil grimaced. "Not good. We have no ideas what private orders my father has already given. Even un-wasped, he'd probably have you shot."

Tarvek shrugged. "Yeah, I get that a lot."

"For what it's worth. You've earned it."

Tarvek winced as he rubbed the site of his recent gunshot wound. "Another thing the two of them will agree on." He looked around. The corridors they were traversing aboard the great airship were becoming progressively quieter. These were places that were not as populated as others. "Tell me again why we're not leaving?"

"We *are* leaving. But I'll bet that every hanger bay has guards by now, waiting to grab you. Probably both of us, actually. No, we're going, but now we're *escaping*."

"Escaping from what?"

Both men spun in shock to see Bangladesh traipsing down the corridor. "Geez," she groused, "I step out to get coffee and when I get back, Boris said that the two of you'd just bolted outta there with no explanation,"

At this moment, Bangladesh stepped under one of the irregularly spaced lights. Tarvek recoiled in terror. "No!" he shouted, "not *you!*"

This greeting was so much an everyday experience that it took the captain several seconds to remember Tarvek at all. When she did, her eyes widened, and a thousand-watt smile lit up her face. "Oh my gosh," she breathed in wonder. "Oh my gosh! I'd know that girlish scream anywhere! It's Prince 'How Dare You'!" She grabbed the petrified man by the shoulders and swiveled him around in delight. "It's really you," she marveled. "I thought you'd jumped to your death! Nicely done!"[111]

Finally, Tarvek couldn't take it anymore. "Wulfenbach, what is she *doing* here? Doesn't your empire shoot pirates? Shoot her now! Right now!"

Bang laughed in delight as she pinched Tarvek's cheeks. "Oh, I've missed you, me proud beauty, yah ha haar!"

Gil nodded sympathetically. "I know, I keep meaning to. I'm continually amazed my father hasn't—" A sudden thought caused him to pause. When he spoke again, it was with a sudden seriousness. "DuPree, come with us."

Before Tarvek could move, Bangladesh wove her arm through his. "Hey," she dropped her voice suggestively, "do you still have those little scars I gave you?" She tugged at his shirt. "C'mon! Lemme see"

Tarvek did his best to ignore her. "Why is she coming with us?"

"Because I don't want her to get wasped."

Tarvek noted that Captain DuPree's fooling about stopped instantly.

"Think about it," Gil continued. "Can you imagine what she'd be like working for Lucrezia?"

Tarvek imagined it. "So *shoot* her!"

"Ha! You're still so *funny!*"

"So where are we going?"

Gil glanced at Bangladesh and took a deep breath. "To my lab."

---

[111]   According to anecdotal evidence, it appears that sometime during their student days in Paris, Prince Sturmvarous was captured by Bangladesh and forced to serve on her ship. Whether this was done at Gilgamesh's behest or on her own initiative remains unclear. From hints we have gathered from multiple sources, he did not have a good time.

Tarvek frowned. "To my *secret* lab. With any luck, no one will find us there."

"Dere hyu iz," Vole said in a put-upon voice.

Gil stared up at the tall Jäger. "How did *you* find us?"

Vole rolled his eyes. "Hyu keeds tink hyu iz so schneaky. Dot's cute, but hyu gots bigger problems, kiddo." He grinned malevolently and leaned in. "Hyu poppa iz alive after all! Heez gots der security forces runnink all offer de place— lookink for hyu." A thick, clawed finger thudded into Gil's chest. "*Hyu* iz to be detained." He glanced over towards Tarvek. "Prince *Schtumvarouwz* iz to be detained." He cocked an eye at Bangladesh and added, "Und enneyvun who haz even *talked* to hyu is to be detained."

The three glanced at each other and then back at the now-visibly amused Jäger. Gil nodded. "And are you here to 'detain' us?"

Vole's amusement broke free into a large, smile. "Ho! No vay, boss! Hy vurks for hyu now, remember?" He gave Gil a mocking salute. "End hy em here to help hyu owt!"

Gil looked confused. Vole's grin grew even larger. "Hyu iz goink against hyu poppa." He shook his head appreciatively. "Dot's gonna be some var! Messy, terrible civil war! De empire vill be in flames! De pipple vill be crushed between de two uf hyu und it vill unleash an ocean of blood!" He raised his hands skyward. "Dis vill be more carnage den hy could heff ever *hoped* for! The destruction . . . It vill be glorious!"

With a sickening crash that she alone heard, Bangladesh felt herself fall in love. While the captain was never known for her forethought and, indeed, openly mocked anyone who mentioned they had long-term life plans,[112] she had long ago dismissed any possibility of a romantic entanglement. Oh, she thought of herself and was occasionally acknowledged as a pirate queen, which meant that, eventually, once she had reclaimed her mother's island kingdom, she

---

[112]   Such as leaving the captain's presence while still alive and relatively unharmed.

would be expected to produce heirs, but she had never been one to demand romance when all she required was sex.

A significant amount of the pleasure she got from interacting with Gilgamesh over the last several months had been derived from mocking him for his infatuation with the Heterodyne girl. The realization that she was suddenly caught up in a similar situation, caused her to experience an emotion Klaus would have easily sacrificed several hundred square kilometers of the empire to see: uncertainty.

Several minutes later, she surfaced from her thoughts and realized that she, as well as the others, were now moving down an unfamiliar service corridor.

Behind her marched Vole, lost in visions of future carnage he continuously choreographed, murmuring in a lazy monotone that threatened to make her swoon with unsavory delight. Before her strode Gil and Tarvek. Tarvek tried to stop listening to the war-besotted Jäger, but kept hearing things that demanded to be cataloged and remembered for later. He quickened his steps and whispered to Gil, "Are you actually listening to any of this?"

Gil shook his head. "Not really. But if that fantasy is what's keeping him from turning us in, then fine. He's obviously enjoying himself."

He walked several steps in silence. "But if you're worried that he's . . . he's correct, then we could just surrender right now. If you're right about all this, I'll just get wasped. You'll probably wind up dead, but at least Europa would avoid a civil war."

"And Agatha?"

Gil sighed. "Yes, that's where our little altruistic thought experiment breaks down, doesn't it? Come on. It's not far now."

Tarvek looked worried. "What makes you think they won't be waiting for you in your lab?"

Gil grinned. "*Secret* lab, remember? I was raised on Castle Wulfenbach, even while they were still constructing it. There were enough crews working at once that it was pretty easy to alter blueprints without anyone noticing and then switch them back before the inspections. As a result, I have a whole private section of the ship sealed off from the main compartments that no one knows about."

Tarvek considered this. "That . . . That's actually pretty cool."

Gil gave a quick grin. "Isn't it though?" He stopped in front of a section of corridor broken by a complicated hatchway. While Tarvek was examining it, Gil stepped to the blank wall opposite, turned a random-looking screw with an odd-looking screwdriver, and a panel down back the way they'd come swung open on silent hinges. A minute later, Gil raised a grate and peered in. Seeing nothing, he eased the grate to one side, then hoisted himself up.

"Okay," he called down. "It's all clear." Which was when several kilograms of excitable arthropod slammed into his back, causing him to scream in shock. He gathered it up and gave it a hug. "Zoing! Good to see you!"

The little creature looked down at him from within its enveloping coat and hat. "Whirrrryu beee?" it buzzed.

"I *told* you I'd be busy. How are the patients?"

Zoing nodded proudly. "No dead."

The group entered a large laboratory. Taking pride of place were a set of glass cylinders, filled with a cloudy liquid. Various gases bubbled upwards. Within the liquid could be seen a pair of figures.

Vole stared within one of them and then recoiled in astonishment. "Iz Meester Ponch!" He examined the other cylinder. "Und Mistress Judy! Hy thought dey vos *dead!*[113] Vell howzabout dot."

---

[113] This was understandable several times over. The constructs Punch and Judy were the personal servants of Bill and Barry in their adventures. Once Bill wed, they retired. After the Heterodyne Boys vanished, the constructs disappeared from Mechanicsburg as well. Many assumed they had followed the Boys into oblivion. In actuality, they had moved to Beetleburg and assumed new identities as Adam and Lilith Clay. However, Barry Heterodyne knew their location, as one night he appeared at their home, a six-year-old Agatha in tow. When he vanished again, after living with them for almost a year, he left Agatha behind, promising to return "in a few months." Instead, eleven years passed. At that point, Agatha was caught up by the Wulfenbachs in the takeover of Beetleburg. They stormed Castle Wulfenbach to rescue her (though there are endless arguments as to whether they *should* have), but in the process they were killed by Otilia, who was trapped within the form of Von Pinn. Their bodies were collected by Gilgamesh, who

Gil straightened up from examining a bank of read-outs and nodded in satisfaction. "Final healing is progressing beautifully. Another day or two and they'll be as good as new. Better, actually."[114] He patted Zoing on top of his hat and fed him a sugar cube from a small bowl on the table. "Good job."

With the bizarre little construct delightedly crunching away beside him, Gil strode over to a large canvas-shrouded device. With a flourish, he whipped the sheet aside, revealing a gleaming insect-like machine, equipped with two separate sets of ribbed wings.

"What is this?" Tarvek was obviously intrigued.

"Nice, isn't it?" Gil checked a meter on the side, pried off a cap that was sealing the end of a pipe, and began pouring something that smelled strongly of volatile petrochemicals into the machine. "It's an experimental flying machine, but really, aren't they all?"

Tarvek studied the cockpit, looking for any sign of supports. "Where's the gasbag?"

"It doesn't have one! I *said* it was experimental."

Tarvek stared. "So it's some kind of falling machine?"

Gil frowned, as if at a particularly embarrassing memory. "No. Well . . . not exactly. Are you familiar with the Bernoulli Equation?"[115]

---

began the process of reanimation. You really should just read the earlier books.

[114] There is much evidence to support this declaration. The Clays were the young Heterodyne Boys' first constructs and, as such, they had notable flaws. Over the subsequent years, these were never corrected. It is unclear as to whether this was a result of a lack of inclination on the Boys' part, or a resistance on the Clay's part to being further "worked on" by the Boys. If the latter was the case, it would be quite understandable, as constructs that went under the knife for simple repairs or adjustments, often awoke to find themselves sporting additional limbs, prosthetics, or an uncontrollable desire to burrow through mountains. When Gilgamesh reassembled and revived them, he automatically corrected many small flaws, and one or two major ones, sometimes without even knowing that he was doing so. This lead to several surprising discoveries, not the least of which was that when he ate spicy food, Adam no longer belched fire.

[115] Ladies and gentlemen, the Bernoulli Equation: $P1+1/2+pv^2/1+pgh1 = P2+1/2pv2^2+pgh2$. We must confess that neither of your professors really understand what it signifies. When an equation starts adding those little letters and off-register numerals, we just throw our hands up and have another drink. This is why, on those rare occasions in our classes when actual math is required, we flaunt university policy and allow our students to bring in their own

Tarvek stared at him. "That's about fluid dynamics, yes? The one that was discredited when that fool, Betancourt, [116] tried to build a supersonic submersible in the Black Sea?" Gil winced. Tarvek continued. "This contraption won't fly at all!"

"Science says it will!"

"Then science can fly it!"

"I assure you, even if it doesn't *fly* exactly, it should reach the ground in one piece long before it explodes." He frowned. "Well . . . I think so, anyway. I haven't really tested it since I made those changes . . . "

Impatiently, he shook his head and dragged Tarvek over to the cockpit. "Look. Here are the controls. They're pretty simple. Can you run a four-gear landwalker?"[117]

Tarvek looked slightly guilty. "Um . . . Once at University, I had to use it to destroy one of my—"

Gil waved a hand, cutting him off. "Perfect! But on this, instead of 'walking,' think of it as '*skating*.' "

"But, I can't—"

Gil swept his hand over a bank of controls marked SAFETY SYSTEMS. "You can ignore all of these—"

Tarvek's eyes narrowed. "Wait a minute . . . "

"Just keep an eye on fuel, altimeter, brakes, and the giant claw."

"Why are you telling me all this?" Suddenly he reared back, eyes wide in astonishment. "You can't seriously— You *are*! For some pointless, no doubt pfennig-dreadful-induced delusion of noble sacrifice, you're planning on *staying* here! Why?"

---

abacus.

[116] Augustín Betancourt (GDE, San Isidro Royal College): In addition to his infamous, life-ending submersible, Betancourt had a long career as an engineer, aeronaut, and intelligence agent. All careers that called for speed.

[117] Four-gear landwalkers were once a common sight at Europa's universities and were frequently trotted out for homecomings, pep rallies, and assorted pranks. Today, of course, they've been replaced by the much more efficient coal-powered third-wheel flex-rod-and-bucket walkers that now dominate what remains of the academic landscape.

Gil looked off to the side. "I have no idea what—"

"Don't you dare try to pull that on me! Seriously, what do you think you can accomplish here? Have you even *considered* how dangerous a spark of your caliber will be if you're enslaved by the Other? It's bad enough she's got your *father*."

"We don't know that."

"*I* know that! And I know that if she gets you, too, the rest of us might as well give up and just burn Europa to the ground ourselves!" Tarvek reached into his coat and pulled out a small notebook and waved it under Gil's nose. "I haven't even given you my formula yet, *and* I'm still not even one hundred percent sure it'll work. But even if it does, you staying here would still be suicide, because if the Other tells your father to *kill* you, he will. And that's the best case scenario! Plus," he smacked the side of the flyer, "I do not believe this thing could *hover*, let alone fly!"

Gil rolled his eyes. "Of course it can't hover."

"Ah-HA!"

Gil sighed. "Lots of things fly without gasbags. You have absolutely no grasp of aeronautics, do you?"

They heard a crash and a grunt from behind them and whirled around to see Othar Tryggvassen leap up from where he had knocked Captain Vole to the ground. "Wulfenbach! We meet again! I have found you at last!" He glanced at Tarvek. "*And* your degenerate clone!"

"His *what*?" Tarvek sputtered. "How *dare* you!"

Gil nodded in satisfaction. "Thank goodness. I hate having to justify myself." He then took a deep breath, snagged Tarvek's sleeve, and ran. "Curses! Foiled again," he shrieked.

Othar looked like a ten-year-old child being given a second Christmas. "What?"

"We must flee," Gil continued as he hustled Tarvek along, "for it is none other than Othar Tryggvassen—Gentleman Adventurer—vanquisher of *eeeeevil!*"

"Hey now," Othar huffed as he pursued them, "you make it sound absurd!"

Gil swung the two of them into the cockpit of the flyer. "We will make a daring escape in my amazing *flying machine!*"

Tarvek struggled like a cat spotting an impending bath. "Not the flying machine! *Not the flying machine!*"

"I think not, villain!" Othar swung up to the flyer just in time to have Tarvek flung directly into his path. The two men went down in a tangle of arms and legs while Gil swept his hands across the activation switches.

"I need to drag you back to your father," Othar roared. "My sister—"

"You did something to his *sister?*" Tarvek tried to stand up. "What is the *matter* with you?"

Gil patted both men on the back. "Don't worry! Tarvek is really good at machinery, and Othar here is a master of escape!" Suddenly, both Tarvek and Othar realized they were connected at the wrists by a pair of shackles. "So if you work together, I know you'll be okay!"

The two men looked up in time to see Gil standing several meters away, a hanger door control in his hand. He gave a wave, hit the switch, and the floor opened up beneath them. Gil watched them go and shook his head. "I'll be very curious to hear how they do," he mused.

"Dot no goot schneak!" Vole stumbled up beside Gil and peered down, rubbing his head. "Goot job, boss. Vell let's get goink. Eef we'z gunna schtart a civil var, ve's gotz to get crackin.'"

"Gil studied him. "Yesss . . . *About* that . . . " and with a sigh, he shoved Vole out into space.

A gasp from behind caused him to turn as he was closing the hatch. Bang stared at him in shock. "What did you do *that* for?"

"Oh, he should be fine," Gil assured her. "They haven't even gotten the engine started yet and, due to his aerodynamic profile, Vole is falling faster—"

Several years of experience caused Gil to instinctively dodge the knife that sliced through the air towards him and catch it with a snap of his wrist. He looked at Bangladesh with a puzzled look on his face. "Now what? Don't tell me you're mad that *you* didn't get to push him."

Another knife cut the air several centimeters from where his nose had been. "I liked that one!"

Gil stared at her. "You . . . like him? Vole? You like . . . " Then it all came together in his head and he gave a whoop of laughter as Bangladesh's face grew progressively redder. "Of *course* you do!" he gasped in glee. "He's a bloodthirsty, treacherous killing machine! Oh, this is priceless!" He easily avoided her hatchet and pinched her cheek. "I promise I won't tell anyone you have a booooyyyfriend."

Exhibiting a level of control that a part of Gil's mind filed away as "worrying," Bang took a deep breath and carefully adjusted her cap. "Yeah, well you should talk, twerp. What about all the trouble you're causing over this Heterodyne wench?"

Gil sobered up. "Point taken." That said, he reached into a pocket and produced Tarvek's notebook, which he had deftly lifted from the distracted prince's pocket. "The first thing I need to do is look at this formula." He nodded and strolled into the next room. "Zoing? Start clearing a space on chemical table three, and get me—"

DuPree's hand dropped onto his shoulder. "Oh no you don't. I'm still working for your father, apparently, and it sounds like he wants you brought in *now*."

Gil snapped the book closed and pinched the bridge of his nose. "I can't believe it."

"You'd better believe it. Now get moving."

Gil shrugged off her hand. "Not you, Sturmvoraus' notes. They're *encrypted*."

Bangladesh gave Gil a small shove in the center of his back. "Too bad, so sad," she sang out. "Now get moving."

Gil paused, faced her, and gently took her hand. "DuPree, please," he said earnestly, "I need you to stay here with me." Effortlessly, he swung the captain through the air and slammed her to the deck. "And let me work!" He received a quick boot in the face in response. Gil somersaulted backwards in time to avoid the second, fetching up next to a bench laden with dusty bottles. "Seriously, DuPree, this is very—" A particular bottle caught his eye. "Oh! *Silver of Vixonite!*[118] I thought I was going to have to make more of this from scratch. That's going to make this a lot easier!"

He twitched his hand to avoid Bang smashing the bottle with her fist, sending it into the air. "Careful, " he admonished her. "This formula is difficult enough without you breaking stuff."

"How do you know that? I thought you said you couldn't read those notes."

Gil caught the bottle as it dropped. "I said they were *encrypted.* I didn't say I couldn't *read* them." He turned away and, as Bang attacked him, slammed his boot into her solar plexus, sending her crashing back into another bench. "Now, would you see if we have any distillation of *Monahan's Viniferous MusEelixir* left?"

"I'll distill *you!*" With a snarl, Bang grabbed a bottle and flung it at Gil's head. Gil plucked it from the air, examined the label, and nodded in satisfaction. "Perfect! Thanks. And next to that should be a bottle of—" Another flask smacked into his waiting hand. "—*Calaxia Oil!* That's right! You're getting better at this. Remember that time you gave me concentrated *Pellicax's Twist* instead of *Saint Michael's Toes* and your whole ship blew up?"

He blinked and ducked as a lab bench sailed overhead and crashed

---

[118] At this time, chemistry was still a hodgepodge of alchemy, zymurgy, necromancy, metallurgy, and cooking. As a result, chemicals still retained the older and, some would say, more romantic, names from antiquity. This was unfortunate, because some names were so popular they were applied to any number of different concoctions, depending on where you were and who wrote down the recipe, often with hilarious/tragic results. One of the great advances of the current empire was the systematic codification of chemicals, which has saved many a researcher's life and dignity. We have, for assorted reasons (mostly because they sound cooler), retained the old naming system whenever possible.

into the wall behind him. "No, no, I've already got one of those."
He checked the book again and frowned as he fished in his work
vest for a screwdriver. "Now *this* part sounds tricky . . . " Absent-
mindedly, he brought the screwdriver up in time to parry the knife
Bang was attempting to drive into his eye. He sighed and looked at
her. "Look, I'll admit this kind of thing is occasionally fun, but this
is not the time, okay?"

"Oh, it's *always* the time for what I'm going to do to you!"

Gil sighed. "Zoing?"

A pair of steel claspers came swiftly down and seized Bangladesh's
shoulders and, holding her tightly, hoisted her into the air.
Astonished, she craned her neck and saw the diminutive construct
piloting a large metal mantis-looking clank which had been covered
in graffiti rendered in a juvenile hand declaring sentiments such as
"Arthropods rule!"

"Gotone," Zoing chirped in glee. "Toldyuit begoood!"

Gil looked a bit embarrassed. "Yes, yes, you were right, I was
wrong."

Upon hearing this, Zoing did a peculiar little waggling dance of
victory. "EEEEE!"

"Hey! Cheating!" Bang declared. "This is cheating. This . . . what
is this thing?"

"Oh, I built it for Zoing a long time ago."

Zoing leaned down. "Izfor pickingup *gorlz!*"

Bang's jaw dropped. "It's for *what?*"

Gil rubbed his neck. "Well, when I was a kid, we heard some of
the older guys talking . . . but we were kind of . . . um . . . unclear
on the finer points, and, well . . . "

Zoing waved his claws in triumph. "Itworkz! Itworkz!"

Bang stared at the two of them, pity evident in her gaze. "That is
just like you. Sooo pathetic."

Gil squirmed in embarrassment. "Just strap her down somewhere,
okay?"

"Somewhere" turned out to be a fully functional medical table, equipped with heavy-duty straps and controls that allowed it to be swiveled in any direction. A shackled Bang stared up at Gil in contempt. "Seriously pathetic."

"I assure you this table is purely for medical purposes."

"*That's* what makes it pathetic." She glanced over at the bench that Zoing was fastidiously tending. "What are you working on that's so important, anyway?"

"Something that should protect us against slaver wasp infection."

Bang's interest sharpened. "But that guy whose notes you're following. That was the Prince of Sturmhalten. You're following *his* formula? Sturmhalten's at the whole center of this thing. The royal family was neck deep in it."

"I know," Gil acknowledged, "That's precisely why I think this has a chance of working. They'd want to protect themselves."

Bang snorted. "They're wasting their time aren't they? Sparks *can't* be infected. Something about their brain chemistry. That's why the Other just kills them."

Gil looked at her askance. It was always disturbing when Bangladesh displayed an understanding of anything more complicated than which was the sharp end of an object. "That was, in fact, the case," he admitted. "Until it wasn't. Apparently one of the Other's pet sparks managed to develop a wasp that could infect sparks, and we think someone got close enough to use it on my father." A sharp intake of breath showed Bang was still paying attention. "We don't know how long they've had this technology, and I'm sure my father wasn't supposed to be their first test, but everything got upset when Agatha was found.

"Tarvek believes this formula will immunize us against slaver wasps. I'm sure you can see how vital that would be, especially if my father is infected. One of the reasons I stayed was that this *has* to be tested, and we're the best—" He turned towards the table, and stopped as he realized that, aside from Bangladesh's coat, boots, and pants, it was vacant. He sighed. "DuPree, are you listening to *anything* I'm saying?"

She slammed into him from his lower left, one of the few directions he had not been prepared for. "Oh, I'm listening." She punched the back of Gil's head, causing his face to bounce against the steel deck. "You've become weirdly infatuated with this girl, who might be the Other full time, as opposed to only *part time*." She ground her knees into the small of his back. "And you were locked away with her in Castle Heterodyne, along with Prince Squealy, who you're now all chummy with when, for as long as I've known you, you've hated him. Which was understandable because, at the moment, he's at the top of your father's Most Wanted List, precisely because he knows all about slaver wasps, since his entire family was working with the Other and her scientists.

"Now you're using one of *his* formulas to mix up a miracle cure for something that's never even been a *problem* before now—and you expect me to *drink* it!" She rested her knees on his inert shoulders. "I think that about covers it."

With a brutal snap, Gil's heel slammed into the back of her head. "Yes," he said. "And no." Bang's eyes rolled up into her head and she slumped forward. "Okay, enough of this," Gil muttered as he crawled free. He levered himself to his feet and grabbed the flask of precipitate sitting on the bench. "I don't care if you believe me or not, this is important. I need you to stay free." So saying, he poured half of the bottle into her mouth. Bang came to with a start, coughing and spitting. Gil patted her on the back. "Sorry about that," he said, not really sorry at all. "But I'm going to drink it as well—" Bang began to twitch. "—in a minute."

He stared in fascinated horror as Bangladesh continued to twitch and shudder while her skin began to throw off small sparks of static electricity. "That's pretty interesting," he said.

Bang threw her head back and screamed. "I *knew* she'd got to you! I really should kill you!"

"No, no," Gil said reassuringly. "I think this is *supposed* to happen." Hurriedly, he picked up Tarvek's notes and began to flip through the pages. "Here we go," he muttered. "*Table H: Temporary Side Effects . . .* Oh! I see!" He looked up at Bangladesh's crackling epidermis. "It's changing your ionic balance. What an ingenious solution."

"Head . . . feels like it's going to explode."

Gil patted her arm. "Don't worry. That means it's working. It should fade in a minute or so."

"That's very comforting," Bang nodded jerkily. "Need to sit down," she mumbled. Gil fetched a chair, which Bang gratefully took and then brought down on his head.

She then grabbed the flask. "I don't know whether to pour the rest of this down your throat or down the sink." She studied his dazed face. "Which would annoy you more?"

CHAPTER 9

Q: Why does the Heterodyne prefer the company of
Jägermonsters to that of hunting hounds?
A: Because a hound feels shame when it does something
wrong.

—A "witticism" found scrawled within the margins of
the original manuscript of Anatole du Lac's *Chronicles
of the Court of the Storm King* (Property of The Storm
King Collection of the British Museum)

⟡⟡⟡

il's ironically designated "flying machine" fell screaming from
the bottom of Castle Wulfenbach and plummeted towards
the mountains ringing the Valley of the Heterodynes.
Technically, it must be acknowledged that the machine itself fell
silently, with the aforementioned screaming being supplied by
Tarvek, who was hammering at an unresponsive control panel. Othar
peered at the wings, which gave a desultory flap. "It *is* working," he
observed thoughtfully.

"But not enough!" Tarvek stared at him wild-eyed. "We're still
falling!"

"Then panic is a luxury we cannot afford."

Othar's calm logic brought Tarvek to his senses. "Okay." He took a
deep breath. "Fine. I'm positively serene. Now, do *you* know anything
about this machine?"

Othar frowned. "Don't you?"

"No! I wouldn't voluntarily go near a thing like this with a three-meter pole! There's no gasbag! It . . . it's like some giant, creepy flapping bug!"

Othar put his hands on his hips. "That's serene, is it?"

"I really don't like flying!"

"Oh, very well," Othar said as he sighed. "Pay attention." Which was when Captain Vole landed on Othar's head feet first, slamming him to the deck.

"Got heem," he crowed. "Pretty schneeky, yah?"

Tarvek felt his sanity crumbling—and not in a good way. "He was the person Wulfenbach said could get us *out* of this!"

A moue of worry was beginning to pucker Vole's face when an enormous fist sank into his stomach, doubling him over. "Ho *ho*!" Othar laughed as he bounced back to his feet. "You won't take me down that easily, evildoer!"

He doesn't have to, Tarvek thought to himself, *gravity is doing it for him.* He suddenly realized the shackle binding the two of them together was gone. "How—?"

"To a Gentleman of Adventure, chains only exist as a manifestation of earthly desire. Therefore—"

This philosophical revelation was cut short by Vole inserting his fist between Othar's jaws. "Peh! Hyu goody two—shoes types iz all vit de beeg mouths. Shot dem op, end hyu go down just fine!"

Tarvek glanced over the side and saw this was evidently correct. "Stop hitting each other," he pleaded.

Othar spat out a claw and frowned as he delivered a right cross that flattened one side of Vole's head. "I think not, creature of evil."

Tarvek stared at the two of them whaling away at each other and his face twitched. "Fine! Don't let me bother you!" He spun back to the engine, slammed open the access panel, and peered within. "Crude," he sneered. "All power and no finesse . . . in a sort of brilliant way . . . a crude, lowlife, debauched way— Ah-ha! Wrench!"

He looked around and saw Vole about to bring a wrench down on Othar's skull. He deftly plucked it from the Jäger's grip. "Thank you."

This so startled Vole that Othar was able to uncoil with an uppercut so strong it added several centimeters to Vole's height before he collapsed, unconscious.

Othar turned, dusting his hands, saying: "Now, about this falling business—" just as Tarvek pulled the starter cord and the engine howled to life.

The wings blurred and the machine surged forward. It bounced off the side of the mountain and tumbled through the air. The two men fought the controls and the machine stabilized in time to careen through the upper branches of several of the taller trees. It broke through into the cleared space surrounding the town and was instantly fired on by Wulfenbach troops, who assumed it was a Heterodyne device, as well as by the town's defenders, who identified it as some sort of Wulfenbach deviltry. An early hit to the rear stabilizers actually proved to be beneficial as it caused the ship to jink and lurch in such a way the subsequent barrage mostly whistled harmlessly past with only the occasional hit.

It was the last of these that finally sent the machine tumbling from the sky to within the town walls. It slammed into the steeply pitched copper-tiled roof of the Lightning Futures Exchange[119] and came to a halt. Tarvek just had time to breathe a shaky sigh of relief before the machine began to slide down the roof. It tipped off into space and began to drop the four stories to the ground below. Tarvek again desperately pulled the starter cord—for the final time, as it snapped off in his hand. However, this was enough to rouse the wings to a final crescendo of effort that arrested the machine's fall sufficiently to

---

[119]   For quite a long time, lightning was the power source of choice for your more over-the-top mad science needs. Unfortunately, one cannot just assume you'll have a sufficiently pyrotechnic storm at the same time one has a potential abomination of science slowly decomposing on the slab. Thus the Lightning Futures Exchange, which banked gigawatts during Mechanicsburg's frequent lightning storms and then parceled them out to its clients when needed. Closed for over a decade at this point, the building was still standing only because the vast rooftop array of lightning rods and assorted accumulators provided a tourist-pleasing show whenever a thunderstorm blew through.

deposit them gently on the cobbled square, at which point the wings ripped free and careened about, smashing windows, destroying market stalls, and raising a great cloud of dust before coming to rest in a fountain where they lay at such an angle that the water began to flow out across the pavement.

Aboard the craft, Tarvek and Othar slowly raised their heads and looked about. When they saw they were provisionally safe, Othar stood tall and clapped Tarvek on the back. "Say," he said appreciatively, "you're better at this than I'd thought!" He hauled Tarvek to his feet. "We'll make a proper hero out of you yet, young villain!"

"I hate, hate, *hate* flying," Tarvek groaned. He had yanked his shoulder out from under Other's hand and tentatively slid a leg up on top of the machine's gunwale, when a voice yelled from behind them.

"Halt!" They turned to see several members of the Mechanicsburg Defense Force[120] approaching cautiously, rifles leveled. Their leader sat astride a compact brass theropod of some sort that was badly in need of polishing. He spoke firmly, but it was obvious he was nervous. "Surrender and you'll be taken safely into custody until we can send you back to your Baron. Resist and we'll shoot!"

Othar gave a great bark of laughter and posed dramatically. "Never fear, good people! I am no agent of Wulfenbach. I am Othar Tryggvassen—Gentleman Adventurer!"

Tarvek rolled his eyes. "Oh, sure, *that'll* sway them." Then he looked at the townspeople, and his surety faltered. All of them were now staring at the two of them with awe in their eyes.

---

[120]   While they do have a town watch, many of your smaller municipalities do not have the resources to support a permanent standing army. Even Mechanicsburg, which has a sizable standing force of assorted monsters, clanks, and semi-autonomous death machines, has the Mechanicsburg Defense Force. Every adult citizen is expected to be able to serve either under arms or in a support capacity in an emergency. They are further required to spend one week out of the year performing maintenance or repair and another week brushing up on military exercises. In recent years, standards had begun to slip badly, and many citizens were able to fulfill their yearly requirements simply by volunteering to deal with tourists.

"*The* Othar?" the leader asked. "We'll take you to the Lady Heterodyne right away!"

One of the townspeople nudged the other. "I'll bet she'll be thrilled!"

"Of *course* she will," Othar breezily assured them. He then reached back into the airship. "Oh, and you'll want to dispose of this." He hauled a comatose and battered Vole into view.

The townspeople gasped and then stared at Othar with even more respect. "Holy Katzenjammer," the leader muttered. He then turned to the youngest man beside him. "Run to the yards. Get a monster wagon[121] over here. On the double!"

One of the soldiers noticed Tarvek and his face fell in disappointment. "Huh. I always heard that Othar Tryggvassen had these cool, spunky *girl* sidekicks."

Tarvek's nostrils flared in barely contained rage. "I am not this oaf's sidekick, I am—" Tarvek suddenly realized that claiming to be the Storm King, hereditary enemy of the Heterodynes, might not be the most politic of declarations at this time. He quickly switched gears. "I am the chief political advisor to your Lady Heterodyne!"

The members of the Defense Force glanced at each other. "We'll let *her* decide that," the leader pronounced and, after Othar had

---

[121] The Heterodynes have not given a lot of things to the world that the world has actually wanted, but the monster wagon that is now part of the standard equipment of almost every town in Europa is one of the rare exceptions. These stout conveyances have been engineered to contain creatures capable of any number of deadly attacks and, *if properly maintained*, have never been known to fail. The Mechanicsburg Monster Wagon Works is one of the few local industries that is highly regarded throughout the civilized world and has been for over two centuries. A suspicious person might wonder why the Heterodynes of old allowed this unarguably beneficial export to thrive. The answer is that each wagon secretly signaled whenever it was used and, as often as not, agents of the Heterodyne, suitably incognito, would appear and offer to buy the now-captured monster from the victimized town. These they brought home and they were studied by the Heterodynes, incorporating any particularly nasty innovations into their own future creations. The Heterodynes knew that staying as feared as they were required capital outlay and continued hard work and were afraid of neither.

nonchalantly slung the still-inert Vole, over his shoulder, the squad formed around them, and off they marched.

It was one of the larger balconies off of the eastern side of Castle Heterodyne, affording a fine view of the Greens, the large park that abutted the grounds of the Great Hospital. This is not to say the rest of the town was without visual interest, as a fair amount of it appeared to be either burning or involved in some sort of fighting. However, in the opinion of the observers, that was somebody else's problem at the moment.

They were a collection of ex-prisoners, who were still marveling at the fact they were free and in no more danger of their heads exploding at any given moment than any other citizen of Mechanicsburg. An apparent invasion was of academic interest at best.

Squinaldo, a dark-skinned man adorned with disturbing tattoos, pulled an iron pot out of a battered chimeneya, sniffed the contents, gave a grunt of satisfaction, and poured out a dollop of steaming liquid into the odd assortment of mugs and cups that had been collected. He then passed them out. "Heya," he declared, "it ain't much, but it's hot!"

Professor Mittelmind snagged a cup with a grin. "Much thanks! Your concoctions are always a treat."

He raised the cup to his lips, but Squinaldo peremptorily raised a hand. "Hoy! Hold on." Mittelmind raised his eyebrows. "Wait for everybody else." The professor recognized the importance of the occasion and, soon enough, all had some sort of drink container in hand. Squinaldo raised his mug on high. "To the Lady Heterodyne," he shouted. "Once again, we are free!"

"Huzzah," the others cheered before downing their drinks.

"Delicious," Mittelmind declared. He licked his lips. "And it isn't even poisoned."

Squinaldo sniffed and swirled his drink in his mug. "I am a new man."

Sanaa vaulted up onto the balustrade, swung her feet out into empty space and just basked in the sunlight. Professor Mezzasalma clacked up beside her, rested his elbows on the stones, and dreamily rubbed his neck where the hated collar had recently been. Sanaa glanced at him. Professor Mezzasalma had been one of the more stable prisoners and had always treated newcomers well. She was pleased he had made it out alive. "So, what are *your* plans, Professor?"

Mezzasalma opened his eyes in surprise and considered this. His metallic feet tapped out the quick quadrille that indicated he was thinking. "To tell you the truth, I am not sure," he said slowly. He glanced over at Mittelmind and Squinaldo. The older man was theatrically clutching at his throat and staggering about, much to the amusement of the others. He smiled. "I never really thought I would get out of here."

From the doorway, an excited voice called out, "Professor!" And a moment later, Mittelmind found himself embraced by a puppy-like Fräulein Snaug. "Astonishing," he said with a laugh. "You're still alive!"

"And you're still a twisted mockery of science, sir!"

Mittelmind chuckled in delight and hoisted her into the air. "Sauce!" Behind her, Moloch stepped onto the balcony and set down a loaded toolbox with a sigh of relief.

Seeing him, Sanaa grimaced and hunched her shoulders. "Oh, geez," she muttered. "It's him."

Mezzasalma looked at her with concern. "Is there a problem?"

Sanaa rolled her eyes. "Ugh. It's that Moloch guy. From the kitchen? He's just such a total spaz and it's obvious that he's stupid in love with me. He's so ridiculously useless."

Mezzasalma spent several seconds glancing back and forth making sure that Sanaa wasn't joking. "You're . . . we're talking about Herr von *Zinzer?*"

The man under discussion now clapped his hands and signaled for attention. Instantly, every eye was on him. "Listen up, people.

The Castle's given me a map of the town's defenses. Most of them are broken or disconnected, but it doesn't sound like anything we can't handle."

Doctor Wrench spat and folded his arms. "Hey. What part of 'free' do you not understand? We're *done* here." He paused and looked up at the looming Castle face in resignation. "Or is the Castle gonna kill us anyway?" At this, the others looked up in trepidation.

Moloch had clearly been expecting this. "Nope. Me and the Castle talked this out. You are totally free to go." The others stared at him. Wrench looked nonplussed. Moloch gave them a second to think about this. "And where are you gonna go? What are you gonna do? Go work for the Wulfenbachs? That worked out *real* well for some of you already, didn't it?" Many of them looked pensive. Moloch nodded. "Get back into piracy? Reopen that little back-alley resurrectionist business? Yeah, no.

"So I've been authorized to offer all of you a place here in Mechanicsburg." They stared at him. "In case you haven't noticed, this whole place is steeped in mad science crazy and there's a new boss who's going to have to do a whole bunch of rebuilding."

Their gazes swiveled in unison out over the besieged town. "But they're fighting the empire," Squinaldo pointed out.

Moloch conceded the point. "Yeah, but here, even if the Baron wins, you'll just be one of her minions. *It won't be your fault.*"

There was sullenness on several faces. Moloch continued, "And I'm sure that, as you're all experienced sparks, you'd have minions of your own." There was now a guarded enthusiasm. "You'll be paid, fed, and guaranteed housing . . . *outside* the Castle." Mittelmind cleared his throat. Moloch rolled his eyes, and went on, "Which has promised not to kill any more of us for fun." He took a deep breath. "So when this is over, I expect all of you to come back inside and help collect and bury the dead."

The great construct R-79 sneered at this. "*Bury* the dead? That seems like a waste. Surely we could use them to—"

Moloch shocked everyone by striding over and smacking the behemoth upside the head. "NO!" R-79 stared at him, fury rising in his face. "You madboys can do whatever sick stuff you want on your own turf." He pointed back within the Castle. "But any one of them could have been you or me! You got *lucky* and you'll acknowledge that by treating the ones who *didn't* get lucky with respect. Got it?"

R-79 stared down at the smaller man who met his gaze full on and unblinking. The giant relaxed and nodded. "For luck," he rumbled. "Where we go first?"

Moloch nodded back and clapped him on the arm, as high up as he could reach. "Into town. There's plenty of work everywhere."

Without a word, the rest of the ex-prisoners began following Moloch. Sanaa realized her jaw was resting lightly on her chest. "Hmmm, yesss . . ." Mezzasalma said with an amused drawl. "A total spaz. I can see how his attentions must be *very* embarrassing for you."

Aboard Castle Wulfenbach, Gilgamesh slowly swam back to consciousness. There was an ache across his face that experience told him would be about the size of Bangladesh's fist. There was an awful taste in his mouth. He was lying on a padded bench of some sort and—he opened his eyes and came face to face with a wasp weasel less than fifteen centimeters away. The two stared at each other, and then the weasel screamed.

Gil recoiled, smacking his head on the bench, and saw the now-thrashing weasel was being held in the iron grip of his father, who stood ominously over him, even more stony-faced than usual. "Ah," he said in a leaden tone, "it is as I feared." Only now Gil became aware there were others in the room: the military and governing elite who tended to congregate around his father in times of crisis. What was it now? Suddenly, the weasel lunged and its toothy jaws snapped closed mere centimeters from his face. The implications crashed in on Gil and he saw the sick judgment on all of their faces.

His father turned towards them. "There is no longer any doubt. The girl is *clearly*—"

"NO!" Gil leapt to his feet—or, rather, would have, if he hadn't been chained by his ankles to the table. As a result, he crashed face-first to the floor at his father's feet. He could imagine the pained expression of barely concealed embarrassment on the Baron's face as his gigantic hand gently, but firmly, pulled him to his feet. "Please refrain from any more foolishness," his father said in a low voice. "You will only be confined until I can give this problem my full attention." He turned to a mixed squad of troopers and clanks. "Take him to the Red Level. Place him under airtight Code Five restraint."

The lead clank's head swiveled towards Gil and its lenses swiveled as it examined him. "Force parameters?"

"Try not to kill him," Klaus said slowly, "but he must not be allowed to escape." Gil found himself shocked. This was becoming deadly serious. The clanks closed in on him and steel hands fastened gently, but inexorably, on his wrists and neck. Only then did his father face him fully. "Gilgamesh, my son, you have my word: no matter what happens, I will do everything in my power to help you." He turned away. "But now I must deal with the Heterodyne girl and her accomplices. They, at least, cannot be allowed to live."

"Father, no! I'm not wasped! How *can* I be? Agatha doesn't even *have* that technology. She *couldn't* have wasped me!"

Klaus paused and turned back to him. Gil blinked. There was something in his father's face . . . "She herself didn't have to do it. You were infected before you even met her."

Before the calm certainty of his father, Gil tried to take a step back, only to discover he could not. "I . . . no . . . " He considered his words. "That's not possible." He stared into his father's eyes. "Is it?"

Klaus continued to regard him even as he snapped his fingers and held open his hand. *An uncharacteristically arrogant gesture* was the observation that skittered through Gil's mind before an aide placed a notebook bearing the Sturmvarous sigil on its embossed leather cover into his hand. He held it up. "These documents were found in a secret lab in Sturmhalten Castle. According to them, you were infected with a new strain of wasp designed to control sparks while you were in Paris."

Gil shook his head. "Sturmvarous said that the spark wasps were *untested—*"

"I warned you against Sturmvarous years ago," Klaus declared hotly. "He and that Heterodyne girl have played you for a *fool!*"

"But-but when could he have . . . ?"

"It was done through an agent. That family never does its own dirty work if they can help it. Someone you encountered serendipitously . . ."

"Zola," Gil whispered.

"This is my fault," Klaus muttered. "I *knew* there were risks in sending you to Paris. They'd obviously been planning this for years."

Gil thought back to his discussion with Zola inside Castle Heterodyne. "Longer, sir. Much longer, if correct." Gil shook his head. "But you're overlooking the fact that DuPree was in Paris at the same time. She was with Tarvek a lot more than *I* ever was. You said she was clean, and if they knew about me, they *certainly* wouldn't have passed *her* up. It would have been easy."

Klaus nodded. "An excellent point. She will no doubt provide valuable insight— if she lives."

Gil felt as if he had been punched in the stomach. "What do you mean, if—"

"She brought you to me and collapsed." He looked at Gil questioningly. "She appears to have been poisoned."

Gil desperately wished he was free enough that he could sit down. "Poisoned?" He shook his head. "No. Nothing in that formula should have done that."

"Formula?" His father asked casually.

Gil continued, his mind grinding up to full speed. "And . . . and even if Sturmvarous' people *did* do something to me, I cannot believe that Agatha—"

"Son!" The anguish in Klaus' voice snapped Gil out of his reverie. "*Listen* to yourself! I understand you think you love this girl and I understand that you can't help it. But she is more a child of the Mongfish family than a Heterodyne." He paused. "Although, looking at the vast bulk of their history, the Heterodynes aren't any better, really. Actually, they're far, far worse. But your Agatha is her mother's daughter and with that family, you can believe *nothing.*"

"But it's absurd to think she could have planned all this! She was first brought here by mistake! We— you, father, *you* brought here! She was unconscious! She didn't ask us to bring her here. She begged us to send her home. I'm supposed to be possessed? I'm supposed to be her thrall? She never *told* me to do *anything!*"

And standing there beside the Baron: Boris Dolokhov, a man possessed of an eidetic memory, started in shock. *Yes, she had.*

It had happened back in Beetleburg, when the Baron had stepped in to take the town away from the tyrant, Tarsus Beetle, who had been secretly experimenting with forbidden slaver wasp technology.[122]

It had been the first time Boris—or the Wulfenbachs—had encountered Agatha. She had been employed as one of Beetle's lab assistants, serving under the Doctors Merlot and Glassvitch, and had been present when the Baron had given his son an impromptu test, during the course of which, he had demanded the schematics to a particularly impenetrable device:

Merlot looked around, then quickly turned to Agatha. "The plans, Miss Clay! They were on the main board. Where did you put them?"

Agatha looked surprised. "Oh," she said. "They're in with—" She swung her attention to the storage room door in time to see a rivet pop out of one of the door's straining cross braces. She swung back and smeared a grin across her face. "A—heh. They're in the files in the storage room, Doctors. How about everyone goes and has a nice cup of tea while I dig them out?"

---

[122] A scene that has been thrillingly detailed in our first textbook: *Agatha H and the Airship City.*

Gil strode forward and pushed her aside. "Bah! I'll get them myself! I'm sure your pitiful filing system will be simple—" He turned the handle of the storage room door and yanked, even as Agatha shouted, "NOOOOOOO!"

Replaying the scene in his memory, by Boris's reckoning, an argument could be made that Agatha's initial suggestion alone (that they all retire for tea), should have been enough to trigger an obedience response from someone wasped. However, to be fair, she *was* nervous and hesitant. But when Gilgamesh had reached for the closet door, her scream of "*No*" had been full-throated and desperate. It should have frozen him in place without question. After almost twenty years of fighting revenants and those ensorcelled by the Other, Boris knew the mechanics of how they worked. Klaus should have known this as well. Klaus' memory was just as sharp as Boris's and, as experience had taught him, the Baron missed *nothing*.

Boris snapped back to the present and glanced at the Baron. A fist of ice gripped his heart as he saw Klaus regarding him. He stared and saw a glimmer of—*was that relief?*—flicker across the Baron's face before he appeared to dismiss Boris from his mind and swung back towards his son.

"And yet," he said in response to Gil's last point, "here she was. On board Castle Wulfenbach. In your lab. A very unlikely coincidence— and I mistrust coincidences. Now, all of Europa is in danger. We will talk more when I return."

Klaus turned away and a small, hidden part of him noted, and immediately tried to forget as unimportant, that Boris had already left. Like a man who has done all he could, the Lord of Europa strode from the room.

Back in Mechanicsburg, there seemed to be an endless line of people vying for Agatha's attention. Mechanicsburg citizens relaying the status of the defenses and the ongoing repairs. Enemy soldiers brought before her while weeping, begging her to accept their surrender and help save comrades still engaged with the town's numerous traps and defenses. A running military analysis was provided by Krosp, who was clearly in his element. A delegation from the Great Hospital, led by Doctor Sun himself, who requested an impossibly long list of supplies as well as a safe place to process the casualties.

Agatha did her best, relying heavily on the people around her, but it was difficult managing discussions when they began to drift into cross purposes. It was a discord she had begun to think would never end, when a loud, familiar voice demanded to know what she was doing, by Ashtara's holy daggers, no less.

Agatha looked up. She was where she had been for the last hour, despite the horde around her, flat on her back, rethreading a particularly troublesome drive chain on a small steam walker. A dollop of dirty oil hit her forehead and oozed its way down her nose. Above her, she saw Zeetha staring down at her and looking remarkably well for a person who'd been perforated by a meter of Skifandrian steel scant hours ago. Agatha bounced to her feet and enveloped the green-haired girl in a fierce hug. "You made it!"

Zeetha shrugged from within Agatha's arms. "Of course," she said breezily, but her grin faltered when Airman Higg's face flickered across her memory. She pulled herself free and hung her head. "The Zumil begs forgiveness of her Kolee."[123] Agatha looked startled. Zeetha plowed on. "I did not take Zola seriously. She bested me and could very well have killed us both. For this, I ask forgiveness, but also beg that you learn this lesson: even your Zumil can still make mistakes."

---

[123]   *Kolee-dok-Zumil* is the contract that bound the lady Heterodyne to the Princess Zeetha. A rough translation could be read as "Teacher trains student," but there is a great deal more to it than just that. A better understanding can be gleaned from the unfortunately titled: *Lust, Honor, Sex & Death Among the Lost Warrior Women* by Professoressa Kaja Foglio. Which, she wants made perfectly clear, hit the publisher's doorstep with the title *An Ethnographic Overview of the Societal Mores and Underlying Philosophical Principals of the Skifandrian Warrior Queens.* The fact that, under its current title, it is currently in its twentieth printing, is irrelevant.

Her face was red and her eyes were closed, so she was surprised when she felt Agatha's arms again encircle her in a fierce hug.

"The next time we fight her," Agatha whispered into her ear, "we do it *together*." Zeetha returned the hug until Agatha patted Zeetha's back and pulled back in surprise. "Where are your swords?"

Zeetha's happiness evaporated. Her fists tightened. "I have to take things easy," she muttered. "The doctor said I will get them back when I am healed."

Agatha whistled in surprise. "I'll bet *that* was a fight."

Zeetha remembered the pain and the shame of being face down on the infirmary floor with Higg's knee in the small of her back, his untouched face looking down at her with a slightly bored expression. Zeetha shook her head. "It wasn't, really." Which had rather been the point. She studied the crowd that was suddenly busy looking elsewhere. She turned back to Agatha. "This seems rather chaotic."

Agatha nodded her head. "I know. I'm trying to help, but another attack could hit us at any moment, and we're not ready."

Zeetha nodded. "Yesss, I can see that. Delegate." She pointed to Van. "He knows more about the town and its resources than you do. Let him deal with that." She pointed to Krosp. "He's supposed to be this big military genius? Let him prove it." She pointed to Mamma Gkika. "Have him work with her. *She* probably knows all about the defensive and offensive capabilities of the town. Let the people around you do their jobs." Agatha saw the three Zeetha had indicated were nodding in agreement.

"So what do *I* do?"

"At the moment? You come with me." And she dragged Agatha out of the workshop and into a street.

"Wait! Where are we going?"

"Somewhere private," Zeetha, still walking briskly, said with determination. "You are in serious need of some princess lessons."

"Now?"

"Yes, now. This is important." Zeetha was clambering up a pile of twisted clanks. With a grunt of satisfaction, she pried a weapon from some cold, metal fingers and tossed it down to Agatha, who managed to catch it, despite its surprisingly heavy weight. "First lesson," Zeetha declared. "Every princess needs a battle-axe." She nodded in satisfaction. "That'll do until we find something more impressive."

"Ah," said Agatha with a smile. "*That* kind of princess."

Zeetha jumped down and again snagged her arm. "Come on, I saw some armor in a burning museum that's to die for." They were off again.

Agatha swung the axe up onto her shoulder. "But I was working."

Zeetha interrupted her. "Like a mechanic."

"I *am* a—"

"Not anymore." Zeetha sighed. "You were flat on your back, so everyone assumed they could walk all over you. They say my mother used to do this. She would try to kill every rogue fafflenarg beast[124] herself, even though she had an army. She's a war queen, for pity's sake." Zeetha poked Agatha in the chest. "*You* are a war queen and you've got me and your boys and Krosp and a whole town that wants you to succeed at leading it. You need to *remember* that and be the leader that they need. "

"Well, of course." Agatha fidgeted. "But I *like* building stuff."

Zeetha rolled her eyes. "Don't I know it. And when you have a month—ha! a week—you can rebuild the whole town."

Agatha stared at her and licked her lips. "Do you . . . do you think they'll let me?"

"At this point, I think they're counting on it. But now is not the time. Let the *mechanics* fix the clanks. There are hundreds of them here, but there is only one Heterodyne and that's you."

They came to a building that had obviously once been some sort of

---

[124]   Fafflenarg beasts (*Fafflenarg gigantus skifandrus*) were unknown to Europa at this time. These days, of course they have become a familiar part of every Europan's table, known to us as Tasty Breakfast Beasts™, even though they are, by law, only eaten at lunch.

military office that had been repurposed. Agatha saw a sign declaring it to be the Mechanicsburg Museum of Armor and Military Science before Zeetha dragged her inside.

After they remained inside for several minutes, Dimo and Maxim, who had been surreptitiously following them, stepped out into the street and looked around. Seeing nothing worthy of their attention, they draped themselves on the front steps. Dimo pulled his cap down over his eyes and allowed himself to bask in the sun. Maxim pulled out his saber and examined it critically. He tsked at a deep notch in the blade and then pulled a whetstone and an oiled silk cloth out from a pocket and began sharpening it. Several minutes after that, Ognian appeared, with three two-liter steins, obviously full, clasped in one clawed hand. He set Dimo's down beside him and then passed one to Maxim. The two clinked the steins together and drank deeply. Ognian came up for air and gave a deep sigh of satisfaction as he leaned back on his elbows.

Maxim frowned into his stein. "Hy tink dey haz dun sompting to der beer vile ve vos gone."

Ognian stuck out his tongue. "Puh. Hyu sound like my ol' poppa." He dropped his voice down an octave or so. "Dey chust ain't usin' de right kind of blood in de blood sausages dese days, blah, blah, blah . . . " He took another swig. "Drink der beer hyu gots in hyu hand, brodder, not der vun in hyu head."

He looked up and saw Mamma Gkika striding down the street in full military rig, heading straight towards them. He nudged the somnambulant Dimo with a clawed foot. "Drink op vile hyu ken, brodder, someting's comink."

When she got close enough, Gkika called out, "Hoy! Hyu!"

Slumping back with the air of a world-weary sophisticate, Ognian tipped his stein in her direction. "Hello, dere, Mamma."

Gkika blinked. This was not the reaction she was used to getting once she was in uniform. "Vere iz our gurl?" She looked up at the museum. "She in dere?"

Ognian nodded. "Ho, yez. Iz ve under attack?"

Gkika stepped up. "Not yet, but—"

Ognian raised a hand as he sipped his beer. "Den ve ain't lettink hyu in."

Gkika's jaw dropped. "Vot?!" Maxim looked nervous.

Ognian sighed. "She's in dere haffink sum gurl tok vit her green-haired friend. She vos not born und raised as a daughter of der Heterodynes. Vot she iz doink now—becomink der Heterodyne—iz a leedle like ven vun becomes a Jäger, hy tink. Even for a schmot gurl like her, iz bound to be a leedle hard. But she vill be ranting und frothing un goink all krezy—like soon enuff."

Gkika stared at him like a person who had just seen a dog quote Plato. She decided to deal with it by ignoring him. "Pah! Hy vant to see her *now!*"

Ognian didn't appear to move, but his triple-bladed halberd was suddenly blocking Gkika's way. "Later," he said.

"Vot iz dis," Gkika screamed. "Hy iz a *general!*"

"Hiz not hyu, Mamma, ve'd do dis to *any* general. Ve vos detached." He patted his chest. "Hy iz a vild Jäger."

Off to one side, Dimo cleared his throat. "Maxim," he asked of the Jäger dithering at his side, "vould hy *regret* tipping back mine hat?"

Maxim considered this. "Dunno. *How* bored did hyu say hyu vos?"

He wasn't *that* bored, apparently, as he simply lay back and listened to the roars and squeals surrounding him. It was obvious to him Mamma was on edge and that a little workout might prove therapeutic. Finally, there was naught but gurgling. Dimo carefully raised his cap to see Mamma standing, panting slightly, with a snarl on her face. Maxim was firmly pinned under her boot heel. Ognian hung from her fist, his eyes bulging as she finished winding his beloved halberd around his neck. Dimo tsked. *That was going to be tricky to fix.* He rolled to his feet. Mamma saw him and her eyes closed to slits. She looked about for a weapon, then saw she still had Ognian in her hand. She hoisted him slightly and nodded in satisfaction.

The two stared at each other.

A window on the front of the building banged open and Zeetha leaned out. "What is going on? Oh! Mamma!" She waved excitedly. "Oh, this is *perfect!* You've got to come up here and see this!" She then examined the scene before her. A look of uncertainty came into her eyes. "Guys?"

Dimo instantly relaxed and cheerfully waved back, as did the other two. "Hello, Mizz Zeetha," they chorused. Seeing that all appeared to be well, Zeetha waved again and closed the window.

"Vell," Ognian said in a faint voice, "hy guess hyu kin go in now."

Mamma looked at him and seemed to see him for the first time. She took a deep breath and effortlessly twisted the halberd open. "Hyu iz goot boys. Hyu go ahead und keep on lookink after her." She spared a glance for Dimo, "But dun do nottink too schtupid, hokay?"

"Yes, Mamma," they said.

With a nod of satisfaction, Gkika wheeled about just as Zeetha was opening the front door. "Und speaking of *schtupid*," she roared at the startled girl, "vot iz hyu doink out of bed? Hyu gots a whole bunch of healink to do und dun hyu forget it!"

"I know, I know! But Agatha needs me, and you patched me up enough that I can at least give her advice." She looked away. "Anyway, that Higgs already made me promise to take it slow, and he . . . he hid my swords." She looked down. "I feel naked," she whispered.

Gkika laughed in admiration. "Dot boy! Alvays vit der tricks!"

"You know him well?"

Gkika nodded. "Ho, yez indeed."

They climbed up a short set of stairs and entered a large open area. The ceiling was easily eight meters high, and the room was lined with weird and improbable suits of armor, all of them, according to neat little cards, harvested from the various armies that had attempted to invade Mechanicsburg. In the center was a series of displays showing automated historical dioramas that, at the drop of a coin, sent minuscule invaders fleeing in terror before assorted Heterodyne creations.

Zeetha screwed up her courage. "Could you . . . tell me about him?"

Gkika turned serious. "No vay, kiddo. If he vants hyu to know ennyting about heem, he'll tell hyu himself. And ennyting hyu hear from odder pipple? Onless hyu hears it from him, dun believe a vurd of it" That said, she changed the subject. "Now vere iz de Miztrezz? Hy gots to talk to her about dot Storm King of hers."

"Tarvek?" Gkika nodded. "Oh, he's a piece of work." She looked at the rows of armor. "But we could've used his opinion here." They approached a large door and Zeetha slid it open. "On the other hand, we're pretty happy with what we found."

Gkika's jaw dropped. "Gott's leedle feesh in trowzers!"

Elsewhere, the man under discussion felt a small wave of nausea pass through him. This was not a result of being discussed, but from being forced to listen to Othar describing Agatha's proposed duties as his "spunky girl sidekick." This was being eagerly lapped up by the townspeople gathered around, even by the man who appeared to be in charge, a man who's name Tarvek had, until now, only seen on a list of hereditary functionaries. He found that . . . interesting.

Herr von Mekkhan cleared his throat. "Well, Herr Tryggvassen, we would be very honored if you were to stay and help out."

"But of course," Othar preened. "As I was saying, with proper training your new Heterodyne will make a splendid hero! Being around will allow me to show her the ropes and—"

Tarvek gratefully turned to Violetta who had been about to tap his shoulder. "Thank goodness, I cannot listen to any more of this." At Violetta's startled look, he rolled his eyes. "Yes, I knew you were there." His look sharpened. "Why aren't you with Agatha?"

"She sent me to look for you."

Tarvek blinked. "She did? Whatever for?"

"Well, at first she thought maybe you'd run off because of her kissing Wulfenbach. I said there was no way a weasel like you would give up that easily. Then she said in *that* case, if you were gone, it must mean you'd run into something either really important or really dangerous, because, um . . . " Violetta looked embarrassed. "She said 'if he's that much of a weasel, then he'd know it's to his best advantage to stick close to me.'"

Tarvek stared at her in shock. "*Agatha* said that?"

"Um, yeah. Sorry."

Tarvek smiled. "No, no— This is marvelous! She might be better at political intrigue than I'd dared hope!"

Violetta shrugged. "She'll be fantastic, assuming she lives. Let's go already."

Tarvek slumped down. "Oh, sure. Great idea. I hadn't thought of that."

Violetta stared. "Wait. Are you telling me *you* can't get away from a bunch of town guards?"

Tarvek just looked at her and then he sighed. "Fine. Let's try a 'down and up.' That might work."

"Seriously?"

"GO!" Without any noticeable transition, Tarvek was off, running at top speed down the street, Violetta hot on his heels.

"Hey," a guard yelled. "Get back here!"

"If you putting in this much effort is some kind of joke—" Violetta threatened.

"Just run," Tarvek said. Half a block away, they saw an open manhole and, without touching the sides, the pair slid down into it and landed in a fetid stream. Pale, ghost-like lizards watched them pass and lazily began to follow. Tarvek led the way, taking random twists and turns, and then suddenly gripping a pipe and swinging upward, slamming a metal grill aside with his feet.

They scrambled up into a dusty basement. A last glance backwards showed a startled Violetta that the pale lizards had gotten a lot closer than she had thought they were. She shivered as she followed Tarvek up a set of rickety stairs. Instead of going out the street door, he turned and began running up another flight of stairs and then a third and then a fourth. At the top of these stairs was a small wooden door that opened out onto the roof. Violetta bypassed the lock without even slowing down. "Was all this rigmarole necessary?"

The door swung open and they plowed into the waiting arms of Othar. "Now where are you going? We still have to find Agatha." He examined a thunderstruck Violetta. "Ah! I see you've found me another assistant!"

"But . . . but *how*," she sputtered.

Tarvek hung from Othar's fist like a man who'd played this part before. "*This* is why he's a hero. He's very good at this."

There was a bit of involuntary screaming as Othar leaped off the top of the building and deftly bounced off walls and ledges before touching down with all three unscathed. "You want the Lady Heterodyne?"

Violetta said, with eyes shut tight, "She told me to bring him to her right away!"

Othar smiled genially. "Ah, but she didn't know that Othar Tryggvassen—Gentleman Adventurer (to his horror, Tarvek found himself mouthing the words as Othar spoke)—was here!"

Tarvek thrashed in midair. "Let us go, you cretin! We should get to her quickly!"

Othar regarded him. "Actually, I'm from Norway."

Tarvek clenched his teeth. "I have important military information! We'll need to re-think all of the town's defenses if any of us are going to get through this alive!"

"Ho," said a new voice, "sounds like hyu vants to talk to *me*, den!"

They had rejoined Van's group and, from the side, a Jäger stepped forward. Unlike most of the Jägerkin, this one took care with his uniform and his hat was polished and worn at a rakish angle. "Vat kind of information hyu gots, kiddo?"

Tarvek glanced over at Van, who bobbed his head. "This is Jorgi, he's our liaison with the Jägers."

Jorgi nodded. "Ve talks vit all der odder monsters too."

Tarvek considered this and then nodded. "Very well, but this is . . . too open."

Jorgi nodded back. "Hokay. Ve see." He turned to Van "Hy'll take dis guy vit me."

Van leaned in. "Are you sure? He's—"

Jorgi raised a clawed hand while looking at Tarvek. "Hy know *exactly* who he thinks he iz."

Tarvek swallowed and any plans about trying to escape from the Jäger were dismissed. "What about my aide-de-camp," he said, indicating Violetta, who was still hanging from Othar's fist.

Jorgi examined her. "Hyu vos Burghurmeister Zuken's assistant. I dunno . . ."

"You'd better take me, you slug," she hissed at Tarvek. "I want you where I can *see* you."

Tarvek considered this and then turned to Othar. "I should mention that Violetta here is a Smoke Knight."

Othar looked surprised. "Really? I've heard of those." He examined a furious Violetta. "That *does* explain why she almost managed to escape several times. It was very impressive."

"Yes," Tarvek acknowledged, "she shows great promise." He caught a small knife that was aimed at his face. "And, she'll deny it, but as far as you're concerned, she's a huge fan."

"WHAT?" Violetta looked stunned.

"Oh, now she's going to get all embarrassed, but she's dreamed about becoming one of your sidekicks for ages."

Othar examined her again. "And she's a Smoke Knight you say? Then she might even last through the summer."[125]

---

[125]   Othar Tryggvassen did tend to run through female assistants rather quickly. Contrary to scurrilous rumors promulgated by his detractors, hardly any of them were killed in the line of duty. Most of them simply discovered the job looked a lot less glamorous up close. One of the principle reasons for this seems to be that while there is no denying he was a great lover of women, Othar was unshakeable in his resolution to never dally with an assistant. For many of his companions, that had rather been the whole point.

"I will hunt you down, flay you, and wear you as a hat," Violetta screamed.

Othar grinned in admiration. "She's certainly got the spunky part down!"

Tarvek and Jorgi moved off down the street. Jorgi glanced back. "Hyu gots to excuse der Town Council. Der oldt guys have been trappink tourists for too long. An' der young guys iz schtill figurink tings out. Dey's schtill tinkink like a bunch of soft townies. Not dat dot's a bad ting. Somebody got's to do de running und screaming. Eh, but this is Mechanicsburg, und dey's its pipple. Dey'll vake up soon enough, and den— vatch owt!" He clapped Tarvek on the shoulder. "But dot vill take time, und since der Storm King vants to make vit der military talk now—"

Tarvek waved his hands. "Shh! That's still a secret!"

Jorgi gave a snort of laughter as he stopped before an ancient door easily four meters tall. He produced an iron key and unlocked it, then pushed Tarvek through. They were in a small dusty anteroom. "Dun vorry, der guys you'll be talkink to dun hold grudges about dot old schtuff." He straightened his hat and knocked on the inner door before pushing it open. " 'Cause if hyu dun learn how to let all dot go— Hyu dun last long enuf to be a general."

The room was long and high, and dominated by an immense table that, to Tarvek's educated eye, had to be easily five centuries old. Sitting around it were four monsters. Tarvek instantly recognized them as Jägergenerals. Zog, Goomblast, and Khrizhan were familiar adjuncts to the Baron. The fourth was a grinning ogre with bright red skin. Tarvek noted his right hand's knuckles were tattooed with the word *LOVE*. On the left, he read *HAT*, and rolled his eyes. This could only be General Koppelslav, who had been stationed on the empire's eastern border for over a decade and who, according to Tarvek's latest intelligence, should be there still.

Interesting. There was also—Tarvek blinked at the sight of Krosp, now sporting a Mechanicsburg souvenir novelty cap designed to look like a hat-wearing Jäger gnawing on the wearer's head. Krosp glanced upwards and shrugged. "It's a *rule*, okay? When you sit at the generals' table, you've got to wear a hat."

Tarvek pointed towards General Khrizhan. "*He* doesn't have a hat."

Khrizhan looked cartoonishly surprised and made a show of patting his baldpate. "Oh, deary me," he rumbled. "Did I forgets mine *hat?*"

The rest of the generals could no longer contain themselves and dissolved in roars of laughter. Krosp stared at them and his fur bristled in fury. "We're about to be under attack and you guys are joking around?"

Tarvek tapped his chin. "Don't blame them," he said slowly, "they're worried. By tradition, the new Heterodyne should be greeted by all the generals, yet you're sitting in here instead." He looked over the assemblage, which had gone silent. "General Øsk died fighting the Polar Lords' doom wyrm last year. That leaves seven generals, but only four of you are here. Where are the others?"

Krosp frowned. "Wait . . . *seven?* I heard there were *six.*"

Tarvek continued. "I'm sure you did. Nevertheless . . . Could there be *dissension* here?"

General Zog stared at him with a sour look on his face. "Hokay," he said grudgingly. "No funny hat for hyu. Come talk vit us."

They made room for Tarvek at the table beside Krosp. Tarvek noted that even if there had been seven of the gigantic creatures, there still would have been space for easily a half a dozen more and, indeed, six immense chairs were lined up against the far wall, each with a small black Heterodyne sigil draped over the back.

Everyone silently looked at Zog, who stared back at Tarvek while slowly gnashing his great teeth. Finally, he nodded once. "Hyu iz right," he admitted. "Der iz only seven uv us now. Not many pipple knows dot." He gestured towards one of the three empty chairs at the table. "General Zadipok should have been here by now. But ve haff not heard from him. It iz, as hyu say, vorryink."

He glanced out the great window that dominated one wall. "General Gkika iz vit der Heterodyne now." He grinned. "No one could take better care uf her."

Both Tarvek and Krosp glanced at the last empty chair. Zog nodded again. "And den dere iz der seventh. He iz a tricky vun. He iz . . . der keeper ov many secret tings."

"Why isn't he here?"

"The Odder inside der Lady," Zog rumbled.

Tarvek was taken aback. "The Other— You know about that?"

"Indeed ve doz. Und as long as dot bad gurl iz in der Lady's head, he vill remain in der shadowz."

Tarvek glanced about. The generals were somber now. He cleared his throat. "Sensible. But . . . let him know he may not have to stay there for long. I have studied the Other's methods, and I believe I can get Lucrezia out of Agatha's head for good."

General Khrizhan leaned back. "Oh-ho! Dot *iz* goot.news"

Zog steepled his fingers and grinned knowingly. "Ah, and den hyu can gets to de keesink, yez?"

"Well, I'm certainly not going to do it before—" Tarvek realized what he was saying and blushed. "Wait! No! I didn't—! That is—!"

Around him the Jägers gave a great roar of laughter. Zog wiped a tear from his eye. "Vell, boyz, dot Wulfenbach keed gots him a rival! Diz iz gunna be fun!"

This provoked another round of laughter. Tarvek turned to Krosp. "Are they *always* like this?"

The cat shrugged. "I'm guessing: yes."

Tarvek turned back to the table. "Anyway, Agatha has Lucrezia under control for now. But we have a bigger, more immediate problem. The Baron—"

The sound of explosions was heard from outside. The red-skinned general leapt up. "Iz too soon for anodder attack!"

Tarvek lunged for the window along with the others, but while they looked at the encircling forces, he scanned the skies above. "Dammit," he swore, "I thought they could get through unsuspected!" Three airships were heading for the town. A larger cargo dirigible, followed by two of the empire's pursuit ships.

"Vy izen't der Kestle shooink dem avay," Zog muttered. Suddenly there was another fusillade from the two pursuers, and the aft of the cargo ship's gasbag erupted into flames.

"Hoy." Khrizhan said in surprise. "Dey's not attackink us. Dey's shootink at der own ship." He looked at the others. "Dot ken't be goot." It certainly wasn't for the cargo ship, which, even with every engine angled to try to slow their momentum, ground deceptively slowly into the market section of the Court of Gears[126] district. Almost an entire block of buildings shuddered at the impact and began to collapse. A huge ring of smoke and dust blossomed and began silently rolling over the town. By this time, Tarvek, as well as the generals, were out the door and running towards the downed ship, followed by a bevy of other Jägers who had been standing guard outside.

Koppelslav pointed upwards at the fast-approaching pursuit ships. "Dey's lowerink lines," he shouted. "Dey's gunna send in troops."

Zog shook his head. "Dey's huntink der own pipple?"

Khrizhan bared his teeth. "Dey vos already *shootink* at dem. Der impawtent ting iz dot deyz landing troops inside our town."

Goomblast looked pensively at the downed airship. "Izn't it gunna blow op?"

Koppelslav smacked him. "Dot only happens in dose cheap Heterodyne Boyz novels, hyu old fool!"

Tarvek glanced back over his shoulder and seemed surprised to see them. "We've got to hurry! I need the people from that ship alive!" He glanced at the incoming ships. Tiny figures could now be seen

---

[126] The Court of Gears is the section of the town where one will find not only the great central factory, but hundreds of individual manufacturers and workshops.

clutching the dangling ropes. "I sincerely hope you gentlemen fight as well as you dress!"

The generals glanced at each other. "Gentlemen?" Zog huffed.

"Us?" Goomblast looked intrigued.

"Fight?" Krizhan began to smile.

Koppelslav shrugged and buffed a spike. "Vot? Dis old ting?"

Tarvek bit back an annoyed retort. There was something wrong here . . .

A squeal of feedback came from the sky and an amplified voice boomed out over the area. "All civilians are to leave the crash site. Anyone who remains will be shot! This is your only warning." With that, several dozen dark-clad figures began lowering themselves on the great ropes, waiting until they were within safe landing distance—

A broad-bladed tool, normally used to edge grass, arrowed up through the air with such force that it severed several lines, and easily a dozen men were sent screaming towards the ground. Krizhan stared upwards in admiration and then turned towards Zog, who had smashed a shop window and was extracting yet another edger. "Hey!" He tugged on Zog's arm. "Hey, does dot count? Does killink dem up in der air count?"

Zog laughed. "Killink hyu enemies *alvays* counts!"

General Goomblast found himself surrounded by a ring of men armed with needle-sharp swords with blackened blades. "Stand down, General," one called out. "We're not here to fight you, but if you interfere—"

"Sorry, boys," the general called out in his unexpected contralto, "but hy am here to fight *hyu*." With a liquid sweep of his arm, he pulled forth an elegant silver rapier and traced a few simple arabesques in the air. "Hyu are invadink our town, hyu know. Ve kent hev dot." He gave them a salute. "Now, how bouts hyu boys surrender like gentlemen?" A look of anticipation filled his great face. "No! Vait! Even better! Hy vill duel hyuz *champion*! Hit'll be terrific!"

The men in black looked towards their leader. "This isn't some *game*," he snarled. "The people in that airship are dangerous traitors, and we have direct orders from the Baron to wipe them out!"

Goomblast shrugged and his sword began moving lazily. "Too bad, but ve gots a guy here who vants dem alive." One of the men crept slightly ahead of his fellows. Faster than the eye could follow, Goomblast pinked his hand, snapped the black blade into the air, and caught it so he could examine it. "Und vhat iz vit dese leedle swords?" He sniffed the blade. "Iz dis *poison*?"

"Enough to take down even a behemoth like you," the leader swore. "Enough! Men, kill them all!"

Goomblast sighed. "Dis hardly seems fair."

"*C'est la guerre*, General." And the men in black flowed forward.

As each came within range, Goomblast's blade flicked out, snapped the guard of their sword, and whipped it into the chest of the man next to them, who dropped his sword, which was caught and so on, until the last man stood unarmed, at which point Goomblast took the first sword he had appropriated and, with a heave, sent it into his chest. "Hy dun mean for *me*," he sneered, "but hy dun expect pipple who'd use poison to understend the subtleties."

Khrizhan tapped his shoulder. "Hy suppose hyu tink dot counts too? Usink der own veapons on dem?"

Goomblast frowned at him. "Ov cawze. De veapons dun care."

On a third front, a wounded man stumbled up to the highest ranking officer left. "Sir! They're wiping us out!"

The man nodded. "Right. Well, the Baron can't say we didn't try. So now we do this my way." He raised his voice to a shout. "Disengage!"

The men stared at him. "But . . . our orders . . . "

"We gas the place from the air like we should have done in the first place."

General Koppelslav roared. "Now hyu guys iz just *askink* for it!" With a sweep of his hands, he swept the great spikes adorning his upper arms free and, with machine gun speed, took down the fleeing men.

Khrizhan appeared by his side. "Und killink den vhile dey iz runnink away . . . Dis also counts?"

Koppelslav stared at him. "Vot der dumboozle iz de *matter* vit hyu?"

Khrizhan looked contrite. "Vell, hy just dun vant hyu guys sayink hy vos cheatink."

Zog frowned. "How zo?"

Khrizhan strode over to a downed Wulfenbach clank and ripped free the great machine cannon it had carried. "Using der own veapons—" He swung the weapon upwards towards the hovering dirigibles, from which faint screams could suddenly be heard. "—vile dey iz schtill in de air." With a roar the cannon's engines spun to life. Khrizhan pulled the trigger, sending a stream of heated metal skyward. The airships blew apart. Khrizhan turned to the rest of the stupefied generals, a wicked grin on his face. "–Vile dey vos trying to escape." Flaming debris pattered down around them. "So, if dot all *counts*—" his grin got even wider "—den hy vin."

A second passed—and then Zog gave a great roar of laughter. "Ho, iz schtill *cheatink*, but in der *goot* vay!"

Goomblast nudged Koppelslav in the ribs. "Hy *knew* hyu could make dem blow op."

From the sidelines, there was a ripple of applause from the crowd of Jägers surrounding Tarvek. He stepped aside as a porthole dropped from the sky and shattered at his feet. This broke his reverie. "Okay, it'll take the empire a few minutes to send something else." He peered down at the now-smoldering airship. He saw a few figures staggering from a hatchway, but— "Why haven't they begun to unload the ship?" he muttered. "They must know time is of the essence."

Jorgi looked over his shoulder. "Dey probably know ve iz out here."

Tarvek took off. "No, something's wrong. Let's go!" The assembled Jägers trotted along behind him.

"Zo vhat's der beeg deal about dese guys?"

"As far as the empire is concerned, they're now some of the most dangerous people alive."

Jorgi looked interested. "Ho! Just like us! Dey'll fit right in. Mechanicsburg is a goot plaze for dangerous pipple what no vun likes."

Yes, Tarvek thought, and the empire, as well as Lucrezia know that.

Jorgi was still talking. "Ve should call de Velcome Vagon! Dey gots dese great leedle sammaches and cute gurls in hazmat suits!" Suddenly he skidded to a halt and stared. "Vaitaminute! *Dose* guys? Dey iz vhat der Baron iz vorried about?"

They were now close enough that the people stumbling from the airship could be identified. They wore the distinctive green uniforms topped with wasp-warrior skullcaps of the empire's Vespiary Squad. Many of them were visibly wounded. One of the officers saw Tarvek and ran towards him. "Prince Sturmvarous! You were right! You were right about *everything*!"

Tarvek nodded. He'd only had a few seconds while he was titularly in charge of the empire's military forces, but certain things had been all too obvious. Passing the squad leader a note under the watchful eyes of Boris and the others had been quite the challenge.

The officer continued, "But it's even worse than we thought. The Baron himself—"

"Yes, yes." Tarvek leaned in. "*I* know, but we don't want everyone *else* to know. Not yet." The officer blinked and took a deep breath as he nodded. Tarvek nodded back. "Now what's the situation?"

"Even before they shot us down, we discovered there were Stealth

Fighters onboard the ship. They've been destroying equipment. We're trying to get the weasels out, but it's difficult."

"Why?"

"Several specimens escaped. They're also killing our people . . . including Doctor Bren."[127]

Tarvek gasped. "Bren? Dead? Then if we lose the wasp eaters, this will all have been pointless!" He spun about. "Jägers! Follow me!"

From somewhere within the airship, there was the sound of something very large giving a scream of defiance. Jorgi placed a hand on Tarvek's arm. "Mebbe hyu better stay here, hey? Hyu regular pipple iz kinda fragile, und hy dun tink der Lady vould like it if hyu got broken."

Tarvek shook the Jäger's hand off and his voice indicated he was sparking out. "Enough! The importance of these creatures cannot be overestimated!" He pointed to the bemused Jägers. "You will follow me and do as I say, or I will have you all flayed, roasted alive, and turned into stoats!" And he turned on his heel and dashed off.

The Jägers followed, though there was some good natured carping. "Hey! Who's he tink he iz, givink us orders like dot?"

"Ve's followink, ain't ve?"

"Yah, vell, dot vun's got a great rantink voice."

They all nodded. It had been a while since they'd heard a good rant. Jorgi summed it up: "No vunder der Lady likes him. He must be vun heck uva demon vit der sveet talk!"

A shaggy Jäger raised a hand. "Hy dunno, dot odder guy gots vun sveet hat."

This had every sign of devolving into a protracted argument, when Tarvek slammed his hand against a buckled hatch. "Jägers! Clear this door!"

With a shouted "HOY!" they thundered past and tore it off its hinges.

---

[127]   Doctor Jupiter Bren (MD, PhD) was the driving force behind the development of the creatures known as wasp weasels.

Jorgi frowned and stepped up to Tarvek. "Hy should varn hyu: not all uv our boyz iz gun put op vit hyu bossink us around like—"

"Jorgi!" The two looked up to see the Jägers that had busted down the door were now grappling with a gigantic wasp eater that was easily six meters tall. A Jäger struggling to break free of a paw snarled down. "Vot iz hyu *vaitink* for? Hyu iz missink a great fight!"

Jorgi threw up his hands and grinned at Tarvek. "Hokay, boss! Hyu vin dis vun. Comink!" He leapt into the fray.

Beside Tarvek the Vespiary officer watched with trepidation. "I *knew* that thing would get loose," he muttered. "Don't even know why Bren kept it around."

CHAPTER 10

For close to a thousand years, Mechanicsburg has been a place apart. The hereditary home of the Heterodynes was a blank spot on the map. Efforts were made to explore and understand what it was that lurked in the mountain fortress, but between the treacherous landscape and the fearsome creatures of the Heterodynes, few who were foolish enough to venture in ever returned.

It was not long before the surrounding kingdoms began to take advantage of the terrible thing in their midst. Witches, murderers, sorcerers, traitors, criminals, and madmen of all temperament and stripe began to be delivered to the great gates that guarded the Valley of the Heterodynes and sent through under fear of death. This was all well and good, but a growing suspicion began to arise that they were not, in fact going to their deaths, but to what many of them would come to regard as home.

—Introduction to Victor Shabazznix's *A Field Guide to the Peoples of Mechanicsburg: Constructs, Hybrids, Sports, Mutants, Beast-Men, Offshoots, Grafts, Mimics, Chimeras, Reanimates, Inhumans, Nonhumans, Subhumans, and Herr Xxississlechix*
(Mechanicsburg Press)

❧

Tarvek grabbed the Vespiary officer's arm and pulled him along. They skirted the screaming, whirling mass of Jägers and megaweasel and slipped down a blood-spattered corridor. The officer pointed. "The wasp eaters are this way." They

329

came to an open door and stopped, appalled. The room was full of crushed and shattered cages. Blood was everywhere. Buried near the bottom, a few intact cages held living wasp eaters that were screaming and dashing themselves on the bars in a panic. Kneeling amidst the carnage was a Vespiary Squad tech, clutching one of the wounded creatures. Tears ran down her face. "I'm sorry, Captain," she sobbed, "So sorry. We've lost so many of them."

Tarvek swallowed and stepped into the room. "Focus," he said sharply. "Collect the rest—"

"*Captain!*" the girl screamed a warning and Tarvek spun, only to see the warning had come too late. Two slaver warriors were sliding into the room, one extracting the arm-blade that it had sent through the captain's back and out his chest.

Tarvek stepped forward. "Hive warriors! Miss, you've got to run!"

Instead, she put one hand on his head, using him as leverage as she vaulted past him. She brought a sword down hard and neatly split the head of one of the warriors in two. The second creature lashed out with its blades, but she slid beneath them while drawing a small weapon from her belt and fired upwards, disintegrating its head in a ball of flame.

Tarvek gawped. The woman rolled to her feet and looked at him with a frown. "Protecting people from those things is *my* job," she said with a sniff.

Tarvek closed his mouth. "Um . . . I'm . . . I'm sorry, you just seemed rather distraught."

Her face collapsed into tears again, even as a third warrior loomed up out of the darkness behind her. "Of *course* I'm distraught!" Without apparent thought, she swung the gun up over her shoulder and fired a shot that hit the warrior between the eyes. "They hurt my weasels!"

Tarvek nodded. "Right. Let's try to collect up as many cages as we can, um . . . ?"

The woman wiped her nose. "First Unit Keeper Ruxala, sir, and all we have to do is open the cages. Lugging them all would take too long, and we need to hurry. You never know what else Doctor Bren was keeping in his lab. These little guys are smart enough to follow us out."

Tarvek held up a hand. "Back up. What else *might* he have had?"

Ruxala continued opening cages. "There should be at least two more warriors, so be careful."

Tarvek paused in the doorway. "Wait . . . you people *brought* them here?"

"Of course. Our job is to detect and destroy them. To do that properly, we have to *study* them. We also use them to train the wasp eaters."

Tarvek relaxed. "That makes sense. You don't have any actual enslavers here, do you?"

Ruxala looked shocked. "Of course not! Not live ones, anyway."

"I'm relieved. Surprised, but relieved."

"Yeah, they don't last long outside the queens." Ruxala dusted her hands together as she climbed to her feet. "There! Come on out, sweeties!" Immediately several dozen of the multi-legged creatures poured out of their cages and began clambering over the delighted woman. Tarvek stood well back. "Huh. I didn't know they were so tame."

She looked at him seriously. "Oh, they're not. They can be quite vicious when they see wasps. But mostly they just hide and ignore people, unless . . . "

Suddenly Tarvek realized all of the wasp eaters were staring fixedly at him. "Unless . . . ?" With a chorus of squeals, they leaped and landed on him. Winding about his neck, rummaging under his coat, and just draping themselves wherever they could. To his astonishment, he realized some were already falling asleep.

Ruxala grinned in delight. "Unless they really *like* you!" Tarvek shifted his feet and almost stumbled as a flotilla of weasels rearranged themselves over his boots. "Lucky me," he muttered.

A series of explosions echoed from somewhere deeper within the dirigible, and a wave of acrid smoke billowed down the hallway. It was followed by another of the Vesipary Squad who was coughing, despite the mask that covered his lower face. He saw the two of them and waved a hand. "What are you people *doing?* Hurry up and get out!"

Tarvek tried to shrug off the weasels. "Bren's lab," he demanded. "Where is it?"

The squad member waved a hand behind him. "I've just come from there. It's full of Wulfenbach Stealth Fighters. They're killing everything they see, but I managed to set most of the experiments free, so they should keep them busy."

And then they'll be our problem, Tarvek thought. Aloud he said, "Did you get Bren's notes?"

"Jeez, I was lucky to get out of there alive."

Tarvek nodded. "Fine. You two get these wasp eaters out of here. They're our first priority." With that, he dashed off down the corridor.

"Wait!" The squad member called out. "Where are you going?"

"I need those notes!"

"I don't even know if Bren kept notes! And there's monsters! And crazy killers! You've got nothing!"

"Nonsense," Tarvek called back. "I've got your gun and your knife."

Startled, the officer frantically patted his uniform and then slumped in embarrassment. "Man," he muttered, "I'm gonna hear about *that.*"

Tarvek turned a corner and stopped short in dismay. Doors to several offices lined the walls. The corridor itself was filled with smashed equipment. One of the offices was filled with swirling green flames. "I hope that one wasn't Bren's," Tarvek muttered.

A chucking squeak next to his ear made him jump—and he realized that one of the wasp eaters was still perched on his shoulder. He eyed it suspiciously. "I don't suppose *you* know where Bren's office is?"

"This way." After his heart restarted, Tarvek realized the voice actually belonged to Ruxala, who had spoke as she darted past him.

"What are you *doing* here?"

She looked back at him, and he saw that she had donned a breathing mask. "You're right. Those notes are important. We'll need them."

"But the wasp eaters—"

"Captain Finucane will get them out." She smiled under her mask. "I lent him my knife." She kicked a hissing gas cylinder into an empty office, where it exploded. "Don't worry, they're not stupid enough to go running into something like this."

Tarvek felt judged. "Excuse me for being stupid."

Ruxala chuckled. "Well, you know sparks. If we don't find those notes, they'll start wanting to experiment on my weasels."

"Only for science . . . " Tarvek began weakly, but Ruxala ignored him. She pointed to an office that was, astonishingly, only slightly on fire. "Here's Bren's office." She looked at the carboys stacked against the wall and stepped back outside. "Hurry up. Some of that stuff's really volatile."

Tarvek was busy emptying a compact bookcase mounted on the wall over the desk. "Oh yes! *This* is what I need." He turned to Ruxala. "Do you see a bag or something we can use?"

She grunted and collapsed, revealing two Wulfenbach Stealth Fighters, one of which was still pulling a knife from her back. He looked at Tarvek and sneered. "I think you'll be needing a coffin."

His compatriot grinned. "Heh, good one! Make that *two!*"

The first one rolled his eyes. "Just kill him and grab those notes. I'll finish the girl."

"No," Tarvek glared at them. "I think not." He turned and leapt directly into the flames.

The men gasped. "What the—? He jumped into the fire?!"

"But why? We were gonna kill him just fine!"

A knife blade erupted from his chest. "You know," Tarvek said as the other fighter swung to meet him. "I've never been much for the whole 'school pride' thing . . . " He effortlessly leapt over the blade that cleaved the air where he'd been, twisting so that his heel impacted the fighter's jaw, sending him to the ground. "But you clods aren't fit to shine a Smoke Knight's knives."

He knelt beside Ruxala. "Ah. Good, you're still alive." He staunched the flow of blood with her cloak. Suddenly he froze. "Of course this means that I'll have to carry you." He hoisted her in his arms, Bren's library piled on her stomach. The wasp eater climbed over his shoulder and sniffed her with concern. Tarvek stepped back out into the corridor and saw one end was engulfed in flames. "That's spreading fast," he muttered to the weasel as he headed for the exit. "Hope they got all your little friends out and at least some of the equipment."

Ruxala whimpered in his arms. "I told you to get out," he muttered to her. "I could have found Bren's office without your help." Another explosion some distance away caused the ship to shudder, and the deck listed several degrees to the right. "Probably . . . Maybe . . . " He turned a corner and found a slain trio of green-clad Vespiary officers. It looked like they had been ambushed while moving equipment. Tarvek stepped over them. "Tsk. Crack Vespiary Squad. All of that training and you get stabbed by morons. What good did it do you?"

He turned another corner and came face-to-face with a slaver warrior. It raised its bladed arms—and was promptly shot by Ruxala, who, as far as Tarvek could tell, was still unconscious. He hugged her tighter. "Okay," he conceded, "the training is impressive."

"Too slow. Sorry, Captain," he heard her murmur. "Tummy hurts . . . " A tear ran down her face.

Grimly he climbed over a pile of debris. "What I wouldn't give for Anevka's strong boys now," he muttered.

"Hoy dere, boss!" To Tarvek's astonishment, he saw Jorgi sitting casually against a wall. *He'll do,* Tarvek thought. "Whoo! Dot vus vun krezy veasel monster hyu find for us, hyu betcha! Goot fun, yah!"

Tarvek looked over his shoulder. "What happened to it?"

Jorgi shrugged and then winced. "Hy dunno. Grishnarf und

Shadsnaf vos chasink it." He looked at the unconscious Ruxala. "Zo—beeg date?"

Tarvek wasn't feeling funny. "Ho-ho. We have to leave. Now. Can you help me out here?"

Jorgi glanced away. "No."

"Come on. Please? I'll get a note from Agatha—"

Jorgi looked apologetic. "Dot really vos vun krezy veasel monster ting. Hy gots broken bones in de shoulder und both legs."

Tarvek sagged. "Oh."

"Hey, dun vorry, ve heals fast." A nearby explosion sent a ball of flame shooting from a doorway, which ignited the hallway. Jorgi sighed and settled back against the wall. "Hokay, not *dot* fast." He closed his eyes and made a shooing motion with his hand. "Hyu keeds better get movin'. Hif hyu vin, hyu treats de Lady goot, hokay?"

Tarvek actually turned and took a step before he stopped. Thirty seconds later, he was running down the hall again, with Jorgi's one good arm clutched around his neck. The Jäger was now chattering away in an effort to raise Tarvek's obviously flagging spirits. This was actually having a positive effect, Tarvek was now moving faster, spurred by the desire to shorten the amount of time he'd have to listen to an endless stream of comments about Jorgi, Tarvek's family, this experience as a test of his stamina, how news of this heroism was sure to be passed on to Agatha, and would Tarvek by any chance have a sandwich in his pockets?

"Stop. Talking." Tarvek gasped. His eyes were wide and frantic.

"Ho! Dun feel bad!" Jorgi reassured him. "Hyu ken gets us *all* sandviches vunce ve iz outta here!"

One of the books slipped from the pile. With a hiss of pain, Jorgi snatched it back with his bad arm.

He examined the book. "Zo, vot iz so impawtent bout dese books, hay? Dey looks heavy." He tested a corner of the cover with a sharp tooth, then flipped it open with one claw.

"Put that down, you illiterate fool!"

"Shaddop, schmot guy, hy ken read."

Tarvek was actually grateful for the small burst of cognitive dissonance. "Good heavens. You can?"

Jorgi sniffed. "Sure. But hiff hyu tells de odder guys, hy rips hyu head off!"

Tarvek nodded. "Of course."

Jorgi slumped slightly. "Mine poppa vos a blacksmith, but he vanted to be a philosopher.[128] He even made mine sisters learn to read so he'd have pipple to argue vit. He vos beeg into duality und de politics ov non-beink as related to Platonic reality."

"Really?"

"Ho! Trick qvestion!"

Tarvek was trying to concentrate on moving forward, but he couldn't resist. "Yet you joined the Jägers."

Jorgi looked at him askance. "Hey, hyu leesten to a guy like dot for fifteen years, hyu vill vant burn down de vorld too."

"Are all Jägers like you?"

"Nah, most uv us just likes hittin' pipple."

"Unlike you."

"Meh, Hy likes it too." He flipped a page with his thumb. "Huh. Diz book iz all about dem veasle tings."

The wasp eater on Tarvek's shoulder leapt down and darted into a side room. It returned, squeaking urgently. "What now?" Tarvek grumbled. "More Jägers? Orphans? Jäger orphans?" The creature chirruped and dashed back. Tarvek followed and found the weasel agitatedly running back and forth to an open-topped cage. Inside was a dead wasp eater, impaled on a long glass shard from a shattered overhead light. Around the body was close to a dozen smaller weasels, meeping pathetically. *Kittens.* Tarvek thought. As

---

[128] This had, in fact, been a popular fad amongst sixteenth-century eastern European blacksmiths

his shadow fell over them, they looked upwards quizzically and their squeaking grew louder.

Jorgi grunted and flipped back several pages. "Huh. Dese tings ain't supposed to heff babbies."

"What?"

Jorgi tapped a set of elaborate diagrams. "Look at dis. Right now, dey gots to use all dis incubation eqvipment." He scrutinized the page. "Ho! Hy recognize dot! Hy broke dot!" He flipped another page. "Oooh! Hy see! Dey vos *vorkink* on dot! Tryink to make dem 'independently viable.' " He looked down at the dead weasel. "Dese must be some new type!" Tarvek stared down at the priceless, squirming kits and hoped he'd be able to fit them all into his pockets.

He couldn't, as it turned out, but the last few fit into Jorgi's pockets quite handily. As they continued onward, nearing the entrance, a different type of shudder ran through the floor, accompanied by a growing set of dull booms. "Hey, boss . . . "

"I hear it," Tarvek snarled.

"Eef hyu just leef me here—"

"No! We're almost out. Nothing here is explosive."

Jorgi shook his head. "Dose dun sound like explosions."

"You're an expert?"

"Sure. Hyu bust op enough schtuff, you learns vhat it sounds like vhen it breaks. Nope. Dot's a monster ting. Beeg vun too."

Tarvek tried to speed up even more. "That giant wasp eater?"

"Wrong direction."

"Maybe another one?"

Jorgi looked worried. "Hy sure *hopes* not. Dot ting vos krenky mean. Vhy hyu schmott guys vant something like dot around ennyvays?"

Tarvek bit back the obvious answer and tried to think like a sane person. It was difficult. "I . . . I don't know. The little ones are already good against the wasps—they'll snap up the swarmers and mob the warriors—but that thing you guys went up against was big enough to take on—"

A huge creature that looked equal parts grasshopper and machine burst through a wall, saw them, and shrieked. It struggled through the hole it had made, lashing out at them with arms like serrated spears. Once free, it lunged towards them, it's horrible maw gaping wide.

"A hive queen! Bren had a *hive queen?*"

"Ho!" Jorgi laughed in delight, "Keepink dot odder ting makes *perfect* sense now!" He blew out a gust of air. "Glad ve got *dot* cleared op before ve died."

But, to Jorgi's astonishment, they were not dead. Tarvek was actually running, still carrying Ruxala, Jorgi, notebooks, wasp eater, and kittens, while barely avoiding the queen's attempts to stab them. "This is ridiculous," he screamed as he ran. "Hive queens are supposed to be *sessile! This is not fair!*"

The wasp eater had clambered back up and draped itself over Tarvek's shoulder, snarling and shrieking at the top of its voice.

Jorgi considered the thing behind them. "Hey! Hy bets a bug dis beeg vould make a nize bug pie! Ven hyu iz done vit it, ken hy gets a couple ov de legs? Hy ken makes a beeg pie und feed a whole bunch'a guys! Hy iz a pretty goot cook! I'll giff hyu some und hyu vill see!"

"You weigh less when you're not talking," Tarvek screamed.

Jorgi laughed. "In philosophy, ve calls dot a logical fallacy. Ooh! Hyu iz almost to de door! Iz behind dot giant wall ov flame . . . hy tink." At this point, Tarvek was willing to accept the consequences of there being no door at all and leapt into the flames without hesitation—

Only to burst free into the clean, cool air of Mechanicsburg. To his horror, the square before him was crowded with dozens of people. Without slowing down, he roared, "What are you people doing here? RUN!" Seconds later, the queen burst out of the burning airship behind him with a crash.

"Whoa," Jorgi murmured. "Dot ting iz schtill comink after us."

"What?" Tarvek felt himself finally begin to stagger. "What is wrong with that stupid thing? Some of those people standing around here look *delicious!*"

A chitinous lance shattered cobblestones scant centimeters behind them. Tarvek spotted a narrow alley ahead. *Maybe it'll be too big to follow,* he thought. It was an idea that might well have worked, if a squad of children, armored in assorted bits of strapped-on kitchen gear, hadn't materialized to block the alley entrance, waving wooden swords and bits of pipe.

"Halt!" One stepped forward. "This alley is the headquarters of the Glorious Mechanicsburg Children's Crusade, Peanut Militia, and Stink-Bombers Secret Society of Justice![129] What's the password?"

"Fine!" With one great shrug, Tarvek shed passengers, books, and weasels. The avalanche sent the boy rolling backwards, but he managed to fall underneath Ruxala, who was still unconscious. The wasp eater leapt gracefully from Tarvek's shoulder and bounced off the boy's stewpot helmet.

"Get these people to safety!" Tarvek commanded. He grabbed the child's wooden sword and spun to face the onrushing queen, then leapt forward with a desperate shriek. The creature recoiled in surprise. Tarvek managed to land a solid blow across its spiny beak. It took a reflexive swat at him, catching him across the chest and sending him tumbling back across the street. Out of the corner of his eye, he glimpsed a terrified mass of children dragging Jorgi out of sight, before a series of stabs had him scrabbling furiously backwards and feinting with the pathetic wooden sword until it was smashed from his hand. He had time to see three great claws rising to impale him—

—and the queen exploded in a burst of blue light. There was a

---

[129]   The G. M. C. C. P. M. S. B. S. S. J. is but one of approximately twenty organized street gangs that roam Mechanicsburg. Many of them are hundreds of years old. While most cities labor endlessly to eradicate this sort of thing, the rulers of Mechanicsburg long ago coopted and deputized them. They are considered an integral part of the town's early warning system.

sound reminiscent of a large lobster being dropped into boiling lava, and a rain of green ichor pattered to the stones around him.

Tarvek blinked at the sky through a coating of goo. "WHAT DO YOU THINK YOU ARE *DOING*?" The voice came from behind him. It sounded mechanical, like a clank. A loud, angry clank. Tarvek sat up and saw, towering over him, a massive armored knight, encrusted with trilobite sigils and spikes. Glowing lights shone through what looked like stained glass panels set into the armor. In its right hand, it gripped a colossal battle axe to which a glowing, cable-festooned cane had been hastily wired. Cane, axe, and armor crackled with the electrical discharge that poured from the glass tip of the cane. The apparition pointed the weapon at Tarvek accusingly. "ARE YOU LOOKING FOR AN EXCUSE TO DIE? YOU IDIOT! I SHOULD JUST—UGH, HOLD ON, STUPID LEVERS—"

Tarvek just stared. The voice sounded familiar, and that cane— "Um . . . Wulfenbach? Is that you?"

The answer was an augmented sigh of exasperation, followed by some clicking, and a decisive "THERE." A set of heavily ornamented panels in the knight's chest swung outward, revealing Agatha, enthroned in a snug cockpit lined with glowing controls. She glared down at Tarvek. "Where have you *been*," she demanded. "What are we supposed to do if you go and get yourself killed?"

Tarvek considered the massive engine of destruction that loomed over him. "Agatha!" He scrambled for an answer, "I . . . uh . . . what are you supposed to . . . ?" he stammered. "In that thing? Whatever you want, I think."

"Just a minute," she said. "I'll be right down."

Agatha slapped a switch and a set of stairs unfolded. A second later she was pulling Tarvek to his feet and examining his face. Tarvek hastily scrubbed at it with his sleeve, removing most of the slime. "Are you hurt?" Agatha vainly tried to brush off his coat. "You look awful."

"You look beautiful."

Agatha's eyes went wide, and Tarvek marveled at the way the blush bloomed upwards from her neckline. Suddenly she turned away. "Um . . . right. Sure," she mumbled, "because I always look stunning when I've been crawling around working on greasy old machinery and . . . and . . . "

Tarvek touched her chin and gently swung her face back towards his and looked into her eyes. "That's right," he said simply. "Always." He leaned forward and guided her lips to his.

The kiss was slow and deceptively gentle at first. Agatha slid her arms around Tarvek's back and leaned into him for what seemed like forever. When they finally, reluctantly drew apart, Agatha realized they were the center of attention. *The Jägergenerals are here*, her hindbrain pointed out, vaguely, *and . . . Othar?* But Tarvek was leaning in for another kiss. She met him halfway. While this kiss was nowhere as timeless as the first, it was equally laden with promise and possibility.

Suddenly there was a theatrical, throat-clearing cough. Othar stepped up and slapped Tarvek on the back, booming: "Well done, sir! You did a fine job in there, you show great promise indeed! The blade that wounded Unit Tech Ruxala was poisoned, but Violetta had the antidote. Admirable rescue. But, I should point out that, as my hapless apprentice hero, you really ought to avoid public displays of affection, especially when there are young children present."

A flawlessly executed uppercut knocked Othar backwards into a convenient fountain. "Foul," he sputtered.

Tarvek stepped away from Agatha and flexed his fist. "That's the *second* thing I promised myself I'd do if I got out of all that alive," he said with a smile.

He then took a deep breath and pulled Agatha close. "And . . . and here goes the other. Agatha— I've just got to say this properly at least once, so I know that you know.

"After that, I'll shut up about it and we'll get to work, so listen carefully. Wulfenbach . . . he loves you. He really does. And you . . .

well, I was ready to give up any hope you might care for me." Tarvek pulled away slightly and looked directly into Agatha's eyes. "But I love you too. For a thousand reasons . . . and I'm not giving up after all. If Gil wins your heart in the end, it won't be without a fight."

Agatha stared up at him and realized that if she had to choose at that moment . . . she'd be in big trouble.

"There!" Tarvek stepped back and clapped his hands in satisfaction. "I said it." He turned to address the silent crowd. "Now, are there any maps of the current defenses? I'd really like a look at them if I could."

Agatha blinked and took a deep breath. Tarvek was right. Time was short. *But,* she silently vowed, *science demands there be more evaluation of this* kissing *phenomena.*

Tarvek had stepped up to examine the suit of armor. "Where did you find this? It's amazing! I suppose it's too much to hope that there's another thousand of them tucked away somewhere?"

Agatha shook her head. "Nothing exactly like that, but there are *heaps* of other things in there!"

As the two moved off, the crowd surged behind them to keep up. Mamma gave Zeetha a gentle nudge. "Hoo! Dis vun fights *durty*! Dot Wulfenbach gots heem sum trouble now, jah?" Zeetha nodded. She looked a bit more troubled about this turn of events than one would have supposed.

The larger part of the crowd was shouting and talking heatedly, mostly at a small cluster of people who were scribbling fiercely in small books. One of the Vespiary Squad members boiled to the head of the line. "Thirty—in gold—on Prince Sturmvarous!" Violetta, who had emerged from the alley, nodded, got his name, and made a mark in her book. The Jägergeneral Koppelslav loomed over Van's shoulder and leered. "Hey, keed. Gimmee vun hunnert on her takink *both* of dem!"

Van licked his pencil point. "That's the dark horse, General. One will get you five."

Violetta jerked her own pencil free of her book and stared at him. "What? You had that at one to *fifty!*"

Van scanned the last few pages of his own book and sighed. "That was before Sturmvarous evened the odds. It's anyone's race now."

Another Jäger, on hearing this, grabbed Van's shoulder in excitement. "Really? Den Hy gunna bet feefty on *me!*"

Van stared at him—and then made a note. "Sure. Good luck."

Meanwhile, in a small dimly lit cubicle aboard Castle Wulfenbach, the officially late Lord Rudolf Selnikov glanced up from the slowly self-turning pages of the book before him. "Oh. Hello," he mouthed. A very good simulacrum of his voice sounded from a small speaker set in the base of the jar that kept his detached head alive and well. "I thought I'd been completely forgotten. Is there any way I could get a goldfish or something in here? I'm dead bored."

Boris considered this request as he sat down. "I wouldn't worry about being bored. There's an excellent chance someone will try to kill you soon."

Several telltale lights on Selnikov's jar switched from green to red. "What? But the Baron said he'd protect me!"

Boris looked offended. "I did say 'try.' Now listen, I need to ask you something and I do not have much time. They think I've gone to get some papers."

Selnikov rolled his eyes. "But of course. Because now I can really concentrate on anything."

"Try. It is about the Other's wasps. The ones made to enslave sparks."

For a man who claimed to be distracted, his Lordship gave every indication of intent interest. "Ah. You know about them?"

"Oh yes. But evidently not as much as you do."

Selnikov discovered that dissembling was considerably more difficult when one no longer had shoulders to shrug. "I . . . I've glanced at some notes . . . "

Boris looked interested. "Notes you say. How long have these creatures existed?"

"I only knew of the one prototype, but I understood it was never released."

Boris leaned in. "Could there be more?"

Selnikov considered this. "Theoretically? Yes, but I doubt it."

"So? How long?"

"Er . . . Maybe a year? No more than that."

Boris frowned. *Long enough.* "Why weren't they used?"

"I'm pretty sure there was just the one . . . "

"Why wasn't *it* used?"

"There was a plan. A schedule . . . "

"But?"

"But the whole thing was overseen by Professor Snarlantz. In Passholdt?"

"Passholdt?" The proper memory surfaced and Boris frowned. "Ah. I see."

"Yes, a bad business all around."

"So, with this new type of wasp, could an enslaved spark resist a direct command by the Other?"

"Of course not. That's the whole point."

"But what if he . . . or she, was *already* in a full-blown spark-induced fugue state?"[130]

Selnikov paused and looked thoughtful. "Interesting. I can't say for sure, but if I *had* to guess—from what little I know[131]—I'd have

---

[130] Known colloquially in the Mechanicsburg region as "the madness place." When a spark is in this state, they are blind and deaf to almost any outside influence that would interfere with what they are doing at the moment.

[131] We, your professors, have tried, for quite some time, to receive permission from the proper authorities to detail within these books the actual mechanisms and processes by which the creatures known as slaver wasps infiltrate and control their hapless victims. We have been informed we will not be allowed to do so under any circumstances, as they do not want us to "give anyone any bright ideas." While we rail against this dictate in the abstract, the real world sensibility of it is inarguable, and thus we shall continue to portray this process in a way that ignorant and shortsighted critics will no doubt continue to call "fabulist hogwash." This is simply yet another way that we, your professors, suffer for our art. We hope you appreciate it.

to say *no*. The . . . Other would have demanded that her control supersede everything else."

Boris considered this. "That's . . . not good enough." He stood up and gently lifted Lord Selnikov's container. "Come, sir, let me find you a place a bit more private."

Several minutes later, Boris reappeared at the meeting that he had stepped away from. In response to the Baron's raised eyebrow, he muttered, "I'm sorry, Herr Baron, I left something in my quarters."

Klaus nodded and turned back. "Please continue, General."

The officer standing before a map of the area sagged slightly. "Continue? I haven't even started! You want us to completely rearrange our strategy! We'll have to reassign almost every unit we have! This new plan of yours will take time, and every military strategist for the last five hundred years will tell you: don't give the Heterodyne time!"

Boris leaned over and side-mouthed his neighbor. "What is going on? I was only gone five minutes! What new plan?"

The man beside him, the leader of the mechanical ground forces, looked disgusted. "Due to new information *somebody* brought in, now our priority is to capture the Heterodyne girl alive!"

Next to him, the air fleet admiral leaned back in her chair and addressed the ceiling. "We're all set to liquefy the place— and now this. And we're supposed to do it with minimal damage, no less! Feh!"

A third man slapped the table in annoyance. "There would have been no need to liquefy anything after my thunder bees had cleared the area."

Boris ignored the growing argument and stared at the Baron. "While I, personally, think keeping her alive is good, Herr Baron, I am . . . confused. You just told your son that the Lady Heterodyne must die. What has changed?"

Klaus' eye twitched slightly. "Boris, if your information is correct, if she is herself infected as some new kind of 'queen revenant,' then she is an invaluable specimen and must be studied." He dropped his voice. "But I do not want my son to harbor any false hope. It would be best if he thought she was dead."

Outside the town, from the assembled Wulfenbach forces, sirens began to blare. More and more of them filling the air until the town was ringed with their wailing. General Zog snagged an adjunct. "Get to Herr von Mekkhan. Those are ordinance sirens. Dey are about to begin shellink der town. Hev pipple get to der cellars."

The adjunct stared out at the dropwalls that ringed the town. "But . . . but I thought the empire was *helping* us."

A low series of *BOOMS* began, followed by the once-heard-never-forgotten sound of incoming shells. Explosions began blooming around the town. A dropwall took a direct hit and shuddered. Zog glanced upwards towards the Castle Wulfenbach that hovered menacingly in the distance. "Hy tink dere iz more den vun var goink on here."

On a street in Mechanicsburg, a group of workers stared forlornly at a burning building. A few scattered boxes and sundry items testified to their attempt to save some valuables, but they had clearly left far more behind. One of them glanced back as a crowd of people shambled up, led by a short man with a stained apron. This worthy consulted a scrap of paper, looked around, and then raised a hand, bringing his group to a halt. "Okay, this is the next one."

The worker frowned, then puffed out his chest, displaying a shining brass Department of Public Works badge. "Push off, you. We're working here."

The little man looked at the group standing about and cocked an eyebrow. "Well, now? So are we."

"Look you . . . "

R-79 loomed up. "Trouble? I can squish . . . "

Moloch rolled his eyes. "No! I told you to *stop* that. Jeez, you just got out. If you beat this guy to death, *I'll* get in trouble."

The city worker stared up at the construct and then recoiled in terror. "Sweet Lady of Solder! You're prisoners from the Castle!"

Moloch slapped his paper onto the terrified man's chest. "Not anymore! Now we're a roving band of heroic repairmen. See?"

Several workmen clustered around and examined the paper. "Hey, this is the same list *we're* working from."

Moloch glanced over at the burning building. It was still possible to see the sign that declared it to be the headquarters of the Mechanicsburg Department of Public Works. "I can see why the Castle thought you could use the help."

Stung, the lead man handed Moloch back his orders. "Hey, we have been under attack, you know. It's not just us. We've had stuff blowing up around us all day. We're trying to get to the substation, but this damn statue fell on it and we've been trying to move *it* for two hours."

Moloch eyed the iron statue of some long-dead Heterodyne and shrugged. "If we let stuff like that slow us down, we'd still be inside." He made a short bow to R-79. "If you wouldn't mind?"

The great construct gave a snort of laughter and strode forth. With three terrible blows, he smashed the statue aside. "Good job," Moloch told him. He then turned to the others. "Now let's get this done before Her Royal Sparkiness shows up and turns us all into fish or something."

The city workers stared at him. "Her . . . You mean the new Lady Heterodyne? You've *seen* her?"

"Oh yeah."

Fräulein Snaug stepped up and said, "Herr von Zinzer here is her chief minion." Every townsperson within earshot froze. The crew chief stared at Moloch as he directed several of the others. "Really?"

"Uh-huh," Snaug confirmed. "The Castle said so and everything."

Moloch caught the tail-end of this conversation and waved a hand. "That is *only* until the job is done, and then I am catching the first airship *outta* here. Now let's fix this stupid thing."

The city workers quickly snapped into action and swarmed over the substation. "Yes *sir*," the crew chief said crisply. "Me and the boys got this one, sir!"

Moloch started to argue, then paused as he saw the crew in action. "What the heck's got into them? If they'd been this organized five minutes ago, we wouldn't've had to waste our time here."

Doctor Mittelmind clapped him on the back. "I believe it is *because* you are here, young man."

Moloch blinked. "Uh . . . How do you figure?"

Mittelmind gestured about, clearly impressed at something he alone could see. "Brilliant. It must have taken *generations*. I don't think it could have been done in any other town in Europa. And who would understand it?" He turned back to Moloch and tapped his forehead, "Ah, but I— *I* know what to look for."[132]

Moloch folded his arms. "Well, why don't you tell me, and then *two* people will know how smart you are."

Mittelmind cheerfully accepted the challenge at face value and spread his hands expansively. "This town is populated entirely by minions."

Moloch considered this. "I guess that makes sense. You probably didn't survive here if you didn't know how to ask 'what color?' when the Heterodyne said 'jump.' "

"Well said. But in any group, there is a hierarchy. Minions are more aware of it than most, and you are now the Alpha."

Moloch stared at him. "Al who?"

Mittelmind chuckled and gently punched Moloch's shoulder. "*You* are now the Lady Heterodyne's chief minion," he explained. "Therefore, all the other minions of Mechanicsburg are *subordinate* to you."

---

[132]   Herr Docktor Getwin Mittelmind (PhD, MD, BFA, University of Salzburg) was a spark who specialized in mad psychology. A specialized field to be sure. He was not locked away in Castle Heterodyne because he built giant anteaters. No, he was locked away in Castle Heterodyne because he could take a perfectly ordinary group of people and within six days *they* would build a giant anteater—*because it was the logical thing to do.*

Moloch waved his hands in denial. "Wait. You're saying that because she pushes me around first, I get to push everyone *else* around? They won't put up with that."

"To the contrary, they have been *waiting* for you—or someone like you—for almost twenty years. Most people never know what their purpose in life is. Where they fit into the great scheme of things. Minions are different. They know *exactly* where they belong and what is expected of them. Oh, it's not always a pleasant life, but studies have shown that psychologically, minions are happier and saner than the majority of the non-minion populace.

"But with the disappearance of the Heterodyne Boys, there was no driver, no authoritative voice to tell them what to do. They lacked purpose. Now there is, once again, a Heterodyne in the Castle, an unstoppable force that controls their lives.

"All very well, but who wants to constantly stand in the presence of an unstoppable force? That is why there is a chief minion, one who knows how to survive in the presence of the master and becomes the main interface that stands *between* the people of the town and that unstoppable force. You are their lightning rod. A conductor of her voice, but one who shunts the madness away from them."

Moloch stared at the work area. Not only was the fire out, but the crew was almost finished with the substation's repairs. As newcomers arrived, he was pointed out to them, and it was if a switch was flipped behind their eyes. They seamlessly integrated themselves into the work crews in an instant. "This . . . this is insane," Moloch whispered.

"Oh yes," Mittelmind agreed. He paused. "I'm sorry, was there more to that?"

Moloch was shaking his head. "Did I say airship? Nuts to that. I'll *walk* outta here. Heck, I'll *run*. There is *nothing* that'll keep me—"

"Excuse me, but..." Moloch turned, and there was Sanaa standing next to him. "Is there anything left for me to do?"

Moloch expected a dozen salacious fantasies to present themselves, but realized all of them had already been surpassed by Sanaa actually talking to him. The mechanic in him, who had long been resigned to a celibate existence, took charge with a sigh. Moloch pointed. "That pump sounds like it has a clogged fuel line."

Sanaa nodded. "I'm on it."

Moloch stared after her and realized he was still thinking clearly. "Weird."

He turned back, and almost ran into Fräulein Snaug who, for some reason, looked furious. "So?"

Moloch stared down at her. "So . . . what?"

Snaug jerked a chin at the receding Sanaa. "So I thought she was your big romantical idée fixe."

Moloch looked back at Sanaa with concern. "Does she have a broken idée? I don't know anything about women—"

"Shut up!" Snaug snapped.

Mittelmind tapped his nose in thought. "This *is* most interesting. For a love-besotted lout, you are quite unaffected."

Moloch's face flushed scarlet. "Does *everyone* know about that?"

"Hm? Oh, not everyone. Just those of us who noticed that anyone who got to your kitchen *after* Sanaa did was served boiled sponge with gravy."

"Oh. Yeah, I guess . . . "

"So?" Snaug gripped his sleeve fiercely. "So? Are you over her now?"

Moloch considered this. "I . . . I don't know. I . . . everything is suddenly so different." He turned to Snaug. "I mean, I still *like* her . . . " Snaug opened her mouth, but Moloch cut her off. "But until these last few days, I never had a chance to get used to working around attractive women like you." Snaug stared at him. "So, Sanaa? Yeah, she's smart and tough and I like being around her, but since I feel the same way about you, I obviously don't know *what* I want, let alone anything about romance." He shook his head. "Stupid, huh?"

When Snaug just continued to stare, he shrugged and turned back towards the work party. After another few seconds, a concerned Professor Mittelmind gingerly poked Snaug on the shoulder, at which she spun around and clutched at him tightly, burying her face in his chest. "Oh, Professor," she moaned, trembling. "I want to kill something so very, *very* much!"

"My goodness," Mittelmind mused. "He *is* a dangerous one."

Moloch hailed Professor Mezzasalma, interrupting an impromptu lecture about the history of flow valves. "How's it going?"

"Just closing it up, my boy." The professor's mechanical legs clambered up out of the pit with ease. "Did you say this was the last one?"

Moloch looked at his list, balled it up and tossed it away. "That's what I *said*, yes . . . "

"Ah! There you are, Herr von Zinzer! Well done!"

The townspeople cowered before the voice that emanated from a rusty grate. "That's the Castle," the elder foreman muttered.

The voice continued, "Bring your team to the guard house just inside the cathedral gate. I have found more work for you!"

Moloch nodded. "But I didn't believe it."

Mezzasalma packed up his toolkit. "Ah, no doubt you foresaw that each repair would allow it to see a further problem, yes?"

Moloch snorted. "No, I just know that it hates me."

Along with the rest of the crowd, Sanaa and Snaug trailed along. They found themselves walking together, although they took great pains not to look at each other. "You seem to know him very well." It was obvious about whom Sanaa was talking.

Snaug shrugged. "Well, *you* certainly wanted nothing to do with him . . . up until now." Without breaking stride she gave a bit of a shimmy and her voice became a rather good imitation of Sanaa's, albeit a bit more breathless: "Is there *anything* left for me to do?"

Sanaa's face reddened. "I was just getting an assignment."

"Such a shame you didn't get the one you obviously wanted."

Sanaa arched her back slightly. "I think I'm more likely to get what I want out of him than you are. If nothing else, he'll be able to thank me afterwards."

Snaug clenched her fists so tightly that her gloves creaked. "Oh, he'll thank me plenty when he sees what I'm going to do to you."

The crew turned a corner and had to step around a collapsed wall. The foreman paused and looked about the town. "We'll be doing this forever," he muttered.

Mezzasalma followed his gaze. "Well . . . Science tells us that there has to be an end at *some* point."

Another shell struck a building, and sent it tumbling to the ground amidst flames and smoke. "Sorry? What part of the town full of rubble are *you* looking at?"

Atop the Heterodyne's Observation Tower, several members of the Mechanicsburg Municipal Watch were trying to ascertain the strength of the Wulfenbach forces outside the walls. "Something out there looks weird," the elder stated flatly.

His nephew stared out at what appeared to be a troop of giant mechanical palm trees and bit his lip. "No, really? Should we even still be up here? It seems a bit dangerous."

The elder swiveled his telescope several degrees to the left. "It'll be worse down there, lad. This here is a place of strategic value. They'll make an effort to take it in one piece." *It was probably a lot more strategic before everybody had airships,* was the unwelcome thought that skittered through his partner's mind. The old man continued, "Besides, *somebody's* got to keep watch so we can warn people if something happens."

Any further nitpicking by the younger observer was derailed by the gigantic hand that softly closed around him. His muffled exclamation caused the older man to spin around and see the matching gigantic winged simian that clung to the tower. Automatically, he scrambled for the microphone. "Giant monkey," he whispered.

The man clinging to the creature shook a fist in agitation. "Cower on your own time, lackey! I am Professor Julius Senear, master of anthropoid aviation! I seek asylum for myself and my beautiful aeroapes!"

The observer blinked. "Asylum? Really?"

"Yes! Yes, I admit it! When I heard that old Klaus was weakened, I attempted to press my advantage! I cannot be blamed for this! There was a power vacuum! I had an unstoppable army of aeroapes! Logic and science demanded that I wrest control of the empire!" Senear slumped and looked out over the devastation. "But alas, it appears I made my move too soon. The Baron has returned and has blown my unstoppable army from the skies."

The old man fixed on the important fact. "The Baron is *alive?*"

"Oh. Yes. And he's angry. He didn't even try to capture us or let us surrender."

"Maybe he's just out of patience."

Senear looked terrified. "Because of me?"

Suddenly, with a *thump,* a battered figure slammed into the tower. It was a man in a smoking exo-skeleton flying suit. "Hoy! You! Doctor Igneas Slaghammer and his beautiful claw seek asylum!"

The old man nodded slowly. "Because of *all* of you."

Having climbed onto the tower, Slaghammer collapsed in exhaustion. "Rejoice," he whispered.

Moloch gently lifted a small child aside just as a piston thudded down onto where it had been sitting. "I'm helping," the child assured him.

"You sure are," he replied. He turned to the civic engineer who was assisting him. "Seriously, unless we want them to 'help' by greasing the gears with their blood, can't we get them out of the way?"

The engineer sighed and hooked a thumb towards the shambling creatures that stood guard. "You gotta convince the Crypt Masters about that."

Moloch gazed at the figure wrapped in rotting bandages. When it saw he was staring, it chattered its teeth at him. He sighed. "And this is a cathedral, is it?"

The engineer looked at him blankly, then at the gigantic jewel-encrusted statue of one of the lesser furies that stood over the altar in the nave. "Yes," he ventured. "What else would it be?"

"I have so got to get out of here," Moloch muttered. Suddenly a series of tremors shook the building. The Crypt Masters snapped into action. "Flee, children! Flee!" With a shout of laughter, the children poured from the room with the ease of long practice. A door burst open, and the Abbess of the Red Cathedral appeared. "Everyone get to the courtyard!"

Outside, they saw the ground itself was heaving and, with a roar, a gigantic mechanical narwhal, horn spinning madly, erupted from the dirt.

Moloch stared in amazement. "Oops," he murmured.

The abbess fixed a cold eye on Moloch. "What did you do to my cathedral?"

"That wasn't us," he hastily assured her.

Professor Mezzasalma clattered up. "Well, bless my boilers," he said with surprise. "That's one of young Iskenshod's[133] *submersibles de terre!*" He nudged Moloch's ribs. "He was a student of mine, you know." He tapped a tooth contemplatively. "It's strange to see one above the surface like this. They aren't really designed for—" Easily a dozen metallic tentacles erupted from around the narwhal and attempted to drag it back under ground. Mezzasalma snapped his fingers. "A-ha! Fleeing from an enemy! Of course! It all makes sense, now."

"Of course," Moloch echoed faintly.

The battle became more pitched and the owner of the tentacles, an

---

[133] Professor Dyson Iskenshod theorized that narwhals, which remain severely understudied animals, actually spent part of their life cycle underground and used their horns to dig. When anatomical studies failed to validate any of his theories, he turned to engineering and designed and built mechanical narwhals that were, in fact, able to function as he claimed they would. As far as mad science goes, this was considered a stunning success by everyone but zoologists, biologists, and anybody who had ever owned an aquarium. When last heard from, he was in the process of attempting to breed normal narwhals with his creations.

ancient mechanical squid, heaved itself into the light. The narwhal proved itself to be surprisingly limber and was making a game fight of it by slamming itself onto the squid's central body. Moloch leaned towards the abbess and raised his voice against the din. "For what it's worth, ma'am, we don't know anything about *that*, either."

The abbess waved a tired hand. "Of course not. Our catacombs are connected to the old Kraken Works[134] caverns. Always knew there were still a few of those devils down there."

Moloch nodded agreeably. "Great. Now that's cleared up, can we go back inside and get to work?"

The abbess considered this. Then, with a roar, three more narwhals erupted from the ground and the courtyard shook with their fury.

Sanaa looked pensive. "How many of them are there?"

Mezzasalma looked thunderstruck. "Amazing! They're able to maneuver on the surface! Clearly these are no *ordinary* giant subterranean mecha-narwhals!"

The abbess rolled her eyes. "This is only going to get worse." She turned to Moloch. "Get your people back to work, and work fast." She gripped Moloch's arm. "When you are done, I have another project for you." Moloch considered telling her there were probably other projects with a higher priority, but one look at the woman's ice-cold eyes caused him to reconsider. He nodded, and the abbess turned to one of the Crypt Keepers. "When they are done with their current task, show these people the Bloodstone Paladins." She turned back to Moloch. "If you can get them working, I want them calibrated for 'sustained smiting.' "

---

[134] The Mechanicsburg Kraken Works was a private project of Nemo Heterodyne. It was built underground so as to have access to the subterranean lakes created and fed by the Dyne, which circuitously flows into the Danube. He planned to become a river pirate, but abandoned the project when he discovered a heretofore unknown allergy to grog. Determined to recoup the vast expenditure the project had accrued, the town leaders marketed bespoke mechanical kraken to the world at large and did a surprisingly brisk business until the fad was eclipsed by airships—a fad that remains ongoing until this day.

Krosp examined a report before him and it so annoyed him that he bit it. "What is he *doing*," the cat snarled.

"He who?" asked Van.

"The Baron, obviously."

Agatha considered this. "Attacking us?"

Krosp flicked an ear at her. "Then he's doing a terrible job of it."

Van looked out the window. "Seriously? Half of the empire's Special Units are beating at our gates! I've just gotten a report of a new subterranean force surfacing near the cathedral."

Krosp nodded. "At *this* point, there shouldn't even *be* gates. Or a cathedral, or a castle! He was all set to vaporize this place. The only thing slowing him down was the presence of his son and heir in the Castle. But according to Sturmvarous, he's already back on Castle Wulfenbach—probably under lock and key. So what is the Baron up to?"

From the corner, General Zog heaved himself to his feet. "If hyu dun destroy an enemy target, iz becawze dere iz sumting in it dot hyu vant."

Krosp nodded. "Yes, but *what*?"

Everyone looked at Agatha. She squirmed. "It might not be me. It could be the Castle, or the library, or . . . or the Jägers, or—"

Zog cut her off, exclaiming, "Occam's razor!"

Agatha slumped. "You're right, of course—"

Zog continued, "Hit vos forged by old Occam Heterodyne!"

"What?"

Zog thumped a fist on the table. "Seriously. Who *vouldn't* vant hit? Dot ting ken cut through *ennyting!*"

Krosp twitched an ear in annoyance. "The Baron has more effective forces just sitting outside the gates—waiting. Why?"

Agatha shrugged. "Does it matter? Every minute we gain because he's throwing incompetent sparks at us allows us make more repairs."

"It matters if the stuff he's holding back can blow through us no matter what we do here." Krosp rubbed his temples in frustration.

"It's just . . . the empire stays together because people know Klaus is too powerful to challenge. By allowing us to remain active, he's putting that perception into question."

Agatha considered this. "Everyone knows the Baron doesn't care what people think of him. He never has."

"That's because he's always been strong enough to do as he likes. But now, according to Sturmvarous, there are uprisings all over the empire. There is a real possibility of irreparable damage to his rule . . . and the Baron is letting it happen! Something is going on here."

"I require a spark." The voice was a faint whisper that drifted through the air.

"Castle?"

"I require a spark."

Agatha felt a twinge of dread. The Castle had been fading, to be sure, but this . . . it sounded like a dead recording, not like the voice of a sentient entity.

"Castle? I'm here."

"I require a spark."

"That's all it's been saying all over the town." Agatha turned to see Tarvek, as well as Professors Mittelmind and Mezzasalma.

"It's completely unresponsive," Professor Mezzasalma said. "It won't even supply repair goals to the maintenance teams anymore."

Tarvek nodded. "We've already shunted every power source we can think of over to the Castle, it just isn't enough."

"I require a spark."

"You've got plenty of them right here," Tarvek said loudly. He turned to Agatha, and she could see the exhaustion in his face. "But at this point, the only *useful* thing I can think to do with them is grind them up and burn them for fuel." There was a startled silence from behind them. Tarvek turned to look at the other sparks and waved his hands apologetically. "No, no, I'm sorry, I was only—"

Professors Mittelmind and Mezzasalma laughed in delight. "My goodness, young man!" Mezzasalma gushed. "I *am* impressed!"

Mittelmind nodded. "Assuming we all survive, you *must* come work with us! You have the makings of one of the greats!"

Tarvek was obviously of two minds about this. "Oh. Lucky me."

Suddenly a great *BOOM* was heard. "Now what?" Agatha asked the air.

"I require a spark."

A Mechanicsburg trooper rushed in. "My Lady," he cried. "The Baron has brought in a battering ram!"

"See?" Krosp hopped down off the table and headed towards the door. "This is *exactly* the kind of nonsense I'm talking about! The empire's got stuff that could *disintegrate* the town walls! They could drop in from above! Burrow up from below!"

"They're already doing that," Mezzasalma informed him.

"So why are they using something so obsolete as a battering ram?"

A few minutes later they all stood on the ramparts and watched as an enormous ram, easily fifteen meters long from tip to tail, again thundered down the causeway and slammed its horned head into the mighty gates. "Yup. That's a ram," Agatha said.

Zog scratched his head. "Hy didn't know dere vos enny of dose tings *left* in der empire's arsenal."

Krosp's tail lashed. "He's cleaning house." He leapt up onto the parapet and looked out at the assembled forces. "Over the last twenty years, he's collected hundreds of sparks and thousands of monsters and machines. They've been on the books, officially listed as being part of the empire's forces, but he's never really used them." He looked at Agatha. "When the Baron uses force, he wants it to be as effective as possible. But here, he's using this as an opportunity to throw in all of the losers that have been hanging around for years."

Zog snarled. "Vat does he tink ve iz?"

Krosp looked at him. "An opportunity."

"Bot for vhat?" He gestured out at the assembled forces. "Look at dese guys." He turned to Agatha. "Hy dun know how goot hyu iz at readink battlefields yet, my Lady, bot dose guys iz seriously mezzed op. Der Baron's deployments vos alvays ordered and efficient." He squinted at them. "Dese guys look like somevun's havink a drunken brawl durink a garbage fire."

Another *BOOM* rattled the stonework. "There's got to be something we can do about that," Agatha muttered.

"Can do!" Tarvek, ensconced within Agatha's ancient armor, climbed to the battlement with a rattle and a clank. "Behold, O Dark Mistress! Your ridiculously fearsome battle armor awaits!"

Agatha stared. "How in the world did you get that thing up here?"

"Hastily improved rocket boosters." He held up a finger. "Quick safety tip: don't click your heels unless you mean it." He leaned out of the window. "Would my Lady like to take over? I've even recharged Gil's lightning stick. You should be able to blow that ram into gyros."

"You go ahead. You look like you're having fun."

Tarvek looked pleased. "Really? But it is your town . . . "

"I'll get the next one."

Tarvek began pulling levers, and the armor swung about. "You know, if we live, I can design you something better than this."

"Better than a two-ton mobile armored death knight? What could make it better?"

Tarvek patted the side. "Better curves? In green?"

"Stop the ram, then we'll talk."

Tarvek swung the great halberd up and, with a crackle, it discharged a blue-white bolt of electricity directly into the again-charging ram. When it hit, the ram leapt forward, again smashed into the wall, then again trotted back for another go. "The devil," Tarvek snapped. "That was a direct hit! They've shielded it!"

Agatha nodded. "I was afraid of this. Everyone saw Gil use his lightning stick, so it makes sense that they've shielded against it."

Krosp interrupted, "They're pulling back the ram."

Agatha grimaced. "Oh, that's not good."

Tarvek nodded. "They were testing us. Now they know what we have. Or at least, what we're willing to use."

Zog considered this. "So hyu tink he's gunna send in an army of beeg sheeps?"

Tarvek looked down and sighed. "No."

"MECHANICSBURG! HEED MY WORDS!"

Tarvek sighed. "I think it'll be something even more ridiculous."

Striding towards the gates was a dragon. Agatha blinked. This wasn't a lumpy, squat dragon like the one she'd seen roaring through the town. This was a sleek red dragon encased in shining golden armor. It reached the center of the causeway and sent a stream of flame skywards. It carried a glittering sword and buckler, which it now crashed together with a deafening sound reminiscent of thunder. "If you would have me spare your miserable town," the dragon bellowed out in a voice that rolled out to the horizon and back, "you will send forth the Heterodyne girl— NOW!" It stamped a huge foot in emphasis, cracking one of the great paving stones. "Or you may attempt to hide her, if you wish, and I will raze your filthy hovels to the ground! Make your choice quickly, or I shall make it for you. For my part, I contemplate the destruction of this vile den of perfidy with great joy!"

Zog shook his head. "A dragon. Dot's not goot. Dose guys iz a real pain in de backside. Hy thought ve took care uf all dem a couple of hunnert years ago."[135]

"It's obviously not very bright," Tarvek said. "It's not like Agatha is actually going to just walk out there."

He turned to her and the confidence in his eyes faded at the sight of her contemplating the dragon below.

"Well, I hope it won't come to that," Agatha said, "but we can't count on the Castle, and we're running out of other options. If it's a choice between me and the entire town . . . "

A scream that sounded like tearing metal echoed from the walls

---

[135] As we have mentioned, dragons are not really considered a viable life form, as they come into direct conflict with humans over things like money and power, which, frankly, is just asking for it. The comments made by General Zog give credence to ancient rumors that the Jägers were instrumental in the hunting of dragons back when it was a sensible career choice.

behind them. Everyone turned to see Franz atop the nearest tower. Stubby wings outspread, scales a-bristle, quivering with rage. "What is this," he screamed. "WHAT IS THIS? You are on *my* turf, pretty boy!"[136] With a clatter, Franz leapt from the wall and hissed menacingly.

The red dragon spread its wings and turned to its companion, a small man astride a surprisingly phlegmatic burro. "What is this? Observe, my dear Gazpacho. 'Tis a poor, baseborn lizard with dreams of dragonhood!"

The man looked at Franz and scratched his chin. "In truth, m'Lord, he *is* bigger than any lizard I have ever seen."

"Pah! If superficial resemblances were the sole measure, then you sit astride his dam!"

"Haw! Good one, m'Lord."

"Oh . . . oh *yeah*?" It was painfully obvious Franz was not used to insults or, indeed, any badinage at all. "Well, we got more than enough real dragon here for one town, so you and your long-eared auntie there can just push off!" He took a deep breath and pointed at the burro. "And by 'auntie,' I mean the jackass." Atop the parapet, the watchers tried not to meet each other's eyes.

"So get outta here. NOW!" This was accompanied by a surprisingly intense gout of yellow flame that erupted from Franz' jaws, catching the red dragon squarely in the face. However, the creature failed to react and, when the flame died down, even its armor was undamaged. Franz blinked in surprise.

"Are you finished, peasant?" The red dragon sniffed disdainfully. "Clearly, you are naught but a sideshow wonder sprung from the fevered blasphemies of some half-witted student of outdated alchemy."

Franz shrugged. "Aren't we all?"

The red dragon frowned. "Fire is not how true dragons duel!"

---

136   Dragons were programmed to be intensely territorial and to challenge all other dragons, no doubt as a way to impress dragon females. This is even more tragic as there has never been a female dragon. Even insane alchemists had survival instincts.

Franz crossed his arms. "Oh great. Let me guess. This is where you spout a bunch of fancy riddles or something."

"No—" The red dragon sprang forward, and a solid punch caught Franz squarely between the eyes. "This is where I beat you to death." Franz slammed backwards into the town gate and collapsed to the ground. He scrabbled feebly as he tried to get back up to his feet.

"Verily, m'Lord," the obsequious Gazpacho ventured, "it hath taken but one hit to make your point."

This did not seem to please the red dragon, who stomped a foot in rage. "No," he roared. "Are you not Franz Scorchmaw, Bone Gnawer of the Heterodynes? First and foremost of dragons?"[137]

This seemed to reach Franz and he lumbered to his feet, a new determination in his eyes. "You'd better believe it!"

Again the red dragon stomped its foot. "Yet you swallow petty insults and move like a drunken bovine! Fight me! *FIGHT ME!* I came for a battle between *dragons,* not this mummer's play!"

Franz launched himself forward. "You want a fight? Then—" Again a vicious blow caught him solidly on the jaw, flipping him up and over backwards into a heap.

The red dragon slumped in disappointment. "So easy," he sighed. "You are naught but a samded spit-frog after all, aye?"

Furious now, Franz rolled to his feet and drove his claws into the pavement below. With a grunt, he ripped free a massive stone block. "You fancy-pantsed, shiny-arsed *twerp!* Yer all sparkle and talk!" He raised the block above his head. "Lots and lots of talk!"

In a flowing move, the red dragon spun and his long tail snapped out like a whip, catching Franz across the eyes, sending him backwards. The stone block dropped squarely on his head. "So slow," the red dragon hissed. "It's as if you were a spineless somnambulist who has but slept for years upon long years!"

---

[137]   The record among humans is unclear about this, but according to the few remaining dragons, it is firmly accepted that Franz was indeed the first dragon.

Franz waved a hand feebly. "But . . . but that's what I'm supposed to do! Waiting for the Heterodyne to awaken me . . . "

The red dragon drew his sword. "Then you will sleep again and await her but a very short while longer—in the undiscovered country."

The watchers atop the wall were startled by Agatha's cry of "Stand back!" She pushed past them, carefully leveling Gil's lightning cane. Tarvek frowned. *But, the red dragon has to be as well-shielded as anything else the Baron would send,* he thought, just as a bolt of blue electricity flashed from the sky and struck—Franz.

The red dragon leapt back in amazement. "What perfidy is this? It seems even your Heterodyne does not like you!"

Within the crackling nimbus of electricity, Franz reared his head high and glared. The red dragon and his squire breaths caught in surprise. Franz' eyes were glowing, as were the array of dials that lined his neck. The needle on the tiny gauge inset into his snout now pointed all the way to the right. A wide, toothy grin spread across his face. "Oh no. That was *exactly* what she needed to do. I feel *great!*" Franz moved towards his opponent with a satisfied rumble, and a fist like a small boulder shot into the red dragon's face, sending the creature to his knees. Franz gazed down at him, still grinning. "Let me show you."

Up on the wall, Agatha was talking to the Mechanicsburg trooper. "Find Herr von Mekkhan. Tell him I need all of Gilgamesh Wulfenbach's power accumulators activated. As many of them as they can get up and running."

"Yes, my Lady!" And the trooper took off. Agatha turned to Tarvek and the others. "All of the Heterodyne creations I've seen—the Torchmen, the mobile fun units, Franz, even Adam and Lilith—they all need to be *recharged*. It's a design flaw I've seen in all my family's works. I'm betting it's the same for the Castle. The 'spark' it needs—it doesn't mean a scientist. It just needs a good, old-fashioned *bolt of lightning!*"

Tarvek looked out over the battlefield and grimaced. "I like your hypothesis. Hope you get the chance to prove it."

On the ground below, Franz stood over the now-cowering dragon and began to remove its helmet. Suddenly, an amplified voice boomed forth. "HOLD!" The two dragons froze, staring up into the sky where eight gigantic figures hovered. They looked like stylized chess pieces, but each of them was easily ten meters tall. They were faced with brilliant white enamel chased with gold and their leader wore a small golden crown. "Cease this obstreperous brawling," he demanded as he slowly settled to the ground beside them. "Your antics shame the Lady Heterodyne!"

Franz glanced at the red dragon. "Some of your friends?"

"Don't be insulting," the red dragon replied. "They're *knights*."

The "king" continued. "We are here to rescue the Lady Heterodyne and her lands in the name of the Storm King!"

Tarvek went white. "That voice . . . "

Agatha poked him in the side. "Those are *your* knights?"

"No!" He considered this. "Well . . . technically, sort of. They *are* Knights of Jove, but I thought you said Gil took them all out with that stick of his."

Agatha shook her head. "Those attackers *claimed* to be Knights of Jove, but that was an army of big metal war stompers. There was nothing like these guys."

General Zog scratched his chin beard. "Vell, dese guyz gots goot timink, ennyvay."

Tarvek gasped. Agatha stepped in. "What is it?"

He swept his hand out towards the besiegers. "The Baron. That perfect mess of a battle array. *Too* perfect. He's just been waiting until the true players revealed themselves!"

Indeed, across the massed armies, sirens began to wail, and before the astonished eyes of the people of Mechanicsburg, the scene before them . . . *changed*.

Smoke cleared. Heaps of ramshackle equipment collapsed.

Disorganized, wandering troops dropped or furled unsuspected trompe-l'œil banners. Where a chaotic disaster of a rag-tag army had been, now stood row upon row of glittering machines and men, monsters and vehicles standing in perfect pre-battle formations. The skies magically cleared, revealing flotillas of airships, bombers, troop carriers, and obvious weapons platforms that completely ringed the town.

Agatha stared. "How did they do that?"[138]

Tarvek waved a hand. "Unimportant. What *is* important is that they were waiting for these fools to show themselves—and now they have!"

Zog interrupted. "Dese guys? Seriously? Der Baron's spymasters iz findink plots against der empire all der time! Vy vould he hold off capturink our Heterodyne for a bonch of goofs like dem? No, Iz too much! Der iz more to dis! Dere iz somting *else* goink on!"

Aboard the hovering Castle Wulfenbach, the Baron examined the tactical situation with satisfaction, then turned to his son. "There now, that is the true situation."

Gilgamesh was currently afloat in a cylinder of heavy oil. It took all of his strength to keep his head free. The Baron continued. "Well? Shall I destroy her?"

"I don't think you can. The Castle. We repaired it."

Klaus shook his head. "Oh, I assure you, I can. You may have repaired it, but there is no sign it is active. I saw it when it was fully functional, you know, and I see nothing to indicate it is capable of effective action. All those years of neglect, followed by the recent

---

138   The Siege of Mechanicsburg is considered the crowning moment of glory of the empire's Phantasmagoric and Misdirection Division. An offshoot of Klaus' psychological warfare division, they specialized in misrepresenting battlefields. Either by trying to convince enemies that there were more Wulfenbach units present than there actually were, or by trying to lure enemies in by disguising the army as a smaller unit, or even something else entirely—like a herd of sheep. Although they had been used throughout Klaus's reign, never again would they have such a stunning success.

burst of activity have obviously left it drained of motive power, to the point where, according to my most recent reports, even its most minor functions have ceased. It can no longer protect itself, let alone the girl—or the town." He pointed at the nearest monitor. "You are not a fool. Look at the field. Surely you can see that this fight is *over*. The only question is whether the girl will live or die. Choose!"

Gil stared at the displays before him, and no matter what simulations he ran in his head, the answer was always the same. His father began to tap his foot, and Gil slammed his fist against the wall of the tube, knowing he had lost. "All right! All right! Fine! Don't kill her! I'll do . . . I'll do anything you want."

Unseen by Gil, Klaus closed his eyes in pain. A part of him had hoped Gil would be able to see a way out. Something he had missed. But no. He straightened his shoulders and turned back to the broken young man before him. "Very good," he said. "There is . . . hope for you yet." Knowing there was no hope at all.

Beside Klaus, Lucrezia/Anevka clapped her hands in delight. "We shall have to come up with something *special* for you," she said mischievously. "Something that will make you as useful as your dear father." An idea struck her. "Oh! I have just the thing!" She patted Klaus on the arm and seemed to take great delight in how he tried to twitch it aside. "You're going to *hate* it," she said with a smile.

CHAPTER 11

Why has the Heterodyne family survived? A legitimate question, when you consider they are universally reviled. The question becomes even more perplexing when you realize they are arguably the oldest dynasty in Europa, surviving when dozens of lesser houses have risen, conquered, and then slumped back into irrelevance. The answer seems to be that they were open minded.

Throughout the centuries, their enemies have consistently proclaimed they are superior to the Heterodynes because they adhere to a predictable set of high-minded beliefs, laws, and/or codes of conduct, while the Heterodynes freely admitted they do no such thing and, incidentally, seemed to go out of their way to embrace chaos, evil, and malice.

While this would certainly seem to give the Heterodyne's antagonists the spiritual high ground, the sad reality is that the people who opposed the Heterodynes frequently did so for less than benevolent reasons. Those who feel the power they possess is granted to them by God, and thus their rightful due, rarely consider the optics of the thousand-and-one thoughtless cruelties they blithely perform on a daily basis have on the (usually) silent constituents who actually make up the foundations of their temporal power.

But while the Heterodynes could be legitimately charged with every high crime, atrocity, and blasphemy under the sun, the one charge you cannot lay at their feet is that of hypocrisy. They freely admitted they were terrible people and made no pretense they were anything else. One of the reasons organized religion has failed to gain the traction in Europa many scholars think it should have, is that the Heterodynes have roared their defiance of all that is good and proper from their mountain fortress for centuries, and have, very conspicuously, NOT been smote by a vengeful deity, or by any of their self-proclaimed earthly representatives. In fact, they seem to be doing annoyingly well.

A large part of this success seems to be that they are, when all and said and done, scientists. And dreadfully good ones, at that. When something doesn't work, they admit it and change it. When they come up with a new, better way of doing something? They implement it. They are, in their own way, devotees of Truth and have no loyalty to any established theory, belief, or institution. This gave them an enormous advantage when dealing with enemies who may very well be aware there was a "better way of doing something," but could not change due to institutional inertia or conflicting beliefs."

—From the introduction to Nikotiva von Schmetterling's
The Warped Tree: The Genealogy of the Heterodynes
(Transylvania Polygnostic University Press)

❧❧❧

"A ttention!" A flotilla of balloonists sailed through the driving rain over Mechanicsburg, loudspeakers crackling. "All citizens are to evacuate by way of the South Gates immediately. Mechanicsburg is about to be destroyed! Attention—"

Atop an observation tower, a Jäger shouted into a small handheld communicator. "Der empire iz valkink shells down der northern road!" On the road itself, a series of explosions were, in fact, leisurely making their way towards the town. It was obvious to the Jäger's experienced eye that this was a display of power and control that was supposed to be seen. "Hy dun tink dey iz gonna blow der north vall *yet*, but vhen dey do, nottink iz goink to schtop dem!"

Agatha, Tarvek, and General Zog were on that wall, to the general's increasing dismay. He, too, calculated that if the Baron's forces had wanted to bring down the walls, they could have done so already. "So they're just going to level the town, going from north to south," Agatha yelled against the ongoing thunder.

"Iz a goot plan," Zog replied. "Vhich iz vhy ve should not be here!"

"So why not attack us from all four sides? They have enough artillery."

Zog beamed and almost patted her head. *Hyu iz a Heterodyne all right*, he thought. "Hy imagine dot dey vants to let der townspipple flee. Iz goot form. Pluz hy tink dey schtill hope to ketch hyu, Mistress."

Agatha considered the Knights of Jove clanks. They had obviously realized that trapped between the city wall and the advancing army was a strategically poor choice. Even Agatha had realized that the great white behemoths standing before Mechanicsburg's dark walls made superb targets. Two of the great clanks had already been destroyed by long-range artillery, and this had spurred the remaining clanks to quickly fly in over the walls. Agatha expressed concern about letting them in, but it was agreed that even if they were inferior fighters, they would cause the empire to waste a few shots, which Agatha thought a bit cold. "What is so important about these guys that the Baron was waiting for them?"

"The empire is in chaos," Tarvek explained. "There are rebellions and uprising all across Europa. This was the plan of some of those fools who were trying to 'help' me declare myself as the Storm King. I thought I'd squashed that aspect of it, but I can see it was just too tempting.

"I'm sure a lot of private scores are being settled and power grabs are under way while this 'popular uprising' is keeping everyone busy.

But all this chaos was caused for someone's benefit. The plan is to have the empire *appear* to revolt, and then the Storm King appears! He allies with the newly discovered Heterodyne, and together they overthrow the old empire and declare a new order. The people who ignited the uprisings calm them down, and thus it appears that the new Storm King/Heterodyne government is supported by the people and is fully in control."

Tarvek shook his head. "Morons. That's not the sort of genie you can easily stuff back into its bottle. From what I saw when I was on Castle Wulfenbach, these uprisings have spread farther and faster than anyone expected. The Wulfenbachs will really have their hands full setting things right."

He gestured up at the chess-king clank as it stood quietly, staring out over the parapet. "The Baron must have calculated it would be easier to calm things down if he could display an actual usurper who, ostensibly, was the cause of the problem." Tarvek gave an evil smile. "Not a bad plan, and the trial would be an excellent place to dump some information I've been hoarding."

Krosp rubbed his head on Tarvek's leg. "I *really* like you."

Agatha stared at the clanks. "Maybe we should move a bit farther away."

"*YOU WILL COME WITH US!*" It was a voice that Agatha would remember for the rest of her life. Rising over the parapet came an eerie figure: long, green limbs folded before it, topped with a golden, conical hat and veil. "*YOU ARE THE HETERODYNE,*" it moaned, "*AND YOU ARE TO COME WITH US.*"

"*Dreen,*"[139] Zog gasped, and without another word, he and

---

[139] The Dreen were the strangest and most inexplicable members of Klaus Wulfenbach's collection of oddities and monsters. Almost everything about them was shrouded in mystery, such as where the Baron found them, why they consented to work for him, or what the actual nature of their powers and abilities were. Most worrying was the evidence they were creatures that existed "outside of time." They frequently displayed foreknowledge of things to come, yet were often flummoxed by events they had just experienced. A lot of this might have been more acceptable if they were avuncular old men who lived in a traveling box or

Tarvek hoisted Agatha up between them and dashed for another stairway— only to find the unearthly creature now standing before them, sepulchral arms raised towards them. "*YOU ARE TO COME WITH US.*"

With a great metallic crash, the leader of the gigantic white knights swatted the Dreen flat beneath an enormous white hand. "*NO,*" it thundered.

A hatch on the titanic chest irised open, and a tall, broad-shouldered man appeared. He was dressed in white and gold and his long hair was contained within a shiny gold circlet. He waved when he saw Agatha.

"Lady Heterodyne," he boomed jovially. "Would that we had met under better circumstances. I, Martellus von Blitzengaard, by the grace of God and the Voice of Europa, am the newly ascended Storm King!" He held out a hand. "Come with me quickly, and I will get you to safety!"

Agatha glanced at a now-appalled Tarvek. "The Storm King? But I thought—"

"Tweedle, you idiot," Tarvek shouted. "Get out of there! You'll be killed!"

The man caught sight of Tarvek and looked surprised. He recovered quickly and sneered. "Give it up, cousin. Whatever pathetic webs of intrigue you are currently spinning are in tatters. You've been replaced."

"Just shut up," Tarvek screamed, "and *jump!*"

Martellus paused, suddenly uncertain. "What are you—" he was cut off as the clank beneath his feet shattered into fragments. Martellus hit the ground with a bounce and rolled to his feet in a large puddle in time to see the shards of his clank continuing to crumble into smaller bits, and the Dreen slowly rising—apparently undamaged—from the wreckage.

---

something, but frankly, they were creepy as Hell.

It again extended a finger towards Agatha. "*YOU WILL COME WITH US.*" It paused as it saw Agatha and the rest of her party disappearing down the stairs.

It swiveled about in time to see Martellus von Blitzengaard tumbling down the same stairs after them. It nodded to itself in satisfaction and turned back towards the Wulfenbach lines. Its preordained task here was accomplished. The Heterodyne girl and this iteration of the Storm King had been brought together. It observed other, less desirable possibilities evaporate into theoretical clouds of mathematics. Events would now proceed as they must.

Agatha and the others were off the wall and moving fast. "Hy dun see dot creepy ting followink us," Zog muttered. "But ve should get to der cathedral. Der are tings dere dot might schtop it." [140]

Behind them, Tarvek and Martellus were arguing. "Replaced?" Tarvek snorted. "By *you?* I'm still the rightful heir and don't you forget it!"

"You are a sniveling weakling and you're supposed to be dead," Martellus snapped back.

"Oh, I'll just bet I am. Too bad that didn't work out for you."

"I was told you were dead when I was called here!"

Tarvek frowned. "Really? And who would call you?" As they turned the corner, they skidded to a stop. Before them was a woman on an armor-clad stallion. She wore an ensemble that was obviously supposed to evoke a nun's habit, but she was also wearing greaves and held aloft a shining sword. Arrayed behind her was a troop of squat horse-headed clanks, all armed with serviceable-looking pike axes.

"Lady Heterodyne!" The mounted woman saluted her with the sword. "I am the Abbess of the Red Cathedral! I and the Bloodstone Paladins stand ready to take their sworn place alongside the Storm King and his Knights of Jove!" For the first time, a slight uncertainty

---

[140] The Red Cathedral of Mechanicsburg has its reliquaries, but the things they contain are not the bones of saints.

filled her face as she peered behind them. "Um . . . I was told they were here?"

Martellus strode forward. "I am the Storm King, here in answer to your summons."

"Where are the rest of you?"

Tarvek raised a hand. "Tarvek Sturmvarous. The *legitimate* Storm King. This fool—" he indicated Martellus "—landed his force directly in front of Wulfenbach's main army. The survivors may have managed to get within the walls, but they're being targeted by Wulfenbach." As he spoke, another of the tall clanks toppled off the wall, a flaming ball of oily smoke billowing out from where its head had been.

The abbess looked at Martellus, who waved this inconvenient fact aside. "Their task was to deliver me here. This they have done." He turned to Agatha. "Obviously this is not the place for flowery declarations. For now I shall let my actions speak for me, and hope that they shall serve as a proper introduction later." He turned and shouted, "Bring me a horse!"

At this point, an obviously put-upon Moloch stepped up with a horse equipped with a splendid saddle and bridle. With a single bound, Martellus took the saddle. He turned to General Zog, who was watching all this with a bemused expression. "General, if you would please show me where we can be of the most use?"

Zog folded his arms and jerked his chin at the ranks of clanks. "Doze tings do belonk to us, hyu know." He glanced to Agatha. "Bot dey vill be uzefull. Heef hyu will excuse me, Mistress?" Agatha nodded, and with a sharp whistle, Zog led the clanks and Martellus off at a brisk trot.

Agatha and Tarvek watched them go off through the rain. Agatha glanced at Tarvek. "He's going to be all sorts of trouble, isn't he?"

Tarvek sighed. "Well, of course. He's family." The last of the clanks turned a corner and were gone. "To be fair, Tweedle's good in a fight, but in this case I don't think he has adequate firepower. I mean, those clanks looked impressive, but they're pretty old. All they'll do is buy you some time, but not much of that."

He turned to see Agatha staring up at the clouds overhead. "I think I have an idea . . . " She turned to Tarvek. "Forget the cathedral, we have to get closer to the Castle. As high as possible, and I'll need Gil's lightning rod . . . " This chain of thought was suddenly cut off by the point of the abbess's sword, which snapped to position directly in front of Agatha's face.

"You are going nowhere," the abbess coolly informed her. "Do not commit the folly of believing yourself a true Heterodyne, young lady."

Simultaneously, Agatha and Tarvek glanced at the Doom Bell. The abbess flinched at the memory. "You may have tricked a broken Castle into accepting you, but we both know you are nothing but a pawn to help smooth the ascension of the Storm King." She glared at Tarvek. "And a pawn that has fallen into the wrong hands at that." She waved the sword imperiously. "You will both come with me to the catacombs, where you will be kept safe until you are neede—" but the abbess never finished her orders. Mid-sentence, she slumped to the ground. Behind her stood Moloch von Zinzer, who had stepped up behind her and smacked her in the head with a length of pipe.

Agatha and Tarvek stared at him. "Trust me," he assured them, "you wouldn't have gotten *anywhere* trying to argue with her."

Tarvek relieved the fallen woman of her sword. "You really are the best minion ever," he told Moloch.

"I am *not* her minion!" Moloch clutched the pipe like a man trying to hold onto his sanity. He turned to Agatha. "Mistress! *Tell* him I'm not your minion!"

Agatha glanced at Tarvek. "He's not my minion."

Moloch stared at her. "You're *lying*," he screamed. "I can tell!"

Suddenly, three grinning figures appeared from out of the rain, and Agatha recognized Dimo, Ognian, and Maxim. "Ho, dere, sveethot," Dimo sang out. "Der general sez dot hyu vanted dis oldt ting!" With a flourish, he placed Gilgamesh's lightning stick into Agatha's hand.

She examined it eagerly. "It looks okay," she said relieved. "I was worried it might be broken."

Moloch gave it a suspicious look. "So what does it do?"

"It tells lightning where to strike!"

Moloch nodded as he pushed the tip away from his face. "And what are you planning to do with it?"

"The Castle needs a lot of power and it needs it fast. I'm going to hit it with a big bolt of lightning!"

Moloch flinched. "From here?"

Agatha pouted. "Of course I can't do it from here. I need to get a lot closer to the Castle." She turned back to the Jägers. "I'm thinking the Heterodyne Observation Tower?"

Dimo rubbed his hand together. "Hoy! Nize choice!"

Moloch sidled up to Ognian. "This place—it's really high up, isn't it?"

"Ho, yez!"

He glanced up as a roll of thunder traveled the length of the town. "And we're going up there in a lightning storm."

"Hyu betcha!"

"I knew it."

The group came to a small overlook. Moloch pointed. "Let me guess. It's that really tall, exposed tower? Way over there?" Everyone nodded. Moloch gave a nod of satisfaction. "You'll never make it. Listen, the Castle had me running all over this town making repairs. Forget the troops outside, there's a whole bunch of forces already in the town. Now all the non-empire stuff is just wandering through the town. They're disorganized, but they're still dangerous.

"Ever since that damn bell rang, the imperial troops have been falling back to the Great Hospital. They pretty much control that sector. Even though the hospital's been destroyed, there's a lot of medical stores in the area.

"There's also that large park they've been using as a staging area. The Castle can't effectively clear the skies anymore, so they've been able to set up an airfield. That's allowed them to bring in enough support that they can hold the South Gate.

"They can't advance against all the town's defenders, so they're no longer trying. They'll destroy the town from the north, which will funnel the remaining enemy forces, the townspeople—and hopefully, you—through their checkpoints. This tower you want is behind one of their fortified perimeters, so you going there will just make things easy for them."

He looked at everyone around him and frowned at their slightly open jaws. He rolled his eyes. "I was in the military for over ten years! If you can't read a battlefield you could accidentally surrender to your own officers, which is super embarrassing, if only because it'll get you shot."

Maxim nodded his head. "Hyu iz vun heckuva useful guy." He snagged one of Moloch's arms. "Hyu gets to come vit uz."

Oggie grabbed the other arm. "Ve'll figger owt a vay to get dere mit hyu alonk!"

"NOOO!"

Dimo glanced at Agatha. "Bot even vit meester expert guide, ve iz gun have trobble gettink over dere. Ken hyu use dot lightning schtick to clear a path?"

Agatha shook her head. "No, it's too fragile. If I use it too much, I could burn it out."

Dimo frowned. "Zo iz *worse* den useless. Not only ken ve not *use* it, but ve gots to *protect* it."

Agatha blinked and then reexamined the stick. "That's true. All right then, I'll improve it. I'll bet there are all kinds of things I can do to make it stronger."

Dimo raised an eyebrow. "As ve iz fightink our vay through a var zone?"

"It will be an excellent way to get parts."

Dimo grinned. "Vhen hyu poots it *dot* vay, hit almost makes sense!"

Meanwhile, Oggie had sidled up to Tarvek. "So hyu iz der new guy efferyvun is talkink about. Vhat happened to der odder schmot guy?"

Tarvek shrugged. "We don't know. I think it'll depend on how smart a guy he really is."

Ognian nodded. "End how schmart are hyu? Vhat do hyu tink ve should do?"

Tarvek looked out over the town, examined what he could see of the surrounding army and glanced up at the machine-filled sky. He turned back to Ognian. "At this point I could make a very good argument for running away and starting a career in piracy."

Ognian's eyebrows shot up. "Hyu *iz* a schmot guy," he marveled.

A few minutes later, they were moving through the rain-soaked streets, when Dimo, who was in the lead, held up a hand. "Qviet," he hissed. "Get back." They huddled in the shadows as a mechanical creature lumbered past on the connecting street. Its red eyes glowed, and a sleek scorpion-style tail swiveled back and forth as it moved. "Iz vun of der Baron's phlogiston-powered mantigoons. He got dem off ol' Professor Ponglenoze last year. Dey'll burn anything to a leedle crisp."

"Professor Wuburtus Ponglenoze," Agatha asked.

Dimo stared at her. "Maybe? *Hy* dunno."

"Doctor Beetle said Ponglenoze developed a brilliant interlock system for regulating energy flows."

Tarvek nodded. "I think I read about that. It's supposed to improve switch efficiency by a factor of five!"

Agatha turned to the Jägers. "Can you get one for me?"

With a whoop, Maxim and Ognian leapt out, dragging a terrified Moloch along. "Wait," he squealed. "Why me?"

Dimo pushed him along. "*Somevun* got to tell us vhat an inter-vhatchamacallit looks like!"

Soon enough they were back, and Ognian handed Agatha a small glittering part. Dimo had an arm companionably slung over Moloch's shoulders. "Hy schtill dun understand vhy hyu hit der driver in der head mit dot brick."

Moloch glared at him. "Because going for the weakest part gets the fight over *quickly*."

Dimo nodded. "See, *dot's* the bit hy dun underschtand."

Agatha clicked the final connection into place and held it up for Tarvek to inspect. "How about that?"

"Nice!" He tapped the cane. "You know what this needs? Some sort of phase-lock inverter."

Agatha bit her lip. "Oooh, now you're talking. But where would we find—"

"HOY!" Mamma Gkika and a squad of Jägers poured out of an alley. They clutched a variety of weapons and local delicacies. "Vhat iz hyu keeds doink here? Dere iz a sqvad of bloater tanks comink up dis road! Ve's plannink an ambush!"

Tarvek rubbed his hands together. "Are these the same bloater tanks featured in Baron von Twangsnekken's book *Twenty-Seven Amusing Thoughts on Urban Warfare and After-Dinner Mints*?"

Gkika looked lost. "Deyz der vuns mit beeg gons on dem."

Tarvek nodded to Agatha. "Good enough."

Agatha finished a quick sketch and handed it to the Jägergeneral. "Here. The parts I want look like these."

Ghika examined the sketch and grinned. "Hokay, boyz, ve's going shoppink!"

Fifteen minutes later, Agatha swung the refurbished stick up into her arms. What had begun the day as a sleek walking stick topped with a glowing blue bulb, now resembled . . . (Note: Um . . . the authors are forced to concede that at this point the Lady Heterodyne's device did, in fact resemble nothing else. It was almost twice its original length, five times its diameter and everyone who saw it unanimously agreed that it looked like *trouble*.) She showed it to Tarvek. "But it still needs something."

Tarvek rubbed his chin. "I see what you're going for, but I can't quite figure out . . . "

"*I* know what it needs," a voice boomed from behind them. They spun to see Othar Tryggvassen with a bedraggled Violetta at his side peering down at the device. "It needs one of those . . . " He snapped his fingers in annoyance. "Oh, how embarrassing, it's on the tip of my tongue. Hold on . . . "

With a leap, he cleared a low wall, surprising a Wulfenbach trooper clank that had been creeping up on them. It lashed out, connecting with Othar in mid-air. Othar grabbed hold of the metal fist, swung about so that his feet were planted on the clank's chest, and tore the arm free. He then proceeded to beat the clank into fragments with the detached arm. As soon as the mangled device fell over, he was rummaging about within its chest cavity. With a grunt of satisfaction, he pulled forth a glowing tube, which he presented to Agatha with a flourish. "You know, one of *these!*"

"Oh!" Agatha was delighted. She snatched it from his hand. "Yes! That's *perfect!*"

Tarvek shook his head. "I keep forgetting he's a spark."

Violetta glanced at Moloch. "Really. So you've completely missed the fact that he's overbearing, self-aggrandizing, and certain death to be around?"

Tarvek looked at her blankly. "Well, no, but what's your point?"

Agatha, meanwhile, had slotted the piece in place and was now grinning disturbingly at the results. "Oh yes, yes, yes, yessss," she crooned. "It is sooo ready."

Tarvek and Othar looked at it and took a step back. "Yeah," Tarvek said, "that ought to do it." He glanced upwards. "Or you could just blow Castle Wulfenbach out of the sky."

Othar clapped his hands in delight. "An excellent suggestion, young apprentice!"

Tarvek ignored this. "Except, of course, that Gil is still up there."

"Even better," Othar declared.

Tarvek briefly considered this, then reluctantly admitted, "But he still has my notes."

General Gkika folded her arms. "Hokay, zo vhat do ve do next?"

"It's time to head for the Observation Tower." Everyone looked down the main avenue. At the far end stood the Observation Tower, but clustered about its base was a full array of assorted Wulfenbach weaponry. "Ha!" Agatha laughed. "I don't think that's going to be a problem *now!*"

So saying, she swung the device up onto her shoulder and squeezed the trigger. A lance of destructive energy spat out from the tip, burning through the assembled Wulfenbach machinery, and struck the base of the tower, causing it to blow outwards in a shower of masonry. With a slow, oddly graceful motion, the tower collapsed to the ground, burying or blocking the rest of the Wulfenbach forces.

There was a brief silence while everyone tried not to look at Agatha. Van stared at the rubble aghast. The only thought in his head: *It was on all of the postcards.*

Moloch was the first to speak. "How is it possible that this surprised *any* of you people?"

Agatha took a deep breath and turned to Van. "So . . . " she said brightly, "Do we have any other tall buildings near the Castle?"

"—that you're not too attached to." Moloch added. Violetta poked him in the ribs, but not very hard.

Van looked like a man who had nothing else to lose. "Oh sure. How about the Red Cathedral spire? Or the Doom Bell?"

Agatha considered them. "Not high enough, not close enough."

"I wasn't being serious!"

Ognian tapped the enhanced lightning stick. "Vhat hif you forgets about der Kestle and just schtart zappink efferyting else?"

Van grabbed him by his vest and shook him. "You'd better not be serious either!"

Agatha answered him anyway. "I'd run out of charge long before I got enough to make a difference. Besides the whole point is to save the town, not flatten it. And the Castle would *still* be dead."

Othar stroked his beard. "If altitude is all you need, young Wulfenbach has helpfully provided us with a flying machine. 'Twould be so *very* trés ironic!"

Tarvek went pale. "Never mention that bucket of bolts in my presence ever again."

"Does the Lady Heterodyne need to go *flying*?" a booming voice asked from on high. They all looked up, and there was Franz perched on a roof above them, eyes glowing. The other dragon's golden helmet sat jauntily askew on his head. "*I* can fly you higher and closer than any building in town!"

Agatha's eyes widened with delight. "That would be *perfect!*"

Van checked her with a gentle hand. "Franz, you can't fly!"

Frank shifted. His short, stubby wings fluttered behind him. "I can *too* fly." A defiant tone had entered the dragon's voice.

"You *can't!*"

"I *CAN*," Franz roared. Then he shrugged. "I just . . . you know . . . *cheat* a little."

Said "cheating" took the form of an elaborate flying machine that resembled nothing so much as a giant bicycle attached to a pair of propellers. It certainly looked improbable, but now, at full power, Franz's legs pumped the pedals with sufficient speed that they were soon aloft. Agatha rode behind him, clutching the spines on the dragon's back and whooping with delight. "It's wonderful," she cried as they swooped over the town. "*I* think you fly very well indeed!"

Franz grinned and pumped a bit faster. "Master Barry made it for me. He said the old system with the birds and the kites was just too silly." They swerved past an astonished Wulfenbach balloonist. "How close do you want to get?"

"I've been thinking about that. Can we actually land on the roof of the Castle?"

"Do you need to be that close?"

"I might. I think that those antenna atop the Castle are lightning collectors. That would be pretty standard, and yet the Castle is almost out of power. I can't believe it hasn't been hit by lightning on a regular basis, it's the tallest thing in town. That means the collectors must be damaged. Unless I fix those, hitting it with more lightning won't do anything."

"Huh. Makes sense. Okay, the roof it is, Mistress."

They flew on in silence for a minute while Agatha looked over the town. It didn't look good. "Franz, how long have you served the Heterodynes?"

Franz grunted. "A pretty long time. A couple of hundred years, I think. I lose track when I'm sleeping. Why?"

"Have you ever seen it this bad?"

Franz shook his head. "Nope. Not like this. Well, even if it doesn't work like it should, this lightning thing should keep 'em busy while you make your escape."

Agatha sat back. "You mean run away?"

"Yeah, of course."

"I wouldn't—"

"Why not?" Franz interrupted. "Too proud? You could give 'em a good rant before you run, you know. Lots of Heterodynes have done it. They were always getting beat back, thwarted, foiled. That's why you rule Mechanicsburg but not the world. Sometimes you gotta know when to set a few time-delayed death traps and run. Rebuild your power. Show 'em all another day. It happens."

"I . . . I can't do that. The old Heterodynes . . . my ancestors . . . whenever they were beaten back, they came here. No one could take Mechanicsburg. That was their strength. If I run away now and *lose* Mechanicsburg, I—we—we have nowhere to run *to*."

Franz considered this. "Maybe Notre-Dame's still got some openings in the Gargoyle Squad?"[141]

---

[141] The Gargoyle Squad of Notre-Dame de Paris has become rather famous as the final refuge of last resort for any number of Europa's spark-produced and then abandoned

Agatha swatted him on the back of the head. "Keep flying!"

They swooped down onto the highly pitched roof. Franz landed with a grunt and a clatter that broke scores of ancient roof tiles and sent them skittering over the edge. The wind and rain were fierce. Franz kept his arm out to steady Agatha as she examined the base of one of the great aerials. She pried open a corroded hatch and gave a cry of satisfaction. "Ha! I *knew* it! There's a row of connectors that have been tripped and should have been reset." She snapped them into position one-by-one and closed the hatch. "Let's get to the other one."

Laboriously they crawled across the top of the tower. Agatha pried open the other panel. "Looking at all the gunk inside these panels, I'm guessing they must have been overloaded when the Castle was damaged all those years ago!" One of the switches showed signs of corrosion. Agatha chipped away at it until she could snap the switch back into place. *I'll be back to clean all of you,* she silently promised them as she tightened the fasteners on the covers. She sat back on her haunches and nodded in satisfaction. "I can't believe no one ever checked them."

Franz shrugged. "If the Castle never said anything, and the masters weren't here . . . "

"Well, they should work now." She glanced up at the rain clouds overhead. "Probably a good thing that tower collapsed," she said primly. Franz snorted in amusement.

"Agatha!" They both jumped as Gilgamesh Wulfenbach called out from behind them. Turning, they saw Gil standing in the bow of a steam pinnace airship, hovering scant meters away. He stood in the bow, one hand on the fore-rope, the other outstretched towards Agatha. When he saw he had her attention, he flicked at the controls with a foot, and the ship gently surged forward. "Come aboard," he called out. "Quickly! You've done your best, but the town has fallen. It's over. I'm getting you out of here."

Agatha reached for his hand automatically, then slipped and

---

megafauna. The Master of Paris claims they help to keep the city protected and dramatically curtail the pigeon population.

skidded down the dark, wet roof tiles. With a grunt, she was stopped by one of the dormers that lined the edge of the roof. As soon as he saw Agatha was safe, Franz glanced at Gil and saw the expression on his face was not fear, but annoyance. "Hold still," Gil said, as he leapt from the ship. "I'll be right there."

Before he could advance, he found himself facing an immense green hand that blocked his way. "Whoa," the dragon rumbled. "Hold on, you. She's okay. I've got her."

Gil went unnaturally still. While keeping an eye on him, Franz gingerly slid his tail back and allowed Agatha to brace herself on it and begin clambering back up. "Careful, m'Lady. Something ain't *right* about this guy." As soon as Agatha was in a secure position, he reached forward. "C'mere, kid. Lemme have a better look at ya." As the dragon's hand approached, Gil waved his own hand and a large hypodermic appeared, which he drove into Franz's palm.

"OW! What do you think you're . . . " Franz suddenly wobbled and then collapsed to the roof, sliding several meters before he stopped.

"Franz!" Agatha knelt beside the great head. One beachball sized eye drunkenly rolled towards her. "Ooorg," he said.

Furious, Agatha glared at Gil, who was picking his way towards her. "What have you done to him? He wasn't going to hurt you, he's one of mine!"

Gil waved this aside with a coldness that Agatha found jarring. "It's only a sedative. He'll be fine. But I don't have time to argue with him, or you. Come with me! Now!" Imperiously, he extended his hand.

Agatha stared at it, and then up at Gil's unrecognizable face. "No." She scooted backwards. "You stay where you are."

Conflicting emotions flickered across Gil's face, settling into an expression evidently supposed to pass for "concern." "You can't be serious. The storm is getting worse! We can't stay up here!"

"Yes! Fine! Get yourself down to the town square. Find Tarvek and Van. You can help them and be out of the storm. We'll talk when I'm done here."

"Agatha, you've got to listen to reason! This has all gone too far!"

"No. Not yet. I'm not finished here. I haven't given up and I'm not leaving this town."

Gil stared at her, and then swept his hand out. "The town? *Look* at your town! Your town is in flames! And very soon, all of Europa will follow it. I've explained everything to my father! He understands! He can help you! If you keep trying to solve this yourself, the Other *will* win. We'll be back to the days of constant warfare! Don't you understand? Mechanicsburg has *fallen!* What else do you think you can *do?*"

Agatha felt a wave of pure wrath wash through her. She raised the modified lightning stick above her head and snapped the main switch. *"This!"* The heavens opened, and the lightning struck the Castle towers.

Over and over again, bolts lanced down and struck the towers with a boom and a crackle that could be heard throughout the town, even above the sounds of battle. In point of fact, the battles paused as the pyrotechnic display continued.

On a rooftop normally occupied by a beer-garden, Agatha's compatriots watched with awe. Professor Mezzasalma stroked his chin and nodded in satisfaction. "Yup. That should do it," he declared.

Violetta leaned towards Moloch. "What will it do?"

Moloch turned towards Vanamonde von Mekkhan. "That's a good question. What *will* it do?"

Van stared at the mechanic perplexed. "I thought it was obvious. The lightning should revitalize the Castle, and then it will take control of the town's defenses."

"Yeah, I've been wondering about that." Moloch looked out over the town and tried to not see it as a town. "How much do you people know about what the Castle can really do?"

Van opened his mouth—and then paused. This man was the Lady Heterodyne's chief minion. He might be new to the job, but just having been chosen to it meant that he *saw* things other people overlooked. Van looked out over the town and bit his lip. "I'm . . . I'm not really sure. My grandfather is always saying I've never really seen what the Castle could do at its height. Earlier today, thanks to the Lady's repairs, it was collapsing streets. Activating bridges and traps. Things like that. But so much of what it used to be able to do has been forgotten."

Moloch rubbed his forehead. "Yeah. I was afraid of that."

"Afraid?" Van felt a premonition of doom settle softly upon his shoulders. "*Why?*"

Moloch waved at the Castle, still wreathed in lightning. "How long did it take to build the Castle?"

Van shrugged. "Centuries."

Moloch continued to look at him, and Van felt compelled to elaborate. "But the core? The recognizable structure and the instrumentality needed to allow the Castle entity to function? About ten years, more or less."

Moloch nodded. "The Baron has been keeping a series of the most whacked-out sparks in Europa locked up in there for over fifteen years. They've been replacing and repairing and improving the place, following the Castle's orders with no questions or supervision. Getting what *it* thought was important fixed." He stared out over the town. "I'm telling you that it's been operating on nothing but the dregs of its back-up power for the last couple of years, and it was *still* able to control all that stuff in the town?" He gave Van a look that Van was growing to recognize as the man's default state of resigned bleakness. "I'm sayin' you got no idea of what it's capable of now."

Van absorbed this and looked back up at the lightning display. "There . . . there's no place we could possibly run *to*, is there?"

Moloch shrugged. "Figured you people were used to that sort of thing by now."

Atop the roof, Gilgamesh flinched as the shingles sparked and crackled around him. "Agatha," he screamed. "Are you *trying* to get yourself killed?"

Above him stood Agatha, surrounded by a small sphere of force that the lightning struck again and again, the bolts rebounding off to strike the accumulator towers. Her hair stood out from her head, and the metal in her outfit sparked furiously, but she stood unharmed and resolute. "Of course not," she screamed back. "How can you possibly underestimate me like this? *You* were the one who supported me! I'm doing what you said you *knew* I could do! I'm keeping myself, my town, and all of us alive and free!" A particularly well-timed bolt hit the sphere and split into two white-hot lances that struck the towers simultaneously. "Any way I can!"

Gil's brow lowered and his voice took on a not-unfamiliar timbre. "It is too late for that! *Listen* to yourself! You're out of control! What if the Other has already usurped your mind and you haven't even *noticed*? You cannot be allowed to run free. Not like this! I— My father will never risk a full return of the Other— or anyone *like* her!"

Agatha stared down at him. Fury and betrayal rising quickly within her. "*Now*? You say that *now* when I am on the cusp of securing the safe place you said I needed? You, who said you were prepared to risk *anything*?"

Deep within Castle Heterodyne, within the Great Movement Chamber, a final circuit closed, and the cavernous room glowed blue from the field of fully recharged Bagdad salamanders. Machinery dormant for almost two decades jerked and began the laborious process of self-repair and retuning. The Castle now had its guiding mind at full clarity and all of the delicious power that it could possibly need-and more kept coming. The repairs went *quickly*.

Gil clenched his hands in fury. "I am risking *everything*! I'm doing so by insisting on keeping you *alive*! I have *seen* what you can do! You're dangerous! As a tool of the Other, you could destroy Europa!"

"You're assuming I'll let her win. I have friends now. Allies. I counted you amongst those, but you can be replaced, if it comes to that. I have ideas, information. My mother's lab, and now, I believe,

I have my fortress. If you and your father want to help me, you can do it here. In Mechanicsburg. On my terms. I won't be anyone's tool. Hers, his, or *yours!*"

With a final crescendo, the lightning stopped. The rain began to noticeably taper off. Gil's face seemed to reflect an inner debate, but he shook it off as he reached into his coat. "We're all tools," he said as he tossed a small item out towards Agatha's feet. It struck the sharply pitched roof and with a *clack* and stuck in place. "You'll get used to it." The device bloomed and a ring of light appeared. From above, a trio of metallic voices chorused. "Hunt mode activated, quarry set." Three of the Castle Wulfenbach gargoyle sentinels[142] dropped onto the roof, surrounding her.

"Clanks," Gil called out, "your orders: take the quarry alive! Do not let her fall!"

Agatha spun towards the closest machine moving gingerly towards her. "Clank! Receive new orders!" She tossed it the lightning rod. "Hold this!" As she tossed the rod, she unhooked a cable, and when the clank caught the rod and attempted to compensate for the unexpected weight and momentum, she held the exposed end to its forehead. Instantly there was a bright blue flash and the gargoyle jerked in place before collapsing to the ground. The other two devices pulled back slightly as Agatha caught the rod as it fell from the gargoyle's nerveless fingers. Before they could again advance, she swung the rod downwards like a golf club,[143] smacked the focusing device, and sent it soaring out into space. The two clanks' heads

---

[142]   Castle Wulfenbach is festooned with numerous mechanical gargoyles. These are not merely decorative, but serve as the first line of defense against air pirates, aeroapes, sky kraken, balloon barnacles, and the occasional meteorite. It is unusual for them to be detached from this assignment.

[143]   Golf is a "sport" that became popular in Scotland in the fifteenth century. Players stalk about a predetermined course, driving small balls into holes in the ground with specially shaped sticks known as clubs. Devotees, of which there are many, claim it is one of the "purest" sports, as it develops nothing in the player that could be useful in the mundane world.

swiveled to track it as it vanished, and then leapt off of the roof to follow it.

Agatha thumped the end of the rod down onto the roof. "Seriously? That was all you brought?" She peered down at the rain-slicked roof and realized it was empty, just as Gil's hands clamped onto her upper arms.

"Now I take you home." For a treacherous moment, Agatha almost allowed herself to surrender, but . . . this . . . his hands felt *wrong*. She felt a peculiar movement from the hand on her left and tore her glance away from Gil's face in time to see the small device he was attempting to get within the grasp of his fingers. She stomped on his foot with the heel of her boot. The pain caused him to relax his grip enough that she could swing the lightning rod up far enough to smack him across the forehead. The device flew from his hand and clattered to the ground far below, showering sparks as it rolled away.

"How dare you," Agatha said. "You're still trying to *subdue* me?"

"Yes, I am!" This time Gil simply tried to smack her. But months of training allowed her to block the intended blow. "Because I have no *choice!*" Again he attacked, but even as she spun out of his grasp, Agatha realized yet again that something was wrong. She had *seen* Gil fight. Had seen him take down Captain Vole and, yet fighting her now, his moves were clumsy and obvious. She looked at his face and saw it was a study in frustration. Not at her, she realized, but with himself. He saw her looking at him and his eyes pleaded with her. "My father wants you dead. He's only giving me this one last chance to try to save you. I want to rescue you!"

Even as he was saying this, Agatha saw his head was shaking from side to side, indicating "no." *Something is seriously wrong here*, she realized.

"I do not need rescuing. I am the Heterodyne!"

Gil's face looked haunted. "You are a fool!"

His head snapped to one side. "That alone won't save you. We're trapped! My father has won!"

His head snapped to the other side. He looked at her coldly. "You talk as if you think the Heterodyne cannot die. I assure you that you can, and you will if you continue to defy me."

Again his head snapped to one side. "I will not lose you," he screamed. "Not again." This last came out almost like a sob.

He's arguing with himself, Agatha realized. *Like there were two—* Comprehension came crashing in on her, encasing her heart in a fist of ice.

She surged forward without hesitation, startling the man before her. She grabbed his lapels and gave him a kiss, fierce and hot. He froze in surprise, eyes staring down at her, before his mouth responded and eagerly molded itself to hers. After several seconds, Agatha grasped Gil's lapels and pushed him back. "*I* will rescue *you*," she said fiercely.

At this, Gil's expression changed to cold fury, and he leapt forward, hands outstretched—and ran right into the boot Agatha slammed into his solar plexus. "Catch," she shouted. Hands windmilling desperately, Gil fell back down the steeply pitched roof and smack into the waiting grasp of the now mostly recovered Franz, who clasped him tightly, arms pinned to his side. The dragon was obviously still a bit woozy, but ferocity filled his eyes, and the hold he had on Gil was obviously not a gentle one.

"So, kid. I don't think we've been properly introduced. I'm the Great Dragon of Mechanicsburg, and you're—?" He snorted and squeezed Gil even tighter. "Eh. You know what? Don't really care."

"Franz!" Agatha's shout caused the great lizard to pause. "Franz, this is the Baron's son, Gilgamesh Wulfenbach. Heir to the empire, and despite everything that's happened here . . . " Agatha looked away as she felt her face flushing. "Despite *everything*, I am somewhat in love with him."

Franz glanced at Gil, so he alone saw the alternating expressions of joy and anger that flicked across the man's face. "You *sure* about that, m'Lady?" Franz waved Gil about for emphasis. "I mean, I *know*

Heterodynes never choose the easy path when it comes to romance,[144] but there is something seriously wrong with this guy."

"I know, but I cannot guarantee his safety here. So, get him out of my town right now, before I utterly destroy him!" Agatha touched her still tingling lips as she watched Franz launch himself off the tower. *Or utterly something,* she admitted to herself.

"Ah! Mistress! *There* you are!" Agatha almost lost her balance as the voice of the Castle boomed out of a nearby grill. "And screaming defiance from the highest tower, just as I predicted!"

"Castle! Are you . . . all right?"

A section of the roof beneath Agatha's feet flattened out. Rods twisted upwards and formed a small decorative balcony railing. "You know," the Castle said wonderingly, "I believe I am!" It chuckled in glee. "Would you like to see me *prove* it?"

"Yes!" A final, gratuitous peal of thunder rolled out overhead as Agatha found herself dancing in place while her town and the invading armies lay spread out before her. "*Yes!* Yes yes yes yes YES!"

---

[144] After learning about Euphrosynia Heterodyne's troubled relationship with the Storm King, Saturn Heterodyne's turbulent marriage, or the present drama unfolding that is a direct result of Bill Heterodyne's marriage to Lucrezia Mongfish, one could easily believe that certain Heterodynes seem to be particularly unlucky in love. Sadly, this sort of thing was actually the norm as far as the family went. The Heterodynes constantly sought to embrace danger, adventure, strife, madness, and relished injecting *sturm und drang* into every aspect of their (and everyone else's) lives. Therefore, it should come as no surprise that, as far as they were concerned, courting and matrimony were simply two more playing fields for this sort of thing. Perversely, one of the greatest books dedicated to the resolution of relationship difficulties and the preservation of marriage is Herr Doktor Danjharl Savage's (PhD, SE, University of Amsterdam) historical overview and analysis of Heterodyne courting: *Don't Do This.* (Corbettite Press/Belfast).

CHAPTER 12

Amongst learned men, there is the conviction that every problem can be dealt with if one applies rational thought and a sufficient knowledge of the germane circumstances. Obviously there are problems that remain intransigent to this worldview, but it is believed this is due to a paucity of knowledge amongst the people attempting to deal with said problem, and that when our scope of knowledge has sufficiently increased, then we will have the tools to deal with them using the proscribed methods.

I myself have now come to the conclusion that this supposition is incorrect. I have seen many things and must state here and now that there are things sane, sensible men cannot deal with and, dare I say it, are perhaps not meant to know.

This, however, does not mean they do not exist, or should not be dealt with. This initially appears to be a paradox. However, the forces that rule the universe have provided us with what, in retrospect, appears to be the obvious solution: men and women capable of dealing with said unsettling problems, who are able to do so by virtue of their reason being already lost. I myself have seen this disquieting truth play out when, as I will recount below, I found myself captured by Jägermonsters and subsequently brought before Robur Heterodyne.

The conclusion I formed from this encounter, and the reason I will return to Mechanicsburg to serve him after I complete this, my final report to my fellow alchemists of the Royal Society, is the terrible, inescapable one that, for our world to continue as we know it, for it to exist at all, it appears that there must always be a Heterodyne."

—The introductory notes to the unpublished manuscript of *An Unsettling Series of Discoveries Regarding the Nature of Time, Space, Existence As We Know It, and a Disturbing Realization of Mine Own Place in the Universe* by Lord Crispen Dugenness. (Currently in the Forbidden Library of the Pope of the Mountains)

๑๑๑

On the streets of Mechanicsburg, the invaders were disorganized. This was not surprising, as even the ones from the empire came from a hundred different units that had been added to the Wulfenbach forces over the years. Many suspected that when the forces invading the city had been assigned, the Baron had selected the most outré fighting units.[145]

They *had*, nevertheless, been rigorously drilled in the empire's fighting methods and protocols, and thus it took a great deal to cause them to pause. The lightning show that took place atop Castle Heterodyne, however, was in a class by itself.

On the Avenue of Mismatched Teeth,[146] the Undead Army of the

---

[145] A suspicion that was quite justified. Empire records show that when Mechanicsburg was invaded, the Baron deliberately selected the empire's most troublesome, unsustainable, and high-maintenance units to lead the charge. One justification was that the members of these spark-created units would be more capable dealing with whatever mad science the citadel of the Heterodynes would throw at them. But the clearly discernible subtext was that if *someone* had to be turned into balloon animals, on the whole, the empire felt slightly more comfortable with it happening to established abominations of science, who might not even mind the change.

[146] Originally devoted to dentists, taxidermists, saw sharpeners, the makers of man-traps, and

Glorious Dawn[147] stared upwards as the lighting struck again and again. After a while, their sergeant managed to tear his eyes away from the spectacle. "All right!" he bellowed. "Back to attention! You'd think you zombies had never seen lightning before."

The troops looked at each other. The one nearest the sergeant spoke up. "Not like that I ain't." Meanwhile the others made a show of shuffling back into some semblance of formation. The sergeant closed his eyes and counted to three. The problem with fully cognizant undead troops was that they had absolutely no fear of consequences. This was desirable when they were ordered into battle, but terrible when one was trying to enforce discipline. The only reason they listened at all was a built-in need to be obliging.

The sergeant tried again. More for his own peace of mind than anything else. "So whatta ya worried about? Yer already dead, ain'cha?"

The zombie considered this. "Yeah, and I wanna stay that way."

"Then let's just—" Suddenly the ground shook. "What the . . . ?

"Earthquake!" the nearest zombie shouted.

"Everyone stay close," the sergeant shouted. He eyed the swaying buildings to either side. "Get to the middle of the road!" Which made things ever so much easier when the road split down the middle lengthwise, and the Undead Army of the Glorious Dawn fell into the darkness before the road closed back up above them.

Elsewhere, a column of Punch-Men clattered through the rain, the giant mechanical hands mounted atop their operator compartments swayed in gyroscopically balanced counterpoint as they ran. "Punch-

---

combs. Today it houses many of Mechanicsburg's portraitists and engravers. No one knows why.

[147] The glorious dawn in question had been the signal that some now-forgotten, long-awaited revolution was to begin. Unfortunately, it rained that day and, for the conspirators, things went downhill from there. The never-activated Undead Army sat, unclaimed, in a storage locker for two years until the empire bought them at auction. This was not the strangest way that the empire had ever acquired new troops, but it was unquestionably the most cost effective.

Captain," his second informed him, "I've lost contact with the ground support troops!"

The captain bit his knuckle in trepidation. "Some deviltry of the Heterodynes." He looked at the burning rubble surrounding them. "I *knew* this was going too smoothly." He made a decision and switched his communicator to Open Channel. "All right. We are pulling out and heading back towards the staging area." He consulted the map above his head. *Fifteen minutes, with no problems.* "From now on, anyone we find alive *stays* that way. I want *hostages.*"

"Oh great," one of the troops muttered. "*Now* he tells us."

"*And* I want us out of the open."

Atop one of the mechanical suits, the great hand twisted and pointed. "There's an alley straight ahead, Punch-Captain."

The captain examined it critically. "No windows, overhanging eaves . . . " The hand atop his suit gave a "thumbs up." "Good job, Lieutenant." The hand waved them onward. "Forward!"

The squad moved forward at a respectable clip. The captain was again consulting the map when his second yelled, "*Look out!*"

He swung his eyes up and saw, to his astonishment, that the exit from the alley no longer existed. Before him was simply another brick wall. "The devil," he swore. "Gloves up! One-eighty and retreat—"

"Punch-Captain!" The voice was from Lieutenant Oshtenpole, who was on rear guard. "There *is* no exit! And it's getting—" His voice rose in terror. "The walls are closing in!"

The captain stared. They were indeed. "But it was just an alley," he moaned as metal spikes slid forth from between the brickwork. "By the devil and his hat! Assume brace formations!" But less than a minute later, there no longer was any alley at all.

Back in the old days, before there were things like "municipal codes," building construction was a more extemporaneous exercise. Which meant that, on the whole, the people doing the building used whatever materials were to hand. This gave the early structures of Mechanicsburg, which were often cobbled together from the salvage and scrap of the Heterodyne's abandoned death machines, a delightful air of uniqueness. It was rare for one building to be similar to another, even one that had been constructed next door. Architectural tours of Mechanicsburg are very popular and focus not on schools of design so much as "Guess What This Used to Be?"

All of which serves to explain, in an admittedly roundabout way, why, while the rest of the home that Zeetha and Violetta were hiding in had crumbled under the withering machine cannon fire that had them pinned down, the remaining wall they now found themselves behind stood firm. It had been constructed from a single sheet of armor plating from a device that had, coincidentally, and entirely unknown to Violetta, once destroyed her family's ancestral castle.

The two women observed the unremitting hail of bullets that peppered the remains of the building around them, and ruminated on the life choices that had brought them here. A fresh burst of fire pounded assorted tilework into powder. "That's another one joined in," Zeetha said with annoyance. "We're really hemmed in, now."

Violetta rolled her eyes. "So what exactly are we trying to prove here?"

Zeetha frowned. "The Baron is attacking Agatha's town. We're helping to stop him."

Violetta looked at her disapprovingly. "One monster at a time? With something you ripped off of a clank?"

"Well . . . That Higgs took my swords . . . "

"Stupid!" Violetta smacked her hand against the floor. "Stupid!"

"Oh, come on. I'm not doing so bad. Did you see that last guy's face when I—"

"Not you, me!"

"What do you mean? Your count is what? Twenty-three? Twenty-four if you count that big steam-walker."

"Why am I here? I'm not cool like you! You're a real warrior! You're good at this and you're fighting for your friend. You're not going to die out here, looking like a complete fool, just to . . . to show off for some guy you hardly even know."

Zeetha stared at the shorter woman even as she gingerly touched the wound that even now throbbed between her breasts. The realization that this was, in fact, *exactly* what she was doing caused her to shake her head in amused self-recrimination.

She clapped Violetta on the shoulder. "Yeah, that'd be the stupidest way to die, ever. Come on, if I'm gonna hear about this guy, we have to get out of here."

Violetta stared at her. "That's an option?"

Zeetha looked around the minuscule safe area they were in, even as new rounds exploded around them. "The first thing we have to do is think positive!"

The shooting stopped.

The two women stared at each other for close to a minute. "Okay," Zeetha said at last. "That's a good start." Gingerly, they tossed a shoe out from behind the protecting wall. There was silence. Zeetha took a deep breath, and peeked out—

And saw no one.

They stepped out onto the deserted street. "But . . . but where are they?" Zeetha muttered. "There were at least twenty of those cannon-hat guys blocking the street. They were here shooting at us. They can't have just disappeared . . . " She became aware of a tight grip on her shoulder. Violetta, looking slightly more shell-shocked, pointed towards the wall across the street.

I don't remember there being a wall there . . . Zeetha suddenly saw the dozens of gun barrels poking out through the stones, along with, she realized, the occasional uniformed hand. She swallowed. "That . . . that's something I'd expect the Castle to do."

"Hello, ladies," the horribly familiar voice seemed to come from directly behind them.

"Castle! Agatha did it! You're back."

"Indeed I am."

"Where is she," Violetta asked. "Is she all right?"

"Indeed she is! She is currently making some minor calibrations."

"HALT!" The two women spun around to see a squad of clanks thumping towards them down the street. When they saw they had their attention, they raised their weapons. "Orders/hear/action/all Mechanicsburg citizens/tasty meat creatures are to be—" What they were to be was never established as, without warning, two entire buildings slammed together, crushing the mechanicals between them.

The Castle blithely continued, "In fact, your feedback would be *very* helpful. Just now? I'll be honest, I thought I was a bit too slow. Would you say you: A. Agree; B. *Dis*agree; or, C. Think there's simply no fun in squashing them if they can't see it coming?"

Zeetha looked appalled, but Violetta leaned towards her. "Relax," she whispered. "In multiple choice? The answer is always 'C.' "

"Hoy! Miz Zeetha!" The two looked around and saw Ognian, Dimo, and Maxim climbing a set of stairs towards them. Maxim saw Violetta and ran a hand through his hair. "Hello again, cutie, hy thought hyu vaz vit dot Othar guy."

Violetta rolled her eyes. Zeetha grinned. "Violetta Mondarev. Smoke Knight now serving Agatha. She was a gift from a guy named Tarvek Sturmvarous."

Instantly, the easy grins of the three Jägers vanished. "A vassal of the Sturmvarous family?" Dimo shook his head. "Hy dun know dot hy trust hyu, cutie."

Violetta raised her hands. "I don't blame you, but Tarvek and I decided we're safer allying ourselves with the Lady Heterodyne. He's in love with her."

Ognian guffawed. "Veez met heem. He's schmott, but he'z gun heffa go through der Baron's son, end hy vouldn't take dot bet."

Violetta glared at him. "*I* would, since I've watched him fight Wulfenbach to a draw at least three times so far."

Ognian's jaw dropped and he glanced over at Zeetha, who grinned. "It was a pity you missed it, guys. They were fighting dirty and everything." The Jägers nodded approvingly. In their opinion, Agatha was worth fighting dirty for.

Maxim leaned in and examined Violetta with a critical eye. "So, hyu'z a Smoke Knight? Wit all der fency poizons and sneaky schtuff?"

"Yes," Violetta said from behind him. "I am."

Dimo didn't bother with not looking impressed. "So vhat are hyu supposed to be doink?"

"I'm charged with protecting her."

Dimo made a show of looking around. "So vhat iz hyu doink here? Shouldn't hyu be by her side or som'ting?"

"Shouldn't *you?*"

The Jägers flinched at this. "Vell," Ognian explained, "ve *vos*, bot den she vent off to activate der Castle. Dot's vhat all dot lightning vos about. De next ting ve know, de Kestle iz tellink us to come op here, fast-like." He shrugged. "Dun know why."

Across the town below, screams and yells could be heard. Vast rumblings and groaning revealed where entire buildings were being flung about. Violetta looked at the Jägers with respect. "I guess the Castle *likes* you."

Maxim considered this. "Hy tink it tinks uf us as part uf der furniture."

A particularly loud explosion echoed off the walls. "And I," Ognian declared loudly, "em *hokay* with dot!"

Dimo, meanwhile, had sidled up to Zeetha. "So vhat iz hyu schtill doink out of bed? Mamma said dot—"

"I've already talked to Mamma. I feel fine."

"Hmm. Und here I thought Meester Higgs vanted hyu to stay dere as vell."

"Don't tell him!"

Dimo snorted and pointed to a figure toiling up the stairs towards them. "Hy dun gots to tell heem notting. He'z gun be here in a minute."

He turned back and Zeetha was gone. Dimo grinned as Higgs topped the stairs. He saw Violetta and went to doff his hat, which seemed to be the first time he realized that he's been dragging an enormous rat creature of some sort. "Hello, Ms. Violetta." He faced the Jägers. "Gents."

Ognian stepped forward. "Heegs! Hey, guess vhat, luffer boy, hyu just meesed—"

He was cut off by Dimo burying an elbow in his gut. "Qviet, hyu."

Higgs frowned. "What's going on, now?" He glanced at Violetta, who looked away with a smile. Higgs sighed. "Ah. She's out of bed again, running around fighting everything she sees."

"Hyu didn't hear it from me," Ognian moaned from the ground.

Dimo smiled. "Goot ting she din' see hyu, hey?" He shrugged. "But dot's hokay, she's a beeg gurl. Iffen she gets herself keeled, mebbe she'll learn nots to do dot again, jah?"

The only sign Higgs gave of being agitated was from the smoke coming from his pipe. "Yeah, you'd've thought," he muttered. "It's not like *I* care, but . . . but she's supposed to be training the Heterodyne, so I don't like it."

Violetta rubbed her nose. "I thought you worked for Wulfenbach."

Higgs stared at her, and his pipe moved back and forth from one side of his mouth to the other. "Yes. Well, Master Gil likes the Heterodyne girl, right? So he'll be . . . he'll be super upset if Miss Zeetha gets hurt and can't train her."

Maxim slapped his back. "Ho! If *dot's* all hyu'z vorried about, dere's *lotsa* pipple dot ken train Miss Agatha!"

Higgs was so annoyed that he took his pipe from his mouth. "No! Miss Zeetha is *special!*" Everyone looked at him encouragingly. "I mean . . . I . . . "

Ognian's hand dropped heavily onto Higgs's shoulder, cutting him off in mid-burble. For once the Jäger's face was completely serious. "Hey, keed." Higgs's jaw shut with a snap. "Ve vaz havink fun tryink to wind hyu op. But now? Just shot op and go *ketch* her." Higgs stared at him blankly, blew out a deep breath, nodded once, and took off at a quick amble.

Maxim gave Ognian a punch on the arm. "Az alvays, hy iz in awe uf hyu mastery uf de art of de romance."

Ognian gave a nonchalant shrug. "Dot's vhy *hy* gots descendants!"

A half a block away, Zeetha dropped off of a roof, rolled to her feet, and then paused. "*Hold* on," she addressed the air. "Why am I running away? I am *Zeetha*, daughter of Chump![148] Should I—a royal princess of Skifander—cower in my bed while my friends fight for their lives? Never!

"And who does he think he is, anyway? I'm going to go back there—right now—and tell him what I think of his impertinent interference!" She glanced out of a shattered window and saw the object of her annoyance sauntering down the middle of an otherwise deserted street. The sight of him caused a wave of emotion to pass through her. "Oh, just *look* at him," she muttered. "Coming after me like he has some kind of . . . of right to tell me—"

From a pool of shadow, a large creature of indeterminate pedigree leapt towards the seemingly oblivious man. Just as it was about to strike, Higgs snagged it out of the air, slammed it to the pavement, and kicked it in the mouth hard enough to break several teeth. With a muttered apology, the creature slunk back into the shadows.

Zeetha realized she was squealing quickly enough that she was able to drop from sight before Higgs's head swung up towards the sound. Zeetha shivered in what she realized was delight, and then bit her knuckle. "But *is* he coming after me?" she wondered aloud.

"Oh my, yes," the Castle assured her. "I believe he rather likes you, actually. Astonishing."

"You again," Zeetha said with a sigh.

---

[148]   An unfortunate name, but still one to be reckoned with.

"Me again!" There was a note of dark amusement in the Castle's voice that Zeetha found disturbing. "He doesn't want to admit it, you know. He's always been a stubborn one."

Zeetha frowned. "But how would you . . . " An idea occurred to her. "Was he born here? In Mechanicsburg? Or is it stranger than that?"

"Hm . . . Perhaps I *should* tell you. But first, let us establish what your interest is in the Lady Heterodyne."

"She is my friend. She saved me from despair, here in this strange land."[149]

"And you train her to fight. Why?"

Zeetha stepped behind a wall as a wounded aeroape crashed to the ground. "You have to ask? Look at what's already happened to her. She's a spark and your Heterodyne. She's going to *need* to be strong. She'll need to know how to fight and when not to."

"So . . . you hope to make her into a fine . . . hero?"

"A what? Don't be stupid! She'll have enough to do just keeping this place in line. All I'm trying to do is keep her alive!"

"I see." The Castle sounded disappointed. "Well then, I will *not* tell you about Mister Higgs, after all."

Zeetha pouted. "What? But . . . "

"Because if I did, he'd have to kill you, and he wouldn't like that. No, it would be amusing, but I *must* consider the best interests of the family."

"Oh."

"Even worse," the Castle muttered, "he would be annoyed with me."

The implications of what Zeetha was hearing caused her to shiver. "Couldn't you just tell me *something*? I mean, maybe just enough so he'd only have to wound me a little?"

---

[149] When Princess Zeetha first arrived in Europa, everyone who had brought her here and knew how to get to Skifander—or even knew that it actually existed—was killed by air pirates. Since no one else Zeetha met in the subsequent three years of her travels across the length and breadth of Europa had ever heard of the place, Zeetha had begun to think she had made the whole thing up in a fever dream. This fear was shattered and her sanity restored when Agatha casually mentioned that she had heard stories of the place from Barry Heterodyne.

A wave of bone-chilling laughter swirled around her. "Why, *I'm* beginning to like you too. You're *fun*." The Castle paused. "I know, would you like to see him fight? I mean, *really* fight?"

Zeetha's breath caught. "Oh! Oh yeah!"

"Ha-ha, that a girl! Very well then, everything is in place and is finally in working order . . . You just find yourself a good seat and watch *this!*"

Zeetha braced herself, but nothing happened. After several seconds, she sighed, and sat on a low parapet—and was knocked to the ground when the wall started shivering. She bounced to her feet and realized the ground was moving. A look around assured her the nearby buildings were vibrating as well, and the people she saw on the streets were either sprawled on the ground or clutching large objects for dear life. She turned to look at the Castle, and saw it erupt with colored lights and gouts of steam that vented hundreds of meters into the sky above.

She stared, entranced, and then blinked. It almost appeared that . . . Another look and she saw she had not been mistaken. One of the toppled towers that had been leaning drunkenly against another, was slowly *moving*. She saw now that *all* of them were. The shattered walls were being repaired block by block. Towers were defying gravity and straightening back upright. Roof tiles were flowing back into place. The dust and the noise increased as everything seemed to move at once. And then, with a final *clunk*, Castle Heterodyne stood tall and seemingly undamaged before her.

Zeetha's breath caught and then she squinted. "The windows are still broken," she observed.

"Can't *do* windows," the Castle grated. It actually sounded like it was under stress.[150] There was a sudden, rising keening noise known

---

[150]   Even after all this time, the mechanics of how the Castle is able to blithely manipulate itself, not to mention the rest of the town of Mechanicsburg, remains one of the Heterodyne family's most closely guarded secrets. The fact that the Castle admits it cannot control glass goes a long way towards explaining Mechanicsburg's thriving glass industry, which is well

to many in the empire as the sound preceding a Wulfenbach aerial bombardment. It was followed by an explosion from atop one of the newly restored towers. Zeetha looked upwards. A Wulfenbach fleet soared overhead. More whistling, and more explosions hammered away at the Castle. All over the surface of the Castle, hundreds of doors and hatches flew open. Before Zeetha's startled eyes, a dark cloud poured forth and angrily spiraled upwards. If she had been closer, she would have seen that this consisted of an innumerable swarm of winged clanks.

Aboard the lead spotter craft, the forward watch *was* able to see— all too clearly—the clanks through his binoculars as the swarm rose towards them. "Com," he roared, "send an urgent alert on all bands! All Wulfenbach ships! Prepare for an attack on your six! Prepare for impact! Repeat: Prepare for—!" Which was when the first wave hit his ship. They smashed through the relatively thin balloon hide and began wreaking havoc amidst the gas cells. The great observation window shattered as a squat clank burst through and raked the nearby instruments with its rusty steel claws. "Thank you for shopping in Mechanicsburg," it cheerfully announced.[151]

"Disengage," the spotter shouted. "All airships are to disengage!"

"Oh no," the clank chuckled in what anyone below would have recognized as the voice of the Castle. "You *had* your chance." It

known for being able to supply everything from delicate laboratory glassware up to pre-made madness-inducing mirror mazes. There was a brief fad for these within the homes of Mechanicsburg's idle rich . . . until they all went mad, of course. Some people just have too much money.

[151] When the Heterodyne Boys inherited the Castle and the town, they realized they had a monumental job ahead of them: converting the Mechanicsburg economy from "pure or chaotic evil" to what Professor Garibaldi Gygax (LLM, The School for Advanced Studies of the Unnatural World, Lucca) referred to as "lawful evil." Realizing they couldn't turn a town of minions, pirates, and henchmen into honest people overnight, they began slowly by turning them into hucksters, which, while it lay upon a bed of solid, accountable mercantilism, still allowed for a generous exercise of low-level chicanery. Repurposing the various death machines that littered the place was a bit more problematic, but as we see here, they were working on it.

ripped the radio free and tossed it out through the window. "Now you get to see why no one should attack the Heterodyne." It snagged the spotter by his flight jacket and dragged him out into the sky. "You're an observer, yes? Then I shall keep you alive, so you can relate exactly what it is you'll see."[152]

And this is some of what he saw:

Gunner First Class Lindar DuQuesne peered upwards. The flotilla of airships that hovered protectively overhead appeared to be under attack by swarms of midges. His unit of mobile artillery was positioned at the base of a small hillock, one of many that encircled the town. The hilltops had been requisitioned by the various commanders who were coordinating the hodge-podge of empire units attacking Mechanicsburg. His unit was on picket duty. He shaded his brow with a hand. "What in crackthunder is going on up there?" he muttered.

"Hoy!" His captain bellowed from directly behind him. "You worry about your own gun!"

Lindar snapped to attention so fast that he almost dislocated his shoulders. "Yessir, Captain, sir!"

The captain clapped a hand on his shoulder and joined him in looking upwards. "But I gotta say," he confided to Lindar, "I been watchin' them cloud jockeys sail clean over the real fighting for twenty years. Now they're doin' the fightin', and we're untouched. Can't say I mind that." He looked at Lindar, who had the reputation amongst the men of being a bit of an intellectual. "Say, ain't there some kind of fancy-pants word for that? You know, for somebody else doin' worse'n us?"

Behind the sergeant, the hillock rumbled and a door opened,

---

[152]   Yes, this was, in fact, Lieutenant Yarl Bollet, who's firsthand account, *The Fall and Rise of Mechanicsburg: One Half-Hour of Terror* (Transylvanian Polygnostic University Press), became, on its release, the most read and, at the same time, most banned book in Europa. A very effective use of viral marketing.

revealing a tall, moss-encrusted clank reminiscent of a man in armor. Its eyes began to glow, and with a hiss, it drew forth a shining steel blade easily three meters long and strode towards them. Lindar frantically tried to bring his cannonette to bear on the advancing figure. *The word you want,* he thought, *is "unnatural."*

Everywhere buried giants were clawing their way to the surface. The great wall that encircled the town shivered. All along its length, enormous metal doors swung aside and armored colossi lurched forward. The first thing they did was to stride up to the dropwalls that girt the town and, with a coordinated effort, begin pushing them back, snowplowing the empire troops and ordinance clustered about their foundations.

One of the imperial generals watching the scene lowered his spyglass and snarled in confusion, "By Janus, what are those things doing? Whose side are they on?" By this time, the giants had pushed the dropwalls easily a hundred meters away from the walls of the city.

The attacking forces accepted this gift with indifference and began to flow into the ever-widening gaps.

"Don't attack the giants until they attack you," the general ordered. He snapped the spyglass closed. "Mechanics,"[153] he said with a sneer. "Bunch of loonies. Always have been." A series of thundering *booms* had him swinging the glass back up to his eye. On the plain before him, he saw the colossi tipping the last of the dropwalls forward. As they crashed to the ground, he shook his head. "First they use our own dropwalls against us, then they knock them down? Overconfident fools. This place may have been an impregnable fortress back in the old days, but times have changed. Still, all the better for us . . ."

Then the ground began to shudder. With surprising speed, the colossi pivoted in place, and strode quickly back to their wall niches,

---

[153] A derogatory term, long used by outsiders, to refer to the natives of Mechanicsburg.

settling back just as the first spikes broke through the soil. Hundreds of troops and associated armaments danced about, trying to avoid the sharp spines appearing around them.

The general saw there was now a ring almost completely surrounding the town, out to almost fifty meters. He snorted. "Do they think we're still just using horses and infantry?" He frowned as he saw several units attempting to retreat from the prickly ground. He pointed them out to his adjunct. "Get those soldier's names," he growled.

Then the retreating soldiers were blocked as the spikes shot upwards, elongating into thick, spike-encrusted branches that trapped men and machinery alike. The branches began to hoist the entrapped figures into the air along with their weapons, clanks, animals, and tanks. Still, the great thorns grew upwards, their bases were now over two meters thick and they began to weave an impenetrable wall of thorns around the town. No one within the thicket managed to escape.

Aboard Castle Wulfenbach, explosions rocked the great airship as, for the second time, it desperately tried to escape the range of Mechanicsburg's defenses. *We should not have come back here,* Klaus swore to himself. *Again I have underestimated her.* "Status," he roared.

"At least one third of the fleet is lost or too damaged to fight, Herr Baron!"

"The smoke is getting worse and there is something weird about it. It appears to be interfering with our instruments! The ships we still have aloft are flying blind!"

"Aye, the town has awakened the Fog Merchants! I hadst thought them but a tale to frighten children,[154] but real they be, and our projectiles shall prove useless!"

"The screamer guns panicked the remainders of our cavalry and mounted units. The Oliphants are still running."

---

[154]   For the record, no ethical teller-of-tales would tell the story of the Fog Merchants to children. It might give them ideas.

"The Mechanized Cavalry was swallowed by some kind of quicksand. They couldn't avoid it—it was like it was following them!"

Klaus ran a hand through his hair. "The Subterranean Fleet?"

"According to their radio traffic, they're in the middle of a battle with giant ants."

Klaus sighed. *Shrinker mines.* "Very well then, it appears there is only one thing left to do." He took a deep breath and when he swung back, was once again in control. "Send a first priority message to all units in the field. I want a full retreat. Abandon the town. Disengage from all Mechanicsburg forces."

"What? Craven, ignoble retreat?"

"All the way back to Balen's Gap."

"We're abandoning the Valley of the Heterodynes? But this is madness, Herr Baron! Madness, I say!"

"It is only temporary. Boris, I will want a list of all of the units still trapped inside Mechanicsburg."

"Oh, that's easy, Herr Baron, soon there shouldn't be any."

Klaus stopped. "What? But the thorn wall . . . "

"There is still an open gap before the southern gates, and it appears that all of our troops still in the city are being herded towards them. The ones already leaving are doing so unmolested."

"AND SHE COULD HAVE CRUSHED THEM ALL," Doktor Chouté cried. "TRULY WE ARE WITNESSING THE BIZARRE, TWISTED KINDNESS OF THE NEWLY FLEDGED DARK PRINCESS OF DOOM!"

"Ah, it *is* possible they are setting the stage for future diplomacy."

"No." Klaus dismissed this possibility. "This is Mechanicsburg. Nothing is ever as it seems, and everything is a sick joke!" He paused, and a look of frustration crossed his face. "Still . . . I must admit that the point of *this* particular joke eludes me."

Meanwhile, down in Mechanicsburg, Airshipman Third Class Axel Higgs shuffled to a stop and stared as the thorn hedge appeared over the top of the encircling wall, the occasional bit of ordinance or soldier lodged within. "Been a while." He made a slow circle in place and realized— "Huh. They left a gap in it. Wonder why?"

At that moment, a mob of retreating Wulfenbach troops roared around several corners and headed his way. A tall general standing atop a mechanical water buffalo waved his staff frantically. "Retreat," he roared, his voice artificially amplified so that it boomed loud enough to be heard over the tumult. "Retreat towards the gap!" Without pause, Higgs pivoted smoothly and began running towards the aforementioned gap as well.

"Helllooo 'Mister Higgs' ", the Castle called from a recessed drain.

"Ah," Higgs grunted. "Should've known."

"Oh, don't be like that," a drain spout whispered. "Look what I've brought you."

The shouts of the crowd behind him grew louder. "Nice."

"Indeed it is. Now go ahead and fight them. *Fight them!*"

"Don't be stupid. Why would I do that? I'm one of them, remember? Just another Wulfenbach man joining in the retreat."

"*Tch.* You are nothing of the sort. Go on, toss a few of them around."

"As if I'd blow my cover just so that you could have some pointless mischief." A thought hit him and he stumbled and caught himself. "No. Wait . . . There's *always* a point, isn't there? What are you up to, you malevolent shed?"

"Why, I have a desire to see you fight! It's always so inspiring!"

"Why would you . . . " Higgs sighed. "Oh. *She's* watching, isn't she?"

"Hee-hee . . . Maybe!"

"Knew she wouldn't stay in bed."

"Why should a wild young lady like her listen to *you?* Ah, but if you showed her something that she *respected* . . . if you fought . . . even just a few of them, why, I believe she'd see a completely new and intriguing side of you."

"Not listening!"

By now the Castle had to actually shout to be heard over the sounds of the approaching mob. "You'll be trampled if you don't."

Higgs shrugged. "Been trampled before." Indeed, he heard the sound of some large mechanical creature growing louder from directly behind him. He realized the shadow he saw enveloping his own meant it was directly upon him. He braced himself . . . but was still shocked when a hand shot down, snagged the back of his jacket and hauled him up and aboard the charging mechanism. "Whoo-hoo," Zeetha sang out. "Come on, flyboy! Time to leave Crazy Town!"

Even dazed, Higgs noted how effortlessly she pulled him atop the shuddering automaton's broad back. The only other thing there was a snug metal howdah-like structure. Its metal door swinging wildly as the machine galloped along. "Sorry about all this," Zeetha said, as she deposited him by her side.

Higgs looked out at the mass of escaping military. "These guys? How is this your fault?"

"Well, the Castle asked if I wanted to see you fight."

A large reptile adorned with a Wulfenbach captain's hat clambered up the side of the running machine. "Mammals! General Siclee is requisitioning this mount! Depart! At once!"

Higgs' foot caught it square on the snout. It fell back into the surging crowd, squealing. "Destroy them!"

"The Castle," he said, annoyance beginning to creep into his voice. "So not only are you still injured and out of bed against doctor's orders, but you're also running around the streets listening to the Castle!"

Zeetha stomped her foot on the claws of another lizard soldier climbing towards her. "Well, I kind of wanted to see it, okay?"

Higgs refused to relinquish the larger conversational issue. "You are not treating your injuries seriously at all! This is not some kind of game!" More lizards showed up, and the airman relished taking some of his frustrations out on them.

Zeetha tsk-tsked as another lizard tried to grab her hair. She grabbed hold of Higgs's sleeve to stabilize herself and delivered a double kick that sent it arcing off to the street below. Higgs nodded approvingly, but then frowned. "And don't 'tsk' me! That's what got a sword through you!"

Zeetha paused. A relevant point, but she had to admit whatever had been done to her at Mamma's had been astonishingly recuperative. "Are you still going on about that?"

"You cannot be so cavalier about this," Higgs snarled. "I've told you and *told* you, there are people here who . . . who *need* you!"

"I'll be fine! Besides Agatha has got *lots*—"

Higgs whirled and grabbed her shoulders. Glaring furiously at her, his grip like iron, "ME," he roared, his eyes locked onto hers. "Me! Not the Lady Heterodyne. Me! *I* want you!" He realized instantly what he had said. "I mean . . . I need you." He looked surprised. "And, I want you, to . . . need . . . me."

Zeetha stared up at him.

"Castle," she yelled. "Are you still there?"

"Oh, I wouldn't miss this for the world!"

"You're *sure* that Agatha's all right?"

"Oh yes, it's all over but the mopping up at this point."

"Good." She jabbed a finger into Higgs's chest. "Then *we* need to talk." Higgs slumped like a man who'd had more than his share of "talks."

Thus he was unprepared when Zeetha grabbed his shirt and slung him into the howdah, stepped in behind him, and locked the hatch. He started to say something and then discovered Zeetha's mouth was in the way. He pulled himself free long enough to take a deep breath and saw Zeetha was already busy stripping off his clothing. "Ah, *that* kind of talk." He began to reciprocate.

The Castle had no receptors that allowed it to observe or interact directly with the howdah or its inhabitants. So, after several rather dull minutes, as far it was concerned, it noted the clank, as well as the bulk of the soldiers, were even now passing out of the town gates. "Try to be back by midnight, at least," it groused.

Atop the battlements of the Southern Gate, several notables watched the escaping army, unaware of the romantic activities taking place in its midst. "That's the last of them," Krosp observed with satisfaction.

Vanamonde took a deep breath and allowed himself to slump against the stonework. Another flurry of activity caught his eye. "With all the Jägers in hot pursuit, I see." He rubbed his temples. "It'll be interesting having them openly around town from now on."

Vidonia blinked and looked around, as if noticing that they were all still alive for the first time. "We really did it, didn't we?"

Van smiled a smile that didn't reach his tired eyes. "If by 'we,' you mean 'she,' then yes, she really did. She won." He glanced out at the chaos before him, as the entire Wulfenbach army began to pull up stakes and exit the valley as quickly as possible. *There'll be some good salvage out there*, he mused. "And by 'won,' I mean 'didn't get crushed by the empire—' "

"*Yet*," Tarvek interjected.

Van waved a hand. "I was getting there."

Tarvek realized he was being a bit of a pill and turned towards Krosp. "The Baron won't let this stand, but at least it looks like we'll all live to see what he sends next."

"I'm just happy about the whole not being crushed part," Violetta said.

Krosp stretched and rubbed the pads of his paws together. "The question is, will he send an envoy or a better army?"

Tarvek ran an eye over the defenses that seemed to be repairing themselves even as he watched. "It'll have to be a crashing good one to take this place now. He's more likely to use trickery somehow—try to catch us by surprise . . . "

"SURPRISE!" called a voice from above. Everyone snapped their heads upwards in time to see Agatha being lowered down in the remnants of Gilgamesh's pinnacle by a squad of Mechanicsburg Torchmen. "Tarvek!" When she saw him below, Agatha leapt the last meter or so and landed in his arms. "We *did* it," she sang out. "We really did it! The Castle is fixed!"

"That I am," the Castle spoke up, "And not a moment too soon! The state of architecture in this town is simply shocking! Hardly a proper venue for Mechanicsburg's renaissance of terror! Might I suggest a giant statue of my dread mistress crushing the Baron under her heel?"

"No statue," Agatha snapped.

"You'd be in a pretty dress," the Castle wheedled.

"No!"

Van shrugged. "A pity. The tourists would've loved it."

Vidonia gave him the side-eye. "I don't think we're going to have to cater to tourists for quite a while."

Van stared at her and nodded slowly. "Oh. No, I suppose not."

Meanwhile, Agatha huddled with Tarvek. "I saw Gil," she told him.

"You did? Here? Where is he?"

"I'm . . . well I'm not sure."

Tarvek studied her face. "What happened?"

"I . . . well . . . he was just being so completely insufferable, and . . . and I was being all mad and stuff and he kept trying to kidnap me and ordering me around and trying to stop me—"

"He *what?* After all we did to help you?"

"I know! He tried to *sedate* me! I got so angry—"

Tarvek stared at her. "You didn't kill him, did you?"

"No!" Tarvek raised an eyebrow. "And I didn't even *try* to! So I . . . I told Franz to get him out of my town."

"Franz . . . the *dragon?*"

"I'm pretty sure he wouldn't eat him." *And even if he tried,* she thought, *Gil wouldn't have let him.* "There was something wrong with him. It was like he was arguing with himself."

"He was obviously compromised." Tarvek swore. "The Baron must have done something to him." He looked at Agatha and shook his head. "I can't believe he was here, and you sent him away! We could have kept him a prisoner! Used him as a hostage! A bargaining chip!"

Violetta broke in. "You think so? *I* don't. Guy like that? In my professional opinion, he'd have escaped and caused you even more trouble."

Tarvek and Agatha looked at each other. There was the ring of truth in Violetta's words, but— "But we should have *tried*," Tarvek said helplessly. "We could have . . . we might have . . . "

Agatha came up behind him and rested her head on his shoulder. "We could have kept him *safe*," they whispered together.

Tarvek reached back and took Agatha's hand. "We're just going to have to rely on his natural, annoying ability to come up smelling like a rose after every single stupid predicament he gets into." He sighed. "I just wonder how'll I'll wind up looking like a fool when he's done."

Agatha turned him around and looked into his eyes. "Not to me, you won't."

Tarvek looked down into her eyes and for a moment wondered why his feet were no longer touching the ground. "So. Compromised, you say."

Agatha nodded, "You know what's wrong with him?"

A bit of Tarvek's euphoria drained away. "I suspect he's under some form of mind control."

Agatha shuddered. She had very much wanted to be wrong. "You said that there was only one wasp capable of infecting a spark. Surely there hasn't been time to make another."

"Right! And *that's* good news for us. The Baron has been collecting and studying the work of conquered sparks for years. He must have access to *lots* of ways to enslave someone's mind. He'll have used one of those on Gil.

"But Lucrezia is a first-class megalomaniac (even for a spark), she's convinced that her slaver wasps are better, and to be fair, she's right!

So at some point, they'll reverse whatever process they have him under now, and she'll wasp him. As soon as she can, I'm guessing."

Agatha stared at him. "How can that possibly be good news?"

"Because once she thinks she has him securely under her control, he'll be allowed more freedom. But Gil has my notes, which contain a formula that will make him immune to her wasps! If he's half the sneak I think he is, he'll dose himself, if he hasn't already, and he'll be able to fight her while operating right under her nose!" Tarvek's grin faltered. "If . . . "

"If what?"

"*If* he has time to make it. *If* he'll take it. If he, well, if he *trusts* me." He looked at Agatha. "There are a worrying number of 'ifs.' "

Agatha took his hand in hers. "*I* trust you. I trust *both* of you. The Baron and Lucrezia may have him now, but they won't keep him long." She squeezed his hand. "We won't *let* them."

Tarvek took a deep breath. "Yeah." He looked down at Agatha and the moment seemed perfect. He leaned forward to kiss her— and she shrieked in surprise. Tarvek recoiled. The swarm of creatures Agatha had seen scurrying towards them scrambled up his back, burrowed under his shirt, and squealed and nipped lovingly at his earlobes. Tarvek whooped and gyrated in place for several seconds before he realized what it was that he was covered in: "Wasp weasels!"

He looked up and saw Ruxula, the Vespiary Squad officer he'd rescued, limping towards him. She had been expertly taped up, but obviously needed the staff she leaned on while walking. When she saw Tarvek recognize her, she saluted him. Tarvek rushed over and all but kicked her feet out from under her in his effort to make her sit down. "You were horribly injured, you know."

"Yep." Ruxala leaned her head back against the cool stonework and closed her eyes. "Can't be helped. The empire is trying to wipe us out. Stop our work. Someone had to check out this town you've brought us to as soon as possible. Had to see how infested it is."

"Infested?" Van looked alarmed. "With what?"

"There's a heretofore unknown type of revenant," Tarvek explained. "It acts like a normal person and will do so for years. But if it's given an order by Lucrezia, or one of the Other's minions, it will obey them absolutely."

Van shook his head in horror. "We don't *have* any revenants here!"

Tarvek sighed. "No, the whole point is—"

"He's right." Everyone stopped and looked at Ruxula. She took a deep breath and sat up. "We're still checking everybody, of course, but the only revenants we've found here are a couple of tourists. Everyone who *lives* here seems to be clean."

Tarvek looked skeptical. "*None* of them? But how is that even possible? Statistically, the spread across the empire should be . . . "

Ruxala nodded. "Yeah. It *is* weird. According to our calculations, at least ten-to-twenty percent of any given population should be infected. But here? Zero." She looked at him quizzically. "We'd been impressed because we'd assumed that you knew."

"I didn't."

"Lucrezia might have," Agatha said slowly. "She really didn't want to come here."

"Interesting," Tarvek mused. "Dispersal is looking more prudent than ever."

"Dispersal?"

"The wasp eaters are too important to keep all in one place, no matter how safe it seems."

Ruxala nodded. "If Prince Sturmvarous hadn't warned us, the Vespiary Squad would have been wiped out already, along with all of our weasels. And so, on his advice, some of our people have already left Mechanicsburg, disguised and hidden amongst the other Wulfenbach forces in the retreat. They'll make their way out of the empire and set up research labs in Paris, Istanbul, and maybe even England."

Tarvek rubbed his hands. "And they'll all be reporting to me."

Violetta snorted. "I wonder whose idea *that* was."

"Oh, he didn't want us to," Ruxala assured her. "We *insisted*." Krosp bit his own tail out of sheer envy.

As Ruxala gave a fascinated Agatha a brief explanation of enhanced mustelid physiognomy, Violetta and Tarvek rested against a parapet. "So," Violetta asked, "what do you think is going to hit us next?"

Tarvek shrugged and began polishing his spectacles. "Really, cousin? You have to ask? The empire is in chaos. Mechanicsburg is still putting itself back together. Agatha may be supported by the town, but she is still nothing but an unsubstantiated rumor to the outside world, and thus not yet completely secure. Who do you *think* will step up to cause her problems?"

A voice roared up from the courtyard below. "Lady Heterodyne! There you are!" Everyone peered down to see Martellus von Blitzengaard, who looked like he had seen a fair amount of fighting if his once-pristine attire was to be believed, sitting tall upon the warhorse he had acquired. He was surrounded by the diminished, but still daunting, ranks of the Bloodstone Paladins.

Violetta nodded in understanding. "Ah. Our family, of course."

Tarvek handed her a chocolate-covered mimmoth. "Right in one."

A small crowd began to gather and stared up at the mounted man in awe. Martellus sat a bit straighter and spoke a bit louder. "Come! We are victorious! Your subjects await you!" He paused and looked around expectantly, and a ragged cheer arose from the spectators. He turned back and swept a hand towards the saddle before him. "Allow me the honor of escorting you to the cathedral square! Come and take my hand!"

Agatha strode down the stairs. "No, that won't be necessary."

Martellus looked surprised. "What? But I have a horse." The horse nodded in agreement.

"Thank you for the thought," Agatha said as she breezed past. "But no."

They turned onto the main boulevard heading towards the cathedral in the distance. Martellus wheeled his horse about, and with a synchronized stamp and crash of arms, the Paladin clanks swung into formation behind them. As they passed, people could be seen emerging from buildings, manholes, and, in one surprising instance, the crown of a tree.

Van looked about and leaned in towards Agatha. He surreptitiously jerked his head back towards Martellus, who was determined to catch up without looking like he had been deliberately left behind in the first place, and murmured, "He *does* look impressive, my Lady. Perhaps for your initial impression—"

"Sitting next to him?" Agatha hissed. "Have you *talked* to him?" Van had the sense to keep quiet. "Besides, if I feel the need to look impressive . . . " Agatha snapped her fingers, and Franz reared his head above the roofline of a butcher's shop that had taken severe damage, a half-eaten cow carcass in one hand. He saw the group looking at him and unsuccessfully tried to hide the carcass by stuffing it into his mouth. "Meff, Mifftreff?"

She glanced back at Van. "Well, you get the idea."

Van nodded. "He is correct about one thing, Mistress, we should proceed to the Red Cathedral. There are important things the new Heterodyne needs to do there."

Agatha glanced about and had to concede that at the moment, she really didn't know what she should do. "What kind of things?"

The seneschal looked pensive. "Well, mostly ceremonial, I'll admit."

Agatha stared at him. "*Ceremonial?* Are you *serious?* We just fought a huge battle! Everything is in chaos! People are hurt! I . . . I should be cleaning this place up! And getting something to eat! And maybe even sleeping!"

Tarvek stepped in and cleared his throat. "There will be time for that, but you must understand that while Mechanicsburg and the Heterodynes may flout most of Europa's traditions, they take their own very seriously."

Van nodded. "It's not *all* ceremonial, my Lady," he said in a low voice. "Your ancestors knew better than to put all of their power under the control of the Castle. Once the Doom Bell has rung, there are additional city systems that need to be 'told' there is an actual Heterodyne present, and they have to be trained to recognize you. Only then will they respond to you. It's a bit of a bother, and one of the reasons they didn't ring the bell much. But once you've done them, it'll allow the rest of us to get things back to normal a lot easier."

There it was in a nutshell. She was no longer simply "Agatha Clay" or even just (just!) "Agatha Heterodyne." She was the Heterodyne of Mechanicsburg. A major power in Europa, and one that would be tested from numerous directions in the coming days.

But she was no longer alone. She had a town; a marvelous, unique town that desperately wanted her to succeed, filled with deviously talented people who needed her like a plant needed the sun. She had monsters, and clanks, and a dragon, and the most awful Castle in existence, who would obey her every command. It was a beginning.

"Ah! There you are!" Agatha's musings were short-circuited as a fresh crowd emerged from a side street, Othar Tryggvassen at its head. He strode up and bowed towards Agatha. "Congratulations! Anyone who can foil the Wulfenbachs deserves the approbation of the continent!" He swung about and regarded the surrounding crowd. "Am I right?"

And then the cheering started. Full throated and joyful this time, it spread outwards, and soon echoes of it could be heard throughout the town. Othar smiled genially and leaned in. Scant centimeters from Agatha's face, he lowered his visor and she saw that his eyes were as cold as ice. When he spoke, his voice reached her alone. "I have heard many things about you regarding the Other. Disturbing things. My apprentice—" he jerked his head towards Tarvek— "has explained things in a way that show you in the best light, but I will want to hear the particulars from you. If you are truly a victim, know that Othar Tryggvassen—Gentleman Adventurer—will do all he can to help. But if you are a willing party to this monstrous evil, know that all of this—" the subtle motion of his hand somehow managed to encompass everything within the Valley of the Heterodynes "—will not save you." Looking into his eyes, Agatha believed him.

He then reared back and clapped her shoulder. "But today you should relish your victory!" With another small bow, he stepped back into the crowd. Agatha bit her lip.

"Yeah, he's going to be a pain in the neck." She blinked and saw Moloch now walked by her side.

She smiled in delight. "You're alive! You made it out!" She spoke to the open air, "Thank you, Castle."

A nearby gargoyle harrumphed. "He earned it."

Moloch was pleasantly surprised at this, but had his piece and was determined to say it. "So we're square? The Castle is fixed and you're queen. Good luck with that."

Agatha nodded.

Moloch took a deep breath. "Then I'm out of here. Just wanted to let you know."

Agatha considered this and turned to Van. Moloch braced himself. "Herr von Mekkhan, please see to it that Herr von Zinzer has new clothes, a good horse, and the equivalent of a year's salary as befitting my chief minion."

Moloch gawped. "You're . . . you're not going to force me to stay?"

Agatha smiled. "That is not how one treats one's friends." She extended a hand, and the two of them shook. "Despite everything, you've proved yourself a very good friend indeed. If you ever return, please come see me at once." Agatha moved on. Moloch watched her go, and found mixed feelings roiling about inside him.

"You're leaving." He turned and found Violetta staring at him, a curiously blank look on her face.

"Yeah. I always said I was going to. This place is crazy."

"Yes." Violetta nodded. "You did. It is."

"You're staying?"

"Yes." Violetta's eyes grew luminous and to Moloch's horror, started leaking tears. "I have to."

Moloch felt something was terribly wrong, and then realized that Violetta being unhappy really *bothered* him.

He found himself gripping Violetta's arms, which at least had the effect of stopping her tears. "You don't have to stay here," he said earnestly. "You're like, the one person I've seen here who seems sane. You should . . . you could . . . come with me." He saw Violetta's face and knew he'd crossed a line of some sort.

"I mean, just until you find someplace better." He looked at her helplessly. "I know I got no right, but . . . but I'm really worried about you, and if you stay here . . . " He pause and then slumped a bit. "You know? I think you'd do just fine. But I'd still be worried about you."

This scene had a growing circle of discrete observers, all of whom were starting to panic at the idea of the Lady Heterodyne's chief minion actually leaving.

It was Ognian who snagged a nearby bottle, shouted, "Lonk live der Heterodyne!" and lurched into Violetta in such a way that Moloch protectively enfolding her into his arms was *completely natural.*

During this timeless moment of revelation Vanamonde took his cue and stepped up. "Forgive me, Herr von Zinzer. But could you stand to stay here in town at least until tomorrow?" He gestured about. "It will take us until then to get you everything the Lady Heterodyne stipulated. We'll put you up, of course, in one of the finest remaining hotels."

Moloch frowned and glanced down to see Violetta looking up at him—hope shining from her eyes. "You could . . . you could dance with me at the party," she whispered.

Moloch smiled back. "That would be nice."

A drain gurgled next to Vanamonde. "Find the second-best dressmaker in town," the Castle rumbled. "The Lady Violetta's façade will be clad in a very pretty dress before the first lanterns are lit in the banquet halls tonight. Do I make myself clear, young von Mekkhan?"

Van nodded in agreement as he moved on. "Clear as crystal, my dear Castle."

When Franz had removed Gilgamesh from Mechanicsburg at Agatha's behest, he had paused on one of the detritus-filled fields surrounding the town, and secured what appeared to be at least a hundred meters of heavy-gauge airship mooring cable, with which he had thoroughly cocooned the furious young man. He had then deposited him on the crest of a hill outside the entrance to the Valley of the Heterodynes, within full view of the Wulfenbach forces that had paused to sort themselves out after their retreat, and then given him a firm shove.

So thorough a job had Franz done, it had not been until they had hauled Gil aboard Castle Wulfenbach that sufficiently strong cable cutters could be located so that the heir to the empire could be freed safely.

To the surprise of the technicians, the Baron himself stepped in and ordered everyone else out while he began the process of snipping cables. Once he gotten into the rhythm of the thing, Klaus spoke. "What happened?"

Gil watched his father's hands as they effortlessly cut the metal strands and listened to himself answer: "She knew there was something wrong with me."

"How?"

"I don't know."

Gil made an effort. It was easier to assert control over his own vocal cords now. "*I* know."

Klaus momentarily paused and then continued. "Is that so?"

The thing that shared his mind began to recede and Gil nodded. "While I was in Castle Heterodyne, I underwent a modified *si vales valeo* procedure that included both Agatha and Prince Sturmvarous as well as myself."

Klaus looked shocked and opened his mouth—

"It was foolish, but I thought it necessary. I can provide you with a full report, as well as blueprints, wiring diagrams, and a few improvements I've come up with since. I think that, with modifications, and under proper supervision, it might be of use in rehabilitating some of the comatose patients in the psychiatric ward. Now, do you want to yell at me, or do you want to hear the important part?"

To Gil's astonishment, a faint smile flickered across his father's face and he said nothing. Gil continued. "The reports of shared immune systems and the synchronization of biometric systems are quite accurate. However the degree to which those involved share mental awareness and an understanding of personalities of the other people involved has been, in my opinion, seriously underreported. I suspect those who were involved in previous experiments were either afraid to chronicle effects they could not substantiate, or else they discovered things about themselves or the people that they were connected to that they thought better left unsaid."

Klaus considered this for a moment and then conceded the point. Gil continued. "The upshot of this is that Agatha *knows* me. Knows what I'm like and was able to tell that the person whom she encountered in Mechanicsburg was not the same person. It's as simple as that."

Klaus sighed. "Yes, the simple things tend to prove the most inconvenient when one is making Grand Plans."

"Father, this connection went both ways. I can assure you that Agatha is a genuinely good person. Oh, Lucrezia is there, in her head. I felt her, faintly, like a maniac screaming impotently in a locked cell, but Agatha—"

"Irrelevant." Klaus spoke with a cold indifference. "The fact is that Lucrezia *is* in her head and can assume control any time she weakens."

"Granted," Gil said, "much like how the copy of you that has been placed in *my* head can usurp *my* body whenever it so desires."

"NO!" There was anguish and fury on Klaus' face now. The cable cutter handle bent within his fist. "The overlay persona will *only* activate in the presence of the Heterodyne girl, or if it senses you going against the well-being of the empire."

Gil's face softened. "Forgive me, father. I know this wasn't really your idea." Klaus said nothing. Gil continued, "We will overcome this, sir. Together, we will."

Klaus sighed as the final cable parted. "I have to tell her you said that."

Gil patted him on the shoulder. "I didn't say it was going to be easy."

The great square that surrounded the Red Cathedral was packed with townspeople, along with the few remaining tourists who were determined to stick it out. Astonishingly, people had managed to excavate enough musical instruments that a respectable band was blaring away, and the Official Song of Mechanicsburg filled the air. Agatha listened and realized with a start that the words she was hearing were not the ones she had heard when she had first entered the town. Van noticed her reaction and shrugged apologetically. "Those are the old words, my Lady. My grandfather had it rewritten so that it wouldn't scare the tourists away." As the crowd began to sing along, Agatha could see how that might have been a problem.

Another section of the square was bustling with activity of a different sort, and from her time in the circus, Agatha recognized the signs of a large communal kitchen being set up. Enormous pots and tables had been produced, and a steady stream of people and constructs were lugging sacks and casks from every direction. Several dozen fires and stoves were lit, and rows of portable food carts, grills smoking, already had the mouth-watering aromas of grilled meat and onions, bread and other savories beginning to spread. Wagons overloaded with gigantic barrels appeared, pulled by cheerful-looking constructs who had the bodies of burly men and the heads of horses. They set up and began to dispense water, beer, wine, and several things that Agatha was unable to identify, though the people drinking it seemed very pleased to get it.

Progress towards the entrance to the cathedral was slow, as at almost every step a fresh crowd of townspeople saw her and spent several minutes roaring their approval, evidently at her mere existence. It was the release of the pent-up fears and frustrations of almost sixteen years, and Agatha realized that there was no way to safely circumvent it.

Along the way, the Castle provided a running commentary about the state of the town, informing her when the last of the fires were extinguished and the final roads cleared. Officials kept appearing, ostensibly to report to Vanamonde but, in actuality, to get close to Agatha and see she was actually, really, finally here. By the time she reached the base of the cathedral stairs, this group had formed a crowd within the crowd. But then, as she ascended the stairs, the people around her began to fall away, until only Tarvek, Van, Krosp, and Mamma remained. Even they halted as she climbed the last few steps. Finally, when she reached the great threshold before the enormous carved doors, she turned and saw the entire population of Mechanicsburg—humans and clanks, constructs and monsters—assembled silently before her. Agatha blew a lock of hair out of her face.

When she spoke, she heard her voice was again amplified and easily carried to the back of the crowd. "I am Agatha Heterodyne. Daughter of William Heterodyne and his wife Lucrezia." Cheers erupted and continued for almost a minute.

She gestured towards the Castle. "The Castle has been repaired and recharged. The prisoners who survived have been freed, as per the agreement, and they are here among you." More subdued cheers this time.

"As you may have guessed, our relations with the outside world are off to a rocky start. I am told this is normal." Nervous laughter skittered through the crowd.

"However this is due to a misunderstanding. I desire nothing more than friendly and profitable relations with the empire, as well as the rest of Europa." Enthusiastic cheering, especially from the merchants.

"BUT, until we clear this misunderstanding up, there will be problems we will all have to deal with. However I know that there is no other place I'd rather be, and no other people I'd rather have in my camp. Thank you."

This time the cheering went on for quite a while and, in several places, showed no signs of stopping. Tarvek climbed up, clapping softly. "Very well done indeed!"

Agatha slumped and smiled. "Really? Because I thought I was going to pass out."

"You're probably starving," Krosp declared. "I know *I* am."

Agatha realized this was one of the most sensible things she had heard in the last hour. "You've convinced me!" She turned to Van. "Let's go take care of all that stuff so I can officially rule Mechanicsburg with an iron fist!" She poked Van hard in the shoulder. "But after that, I'd better see some cake."

Tarvek glanced at her. "You know, there's more to being an evil despot than getting cake whenever you want it."

Agatha thought about this and was filled with a sudden conviction, one that would stand the test of time through everything else that happened to her through the years. "If that's what you think, then you're doing it wrong."

END

APPENDIX

The Original Mechanicsburg Song

As we mentioned towards the tail end of our last chapter, the Lady Heterodyne heard the townspeople singing. Initially, she thought she was hearing the familiar "Mechanicsburg Tourism Song," which can be heard throughout Europa wherever travel agents are established, and the full text of which can be found in our previous volume (*Agatha H and the Voice of the Castle*). This iteration of the song was composed close to twenty years ago by the popular balladeer, sophisticate, and *bon vivant*, Thomas (Tom) Smith.

That, however, is not the *original* song, which is what the Lady Heterodyne actually heard.

Monsieur Smith was indeed hired by the newly empire-empowered Mechanicsburg City Council for his musical abilities, but his task was to *alter* the original anthem that had been sung by the town's inhabitants, in one form or another, for over three hundred years, as it was felt this song would not portray the newly domesticated town in the most desirable light to outsiders.

These days, while the more palatable song is still known abroad, within the Valley of the Heterodyne, it is the original that has returned to everyday usage. We present it here, published for the first time.

Mechanicsburg, Mechanicsburg,
You're wise to fear Mechanicsburg!
A name that causes nightmares from
Zelenograd to Rome.

Mechanicsburg, Mechanicsburg,

428

The Heterodynes' Mechanicsburg,
The scourge of Europa and
The place that we call home.

How mighty are her mighty walls,
How deadly are her clanks,
How impassible her mountains tall,
With monsters in their endless ranks.

The Heterodynes, they rule us all.
We load their guns, we forge their steel,
We know their house will never fall,
They keep us safe beneath their heel.

Mechanicsburg, Mechanicsburg,
We live to serve Mechanicsburg,
With blood and sweat and hearts and mind,
With every erg and ohm.

Mechanicsburg, Mechanicsburg,
The greatest burg you've ever heard of,
Scourge of Europa and
The place that we call home.
Scourge of Europa and
The place that we call home.

ABOUT THE AUTHORS

Kaja Foglio attended the Fine Arts Department of the University of Washington, where she learned how to see past the façade of cultural stereotypes surrounding an object, be able to discern the artistic principles that said object was attempting to express and then elucidate these principles with an awareness of the artist's purpose while acknowledging (without necessarily condoning) said artist's own cultural biases and place in history, and not be embarrassed to ask people for money for doing so. Her first professional art job was for a small, independent, Seattle game start-up called Wizards of the

Coast, for whom she produced several iconic Magic: The Gathering cards. The company she set up to sell art prints, Studio Foglio, later morphed into a publisher of books and comics, for which, thanks to the rigors of her university training, she is not at all embarrassed to ask for money.

Phil Foglio has toiled in the fields of science fiction, comics and gaming since the 1970s. He won a pair of Fan Artist Hugo Awards in '77 and '78. He produced *What's New With Phil & Dixie* for Dragon Magazine, adapted Robert Asprin's *Mythadventures* for WARP Graphics, and independently published his own comic series *Buck Godot-Zap Gun For Hire* and *XXXenophile*, as well as doing work for DC, Marvel, Dark Horse, and a depressingly long list of no longer existing companies. He has done work for numerous game companies, including Wizards of the Coast (Magic: The Gathering and Roborally), Steve Jackson Games (S.P.A.N.K. and GURPS IOU), Cheapass Games (Deadwood Studios and BRAWL), and Spiderweb Software (Avernum). He co-wrote the frankly silly science-fiction novel *Illegal Aliens* with Nick Pollotta. In his spare time, he did some medieval dancing and improv sketch comedy.

Phil & Kaja met thanks to a diligent comics shop owner. They have been working on the Girl Genius series since 1993, which puts it in the running for "Worst Get Rich Quick Scheme Ever." They were the first ever creators to take an established comics property and begin putting it up for free online, which to everyone's surprise (including their own) immediately tripled their sales. As a webcomic (http://www.girlgeniusonline.com), Girl Genius won the first three Hugo Awards for Best Graphic Story. They enjoy traveling, the opera, gardening, and various video games.

MORE GIRL GENIUS NOVELS

⁓◦❁◦⁓

AGATHA H AND THE AIRSHIP CITY: GIRL GENIUS, BOOK ONE
Hardcover / $24.99 (available now)
978-1-59780-211-6
Trade paperback / $14.99 (available now)
978-1-59780-212-3

The Industrial Revolution has escalated into all-out warfare. It has been eighteen years since the Heterodyne Boys, benevolent adventurers and inventors, disappeared under mysterious circumstances. Today, Europe is ruled by the Sparks, dynasties of mad scientists ruling over — and terrorizing — the hapless population with their bizarre inventions and unchecked power, while the downtrodden dream of the Hetrodynes' return.

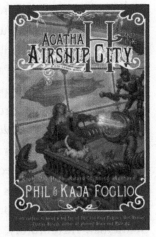

At Transylvania Polygnostic University, a pretty, young student named Agatha Clay seems to have nothing but bad luck. Incapable of building anything that actually works, but dedicated to her studies, Agatha seems destined for a lackluster career as a minor lab assistant. But when the University is overthrown by the ruthless tyrant Baron Klaus Wulfenbach, Agatha finds herself a prisoner aboard his massive airship Castle Wulfenbach — and it begins to look like she might carry a spark of Mad Science after all.

AGATHA H AND THE CLOCKWORK PRINCESS: GIRL GENIUS, BOOK TWO
Hardcover / $24.99 (available now)
978-1-59780-222-2
Trade paperback / $15.99 (available now)
978-1-59780-223-9

In a time when the Industrial Revolution has escalated into all-out warfare, mad science rules the world . . . with mixed success.

With the help of Krosp, Emperor of All Cats, Agatha has escaped from the massive airship known as Castle Wulfenbach. After crashing their escape dirigible, Agatha and Krosp fall in with Master Payne's Circus of Adventure, a traveling troupe of performers dedicated to staging Heterodyne shows—dramatizations of the exploits of Bill and Barry Heterodyne and their allies—who are unaware of Agatha's connection to the Heterodyne line.

Pursued by the ruthless Baron Klaus Wulfenbach, his handsome son Gil, and their minions (not to mention Othar Tryggvassen, Gentleman Adventurer), Agatha hides in plain sight among the circus folk, servicing their clanks and proving herself adept in performing the role of Lucrezia Mongfish, nemesis to—and later wife of—Barry Heterodyne. She also begins training under Zeetha, swordmistress and princess of the lost city of Skifander. Together, Agatha, Krosp, and the performers travel across the treacherous wasteland of war-torn Europa, towards Mechanicsburg, and the ancestral home of the Heterodynes—Castle Heterodyne.

But with many perils standing in her way—including Wulfenbach's crack troops, mysterious Geisterdamen, savage Jägermonsters, and the fabled Storm King—it's going to take more than a spark of Mad Science for Agatha to get through . . .

AGATHA H AND THE VOICE OF THE CASTLE: GIRL GENIUS, BOOK THREE
Hardcover / $24.99 (available now)
978-1-59780-295-6
Trade paperback / $15.99 (available now)
978-1-59780-833-0

In the third installment of the Girl Genius novels, *Agatha H. and the Voice of the Castle* begins as Agatha Heterodyne returns to her ancestral home, the warped little town of Mechanicsburg. There she must claim her inheritance by convincing the artificial intelligence that animates her family's castle that she is, in fact, the new Heterodyne. But this apparently simple task is made complicated in several ways: An imposter claiming to be the legitimate heir appears. The Empire is convinced that Agatha is the person responsible for the Long War (and to be fair, they are not entirely incorrect). And, worst of all, the Castle itself is insane.

From the Hugo Award–winning *Girl Genius* online comics comes this third book in the Agatha H. trilogy; and just like the first two, *Agatha H. and the Voice of the Castle* will grab you from the first page and not let go!